# A

# LETHAL

# SENTENCE

I Dedicate this to my brothers
Joseph and John.

Contents

Chapter One.  School                       Page 4

Chapter Two. Friends                       Page 56

Chapter Three. School Friends              Page 118

Chapter Four. Dating Friends               Page 171

Chapter Five. Relationship                 Page 228

Chapter Six. Us                            Page 261

Chapter Seven.  Fun                        Page 324

Chapter Eight. Memorable                   Page 375

Chapter Nine. Work                         Page 430

Chapter Ten. Living                        Page 480

Chapter Eleven. Occasion                   Page 541

# Chapter One

## School

## Morissa College

In the year of nineteen eighty-eight Morissa Brown is starting her first year of college. The college she has chosen is located outside of Albany New York. Her Father Mr. Brown has driven her up to her dorm. Morissa has been dreaming of being a teacher. Mr. Brown and Morissa sit in their car having there last talk, before Morissa walks out of the car and in to her dorm.

Mr. Brown: "Morissa I can walk up to the room with you. I would like to do that."

Morissa: "It is ok dad. I know the way. I am sure you would like to get back home."

Mr. Brown: "That's not what I was thinking Morissa. It is something that fathers like to do for their daughters. You are my only daughter."

Morissa: "I know dad. Thank you for wanting to do it for yourself. I need to do this by myself for myself. I need to get away and grow up. It may be symbolic. I just need to walk in there by myself dad. I need to do it for myself dad. I been waiting for this day a long time. I don't think you did a bad job raising me. You did the best you could. I love you dad for doing what you did for me. I know now that the little girl who ran to you for help is doing a slow walk away from you. That next step away from you is right here. Now it is time for me to start walking those steps that take me further away from you. I chose a school far enough so that it will not be easy for you to come up and see me. Just far enough away where it's not easy for me to see you.

There is something out there for me and I need to find it. The only way I'm going to find it dad is too walk into that building by myself. Then start being myself."

Mr. Brown: "Morissa my parents often wondered how I would turn out when I got older. My father said before he died that I turned out just the way he thought I would. When you were born my mother told me the biggest responsibility in my life wasn't too myself anymore. She said the biggest responsibility in my life was too her granddaughter. That was you Morissa. Both my parents were proud of you. You are a good person Morissa. In spite of me and who I am. You made it easy for me raising a daughter. I never once had to worry about your judgment. Or had to be worried about anybody else's judgment around you. Every father has a fear of the boy his daughter will bring home one day. I never had that fear. When I talk to your mother, I always tell her that she did a better job with you then me."

Morissa: "I know that. She tells me that all the time. I talked to her last night. She said to take it easy on you today. She said it was going to be hard for you to let me go."

Mr. Brown: "She is right this is harder than I thought it would be. Morissa you never told us why you chose to live with me. Your mother has her family money and that place on the west coast. That would have made a much easier and better life for you. I have some money. Enough to take care of both of us. One day you will have to tell us why you chose to come and live with me."

Morissa: "Dad you two separated when I was 12. If you two had separated earlier may be I would of went with mom. At twelve I wanted to learn to be independent. I wanted to learn how not to rely on anybody. Not to rely on anybody's money. I did think about my friends.

That night I sat in my room trying to make the decision of which parent to go and live with. Moms' money and that nice place on the beach was tempting. Your independence and the ability you have to survive and think on your feet, help me to pick you. I hope I learn something living with you. That job you call a side job and the way you handled it made me want to be more like you."

Mr. Brown: "I would have never thought that. I thought you hated what I did. It would be nice of you to let your mother know that. She has that guilt of you not wanting to have much to do with her. She thought you held the breakup of us against her."

Morissa: "Dad. I do. I did. I will always look at her as the reason you two separated. From what everybody told me you two fell in love at first sight. You two were always together and always wanted to be together. You weren't married when you had me. You got married after I was born. She wanted to change you dad. When I was young, I thought it was just the way my parents were. As I got older, I saw her trying to change who you were. I think you can't change people you have to let them be who they are. You have to accept who they are. You have to accept their flaws."

Mr. Brown: "Morissa. I don't know how to answer that. Your mother and I ran our time together. Your mother was trying to do what was best for everybody. It was as much as my fault as hers. I keep thinking you were missing out on life when you stood home on weekends living with me. Other girls were going out on dates you were home reading a book. As a father of a teenage daughter, I was glad to know you were safe at home sometimes. In the back of my head, I was thinking you were missing out on some fun. I think you missed out on some life growing up lessons. You will have some steady boyfriends here. You are going to like some of them a lot.

You may even fall in love with one of them. You are going to get to know them really well. After some time with them, you're going to see the flaws in them. Some of those flaws you are going to want to change, to make that person a better person in your eyes. Somewhere in a relationship you are going to get to thinking if the work and time to change someone is worth it."

Morissa: "I didn't like any boy enough to become serious with them back home. The school I went to was too small. Most of them felt more like a brother. I may meet somebody here we will see. I want a college degree. I want to be a teacher. I want to be independent. Any guys I'd date I will just let mother nature take its course. With that dad it's time for me to leave you and walk by myself in to that building."

Morissa father gets out of the car and goes to the trunk then opens it. He pulls a couple of bags and a suit case out. Morissa takes her bags and suit case. She gives her father a kiss on the cheek good bye. She turns to the school building and walks up to the building. She pulls a door open and walks in side.

Morissa father watches his 17-year-old daughter walk away without looking back at him. He watches her disappear into the building. He closes the trunk and gets back in his car and drives away.

A 17-year-old Morissa just walked in to her dorm room with her suitcase and bags in hand. Morissa was dropped off by her father and walked up to her dorm room by herself carrying her bags. It was the way she wanted to start her college school year and college life. There are some other bags of hers and thing she had shipped up before in her room.

In her room is her new roommate. Her name is Sue. Sue is a cheerleader. She has been at the school for two weeks with the cheer leader team. Sue is the perfect picture cheerleader. She has some gymnastic skills.

Sue has already met all the football players and all the place to party after a game. Her majors are gym and cooking.

Sue: "Hi Morissa. Happy to see you. So where is the family entourage? It is your first year. It is supposed to be a good drama moment when the parents leave there kid off at college for the first time. Please don't tell me they just dumped you and ran. It ruins the experience of the first time. A young woman should never be neglected of a good first time, any time."

Morissa: "No nothing like that I just want to do this by myself. This is just something I been thinking about. I had this pictured in my mind for the past six months. It wasn't as hard as I thought it would be. No tears no drama."

Sue: "I think you missed out. A specially for a girl. We should have that kind of drama. It is good for the female psyche. It keeps us in a female mind set."

Morissa: "Sorry. Sometimes we have to put those female things a side and just do what comes in our head."

Sue: "Ok I understand. Sometimes I do those things in my head to."

Morissa: "Meeting you last week was a help for me to do this. I did like meeting you. I think we are going to get along just great. I think us being a little different is going to be nice. We will be able to understand that there are some differences between us. If we were the exact same any little thing may cause a problem. We can look at each other and just leave it up to us being different."

Sue: "Morissa you just lost me. I think we are going to be good friends because we are friends now. We don't have to worry about us not being friends. If we did meet later. Because we have already met and are friends now."

Morissa: "Yes you are right. I am going to start to un pack and set myself up here. I have the weekend my classes don't start till Monday. "

Sue: "If you don't have enough space, you can rent a storage locker. I had to do that. This school doesn't let us first year students live off campus. Next year I am going to have a house to live in. My parents are going to rent one out for me if I pass this year. I took the easiest courses I could possibly take. Next year you could come and live with me and my other cheerleader friends. That will be so cool, me you and all my friends. Sounds like a party to me."

Morissa: "I have a lot of school to get pass this year. Next year is a long way off for me."

Sue: "Tomorrow is going to be here tomorrow. There is a big football game tomorrow. All the students will be there. I want you to sit by us the cheerleader so I can wave to you."

Morissa: "I am going to be walking over the campus to learn where everything is. I am not a real big sports fan. I am not going to have much interest in whether the team wins or lose."

Sue: "Morissa you can't say that. You have to want them to win. You have to go. If you want to find a college boyfriend you're going to have to get out. Those games have a lot of guys at them. After the game there is always a big party somewhere. That is where you can meet some nice-looking guy to date. It is one of those things you go to college for.

The guys outnumber the girls here so it is a place full of testosterone filled guys. Or the girls outnumber the guys here. I don't remember. You are a pretty girl with a nice figure. You will not have any problems finding a guy to date here. Unless you have a boyfriend home you promised to be true to. Then I will understand, kind of, I think."

Morissa: "No boyfriend home. No boyfriend anywhere."

Sue: "You do like guys, Right? I would understand if you were into girls. I have some friends like that."

Morissa: "That is good of you. I do like a good-looking guy. I do prefer the male race if that is what you mean."

Sue: "Good because I will help you find some real cute hunk. I know the hole football team. By the end of the year, I will know every jock who wears one."

Morissa: "Sounds like fun. You can just find me here studying. Don't let me get in your way of fun. Any time you need the room for a night just let me know and I will sleep in the library."

Sue: "Ok. But I am not going to be doing it in here. I want a first-class hotel room. Nobody is getting on me without making it a romantic night. How about you Morissa."

Morissa: "I hope to do better than a one-night stand. You will not find me between the sheets with some guy in here."

Sue: "Sure. Have you had a lot of boyfriends Morissa?"

Morissa: "I came from a small school. I knew them all since we started school. When I kissed one of them it was like kissing a brother."

Sue: "You poor girl. I will have no problems finding a lot of guys for you to kiss."

Morissa: "Thank you but just call me old fashion. I can get my own guys to kiss me know problem."

Sue: "There is a big home game in two weeks. I will have you front and center so boys can check you out."

Morissa: "Thank you I look forward to it.

Something about being put out front to be checked out by a bunch of guys sounds great. You will have to excuse me for now. I need to unpack and start my time here. If I seem a little withdrawn, please excuse me. I know your trying to be nice to your new roommate."

Sue: "Ok. I got you. Just let me know when I can help. I am going to a friend's room for a while. We went to high school together. I think we even dated the same guys. But a girl never really knows does she."

Morissa: "I guess. See you later."

Morissa talking to herself. After Sue leaves.

My new roommate. My new roommate is an air head. How did I get so lucky to have her? School has what I am here for. I want a degree. I want to graduate here and be a teacher. I want that degree so I can get a career doing what I have been dreaming of doing. I don't need to be part of a carnival of the guys choosing girls. I could see Sue pointing me out. "Step right up boys she's in the front row like a pound of ground beef, in a freezer case."

I kissed a couple of guys. I've dated a couple of guys. That's the end. If it goes further here. Then it will be. I'm not looking for anything but getting that degree.

My clothes my closet and my dresser. The space on the bed. My desk to the side. The nice little bathroom I get to share. My bed. It's a nice bed it feels nice sitting on it. I will try laying down on it. It's a nice bed.

How many people have slept in this bed? I may not want to know. I have my own clean sheets and there is a washing machine and dryer in the basement.

I guess I will unpack now and put my stuff away. I didn't bring a lot of stuff. I don't like a lot of stuff. I Think my roommate has more stuff under just her bed then everything I brought with me. They say opposites attract and so we should be friends. I will have to remember that. I think Sue just wants another friend.

Morissa starts her school year and gets right to work. She goes to her classes. She goes to her meals. She goes back to her dorm room and studies at the end of the day. She stays to herself most of the time. Sue has asked Morissa to go out with her and her friends a couple of times but Morissa just stays to herself. Morissa is nice to Sue's friends when they come into the room. Morissa will stop studying and talk to sues friends and tell them how much she likes Sue. That she will join them later in the year when she feels settled in.

Morissa second week the football team is at home for the big game. Sue has invited Morissa to go to the game. Morissa did not want to go to the game. Morissa did go to the game feeling that she needed to go so Sue wouldn't ask her again. Her school work was done for the week and it would be her first break away from the dorm room and class room. Morissa went to the game and sat in the front row and watched a football game with a lot of people who were all Sues friends. After the game Sue invited Morissa to a party off campus at a bar. Morissa went with more of Sues friends. She had a couple of drinks of soda.
Accouple of guys came over and introduced themselves to her. They offered to buy her a drink, then went on to other girls. One guy bumped into Morissa. Morissa nearly spilt her drink. The guy apologized to her then offer to buy her another drink.

Morissa without making eye contact tells him "don't bother yourself I had enough." He said a simple ok then went back to his date. The day turn to night.

Later that night Morissa and Sue with a couple of girls went back to the campus and back to their rooms. The next day Morissa went back to studying her school work. Sue left the door opened for Morissa to join her anytime.

The next couple of weeks Morissa stays working at her school work. She just went to one other football game. When thanksgiving break came Morissa got a ride to the local airport and flew to her mother's house in California. The ticket was pay for by Morissa's mother. Morissa spent that thanksgiving school break with her mother. She called her father thanksgiving night and the two talked for a while. When thanksgiving break ended, Morissa flew back to school.

Morissa stayed working at school till Christmas. At Christmas Morissa father drove up and picked Morissa up and brought her back home. She spent Christmas with her father. Christmas night Morissa called her mother and talk to her for a while. Morissa went back to school at the end of her Christmas break. Morissa went back to school work and her dorm life. The football games were done for the year.

Morissa and Sue developed a good friendship. They talk to each other at night about a lot of different things. Sue would invite Morissa to some parties. Morissa would pass them up and just stayed in the dorm and the classes for the winter. When spring break came Morissa had to make a decision.

Spend the break with her father and see some friends from her high school years. Sleep in her old room and her old bed. Have a couple of weeks to decompress.

Should she go and spend time with her mother. Her mother with access to a warm beach. She could sit on the beach and read a book and unwind from school. Her mother would cover whatever she spent on her vacation.

The last option was to go where all the college kids go on spring break. Sue offered her a free time with her and a couple of Sues friends in Florida at a place her parents owned.

Morissa chose her mother's place. She flew out to California. She spent her spring break mostly alone on the beech reading a couple of books. At night she and her mother would go out and eat at a restaurant. Sometimes they would have dinner on her mother's back deck and watch the sunset. At the end of spring break Morissa returned to school. She went right back to her class room and dorm room.

Morissa and Sue stayed friends. Sometimes the two would find themselves talking all night about anything and everything. Morissa learn that Sue was into competitive gymnastics. Sue was top in the state high school ranks till she broke her leg. It was the end of her gymnastic career. She became a cheerleader. She misses the competition that she loved in her younger years.

In the last couple of weeks of the school year Morissa had to make a decision of where she would spend her summer vacation. The time with her mother at thanksgiving was so relaxing. Her mother just let her be. Morissa wasn't a little girl anymore. Her mother just let Morissa do as she pleased. The spring break was a bonding time for her and her mother. The time with her father at Christmas wasn't as relaxing. Her old friends were off living a different life then she lived with them a year earlier.

Her next decision was where she would be living her next year at college. She could go and live with Sue off campus. The thought of trying to study for school with Sues party life would be part of her life. The money to live off campus wouldn't be a problem. Her mother would pay the bill if Morissa asked.

At the end of her first college school year Morissa has her father pick her up and bring her back to his house. She spends a week there then flies out to California to be with her mother. Morissa will spend most of her summer at her mother's house. At the end of summer, she will go back to her father's house. He will drive Morissa back to school for her second year.

Morissa is mother lives alone. She has one man friend sometimes. The man friend will stay over her house or she will spend time with him at his house.

Sommer time. Morissa is living with her mother in her beach front house.

Morissa and her mother spend a lot of time together bonding and making up for the years Morissa spent with her father. One night on the deck eating dinner she and her mother have a sit-down talk.

Miss. Brown: "Morissa have you decided where you're going to spend your next year of college. Are you going to go back and live at the dorm? Or are you going to go and live off campus with your friend?"

Morissa: "No mom. Not yet. I still have time to make that decision. Part of me wants to go and live off campus and try to be like the other girls. The smarter part of me wants to stay on campus and stay with my schoolwork. I want that degree. I want that degree really bad mom.

Miss. Brown: "I know you do Morissa. Don't think you can't do both. You're a very smart person. When you were born, I wanted to see what you would be like as an adult. I wanted to see if I would do a good job raising you. Morissa you are what every parent dreams of how they want their child to turn out to be. I am so proud of my child. Morissa like I said before I didn't raise you. You raised yourself. I never had to give you any rules.

I never had to check up on you. You raised yourself better than your father and I could've done. You are always levelheaded. You never asked for more than what you need."

Morissa: "Thanks Mom. I didn't need anything you two didn't give me. I did want you and dad to stay together at one time. Like most young kids do when their parents break up. I got over it fast and understood that it was just the way it was going to be. I was a happy kid mom. I thank you for letting me stay with dad."

Miss. Brown: "I did mis you so much. I would go places and think how much I would have loved having my daughter with me. I would see other mothers and daughters your age and think I was missing out on something. As I see you now. I knew I did the right thing letting you stay with your father."

Morissa: "Mom I'm 18 now and I never had a steady boyfriend. Sometimes I wonder if I am normal. Sometimes I think I'm too good. I wonder what happens to kids who are too good. As I look back at all my high school days. I wish I did some bad things like the other kids. I wish I stayed out and got drunk and had to call somebody to come and get me. I haven't had real sex yet. Technically I'm still a virgin. I wish I got that over with. It is still something that I have to deal with. I wish I didn't have to think about it anymore."

Miss. Brown: "Morissa don't worry too much about that. If you did lose your virginity, you'd be doing the second guessing of I should've waited for a better person to lose it to. There's always the what if, after when you do. It will happen for you. It is just the way it worked out for you."

Morissa: "Mom that is why I think I am going to go live off campus this school year. My courses this year will be easier than my last year. I will have more free time. My roommate Sue and a couple of her friends have a house.

As I told you before they are offering me a room in the house to live with them. I think I will go live with them. If it doesn't work out, I will just call you up and have you bail me out. I think you may enjoy giving me a talk about being more responsible. I may have deprived you all those years of not letting you have that talk with me. Most mothers have to have that talk with their daughter a couple of times, I'm sure."

Mom: "That would be our first. So long as you're safe it will work for me. If you want your own place off campus let me know and I will get you your own apartment close to the campus. I can even get you a two bedroom in case I stop by. I could have a place to sleep. Or you could have another girl stay with you."

Morissa: "Thanks mom I will keep that in mind. Staying with the other girls is what I may need to do. Living on campus is convenient. Going off campus is just to be with other girls my age. I may need that experience later in life"

Mom: "Your college years should be some fun years. Knowing that you're staying with other girls your father and I will feel more comfortable than if you are out on your own. When I was in college, I spent my last two years living off campus. It was before I met your father. The girls I stayed with were a lot of fun and we became very close.

Some of them had steady boyfriends and would spend most of their time with the boy. Some nights it would be just us girls and we would have an all-night party. To us it was always party. I think, as I get older it is just part of growing up in getting the partying and wild side of you out. It's learning that there's a responsibility for your actions. The next day depending on how much we drank there was a price to be paid. It was the hangover. It was, how far did I go with that boy. It was the mess we created. It was if we missed time at school and how to explain it to the parents."

Morissa: "Mom you never told me about your time in college. You never told me about the times that you were bad. This is your chance now to clear your conscience and tell me all about those things you never told dad. I don't want to hear about you and dad. Those types of things may make me sick. But you can tell me about the other guys and all the other things you may of or may not have done. "

Mom: "Morissa when you have your first child, we can have that talk. Till then we cannot have that talk. There are some things I did I will never tell anybody. Somewhere along the line of your life you may or may not have things you don't tell your child. There are things I did I never told your father. There are things he probably did that he never told me. Everybody has those things."

Morissa: "Mom. If you had to work for a living, what do you think you would be doing? I am going to college so I can teach. There's nothing more I want then to become a teacher. What did you want to do?"

Mom: "Morissa I wanted to be a writer. I would always write. I'd told my parents your grandparents that I was going to college so I can be a writer. A college degree would get you in the door of a place that needs a writer.

Once you're in that door you need to be able to create words to a story. I got my first job at a newspaper from some help from my father. After a year it occur to me that I just didn't have with the other people who are working there had. They had the talent and drive to do it. I just had a father who got me the job and paid for my degree. I didn't earn ether. After that job is when I met your father as you know. With money to my name and a blank check from my father I retired and married your father. My writing was put off and I never went back to it."

Morissa: "I would like to write a book one day. I think everybody would like to write that great American novel. Mom I have nothing in my head on what I would write about. I cannot even come up with what story I would write about. May be I will be the teacher of the next great writer. Then when he or she accept there award I hope to get a thank you."

Mom: "Morissa from what I learned through college and my one year at a newspaper. You have to have an interest in something. Then you have to find the words to tell your story to other people who may want to read what you have written. It's all about the words and how you use them. Then it's all about how interesting you make the people and the words you created to your readers. What type of story you write doesn't really matter? It's how you tell the story. People are the most interesting parts to a story. People want to relate themselves to people in your story. Readers want to relate their life events into your events in the story. Then again what do I know. I never written anything."

Morissa: "Maybe I will marry the next great writer."

Mom: "Give me a grandchild like that, then I will be the grandmother who will be the show off of all the grandmothers."

Morissa: "Mom let's not rush this. I don't even have a steady boyfriend yet."

Mom: "Morissa do you want to travel anywhere this summer. You still have a lot of summer left before you go back to college?"

Morissa: "No Mom. I just want to hit the beech sit back and relax for the summer. If I change my mind, I'll ask you. If you come up with something let me know maybe, I will change my mind."

The next day on the beach. Morissa is sitting on a beach chair. She has a New York baseball cap on with dark sun glasses. She has a pair of jean shorts on and a halter top. An hour or so on the beech her attention is drawn to a young man about her age. The young man is standing in front of her. She looks up at him as he is blocking her view of the water. The young man is about six foot two and two hundred and eleven pounds. His hair is blond and his eyes are blue. He is tan and muscular. She smiles at him as he is looking down at her. Morissa takes her hand and motion for him to move a side. He smiles down at her and says." Haven't we met some where before Morissa."

Morissa: "Excuse me. Haven't we met somewhere before Morissa? Is that what you just said? How do you know my name?"

Guy: "We met last year at a party after a football game. I remember you being at a bar with a bunch of other girls. I can't say I remember all the other names. I did remember yours."

Morissa: "I am sorry I don't remember yours or you."

Guy: "My name is Everett."

Morissa: "I am sorry I still don't remember you."

Everett: "That's ok we didn't talk. You were with Sue and her friends. I was with my girlfriend. I remember seeing you talking to no one. You just sat at the bar. The time you were there you didn't talk to anybody. I thought that was strange. I came over to you and purposely bumped in to you. You didn't even look up at me."

Morissa: "I think you are strange for looking at other girls when you are on a date. I bet your girlfriend didn't like it."

Everett: "You are right. She caught me looking at you a couple of times."

Morissa: "What did she tell you."

Everett: "I don't remember the exact words. Let's just say she didn't like it."

Morissa: "You may want to stop talking to me and leave before she comes and catches you again."

Everett: "We broke up.  Too much drama."

Morissa: "Oh that's too bad for you. If we have the occasion to bump into each other again back at school, I will remember you.  I think. You have a nice day. Bye now."

Everett:" You do remember me. How did you know I went to your school?"

Morissa: "You knew Sue. Sorry I really don't remember you."

Everett: "Maybe you would like to get to know me. You may even get to like me."

Morissa: "Yes I may get to know you when I see you back at school. Ok bye."

Everett: "How about right now? I could take a chair right next to you and we could talk."

Morissa: "Sorry sailor there is no chair next to me, maybe next time."

Everett: "It you don't mind I could take a seat right by you there in the sand."

Morissa: "If you like. It is an open beech I can't stop you. I really was enjoying this book it is so entertaining."

Everett: "May be you could reed me the book. May be I could be more entertaining than the book?"

Morissa: "You could talk to me about your old girlfriend. May be not, I don't think I will find that entertaining sorry."

Everett takes a seat by Morissa.

Everett: "I could talk about you."

Morissa: "About me you say. I am so flattered. You don't know anything about me. You may know my name but that's it. If you did know anything about me you would know I am a boring person."

Everett: "You just finish your first year of college. I know that because the girls you were with that night were in the same year. You like to study because I saw you walking in and out of the library. You're wearing a New York hat so I think you are from New York, and out here on vacation."

Morissa: "Sorry, see that beech house behind me. That's my mother's house. So that means you must be wrong."

Everett: "I spent every summer on this beech for the past twenty years. My father owns a house down the beach. I have only seen a man and a woman in that house for as long as I can remember. If you lived in that beech house you must have been locked in the basement."

Morissa: "Your right I am sorry. My mother owns that beech house. I am staying with her for the summer. I would visit her on the winter breaks for the past ten years. She and my father are divorced. I would see her then.  I live in a small town called Port Chester New York."

Everett: "I know where that is. My father has an office in Greenwich Connecticut."

Morissa: "Small world isn't it. We could have met at school and we didn't. We could have met at the bar that night and we didn't. Three thousand miles away from school and we met here.  What are the odds of that?"

Everett: "Sorry I can't tell you I don't major in math."

Morissa: "What is your major?"

Everett: "Sports I can throw a baseball. That landed me a scholarship."

Morissa: "May be you will be a pro someday."

Everett: "No I will never be a pro. I can't throw the ball fast enough. I don't have much movement on it. I am just good enough to throw batting practice. I was the third string quarter back till I got kicked off the team.  I gave some information to a better on another player. Somebody found out, Then I was kicked off the football team.  And if I don't do anything wrong again, they will let me finish school. I have just two more years."

Morissa: "So you're a bad boy kind of."

Everett: "No I am that kind of guy a father would let date his only daughter."

Morissa: "Are you now. Was your last girlfriend an only daughter? Did you ask her father if he would let you date her?"

Everett: "No she had another sister at the school. I think her sister was watching me sometime to see if I was cheating on her sister."

Morissa: "So you can't be trusted. When you have an older sister looking out for a younger sister you have something to worry about."

Everett: "Do you have an older sister.?

Morissa: "No I am the other one you have to worry about. I am the only daughter of a crazy father. He may be watching us right now.  You may want to get away while you can."

Everett: "I will stay and take the chance. If you don't mind me sitting here?"

Morissa: "It is a free beech."

Everett: "What would you like to talk about now?"

Morissa: "I would like to finish reading this book. I was kind of enjoying the sun and the view of the water and the book. Till you stepped in front of me and started talking."

Everett: "We could do it again if you want?"

Morissa: "Do what again we haven't done anything."

Everett: "We could have the boy meet girl all over again. This could be the moment we remember our whole lives. We could be living it right now."

Morissa: "Are you kidding me. Is that some kind of pick-up line? I probably heard better ones that night in the bar. I am sure none of them was from you.

Everett: What are you doing later Morissa. May be we could get something to eat later."

Morissa: "I was going to have a pizza on that deck with my mother. It would be kind of awkward to have you there. A guy I just met. You know how those things are. You may think of her as my big sister. I would hate to put you in that spot. You may even be looking at her when I was talking to you. I heard you do those kind of things."

Everett: "I think you would know how to handle it."

Morissa: "I never had to handle it. I will never have to handle it."

Everett: "You know what I learn being a backup for the backups at baseball and football Morissa?"

Morissa: "What did you learn being the back up for the backups?"

Everett: "One-word. Practice. That is, it. Practice. You may think you know How to act when something unexpected happens. You may think you have a plan for anything that may or may not happen. But till you face it for real you never know if you are going to be able to handle something that may or may not happen. You may want to practice for any event that may happen if it happens.

Morissa: "Do you have practice at girls turning you down?"

Everett: "Yes. But when a girl spend some time with me, they do get to like me. I have that little puppy effect. You know once in a while you have to tell a little puppy what they did was bad. But a minute later you want to give them a hug."

Morissa: "You may not believe this. I don't see you as a little puppy. I see you as a problem. I see you as high maintenance."

Everett: "My mother likes me."

Morissa: "I don't know how to answer that. You are the first guy to give me that line. My mother likes me.  I hope she likes you."

Everett: "She said I was her favorite child."

Morissa: "My father said the same thing to me. Then again, I was his only child. I guess you are the only child to?"

Everett: "Yep. You guess right. You know what that means?

Morissa: "You are going to say that means we have something in common. Right?"

Everett: "It means we don't have to worry about any big sister watching us Morissa."

Morissa: "You forgot about my mother, didn't you?"

Everett: "No I didn't. I think your mother would like it if I ask you to get something to eat with me later."

Morissa: "Why do you think that. I know my mother better then you."

Everett: "If I ask your mother if I can get something to eat with you later. And if she says yes. Then you will be obligated to have something to eat with me later."

Morissa: "I don't think you are brave enough to ask my mother that. Then if you could find her that would be something else. Then if she said yes. I still may tell you I don't want to."

Everett: "Do you know what else I learned being a back up to the back up?"

Morissa: "What else did you learn being the back up to a backup?"

Everett: "A catch phrase."

Morissa: "Oh boy."

Everett: "Morissa I think at this point in our relationship we shouldn't keep secrets. I am going to tell you. It is the most important thing any man has ever said. Every great feat that was ever undertaken, this phrase was used. This phrase of such importance. Nothing ventured nothing gained."

Morissa: "Everett can I ask you a question. Were you ever hit on the head to hard?"

Everett: "Yes more than once. Morissa, can you at least give me a chance. It is just a simple let's have a meal together."

Morissa: "Ok Everett. You seam harmless enough, I hope. The day you find my mother and ask her. And if she says yes, we can have a meal together some day maybe. So please let me get back to this book."

Everett: "This whole time we been talking your mother has been sitting on the deck watching us. IF you turn around you will see her."

Morissa turns around and sees her mother laying in a chair with dark sunglass on. She is not sure if her Mother is a sleep or awake watching them.

Morissa: "Is that why you are facing the beach house and not the water.  Ok mister back up to the back up. Ok mister nothing venture nothing gain. Here is your chance. You can walk right up to her and ask her. Then if I see you walk away with your head down. I will think of you as that little puppy dog. I may want to feel sorry for you.  I don't think there will be any hugging going on."

Everett stands up. He starts his walk up to the beach house and Morissa's mother. Morissa stands up and turns to the beach house.

Everett walks up to the deck and gets Morissa mother attention. He starts to talk to her. Morissa cannot hear what Everett is asking her. When Morissa mother looks down to Morissa. Morissa is shaking her head no and mouthing the words "no way. Don't say yes." Then Morissa sees her mother then say the words yes, and nods her head up and down. Morissa turns and falls back in to her seat. A couple of minutes later Everett walks back down to Morissa. He takes the same seat in the sand facing her. Morissa has her glasses on and is back to reading her book as if nothing has happened.

Everett just sits there not saying anything. Morissa breaks her silence and the act of reading the book and puts her glasses up.

Morissa: "What did she say Everett?"

Everett: "She said that I have grown up a lot since I used to deliver papers to her. During the summers here I would have a part time job, bringing the morning papers out to the beach house. I was the only one that would walk on to her deck and put it by her door. She never forgot me for doing it."

Morissa: "I was set up, wasn't I? What are the odds of you being here from my school? You being here when I am sitting here reading a book. Then to have my mother remember a paper boy who used to bring papers up to her door."

Everett: "Your mother said she was going to go out tonight. That I should bring over some buffalo chicken pizza around 6:00. Because that is your favorite."

Morissa: "I guess I lost. Everett, You know I may not be at the house when you show up."

Everett: "I know. If you told me that you didn't want me there, I wouldn't be there. I haven't heard that yet. At six o'clock I will have pizza in hand. If you are on your deck, we could enjoy some pizza and a setting sun. If you are not, I will be right here eating crow and the pizza watching the sunset alone. I can't think of a better way to have a first date."

Morissa: "Nobody ever said anything about a date. If I am there it will be just eating some pizza with a guy at school. It could have been any guy at school. That is all."

Everett: "Ok. I will take my leave now. It will be nice to see you later Morissa."

Everett gets up and puts a x in the sand in front of Morissa. Morissa looks at him and ask him why he did that.

Everett: "I just mark the spot where we met."

Morissa: "That's a little much isn't it?"

Everett: "Could be. You never can tell about somethings."

Morissa: "Bye Everett."

Morissa goes back to reading her book. Everett waves to Morissa's mother. He then walks away toward the other end of the beech where his parents have a home.

Morissa thinking to herself. "What did I just do? The guy was just trying to be nice to me. He was just trying to meet a girl. I could have been a little nicer to him. It is just something to eat with two people. Why did I make it so hard for him? I guess he really wants to spend some time with me. He is a good-looking guy. A little quirky, I guess. He is more like that puppy dog then he knows. My mother what a help. She will be telling my father about the paper boy she fixed me up with.

It would be nice on the other hand to talk to someone from the male race. It may be good for my ego. I don't have to worry about any perception of a date. It isn't a date. I made that clear. What should I wear if I do this? Should I dress up or dress down.  Casual would be good. Shorts and a shirt. May be a summer dress. Hair up or hair down. Sneakers, flip flops or bear feet. Perfume on or not. Should I bring anything. May be a couple of beers? We don't have to worry about driving he can walk home how nice.

What will he be wearing? I hope nothing that will show he is thinking he is on a first date. I hope he shows up like he was on the beach. Shorts and a shirt. What was he doing on the beech? He said his house was down the beach.

Did he see me before and planned all this out? He was pretty good at talking to me. He had enough confidence and I liked it.  He had this planned out. He waited till he saw me on the beech then walked up to me as if it was just a coincidence. I should show him and not be there on the deck.

I may be over re acting or over thinking it. It was just something harmless. If I do have a meal with him to night, what are we going to be talking about. School, I guess. I wonder how many girls he has dated that I may know. I wonder how well he knows Sue. He may not even know her. I think everybody Knows Sue She is just one of those kind of people.

May be I will surprise him and dress up like an old woman with a lot of clothes on and scare him away. Or I could dress up with a lot of cleavage showing. What to do. I shouldn't be having this much trouble about a simple meal with a guy from school I just ran across at a beech. It probably happens more than people know.

May be I will wear a pair of white ankle pants. What shirt to wear? I could wear just a halter. No wrong impression. I will wear the New York football jersey I have. That will show him that it is just a casual meal nothing more. Yes, that's it Casual.

What was I saying that we would talk about? Was its school or was it Sue. Maybe sports. I don't know much about that. Or even like that. He would be better off talking to my father the bookie. Should I tell him that. I don't think so. I will tell him about him selling cars.

Money, can he come from a family with money. Does it matter. Father with an office in Greenwich Connecticut with a house on a California beach. His parents are loaded. And if so, who cares. He plays sports. But he is not good enough to play during a game.

Did he say he sold information about a player getting hurt? I wonder if he is in to gambling. That could be a problem. A problem for what. We are not dating. This is not come and meet my parents for the first time. He already knows my mother. My mother likes him he can't be all that bad. At least he was a good paper boy. That should mean something. Something for what.

Ankle pants are out. I think I will wear a pair of ripped jean and that football jersey that will just say a casual meal. I wonder when I should go and prepare for the casual meal between school mates. I have over four hours to do that. I will have lunch before that.

I hope my mother does leave. I would hate her to be hanging around us. If she stays in the house, would she be watching us. I hope not. I been on dates with other guys why is this one seam so strange. Is it him? Beer what if he doesn't like beer then will I make it more awkward. May be he is an alcoholic and can't drink any more. I could be putting him in a tough place.

He may not want to show that to a girl on a first date. I have to keep telling myself this isn't a first date.

Why did he draw that x in the sand? That was very clever. I like that. I wonder if he did that for another girl. I wouldn't like it if he did. I had to be the first. I never heard a guy doing that for a girl. It was clever. I just can't wait to tell the other girls about that. I bet no guy did that for them. I have to stop thinking about this. Back to the book.

Later that afternoon. Morissa is sitting on a beach chair on the deck of her mother's house facing the water. On her left side is a cooler. To the left side of the cooler is another beech chair. The time is five o'clock Morissa is dress up in a white summer dress. She gets up and walks back in to the house. The house is empty her mother has gone out with her boyfriend. On the kitchen table are bags of different kinds of potato chips.

She walks to her room and changes again. At six o'clock Morissa comes out of her room dressed in a pair of shorts a large sweat shirt and a pair of flip flops. Her long auburn hair is down past her shoulders. She walks out to the deck waiting for Everett to show. At five after six Everett could be seen walking up the beech with no pizza in hand. He is wearing the same clothes as before. He walks on to the deck and stand beside Morissa and ask the question is this chair taken? Morissa tells him it's his if he wants it. Everett thanks her and takes his seat.

Morissa: "Thank you for coming Everett. I am sorry I gave you a hard time."

Everett: "It is ok. It was kind of fun."

Morissa: "I thought you were to bring the pizza?"

Everett: "It will be hear soon. We are going to have it delivered. This way it is still hot."

Morissa: "Sounds like you been thinking a lot about this."

Everett: "Yes. I have to say I was. How about you?"

Morissa: "Sometimes a girl doesn't know what to wear to such social events like this.  I spent the afternoon trying to figure out what outfit I should wear for this ball.  Would you believe that."

Everett: "If you say so. I see are pizza coming. Can I ask what is in the cooler?"

Morissa: "There is some beer, wine coolers and soda. I wasn't sure what you would like."

Everett: "Pizza and beer is the best. I am not much of a drinker. I don't have to drive so I think I am safe tonight to get home safe."

The pizza man delivers the pizza with some breadsticks. One pizza is buffalo chicken and the other is mushrooms. Morissa goes inside get some paper plates and paper towels and brings them out to Everett.  He opens the buffalo chicken box and Morissa takes a slice out then thanks Everett. She takes some napkins and takes her seat. Everett takes a slice of the mushroom pizza and takes a bite. Then he ask Morissa what she would like to drink. Morissa ask for a wine cooler. The two start to eat and drink there drinks. They just look back and forth not saying anything for a while. Then Everett starts talking.

Everett: "This is how the rich people must live. Pizza, beers and a water front view."

Morissa: "That could be had by almost anybody. Just buy a pizza and a beer and drive to any water front. It's not different. You can change the zip code and water is just water."

Everett: "You can change the zip code. You can change the pizza. What will make a memorable view is who is sitting beside you. Thank you for doing this with me."

Morissa: "It is ok. Thank you. Maybe we will have a good time."

Everett: "We could have a real good time Morissa."

Morissa: "My mother could be back at any time Everett."

Everett: "Trust me Morissa."

Morissa: "This pizza is really good. Where did you get it? I don't recall any pizza place around here having anything this good."

Everett: "Thanks Morissa. I made it. I had a friend fake to be a delivery guy. I love to cook. I have a lot of people tell me I should of went to culinary school."

Morissa: "Why didn't you?"

Everett: "I wanted to play baseball. I love pitching in a game. In high school I was consider very good. Then I went to college and went up against good college pitchers. I found out quickly I was a good high school pitcher. Sometimes they let me throw batting practice. For now, that is enough to keep me at our school. I have taken some culinary courses. I met Sue your roommate there. She is all about who knows who. And when the next party is to be and where. I don't have to make any hard decisions for a while. I am just trying to keep my life simple. How about you Morissa."

Morissa: "I want to teach. That's what I want to do. I think I always wanted to do it. I shouldn't have any problem getting my degree. I can speak Spanish that will help me get a job somewhere. I don't know if I will get my masters before I start teaching."

Everett: "Where would you like to teach. Do you have any place that you would like to live in?"

Morissa: "I haven't thought much about that Everett. This summer being here I was thinking of California. There are a lot of schools out here with Spanish speaking kids.  Let me ask you if you could pitch for a team which team would you pitch for?"

Everett: "The Yankees or the Dodgers. The Yankees. Just to take that field must be some great feeling for anybody who gets the chance to play on it. I never will have that chance."

Morissa: "There has to be something else you would want to achieve in life beside that. Isn't there something else that you could try to do?"

Everett: "I had to think about that when I saw how good the other pitchers were. My mother gave me the idea to open a restaurant. I been thinking about that. It would take about ten years to do it, I guess.

 I would have to spend four years in culinary school. Then learn the business at somebody else restaurant, Even before I could try it. Or I could just open up some diner somewhere with the money I could borrow from mom and pop."

Morissa: "I would think that anybody who did ether of those things achieved something. Any place a person opens up as a business is something that they can be proud of."

Everett: "Thanks Morissa. I am the son of two parents that is always looking to borrow money from them. I like to think that one time I could pay them back and never borrow money from them again."

Morissa: "What do you borrow money from them for. If I can ask?"

Everett: "Anything that I do. A couple of times I bet on games and lost more than I could pay back. I had to go to my father and have him bail me out. He does it every time and I keep thinking it will be my last time."

Morissa: "I heard a lot about bookies and you see those guys in the movies."

Everett: "Not the bookie I know. This one will give you time so long as it's not big-time money. He knows who can pay it back and how much. You can't make big bets with what you don't have. I told him something one time that I shouldn't of and I got kicked off the football team. No big deal. I would have never made the real team."

Morissa: "This other mushroom pizza is very good to. You could open a pizza place and do very well, I am sure. Just find a college and you will have a line out the door all the college year. During the summer break you can close up the place and go away for the summer."

Everett: "Sounds like a plan. It sounds like a simple plan that may work out well. In the morning I could sell coffee and energy drinks to those people who drink it like water."

Morissa: "I can't believe I ate so much of that pizza. I never had more than two slices. I just finished my fourth slice. Do you cook pizza for a lot of girls?"

Everett: "I only had two real girlfriends. The last one said that I was better at making breakfast then pizza. Maybe you would let me make breakfast for you some day?

Morissa: "Before on the beach you said you knew I was Sues roommate. I didn't tell you that. How did you know?

Everett: "I asked Sue the next class I had with her who you were. She told me that you were her roommate. Then she told me I had a girl and that you were to shy.

Then she told me that you were hands off to any guy who had a girl friend or she would tell all the girls that I was a cheater. She really likes you."

Morissa: "I like her to. At first when I met her, I didn't think we would get along. We get along just great now. She knows when I just want to be left by myself. She is so honest with everything. At first you look at her and it the bleach blondie bimbo type. She really isn't like that. She is just trying to have fun. She is that simple. She passes all of her class with little effort. I think she is a lot smarter then she lets on. Let me rephrase that. I said she so honest in one sentence then I said she smarter then she lets on. I can't rationalize it but that's her. She's smart but doesn't show it. She is so honest."

Everett: "Everybody likes her. She is always the center of any party. That leads me to ask you why I haven't seen you at any of the parties?"

Morissa: "I don't need them. I just want to work on my school work. Some times when I need to clear my head I will go for a walk on campus. I call it my party time. I don't need any entertainment."

Everett: "Morissa you're a parents dream kid. My parents think of me as there punishment for something they did in a previous life. There always having to bail me out every time they turn around."

Morissa: "I don't try to be a parents dream kid. I am happy with the way I am. Sometimes I think I should be a little more outgoing. At the end of the day when I go to sleep. I am happy with myself when I get up the next day"

Everett: "At the end of the day. I am more often than not, trying to figure a way out of the trouble I got myself in."

Morissa: "What do you do that creates the problem that gets you in to trouble?"

Everett: "Money. It is all about money. I bet more than I have. I gamble and lose more then I win."

Morissa: "Can't you stop doing it."

Everett: "I do it for a time. Then I go right back to doing it again. I plan on stopping it totally when I leave college. Till then I hope to get by. Maybe I have to be totally cut off by my parents and friends. Then I will quit"

Morissa: "That is a heck of a plan you have their Everett. I wish you luck with it."

Everett: "Morissa we have a couple more slices of pizza left in the box. Do you want another slice?"

Morissa: "No thank you it was really good but I had enough. If you don't mind, I am going to put the boxes in side. It is the smell of pizza after I eat so much of it that is bothering me. I will be right back"

Everett: "Ok I will be right here when you get back."

Ten minutes later Morissa returns and takes her seat. She looks at Everett and smiles.

Morissa: "Everett thank you for the pizza and trying to spend this time with me. I am sorry I left the chips in the house. I like it out here talking to you."

Everett: "May be we can do it again some time?"

Morissa: "Maybe. Will see."

Everett: "What are you going to do tomorrow?"

Morissa: "I am going to go shopping with my mother. She will have me out all day and in to the night. It is what she does."

Everett: "Does she have a job?"

Morissa: "She think she does but she really doesn't. Her boss is her father. He is some money manager that makes more than the people he manages money for? My mother is on his pay roll for something so he can write it off. What do your parents do Everett that lets you play with their money?"

Everett: "My father is a lawyer with an office back in Connecticut. My mother was a freelance editor. My mother was a TV writer years ago. She made a lot of money doing it. Then she wanted to be free of any schedule. She has retired."

Morissa: "I like to do what your mother did."

Everett: "I could introduce her to you."

Morissa: "Thank you. I'll keep it in mind. Everett what are you going to do tomorrow?

Everett: "I am a life guard on this beech. I been doing it for the last couple of years. I make enough to last me for a little while in school. If I could do it seven days a week all year round, I'll be set. When late summer comes, I go back to school. I don't have a job at school to help keep my grade point up"

Morissa: "Maybe I will come by and see you while you're in your life guard tower. If I am lucky maybe you will be saving someone."

Everett: "Maybe I will get lucky and save you."

Morissa: "Sorry Everett. I am probably a better swimmer then you."

Everett: "We will have to try that one day. We have to have a race."

Morissa: "Be careful. I would hate to go back to school and tell Sue I beat you in a race. Then the whole school would know that a girl beat you."

Everett: "We would have to bet something."

Morissa: "Like what?"

Everett" "How about breakfast?"

Morissa: "I heard you already had that meal. I don't want to be the second dish. If you know what I mean."

Everett: "What do you have in mind?"

Morissa: "That pizza was too good. I am starting to wonder if you really made it. A girl can't be too careful you know. See that dock out there in the water?"

Everett: "Yes. I see it."

Morissa: "Saturday morning I will meet you out there by the water's edge. I will race you to the dock and back to the shore. If I win you have to make me dinner. If you win, I will make you dinner."

Everett: "Can you cook?"

Morissa: "Can you swim?"

Everett: "I am a life guard."

Morissa: "Can you swim fast?"

Everett: "Fast enough to catch somebody before they go under for good. How about you?"

Morissa: "High school swim team."

Everett: "Sounds good."

Morissa: "Ok. Saturday morning at eight AM. I will meet you down there by the water's edge. Out to the dock and back to the shore. Loser has to make dinner. Deal?"

Everett: "Deal."

Morissa: "I will start thinking about what I want for dinner. Any suggestion?"

Everett: "Japanese or Italian. People like what I can cook from those two the best."

Morissa: "I will let you know Saturday after I win.:

Everett: "What if I win."

Morissa: "I'll keep my end of the bargain. I been cooking my own meals for years now. I live with my father and he would come home after I have eaten. Most of the time I would cook something for him or reheat the meal when he came home."

Everett: "Be careful of that dock when you get near it. There are four chains that are anchor to the bottom of the dock. They hold the dock in place. Swimmers that are new hear will often swim right in to the chain. Some of them will panic when they hit it thinking that it is a shark. If they hit the chain to hard it leaves a mark on their skin. Then when they get back to the shore the swimmer will see the chain mark and think a shark bit them."

Morissa: "Anybody get seriously hurt doing that?"

Everett: "Not in a long time."

Morissa: "Are there any sharks out there?"

Everett: "Yes there are. They are always out there somewhere. They don't like coming to close to this shore for some reason. We have some shark detectors out there."

Morissa: "What is a shark detector."

Everett: "It is something that the life guards tell the tourist. It makes them feel safer."

Morissa: "Nice. Tell me about what happen a long time ago on the dock."

Everett: "One kid died several years ago. He and a couple of friends swam out to the dock late one night to drink and got drunk. One by one they passed out that night. One of the boys rolled off the dock and fell in to the water."

Morissa: "That is so sad."

Everett: "Yes his family never got over it. Some people think he rolled of the dock when he was drunk. He did have some chain marks on his skin when the autopsy was done. The doctor said he could have hit the chain when he rolled off the dock that night."

Morissa: "I feel so sorry for his family."

Everett: "The water is going to be cold early in the morning. Do you want to do it later in the day?"

Morissa: "No. I am used to the north east water."

Everett: "You may not be as shy like you act Morissa."

Morissa: "It isn't that I am shy. It is just who I am. I don't try to be anybody but me."

Everett: "I could get to like you."

Morissa: "A girl can't be too careful my mother always tells me."

Everett: "What does your mother also tell you."

Morissa: "Never date anybody name Everett."

Everett: "No she didn't."

Morissa: "Were you there when she said that?"

Everett: "Everett and Kermit sound a lot alike. Maybe she did say Kermit. Maybe she doesn't want you to date a Kermit."

Morissa: "Good come back. No guy I have told that joke to had a better answer."

Everett: "Your mother does like me. She helped me spend this time with you."

Morissa: "She like the paper boy who didn't throw the paper at her glass patio door from the beech. Not much more then that I have to tell you."

Everett: "You will get to like me. If you give me a chance."

Morissa: "I could go out in to that water and get to like a shark just as much. I know it is safer to stay away from a shark. I may be safer to stay away from you."

Everett: "I am safe you can trust me."

Morissa: "I can? Can I? I met you a couple of hours ago. I let you spend the last couple of hours with me alone out here. I let you fill me full of pizza. I have been here drinking too much with you at arm's length. You told me you lied to tourist because it is funny. I already have committed to a second meeting with you. You have me betting on a race with you. I am starting to think your one fast operator. May be I should just say good night here and now."

Everett: "Let's look at it like this. We go to the same school. We have the same friends at school. I met your mother before. I just made you a nice meal in a place that was very comfortable for you. You feel safe enough with me to get a little drunk. I been a perfect gentleman being so close to you. I do give the tourist something to write home about. I would have met you in school again this fall.

The bet is an opportunity for you to have another meal. I could say I been waiting for you my whole life to come along. You could say good night here and now. Your smart enough to know when it is time to end it."

Morissa: "Now I believe it."

Everett: "Believe what?"

Morissa: "I now believe your father is a lawyer. The comeback with that name of Kermit. That line that came back so fast. You should be a lawyer like your father."

Everett: "That makes more sense then you know. Somehow, I always managed to get myself out of trouble like a lawyer. The reasonings I gave sometimes had my father in fits on how to deal with my reasoning. He never came down too hard on me. We have just been talking a couple of hours in you had me all figured out. When you do become a teacher. Take it easy on that little boy who said the dog ate his homework. When you look at his face when he tells you that just think of me. Because right now I feel like that little boy. Just like a lost little puppy dog that's kind of like me. I just need someone to like me."

Morissa: "When I race you Saturday, I better not see a little boy with a puppy dog face. You know the sad face that girls like to see a puppy dog have."

Everett: "Maybe that's why your mother likes me. She sees me as a lost puppy dog?"

Morissa: "I have to tell you again. She like the paper boy who didn't throw the paper against her glass patio door that's all."

Everett: "Later when we all are talking at a table about the good old days. I am sure you will be surprised about how much she likes me."

Morissa: "I am starting to worry about you Everett."

Everett: "Why?"

Morissa: "I think you had too much to drink. You are becoming delusional. Maybe you should stop drinking."

Everett: "We just met and you are worried about me how nice."

Morissa: "Are you really like this or is it an act?"

Everett: "It is me. The better you get to know me the more you will like me."

Morissa: "Do you tell that to all the girls? Or am I just the lucky one to day?"

Everett: "I am the lucky one to be here with you tonight. Just think of it we are able just to sit out here. We are watching the waves roll in and out. The stars and the moon are burning bright in the sky. We don't have any class to be at tomorrow. We both know your mother will be home soon so there is no need to try anything. Somehow we are able to keep the conversation going and enjoying it."

Morissa: "Stop. What do you mean try anything?"

Everett: "Like the first kiss. We both know it will happen. It is the timing of it. Will it happen before your mother comes home? Or after she comes home."

Morissa: "It just may not happen Everett. You never know how these things work out."

Everett: "Yes I know. Sometimes it is just a kiss on the cheek. Sometimes it is just a hug. And sometimes. Well, you never know how things turn out."

Morissa: "I could tell you how it is going to turn out right now. I would but a good girl never talks about what she does or has on her mind. Now you think about that."

Everett: "I will be thinking more about it on my walk home tonight under those stars."

Morissa: "Yes you will be."

Everett: "Morissa why do you want to become a teacher?"

Morissa: "That is changing a subject fast."

Everett: "It is the way you talk. Your so guarded. I think when you are in front of a class a teacher has to be who they really are. If you try to be somebody you're not or try to be to guarded the class will see it. You could be the greatest teacher ever to teach I don't know. The way you don't want to open up. Or the way you make defenses for your answers. You may be too afraid to be a teacher."

Morissa: "How do I answer that. I think you just insulted me. I think you are trying to analyze me. I don't like what you just said."

Everett: "This is our first real talk Morissa. I am enjoying talking to you so much. Some of your conversations are all a measured response. Somewhere in how you are talking to me is the person named Morissa wanting just to talk to a guy who is a stranger. I am not going to put any pressure on you to night. This is just about two people enjoying their time to gather. The way it usually works at are age. The words are the best way to learn our likes and dislike. It is when a boy and girl or man and woman are talking together. It is the challenge to find an honest conversation is what we like the best."

Morissa doesn't say anything back to Everett. She looks at him then takes another wine cooler and downs some of it.

She puts her head back on the chair and reclines it fully back. She closes her eyes. The two don't say another word for about a half hour. Then Morissa says the first words.

Morissa: "What do you want to talk about now Everett."

Everett: "I don't know. We could talk more about the sharks here."

Morissa: "We have the best sharks off long Island. Did you ever see that movie about a great white shark? That proved we have the best sharks.'

Everett: "No that doesn't. It was just a movie. Australia has the biggest and meanest sharks."

Morissa: "Were you ever there?"

Everett: "Yes when I was five. A life guard told me a shark ate a boy my size the day before. I was so scared."

Morissa: "Is that true?"

Everett: "Yes. I was with another boy about ten years older. He told me he would protect me from any sharks. He did that. That is why I am here today."

Morissa: "That was nice of him. I hope you thanked him."

Everett: "Yes I did. Don't worry about the sharks Saturday. I will protect you from anything that may bite you."

Morissa: "It may not be the sharks I will be looking out for."

Everett: "Morissa I'm safe. We could now go for a walk along the beach under the stars and burn off some of those calories."

Morissa: "Ok Everett let's do it. A walk on the beech sounds nice. Let me go inside for a minute and I will be right back."

Morissa goes inside then quickly returns. She is wearing a pair of dark sunglass and a New York baseball cap.

Everett: "Why the so dark sun glasses and the baseball cap?"

Morissa: "The glasses make the drunk better. The hat is because I look good in it."

Everett: "Ok we are off."

Morissa and Everett walking along the water's edge side by side.

Morissa: "Everett I love the water. My friends and I used to go down to the local beech at night and sit on a stone wall by the water. That place has a small beech and a dock for boats. In another part of the beech there is a kid's playground, a tennis court and baseball field. You would never know it was there driving past it. It is just a nice place to hang out in. We would spend hours on a stone wall by the water talking about anything. Then we would just call it a night and go home. And You may think it is just for some millionaires. It's not we were just an odd bunch of friends. Would you like me to tell you about them?"

Everett: "If you like."

Morissa: "The best way for me to tell you about them is to tell you we liked each other. Their names Were Gerald, Pat, and Tony."

Everett: "All boys."

Morissa: "No Tony was a girl. I was always so happy to be with them."

Everett: "Do you see them now that you are in college?"

Morissa: "Not as much. They have their own lives. When I do talk to them. We always say we have to get together on the wall again. Do you have any friends like that Everett?"

Everett: "I had a best friend years ago. After he went away, I never had another close friend like him."

Morissa: "How about girlfriends Everett. You are a good-looking jock kind of guy. You must have had a lot of girl friends?"

Everett: "Jock not really. I could swim better than most that's about it. I like sports. A lot. I like betting on the games but jock not really. I had a few steady girlfriends it never last more than a few months. Every girl I dated we broke of the relationship for different reasons. How about you Morissa. Tell me about your love life."

Morissa: "I dated. I never had a boyfriend for long.  I like them at first then they change on me. I am a girl that guys don't want to date."

Everett: "Maybe we can work on that."

Morissa: "I don't want to work on that. I just want to be me."

Everett: "We all have to give and take in a relationship. Whether it is just being friends or some serious relationship it will always take work to keep it going. A marriage takes both side working to keep that marriage going. Relationships are nice to be in. To have somebody who is always thinking about you. To have somebody you are always thinking about. The price to have that is the work it takes to keep it going.  You have to be able to change for that other person. That other person has to be able to change for you. Then you have to be able to except who that other person is even if they don't change."

Morissa: "I thought you were just looking for the next pretty girl to come along. Where did you pick that up from?"

Everett: "My mother told me that."

Morissa: "I agree with her. Everett why can't you do better at gambling?"

Everett: "I over analyze the bet. Sometimes I will just look at a bet and work it out so many different ways I never get it right. I just walk away losing. More often than not if I go with my first hunch I do better.

 When I start over thinking it, I think of the what ifs too much. I lose more often than not. Unfortunate for me I seldom am able to put the right parts together at the right time enough to win more then I lose."

Morissa: "Why do you have to make those bets. From what you told me your parents have money. You don't need the money to live."

Everett: "It is the excitement of it. It is something like the time on that stone wall by the beech with your friends. It is that way with me and some of my friends. When we see each other, it is a good time with us when we are talking about what game to bet on. It is the talk of how much money to bet. Where to bet and everything else that goes with it. Then it is the talk of just what happen."

Morissa: "It sounds like what girls do after they date a guy. We just talk about what we wore. We talk about what we talked about. Where we went. Same things."

Everett: "What will you tell them about us tonight?"

Morissa: "Probably nothing. This wasn't a date."

Everett: "If this was a date. And you did tell your girl friends about are night tonight what would you say?"

Morissa: "I would tell them the truth. So far, I would say you are very nice and I had a good time talking to you. I do like talking to you Everett."

Everett: "Thanks. What would you like me to talk to you now about?"

Morissa: "I think you and I should turn around and head back now. It is after midnight and we should get back home."

Everett: "Ok"

Morissa: "Don't you live somewhere down here?"

Everett: "Yes. See that white beech house with the red roof. That is my parents' house. They also have a house in Pomona."

Morissa: "It so big. Just you your father and mother. That is a lot of house."

Everett: "Yes my mother likes it a lot. When my father retires, I think he may live somewhere else."

Morissa: "Sounds like my parents."

Everett: "Sometimes when my father is here. You can find him on the beech fishing then later that night he'll cook what he caught. He taught me how to cook. We get along great sometimes. Then it is the time that I get over my head and he has to bail me out. That is the problem between us."

Morissa: "How about your mother. How well do you get along with her?"

Everett: "Good. Sometimes she had to bail me out without my father knowing. She is the peace keeper in the family."

Morissa: "I am starting to wonder about how much money you bet that you shouldn't."

Everett: "Sometimes too much. Right now, we are in the summer time. There isn't as much action now as in the fall. It's the professional football, college football and play off base ball that gets me in trouble. If I make it past the last football game even. It was a good year for me."

Morissa: "How many good years have you had?"

Everett: "One so far and about eight bad ones."

Morissa: You started when you were about twelve years old?"

Everett: "Yes. It started off with some simple bets among friends. Then it was the big time and a friend who knew a bookie."

Morissa: "You know those bookies are like sharks in the water. Your just food for them."

Everett: "I know."

Morissa: "I wish you luck Everett. If I, was you? I would get some help to stop that?"

Everett: "I will probably stop it when I finish college. That is when most of us stop."

Morissa: "I will be with my mother shopping and eating a lunch somewhere tomorrow. Or should I say later today. Where will you be today Everett."

Everett: "I will be a life guard sitting on a tower watching the people trying to have a day at the beach. If you get a chance you can come by and see me. I will be by one of the towers by the dock."

Morissa: "We will be out all day. It is what she likes to do."

Everett: "Do you and your father get along?"

Morissa: "We do. I have spent more time with him over the years. He is great. He lets me do what I want. I can come and go as I please. I don't need any more money than they give me. I have an easy life, I guess. I haven't done anything to have him second guess my decisions."

Everett: "You are the kid my parents wish they had."

Morissa: "I am probably the kid every parent wish they had at one time or another."

Everett: "When you start teaching you will be lucky to have just one of you in a class room. We both know that teachers are stuck with teaching what a parent created. Most of the time the parents are just giving the teacher a problem that they can't handle."

Morissa: "Yes I know. It is what every teacher has had to deal with since teachers have started to teach. If you want the good part of teaching then you will have to get past the hard parts. Just like every other job. In teaching you have the satisfaction of seeing someone learn something that you taught them. What could be better than that."

Everett: "May be some day you will look at me. Like you taught me something. You will be so happy if you can take me and say you taught me something."

Morissa: "I think you may be somebody that is better off with you helping yourself."

Everett: "Yes I understand."

Morissa: "You know we are right at the point closest to the dock. We could have that race to the dock right now Everett."

Everett: "We could but it wouldn't be smart. We have had too much to drink and eat. The water is to dark. You will have your chance the day after tomorrow."

Morissa: "Sounds like you are trying to be the responsible one here."

Everett: "I do have a dark side, I guess. This is my responsible side.

Morissa: "I may like this side of you better."

Everett: "If you like boring to, Then that side of me is in side of me somewhere."

Morissa: "We'll see."

Everett: "Morissa we are almost back at your house. We could walk down the other side of the beech if you like."

Morissa: "I would, but you have to be the responsible one tomorrow and go to work. I would feel bad if you mis work because I kept you out all night."

Everett: "I have you back at your house. It is that time that we say goodbye. Since this wasn't a date, we don't have that pressure of the first kiss, do we?

Morissa: "No we don't do we."

Everett: "I could be the responsible one here and say good night turn around and walk home."

Morissa: "Everett. I had a nice time with you. I enjoy talking with you and having that walk on the beach. I would like to do this again. I will see you Saturday morning at eight by that dock.

Morissa gives Everett a kiss on the cheek.

Everett turns and walks back home. Morissa watches him walk away then takes the remaining bottles out of the cooler. She flips the cooler upside down then takes the bottles back inside the house. She then goes up to her room and turns in for the night.

The next day Morissa and her mother spend the day together shopping and having lunch to gather. Morissa tells her mother about her time with Everett. She tells her how nice he is and how he comes across as being so honest with her."

Everett spends his day as a life guard. He has to be the responsible one on the beach. Everett is a person who knows how to handle the people he is watching. He has learned his job from some state regulated classes.

Most of his ability comes from a lot of experience. While some parents are off doing something else. Everett is the one watching over there kids. There our people on and off the floating dock all day. Everett will swim out to the dock a couple of times to make sure that everybody stays safe on it. Everett has saved serval people over his time as a lifeguard.

The day ends Morissa comes home with her mother. She goes out to the beech deck and reads a book, thinking about Everett. Everett day ends he spend the night out on the deck reading a book.

Chapter Two

Friends

The next day Saturday

Morissa is the first to show up on the beech by the floating dock. She has a pair of shorts on over a blue one-piece bathing suit. She spends her time waiting for Everett stretching and warming up for the swim. Everett shows up fifteen minutes later in his pair of life guard swimming trunks.

Morissa: "Nice of you to show up Everett. I was starting to think you wouldn't show up. Maybe a little scared?

Everett: "Yes. Let me know when you are ready."

Morissa: "Don't you want to warm up. I used to swim in high school. I was pretty good. I was able to beat most guys my age."

Everett: "Ok let's do this. Do you want to get in the water first or have a running start?"

Morissa: "I am getting in to the water. You can run and then start swimming. That is what life guards are used to."

Everett: "Ok let's get in that cold morning water."

The two start the walk in the water. Morissa takes some of the cold water and splash it on herself. Everett just looks at her. Morissa removes her shorts in the water and pops back up and tells Everett she is ready.

Everett: "Ok you say go. Then the first one to the dock and back to the beach wins."

Morissa: "Ok I got it. Get ready get set and go."

Morissa takes the early lead. Then Everett catches her half way before they reach the dock. At the dock the two are tied. The race back Everett pulls ahead and reaches the beech before Morissa is three quarters of the way back. Everett is standing on the beech holding her shorts as a tired and winded Morissa hits the beech. It takes her accouple of minutes to catch her breath. Everett hands Morissa her shorts."

Morissa: "You are really a fast swimmer. I haven't seen many people who can swim that fast. congratulation on the win.

Everett: "Thank you. You are not the first person who I beat."

Morissa: "You should swim for a school. You may even be good enough for the Olympics."

Everett: "Yea, I may be. Maybe. Probably may be fast enough. Maybe. But right now, You should get back to your house and get dried off. You are starting to shake from the cold water.

Everett walks Morissa back to her house. Then he returns to his house. In a couple of hours Everett is at his life guard station. Morissa finds Everett at his tower working and tells him what time he should come for dinner.

Everett starts thinking about what Morissa will be making him for dinner. His thoughts of did he make it look to easy. Did he embarrass her. Should he have just let her beat him. The thought of trying to do the right think. The right thing trying to get her to like him. Trying to do the right acts that a new boyfriend will try to do. The work of his day and the patience to the problem swimmers takes his mind off the race and Morissa. As his day ends, he starts to think again about what dinner Morissa will make him.

Everett's day ends and he walks home. He takes a shower and starts to get dress for his dinner with Morissa. Morissa spends her day on her deck getting a sun tan and reading a book. An hour before Everett was do for dinner Morissa gets up and goes inside. She gets ready for her dinner with Everett. She takes a shower and gets dressed for The dinner with Everett.

Everett leaves his house and walks up the street. He is dressed in pressed black pants and a white shirt and a sports jacket. He walks up the street that runs up in front of the beech house. Everett knocks on Morissa front door. Morissa answers the front door. She is dressed up in a pair of blue jeans that has some rips in them and a white button-down shirt.

Morissa gives Everett a kiss on the cheek and tells him how nice he looks. Then Morissa grabs Everett hand and takes him for a walk up the street.

Everett: "You have me a little confused Morissa. Where are you taking me Morissa? I thought you were going to make me dinner."

Morissa: "We are going to have dinner together."

Everett: "This is how you are going to make me dinner."

Morissa: "I am going to make you dinner."

Everett: "Are you taking me shopping?"

Morissa" "I am taking you to a place that I will make you dinner Everett. Don't you trust me. Where else would I be taking you."

Everett: "I don't know. But I am a little surprise. I thought we were going to have dinner at your house."

Morissa: "You did. Did you. Well. I have something else on my mind. Would you like to know what I have on my mind Everett?"

Everett: "You could just tell me and the mystery would be over."

Morissa: "Everett I can't make everything so easy for you, can I? Wouldn't you like to have a surprise? Maybe it would be a surprise that you would like. Just think about that Everett. You were probably thinking what I was going to make you all day. Everett, to tell you the truth I didn't even think about what I was going to make you for a meal. I was just reading a book all day and that's were my mind was."

Everett: "I was thinking was it going to be Italian or maybe some Asian. May be you would make me a seven coarse meal. Then I was thinking whatever you would make it was just going to be you and I"

Morissa: "I have a confession to make. It may not be just you and me. There may be another man who may join us. Maybe more than one man. What do you think of that?"

Everett: "I don't know what to think. I thought it was just going to be you and I."

Morissa: "I could probably guess what was on your mind. But I don't know how many other men will be there. But there will be some other females to talk to. If you get tired of talking to me you can talk to them. There may be more females there then males. It can be a smorgasbord of females. You may meet your future girlfriend there."

Everett: "I was hoping that I have already met her."

Morissa: "I bet you did. Everett take your mind off what you were hoping for your self-tonight. Start thinking of what you may do for somebody else.

Think how somebody could be made a little happier by something you could do for them. Sometimes it is the little things you could do for someone.

The little things that may help a person. Isn't there any time in your life that you wish you could have helped somebody?"

Everett: "We all have that feeling once in a while. We all look back and wish we helped someone that needed help."

Morissa: "Everett you are going to get your chance to help some people tonight. See that building up there. That is a senior center. It is there time for them to be served dinner. I have volunteer to help them with their dinner before I made that bet. Now I can pay of my bet to you and do what I volunteer to do."

Everett: "I really underestimated you. I thought you would be thinking about trying to impress me on how well you can cook. That is how I thought you would react to my pizza. You should be trying to outdo me. That is the way it should work."

Morissa: "That may be how you think. That may be how you want a girl to react to you. That is not how I think or how I am going to react to a guy. If you like you can leave now and walk away. I would like it if you gave me a chance and come in side with me. I usually spend a couple of hours here a week during the winter holidays when I visit my mother. Everett, please come inside with me."

Everett: "Any time I could spend time with you I will take it. Let me get the door for you and I will walk in to the valley of the seniors"

Morissa: "Thank you Everett it means a lot to me you joining me tonight."

Everett: "Ok."

Morissa and Everett go inside the senior center. Morissa introduce Everett to the people who run the center. They ask Everett if he would like to help set up the chairs and tables. Everett does what he was asked.

Morissa disappears in to the kitchen and helps makes the meals for the dinner. Everett works on the tables and chairs. He sets up some garbage cans. The seniors start coming in and getting their meals from a feeding table. The seniors take those seats that they always sit at with the same people. Morissa is at the serving table giving food to the seniors. Everett runs out of things to do. He goes up to Morissa with an empty plate. Morissa puts some corn beef and potatoes on his plate. Everett then gets a piece of cake and a drink. Then he finds a seat by an older man named James. James is sitting alone. Everett introduces himself to James.

James: "Good afternoon young man. How is your day going to day?"

Everett: "I am alright. A little Confused on what I am to do next here."

James: "You don't have to do anything next but eat."

Everett: "Thank you. That's not what I was thinking about. I came in here with a friend. I was hoping to have somebody tell me what I am supposed to do here."

James: "You don't have to do anything here. You don't even have to eat. Sometimes I just come in here to find someone to talk to. I may have a cup of coffee and see if I can find someone to talk to. Sometimes one of us may have a question on social security, health care or where we can get a good senior citizens discount."

Everett: "I will keep that in mind when I need anything like that."

James: "I guess you are a young volunteer here."

Everett: "I guess for tonight I am."

James: "Thank you for being here."

Everett: "Your welcome. But I haven't done anything."

James: "You're here. That is nice of you to be here. Some of the people here do need the food that is given here. The meal people get here will be the best meal they will have all day."

Everett: "I just had some of the meal of the day. I can't say it was all that good."

James: "Sometimes the meal just being hot is what makes it taste good."

Everett: "Can't you make something hot at home. Just heat up a can of soup."

James: "It sounds so simple to you doesn't it. Just heat up a can of soup. It would be. It would be that simple if somebody had a can of soup to eat up."

Everett: "Can you tell me when this ends?

James: "It ends when you leave. If you're asking me when they stop feeding us. It will stop when they run out of food or people to feed. In my business day that was called supply and demand. Now it is called last call for food."

Everett: "I got it."

James: "Do you know anybody that needs to come in here and eat?"

Everett: "No. I lived down on the beech my whole life and never thought of this place. I must of past this place a thousand times."

James: "I used to pass it to. Now I come in here a couple of times a week. I like the desserts we get here.

Sometimes a local restaurant will donate some left-over dessert or pastries that didn't sell. It is a treat that is greatly appreciated by us. Some of the people here can't afford such nice things."

Everett: "Really. I thought they throw that stuff away or save it till the next day."

James: "They used to. Now thanks to some good people we get some of it."

Everett: "I have seen a lot of food go to waste at all the schools I went to. If you took all that wasted food and feed people with it you could feed a lot of people."

James: "Yes I remember my school days. I remember being in the army and how much I hated that food. At that time, you don't think about it. But there was always food. We never missed a meal. How simple it was just to get a meal. It is much harder as you get older."

Everett: "I guess it can be."

James: "Here comes my girlfriend. She finished serving the people now she is coming over to talk to me."

Morissa comes over to the table with Everett and James who are talking. She takes a seat by James who is sitting across from Everett. In her hand is a plate of the day's dessert. It is wrapped up in plastic on a paper plate.

Morissa: "Here you go James. A plate of the house special dessert. Just for my special boyfriend."

James: "Thank you Morissa. That is nice of you. I hope I am not taking it away from anybody?"

Morissa: "Not tonight. Not that many people tonight. There is more back there if you need more?"

James: "If I eat any more of this, I may get fat then I may lose you."

Morissa: "James, you will never lose me. I see you met my new friend Everett."

James: "Yes nice young man."

Everett: "I didn't know you two knew each other."

Morissa: "Yes we have been seeing each other for years now."

James: "Morissa likes to come in here and keep me company. Her mother bought her in here one thanksgiving. She came over to me one meal with some dessert and we been friends ever since. She is just a good person don't you think so?"

Everett: "Morissa and I just met. I am hoping that she likes me as much as you one day."

James: "You will be doing good if she likes you. You may never find a girl better than her. A man will be lucky to find a woman better looking than Morissa.

Morissa: "Thank you James you just the sweetest talking man I know. I bet that is how you won your wife's hart."

James: "I was so lucky she said yes to me. It wasn't my sweet talking to her that had her saying yes to me. I remember my tongue being tied in knots. I think I asked her three times four different ways before she said yes to me. She told me years later she said yes the first time but I was so nervous that it didn't register with me."

Morissa: "I am sure she was happy you did ask her."

James: "She gave me four sons and six grand kids. I hope she knew how happy I was to be married to her."

Morissa: "I wish I met her. I would have told her she found a good man."

James: "She would have liked you Morissa. She always wanted a girl. You would have been the girl she would have been proud of."

Everett: "James where is your wife tonight?"

James: "She died about ten years ago."

Everett: I am sorry I didn't put it together."

James: "It is ok. I have to tell everybody who ask where my wife is."

Morissa: "James often tells me stories about him, his wife and kids. We would sit here till they have to close this place up. Sometimes when James is up to it, he will even walk me home."

Everett: "James Morissa made a bet the other day. It was a swimming bet. Who was the fastest swimmer? The loser would make the other person dinner. She lived up to her bet. She made me dinner. If I lost the bet, we would have dinner at my house. I am a pretty good cook. I would of really went all out to impress her."

James: "Yea if I was fifty years younger, I would be trying to impress this good-looking young lady to."

Morissa: "I don't think I ever been so flatter James. Thank you."

Everett: "I tried flattering this good-looking young lady. I don't think it is that easy with her. I think she is looking for something else beside the words."

James: "She told me what she is looking for. But I can't tell you. If you want to win her heart you will have to be what she is looking for."

Morissa: "James is a gentle man. He would never talk about what a lady may have told him in secret. Gentleman are so hard to find now a days."

Everett: "If I can ask you James what did you do when you worked."

James: "I was a bank owner when I was young. Our family own two banks. Then I sold them and managed one of them. Then I worked on people 401k after I retired."

Everett: I guess you did pretty good for yourself James."

James: "I did. I am a millionaire a couple times over."

Everett: "I don't understand why you come here. You don't need the food."

James: "You are right I don't need the food. I think it may be time for me to leave. It was nice meeting you Everett. Morissa thank you again for helping these people who need help."

Morissa: "I like doing it. I like seeing you James take care."

James gets up. Everett and him shake hands. Morissa gives James a kiss on the cheek. Morissa and Everett sit back down at the table.

Everett: "I don't understand if he has the money, he says he has. Why does he come here?"

Morissa: "He comes here for the conversation and the dessert."

Everett: "Then he is taking food from the people who may need it."

Morissa: "No one who gives or works here keeps a score card on what people eat or take out of here. He donates a lot of money to the food banks. He will pay to feed people who needs the food.

He use his money and influence to help seniors who needs help. He lives alone now. He visit his kids and grandkids as much as he can. He likes coming here. It gives him what he wants. That is having this place to go to and he gets to talk to people. He does miss his wife a lot. I like him a lot Everett he is a good man."

Everett: "Well I guess are bet is over now. You did make me a meal. What would you like to do now?"

Morissa: "There is only one thing left for us to do. Can you guess what that is Everett?"

Everett: "Clean up?"

Morissa: "Yep."

Everett: "What would you have done, if you won the race and I would have had to make dinner for you? You would have been at my place not here."

Morissa: "I had a plan for that Everett. I may tell it to you some day but you could start folding the chairs and tables back up. I have to help them cleanup in the back. It shouldn't be another fifteen minutes then we could walk back home.

Morissa and Everett finish their work then leave together.

Morissa: "Everett thank you for being a good sport about this. You could have left you know. I didn't exactly live up to my end of the bet."

Everett: "We ate together twice Morissa and we can't say we even had a date yet."

Morissa: "Yes I know. I will tell you what. Do you have to work tomorrow?"

Everett: "Yes I do. Why?"

Morissa: "We could have our first real date tomorrow. I will live up to my part of the date an make you lunch and bring it to you. How would you like that?"

Everett: "That would be nice. I never had anybody do that for me. I would really like that."

Everett and Morissa help clean up the center and start there walk back home.

Morissa: "We are at my house now. Could you do me a favor to night Everett?"

Everett: "Sure what can I do for you."

Morissa: "It is a Saturday night and the night is still young."

Everett: "I am all yours tonight what would you like to do?

Morissa: "The other night when we were on the deck and talking that was one of the best times I have had in a while. Didn't you like it?"

Everett: "I did like it. I had a good time."

Morissa: "Good I would like to do it again. But with one thing different.

Everett: "What do you want to do different?"

Morissa: "No alcohol. Just us talking with no alcohol. Do you think we could do that? Two drunk people can talk to each other with little effort. Do you think we can do that Everett?"

Everett: "Sure. We can talk about our past dates."

Morissa: "I hope that is you trying to be funny."

Everett: "Ok it is. Are we going to do this on your deck or mine?"

Morissa: "We could swim out to the dock and talk out on that dock."

Everett: "Morissa I don't like that dock. You can think of it as it is part of my work if you like. I just don't like that dock."

Morissa: "Ok it is your deck then. Just let me run in side for a moment I want to grab a bag of Milano cookies."

Everett: "Sounds close to a date Morissa. I will be on the deck waiting for you."

Morissa: "Ok be right with you."

Morissa runs in side and comes out with a bag of Milano cookies and a couple of tea bags. She meets Everett sitting on the back deck. The two walk back to his house. Everett gets two deck chairs and puts them at the end of the deck facing the water. He takes her tea bags and goes inside the house. Twenty minutes later he comes out of the house in short, an old football jersey and bear feet. In his hand is a platter of cheese with a large mug of tea. He hands it to Morissa. Then he goes back in side and gets a small folding table and sits it down next to her. He takes the tea from her and puts it on the folding table with the cheese. Then he goes back in side. When he comes out, he has a root beer in his hand and some napkins. He hands the napkins to Morissa."

Morissa: "Thank you for the tea and thinking of the napkins. That is really considerate."

Everett: "Your welcome Morissa.  Strange my mother has a thing for Milano cookies and tea."

Morissa: "Who's jersey is that, Everett?"

Everett: "It was my high school jersey. Way back in the good old days"

Morissa: "Everett I am starting to get a picture of you as a high school jock. You played high school back up quarter back. You can swim faster than most people. I bet you even dated a high school cheer leader. Did you bring the prom queen to the dance?"

Everett: "No I didn't do that. The high school team didn't win a game all year. We weren't very good. I went to the prom with a girl who was just a friend."

Morissa: "Everett You are just not who I first thought you were."

Everett: "I am just the average college guy Morissa no different, no worse, no better."

Morissa: "This tea is so good'. You used a different tea then the tea bag that I bought."

Everett: "Yes I used one of my mothers' bag. I am glad you like it. My father picked it up in France last time he was there."

Morissa: "I would like to meet your mother, Everett."

Everett: "Morissa that may be pushing it a little. We haven't even had a real date yet. May be we should start dating before I bring you home to meet the old folks."

Morissa: "Our first date will be tomorrow when I bring you your lunch."

Everett: "Sorry Morissa that is not what I call a date. That is more of a meeting. May be a delivery service. But definitely not a date."

Morissa: "Ok what do you think, constitutes a date, Everett?

Everett: "What we did the other night. A boy and a girl enjoying the time with each other. I use to think it was taking a girl out to dinner and maybe a movie. I now think of that as a formality to get a girl to be comfortable with you before you try to have sex with her. The dating ritual that has gone on since there has been dating."

Morissa: "Have You ever seen old movies where you see two people are lying in bed to gather. Have you ever noticed that the two people are smoking? That was a way it show the audience that the two people have had sex."

Everett: "The real old TV series they couldn't show a husband and wife in the same bed. The good old days."

Morissa: "It is so different now."

Everett: "It is different now everything is so open. People don't have to hide who they are or what they do behind closed doors anymore."

Morissa: "I still like some privacy. I do like being behind close door sometimes. Some things I do or will do I would like to keep private."

Everett: "Would you like to confess them to me now or later Morissa."

Morissa: "You may never get to hear that confession, Everett."

Everett: "Morissa can I ask you a question about James back at the senior center?"

Morissa: "Sure ask away."

Everett: "Do you write him when you are a way. If you only been here during the winter holiday you two seem pretty close."

Morissa: "Your right. I do write him Everett. I tell him a lot about me. He never writes back to me. He ask me to do it accouple of years ago. If you ask me, how do I know if I could trust him. My mother knew his wife. I never met her. That's why I am so close to him. He really tries to help some of the older people who go to that senior center. He gives too much some times. Some people will take advantage of him. I asked why he keeps on giving after some people have taken advantage of him. He told me if you want to keep score of what you give them don't give. He gave me that line to."

Everett: "That makes sense. You two seemed close just for seeing him at the center a couple of times a year."

Morissa: "I like him, Everett. He may be the best man I know?"

Everett: "How about your father?"

Morissa: "I love my father. We get along great. But my father has a lot a flaws."

Everett: "So does James. You just don't know his flaws or can see them. If you knew his flaws or could see them than you may feel differently."

Morissa: "We both know that. That is why he doesn't write me back. He is a good man and that's all I want to know."

Everett: "It simple but I do understand it. You are lucky to have him. When you write him, you can tell him things you don't want to tell anybody else. Your close friends can't help but to analyzed, criticized, or praise you. It lets you clear your conscience we all wanted do that."

Morissa: "Right now I don't know a better man. I may never meet one Everett."

Everett: "You never will Morissa. He is only half of a man Morissa. You see only the good side of that man. If you want to see the whole man you have to see his bad side to. That is the hole man. The good and the bad. If you are waiting for that perfect man, you may be waiting till you are a very old lady. They don't exist. You may have to settle for just good looking could have been, kind of a has been jock someday."

Morissa: "Thank you for that advise. Do you know where I can find some good looking has been jock that wears his old football jersey. He can't be perfect, keeping in mind he has to have some flaws. But in his heart, he has to be good."

Everett: "Sorry Morissa all those types of guys are in those old movies of long ago. They will never come back. You will just have to give up."

Morissa: "I am so young. Yet I can see myself as a spinster someday."

Everett: "You are a good-looking young woman Morissa. You will find somebody sooner or later."

Morissa: "I was starting to think you may have been interested in me."

Everett: "You fooled me before. When I saw you feeding those people at the senior center. My vision of you was broken. I thought of you as a heartbreaker. A good-looking woman who was looking for the right guy. I think I found a person who looks to give what she can.

Morissa: "Thanks Everett. What would you like to do now?"

Everett: "Morissa. I think it is time we have a real first date. Not the lunch you promise to bring me tomorrow."

Morissa: "Our you asking me out on a date Everett?"

Everett: "Yes Morissa. How would you like to go out with me the day after tomorrow? I could take you to a brunch in town. Just you and I."

Morissa: "I would like that, Everett."

Everett: "Ok. I will pick you up at Ten?"

Morissa: "What would you like to do Now Everett?"

Everett: "Morissa are you going to live back at the dorm when you go back to school?"

Morissa: "I have been thinking about that. I may go and live off campus with Sue."

Everett: "I have to live on campus. Or should I say that I agreed to it with my parents. I promised them that I would live on campus. I had to make that promise for them to bail me out last year. I have a thing for getting over my head. When I do, they have a thing for giving me rules to follow. I know it sounds like I am being punish like a five-year-old. I know when to follow some rules and take the help."

Morissa: "Part of me wants to go and live off campus. Then just try to have a normal couple of years as a college girl."

Everett: "Sue will take care of you. She will watch over you like a mother hen, I am sure."

Morissa: "I don't need any one to watch over me like a mother hen. I have done a good job by myself."

Everett: "There could be a lot a trouble for a young helpless female out there. There are a lot of guys just looking for someone like you to come along."

Morissa: "Like me. Can you tell me what like me means? Could you describe what I am to you in your eyes."

Everett: "You are very pretty. You come across as somebody who has not had to deal with a lot of real jerks that are only looking to make it with you."

Morissa: "I am glad you cleared that up for me. I thought most guys my age were only interested in my mind. "

Everett: "I may even help keep an eye on you. Would you like me to do that?"

Morissa: "Here I was thinking that you were the big bad wolf. I am so relieved to know I don't have to worry at all about you. Every time that I look at you now, I will think of you as a harmless sheep. I have to tell all the girls when I get to school that you are just harmless."

Everett: "I never thought that I would have had that problem at school."

Morissa: "You know I am only kidding,"

Everett: "Yes I know."

Morissa: "Can I ask you what happen to your last girl friend? "

Everett: "There is so many people to date at college for people our age. Sometimes you just want to do more than just see one person."

Morissa: "Can I guess it was you who just wanted to see other people?"

Everett: "It would be wrong for me to kiss and tell. Let's just leave it."

Morissa: "Ok. It isn't any of my business anyway.  I am sorry I am asking"

Everett: "That's ok Morissa. I will not ask you about your last boyfriend."

Morissa: "I can tell you he was a real jerk. Let's just leave it like that."

Everett: "Morissa if you don't become a teacher what else would you like to do."

Morissa: "I don't know Everett. I had a part time job in high school. I hope I don't go back and have to do that again. I should be able to get some kind of decent job with a degree."

Everett: "I wish I was thinking like that. I should be concern what I will be doing when I graduate."

Morissa: "It may come to you Everett. That is part of what we go to school for. Sometimes people just fall in to a job or a career."

Everett: "You like those cookies don't you."

Morissa: "Yes. I have always liked them. They help me to relax."

Everett: "Do you need them to relax around me?"

Morissa: "No. I like being around you. You are very easy to talk too. You have that ability to make people at ease around you."

Everett: "May be I can be a politician. I can run for the senate. My mother would love that. I could see my mother going around and telling all her friends. My son the senator."

Morissa: "What would you do if your wife was a senator.?"

Everett: "It wouldn't make a difference to me. I would just do what I would be doing. Whatever job I would have I would have. I wouldn't give it up. I don't understand where you are going with that question."

Morissa: "Wouldn't you be there to support your wife."

Everett: "If my wife becomes a senator, she became one without me. I like to think that I will be there for her if she needs me. If she is doing that, she is doing it with or without me."

Morissa: "Everett you are not like I thought you would be. I have to admit my perception of you when I first saw you is different now."

Everett: "I hope in a good way."

Morissa: "I'll tell you it isn't in a bad way."

Everett: "That's good Morissa. I am not a bad guy when you get to know me. You may even get to like me. Maybe a lot I hope."

Morissa: "I don't know if it is an act or not. Sometimes you come across as a little boy. It is something that makes me want to reach across and hug you."

Everett: "You may not believe this. I was told that before. I wish I knew how to turn it on more often. It isn't anything that I try to do. It is something that I do without trying."

Morissa: "I am glad to hear that. I don't know if I would be able to trust myself around you. If you could use that when you wanted to. It would be something that could make me make a bad decision about you. I may trust you when I shouldn't because of that ability."

Everett: "You're going to have to trust somebody sooner or later Morissa. It may as well be me. My mother likes me."

Morissa: "I hope so. You told me that before"

Everett: "Morissa when you graduate where are you going to live? You could live out here and teach or go back to where you grew up?"

Morissa: "I haven't thought about that much. My first thoughts are that I will stay in New York and teach. I do like being out here in California the weather is so much better."

Everett: "Living here is nice, the weather is great but always the same. I like the change in the weather in New York. It is different. I like that difference."

Morissa: "Everett, I think it is time to get back now. Can you walk me home? I have to see a guy tomorrow and I want to be ready for him?"

Everett: "Sure who's the lucky guy?"

Morissa: "It is you. Like you forgot."

Everett: "Sure. Let me have your cup and what is left of those cookies and I will be right back."

Everett brings the cup and cookies in side with the uneaten cheese. When he comes out Morissa is on the beach with her shoes in her hand and pants rolled up. Everett and Morissa walk down to the water's edge. He takes Morissa's hand and pulls her close to him. He gives her a long kiss on the lips. They look at each other for a minute. Then Everett still holding her hand walks her back to her house. They don't say anything to each other. At the deck still standing in the sand Everett gives Morissa a short kiss then let's go of her hand. Morissa doesn't say anything as she looks at him. She walks backward up on to the deck. She stops on the deck looking down at Everett. Morissa jumps off the deck in front of Everett and gives him a kiss on the lips. Then she says good night and runs in to the house. Everett didn't have a chance to say anything before Morissa disappears in to the house. Everett turns and walks home for the night.

The next day about Noon Everett is sitting in a life guard stand.  Everett has his orange life guard shorts on and a white tee shirt. Morissa walks down the beach with a lunch basket in her hand. Morissa has on white shorts and a white tee shirt.

Morissa: "Hi Everett. I am here with the lunch I promised."

Everett: "Hello Morissa. Thank you for remembering me today. Why don't you carry yourself up here and take a seat by me? The rain this morning and the rain coming later has kept a lot of the people away today. I think it will be ok if you join me here."

Morissa: "If you think it is ok."

Morissa climbs up the chair with Everett's basket lunch.

Morissa: "I never been up in one of these things. You really can see everything."

Everett: "What did you bring me today Morissa?"

Morissa: "It is called a safe lunch. Roast beef on a hard roll with salt pepper and mayo. It is a sandwich that is hard to make wrong and everybody likes."

Everett: "You like to play it safe don't you. You could have re heated the leftover pizza and bought it. That would have been safe to."

Morissa: "It did cross my mind. The problem with that. My mother had it for breakfast this morning."

Everett: "I hoped she liked it."

Morissa: "She did. She wanted more."

Everett: "I can make a good pizza. It isn't much of a talent. But your mother has a better talent."

Morissa: "What may I ask. Do you think her talent is?"

Everett: "I think she makes the best-looking daughter. What a gift to mankind."

Morissa: "Flattery to a girl's mother will get you places."

Everett: "It is nice to hear you and your mother get along so well. You must of mist her, living so far away.

Morissa: "I did. That is where my friends were at the time my parents split. Part of me liked my father independence. I wanted to be like that. Independent. I was going in to my teen years. I didn't blame them for it like some kids do. I just understood, that is what they wanted. As the years past I saw two people. My parents who were friends. They kept everything simple. I also like the way my life was.

Everett: "What is your father like?"

Morissa: "If I was a guy, I would of like to be like my father. He had this way about himself. When I was really little. When I was out with my father, I thought he knew everybody in the world. Everybody liked him. I wanted to learn to be like him. I thought if I was like him everybody would like me. It may sound silly being our age now. Back then that is what I wanted."

Everett: "My parents' kind of went thru the same thing. My father business partners open up an office in Connecticut and he spent a lot of time there. Not good for a marriage. My mother gets past whatever he did, or who he is doing with alcohol. Right now, it is good between them. My father has his work. My mother has me, her social life and a bottle."

Morissa: "Everett, There isn't anybody in the water. Can you guys just call it a day and leave?"

Everett: "No it isn't are call. It is always some higher state person that can call it a day for us."

Morissa: "Do you have any best friends?"

Everett: "I had one long ago. He went away and I haven't seen him sense. I have a lot of people I know. Best friend I don't have. There is my roommate at school we get along really good. But I don't think of him as a best friend. How about you Morissa?"

Morissa: "I have three really good friends. One girl her boyfriend and another guy. I went and saw them during a school break. They were happy to see me but they had plans to be doing other things. We made plans to get together. I don't think it's going to happen anytime soon. It is just the way it works out with the people you know. We now have different lives to live."

Everett: "I like the way you tell that. It sounds like something you would read in a book."

Morissa: "Everett do you like music?"

Everett: "Everybody likes music. We may not like the same music but everybody like some kind of music."

Morissa: 'I like listening to the words in some songs. If I hear a song that tells a good story, I like it even more. A good song with a good story is hard for a person to create. To get those two parts to be married and join together. Sometimes it is such a beautiful marriage of music and words. Such talent. Such talent to let the listener be part of that marriage. It doesn't have to be a real story. The words in the songs are there pictures. We have the music to give us feelings to those words. What a gift they give us. They give us a place for our minds to wander. You can go back to the sixty songs and listen to what they were saying and apply it to things that are happening today or tomorrow. It is not one group of people saying anything more import than any other group.

Most of the words tell of the same stories. Different types of people with different types of music with the different words arranged differently. They all give us a story. I love listing to music."

Everett: "You will have to show me what you like listening to."

Morissa: "Thank you for not trying to give me your opinion on it. Thank you for just listening to me go on. When I tell some people what I think, I get them trying to break it down for me. They want to show me how much they know. Like it is some kind of math calculus or quantum physics. It's hard enough to explain."

Everett: "Thank you for the sandwich it is pretty good."

Morissa: "What do you usually do for lunch out here?"

Everett: "I have a good breakfast. Sometimes maybe a lite lunch. I don't want to eat too much. I may get tired if I eat a lot. There are times you can't close your eyes for a moment. You have to be always looking for something wrong out there. If you're looking for everything that is right, you could mis something wrong. Sitting up here is about keeping anything wrong from happening. It is a job. It is work. It is about everybody going home with no more of a problem then a bad suntan."

Morissa: "Did you ever see something bad happen?

Everett: "Every day I work. Everybody left the beach alive."

Morissa stays with Everett for about an hour. Everett and Morissa make plans to see each other the next day.

Next day Sunday. Everett shows up to Morissa house. He has on black pants and a black shirt on. He walks up to the front door and knocks on it.

Morissa mother opens the door and says hello to Everett. Morissa mother and Everett talk about her remembering Everett being a nice boy who would put the paper by her door. It was her first year living in the house. Everett tells her it was his last year of delivering papers.  The next year he started working with the life guards. Then he became a life guard. Morissa comes down the stairs and walks up to her mother and Everett.

Morissa: "Hello Everett."

Everett: "You are looking very nice. I like the way you did your hair."

Morissa: "I told you Mom he would notice. Thank you, Everett."

Morissa's mother: "Everett don't worry about any curfew with Morissa. You just show her a good time."

Everett: "I will deliver her back at your door later today. Morissa, will you do me the pleasure and join me today."

Everett takes Morissa outside and start there walk on their real first date.

Everett: "You are looking better than the first day I saw you at the bar. That pink dress gives you a look of innocence."

Morissa: "Thank you Everett. I wish I could remember you. But I don't remember you.  If I saw you, I would have remembered you."

Everett: "I spent a lot of time in the boy's room. I guess I drank too much."

Morissa: "Where are you taking me Everett. All the restaurants are the other way then where we are walking."

Everett: "We have a little stop first before we eat."

Morissa: "I guess you like to surprise your dates. Do you do this a lot with all your dates?"

Everett: "I never took a date where we are going. I use to walk there at least once a week as a kid."

Everett has Morissa in front of the local library.

Morissa: "This is really a surprise. Is there some meal being served here?"

Everett:" No. Turn around. And look at that building."

Morissa: "I think it is a bar. Is it even open?"

Everett brings Morissa up to an old bar.

Morissa: "This is a bar Everett. You bought me to a bar. You could have taken me to a bar last night."

Everett: "Trust me Morissa. I am going to teach you that you can't read a book by its cover."

Morissa: "Everett. I do trust you."

Everett takes a set of keys out of his pocket and opens the door. The two walk in to the bar. Everett reaches over and flips a couple of light switches on. Then he hits the keys on the security pad. Everett ask Morissa to have a seat at the bar. Everett walks around the bar and turns on some more lights. He walks in to a back room and turns on some lights. Morissa is sitting at the center of the bar when Everett walks back to her. He is wearing a white bartender apron.

Everett: "Hello young lady what can I get you today."

Morissa: "Everett: "What are you doing? Can we get in to trouble being in here?"

Everett: "If we don't make too much of a mess. If we don't drink too much. If you pay the tab, we will be ok. I have to let you know I have just a five-dollar bill in my wallet. I think that may limit us on the amount we can drink here."

Morissa: "May be we should leave."

Everett: "Morissa I promised you a meal. I am going to make you a lunch or a brunch."

Morissa: "You could take me somewhere. We could go back to your place."

Everett: "Morissa let me be honest with you. My father partners are in to real-estate. They saw this bar for sale years ago. They bought this bar. They put some money in to this place. There waiting for the right offer to come along and sell it. I have had talks with my father for me to buy it when I graduate. Right now, my father partners want to sell it. It hasn't made any money yet for them."

Morissa:" Your parents have some money from what you tell me."

Everett: "Yes they do. Sometimes I go to them too often. I hope my father and his partners keep it long enough for me to buy it when I graduate. When I graduate college, I will get a check. That check will let me put a down payment on this bar."

Morissa: "Why wouldn't your parents just buy it for you? That is what some parents would do."

Everett: "My father has partners other than my mother. They are called business partners. Those partners would like a nice check."

Morissa: "I understand Everett."

Everett: "I am going to put on some music. Can I get you something to drink?"

Morissa: "It is too early for me to drink. Maybe some ice tea."

Everett: "Fine. Come in the back with me and I will start making your brunch. We will see if we can find you a tea"

Morissa: "Ok Everett let's do it."

Everett and Morissa walk in to the back room. The back room is an updated kitchen. There is a new white ceramic tile floor. The wall has new cabinets. Two new stainless-steel sinks. There are new stainless-steel kitchen appliances.

Everett: "Morissa I don't know much about you. Are you allergic to anything before I make you something to eat?"

Morissa: "No. No allergies. You can make me anything."

Everett: "Ok I am going to make you some eggs benedict"

Morissa: "Sounds good."

Everett: "Great. Could you go to the refrigerator and get me some eggs? I think I saw an ice tea in there."

Morissa: "Ok. I see the ice tea. I am going to sit on this stool and watch you if you don't mind. I never had a guy make me a meal before I met you. You made me a pizza the other night. Now you are making me another meal. Now I get to watch you do it. Do you do this for all your girl dates?

Everett: "I have cooked meal for other girls and guys. I have to tell you. I never took a girl here. You're the first one.

Morissa: "I guess that makes me special in some way."

Everett: "It does Morissa. I like my egg benedict with caramelized onion. How do you like yours?"

Morissa: "Homemade With Hollandaise please."

Everett: "I have this pan hot enough now; I am going to cook the bacon and make the eggs. I hope you like your bacon from Canada and extra crispy. I have a toaster here? That is where we will cook the English muffins.

Morissa: "Sounds good."

Everett: "Ok Morissa the first thing we need is some fresh eggs. I hope the ones in the refrigerator are fresh, Time will tell. They have been kept cold till now. I have these cold eggs here. I will crack them into a strainer. This cuts down on the white parts in the water. It means a better yok for poaching. A little salt in to the water. Just a little you can't put too much in you know."

Morissa: "You have it down pretty good."

Everett: "Practice."

Morissa: "You must have had a lot of it."

Everett: "My mother let me make her breakfast a lot.  To make hollandaise souse it is best to whisk it. I need one teaspoon of water then whisk it to the right consistency. Morissa if you could go back in to the bar. There is a coffee pot in there. Could you bring it in here please?

Morissa: "Sure no problem I will be right back."

Everett: "We could have some fresh coffee with our eggs. Or we could have a cold beer. Which one would you like to have?"

Morissa: "Coffee now will be ok. May be later the beer it's too early for beer now. I'll be right back.

Morissa goes out to the bar and finds the coffee pot. She brings it back to Everett who is working the eggs and the bacon. He ask her to fill it up with water.

Everett gets some coffee grinds and set up the pot to percolate the coffee. Morissa sits back down on the seat watch Everett move back and forth from the bacon to the eggs. Then to the coffee pot. He reaches over and gets two plates. He puts them on the hot side of the stove. Within accouple of minutes Everett has the eggs with English muffins on two plates. He gets two beer mugs and brings them over to the coffee pot. He brings the pot and the mugs out to the bar. He comes back and gets a bottle of Orange juice from the refrigerator. He then brings it out to the bar. Morissa just watches him walk back and forth from the kitchen to the bar. Everett comes back in with a white towel over his arm like a waiter. He leans forward puts his arm out. Then he ask Morissa to be his guest at a table. He walks Morissa out to a table in the center of the bar. He pulls out a seat for Morissa to sit at. She takes the seat and thanks him. Morissa looks at the table in front of her. There is a clean white table cloth laid out on the table. The coffee pot is there with the beer mugs. The two glass have some orange juice in them. A small butter dish with fresh butter with a butter knife lays to it side In the center is a large flower glass with flowers in them. There is one light on now in the bar. That light is a pool table lamp right above the Table that she is looking at. Everett goes back in to the bar and comes out with the two plates with their breakfast on it. He stand next to her and points to the chair across from her. He looks at Morissa and ask the question.

Everett: "Is this seat taken? Do you come here often? Haven't I seen you some where before. You are a very good-looking woman maybe I could take this seat. My name is Everett. Maybe we could share a meal? You don't have a steady boyfriend, do you? I am sorry what did you say your name was?"

Morissa: "You are just somebody I never would have expected this from. Why all this just for me."

Everett: "I like you Morissa. The first moment I saw you I liked you. If I wasn't dating someone else. That is over now so let's just enjoy this meal before it gets cold. Please try the eggs and let me know what you think."

Everett waits for Morissa to start eating.

Morissa: "This is the best breakfast I have ever had. You really are a good cook. The pizza and this breakfast. You are doing a lot just for me Everett. You have gone a long way out of your way for a first date."

Everett: "I am glad you like it. I have a confession about doing this for you. I have an alternative motive Morissa can you guess what that may be?"

Morissa; "I am afraid to guess. You didn't have to do all this. It could have been simpler."

Everett: "It may not be what you're thinking I have on my mind. Morissa, I like doing the unexpected and may be a little bit of showing off some times. Like when I bet you swimming. I went home after I did that second guessing myself, if I should have beaten you swimming that fast. I am trying to impress you like guys like to do on a date you could rest a sure."

Morissa: "You do like showing off at cooking. I can tell. if you do get this place after college, you could turn it in to a café. It wouldn't take much. We are close enough to the beech to get the beech traffic."

Everett: "Yes I talked about that with my father. If they get an offer my father's partners like. There isn't much I can do. They will have to sell it."

Morissa: "If that happens you could get another place."

Everett: "We will see. I don't want to talk about that right now. Let's talk about something else."

Morissa: "Like what?"

Everett: "Let's talk about you."

Morissa: "Me? Why me."

Everett: "Girls love to talk about themselves."

Morissa: "I was starting to get to like you."

Everett: "Let me rephrase that. Girls like to have conversation so let's have a conversation."

Morissa: "Lets."

Everett: "Let's talk about you being a teacher again. All those little brats running around. They are always looking to give a teacher a hard time. I couldn't take it."

Morissa: "Was that you when you were a little boy."

Everett: "No I wasn't the problem student. I got in trouble sometimes but I was a fairly well behave child. My parents didn't get any notes from any teacher saying I was the problem child."

Morissa: "I want to teach children. I want to see them learn something that they will have for the rest of their lives. As they grow, they will carry a part of what I taught them."

Everett: "I would be afraid to teach any kid. I would be afraid that if I told them something wrong, they would carry that around there whole life. I have a hard-enough time trying to live my life without it affecting somebody's else life. I think there is a thin line between teaching someone.

Then trying to change someone. Sometimes I saw teachers just trying to change kids so the kids would act the way the teacher thought the kids should act. I think that falls in to that they wanted to control those kids. It wasn't teaching but just control. When those teachers left at the end of the day, did they pat themselves on the back because they control the kid. Did they teach the kids or just controlled them for the day? There is a big difference there."

Morissa: "It sounds like you thought of that before. You explained it very well. I don't agree that it is done by all teachers. It isn't always like that"

Everett: "I think I have great parents. They never tried to control me. They let me make mistakes. They never worried about me being me. Some parents get tied up with having there kid embarrass them or cause a problem for them. Some parents have kids that can do no wrong in their eyes. When there told there kid did something wrong the parent always looks to blame someone else around there child. Like the school. A teacher or another student. If I was a teacher, I would not last long. I would have a parent coming to the school to get on me about something I said to their kid."

Morissa: "I know I will have some problems. Every teacher has problems or the problem child. Somewhere in my teaching of kids. I hope to be the one who help someone who needs it. I am taking a lot of classes to learn how to teach."

Everett: "Helping or teaching is one thing. Changing some kid to what you may think is right, may not be what you want to do."

Morissa: "Do you think if I was your teacher, I would have done a good job with you?"

Everett: "I think from the last couple of days with you. You may start off with some problems, after that you are going to be a great teacher Morissa."

Morissa: "Thank you."

Everett: "How is the food?"

Morissa: "I could have a real problem with you Everett."

Everett: "What problem could that be may I ask."

Morissa: "The food you cooked for me is to good. I am eating too much of it. You keep cooking for me I am going to lose my figure. Then where will I be. I may never get another guy to date me."

Everett: "Ok Morissa I will never cook for you again."

Morissa: "Let me rephrase that. I need to eat less of what you cook for me. I may even start running on the beech so I could keep eating what you cook."

Everett: "You did a good job of finishing off all the beacon and your breakfast."

Morissa: "I was hoping you didn't notice. Then I was hoping you didn't say anything. But you had to say something didn't you."

Everett: "Sorry. I am glad you enjoyed it."

Morissa: "You have shown me a real nice time with you I really enjoy being with you."

Everett: "Morissa. I am sorry to tell you it is time we did something together now. I am not sure how to ask you to do this. Husbands and wives have been doing this since the first, I do was said"

Morissa: "What do you mean to do something together. Can you explain it to me please?"

Everett: "I would be happy to. The bar has to be put back like we found it. I need your help to clean up what we did here. What else would I ask you to do?"

Morissa: "I would love to dry your dishes, Everett."

Everett and Morissa clean up the Bar and the kitchen and put everything back as they found it. Morissa is waiting for Everett by the front door as Everett is walking around the bar making sure everything is as they found it. She has her back against the door and her arms folded in front of herself. She is thinking how much she likes Everett.

Morissa thoughts.

I just met him and I like him. He is so nice. He is so good looking. This can't be for real. Is this an act he is putting on? He can get a lot of other girls without the effort he is doing for me. He must like me. He must really like me a lot. I wonder how soon he is going to want to bring our relationship to that next level. That level I never been at.

I'm sure he's been there a couple of times at least. What will he think of me when he finds out I never been that far with a man? I know what guys at that age like.

Everett: "Ok Morissa we are done here. Let's lock it up and move on. I have something else for you today."

Morissa: "Where did I find you?"

Everett: "I was the one who found you on the beech don't you remember, or was it that bar?"

Morissa: "Yes I guess you can say that."

Everett: "We need to leave now. Do you feel like taking a walk? I have this place I need to stop by and pick something up. Then I would like to take you somewhere."

Morissa: "Ok Everett. Please no more food. I can use the walk to burn off some of these calories. If I could cook like you, I would weigh a ton. How do you stay in such good shape with the way you cook?"

Everett: "Lucky, I guess. Genes or genetics, I guess. Come on now. I am going to lock this door and we need to go down a couple of blocks."

Everett set the alarm code and locks the door. He and Morissa start the walk along the side walk. They walk hand in hand looking in side of some store fronts. They have the look of a couple that has been dating for years. They walk up to a pawn store. Everett looks at Morissa and ask her if she has ever been in a pawn store before. Morissa tells him she has. The two walk in to the pawn store. Everett takes Morissa up to the counter. At the counter is the business owner named Jason. Jason is in his sixties, fat and bald.

Everett: "Hello Jason. How are you today?"

Jason: "I am just fine today Mr. Everett. I see you have a lady friend with you today. She is a nice-looking piece."

Everett: "This is my friend Morissa. Be nice to her Jason. Don't worry she isn't going to steel your dozen donuts that you have under the counter fatso."

Jason: "I am nice to everybody that comes in here. Maybe some more than others. I could be really nice to you Morissa."

Morissa: "Thanks I'll pass I don't see anything in here that would interest me."

Jason: "Have it your way princes. I am sure the young jock to your side has something that may interest you. Have you seen it yet?"

Everett: "Jason you're a real creep. Here is what I owe you now please get my bag. "

Jason: "I have it right under my counter by my dozen donuts. I hope I didn't get any donut crumbs on it."

Everett takes a folded white envelope out of this back pocket and gives it to Jason. Jason takes the envelope looks at it without opening it. Then Jason reaches under the counter and pulls out an old black doctor bag. He then hands it to Everett. Everett takes the bag and puts it on the counter. He puts two hands on it and says There going to bury me with this bag. You will never see it again"

Jason: "Are you going to check to see if it is all in there."

Everett: "I trust you, Jason. There is nothing in there that is worth anything to you or anybody else and you know it. Are you going to count the money or do you trust me"?

Jason: "Everett, I trust You. No one else would have given me that much money for that bag or what is in it. That is the friend in me. After you leave, I will count it, that is the business man in me my friend."

Everett: "By Jason. You could go back to your donuts I have my bag and you have your cash."

Jason: "By Everett. I hope to see you before the Army, Navy game this year. You had me wondering about your luck late in to last football season. That was too long for you. I could tell your luck has gotten better by that nice trophy you brought in here."

Everett: "Let's go Morissa."

Jason: "Morissa. I have a tiara in back that will fit that pretty little princes head. I may even come up with an outfit to match. I bet I can now guess your dress size after looking at you. I will be thinking about you all day princes."

Everett: "Jason I could come across the counter and beat you with that baseball bat you have under the counter. Before you could get a donut in that fat face of yours."

Jason: "Buy friends."

Everett and Morissa walk out of the pawn store.

Everett: "I am sorry to bring you in there Morissa. Sometimes he could be half way normal. I guess he had one to many of those donuts."

Morissa: "It wasn't anything he said. I heard worse at school. It is the way he says it. It is him being a fat Sixty-year-old man trying to be so creepy."

Everett: "I will make it up to you later. We have one more place to go. I promise you it is a better place."

Morissa: "Everett, can I ask you what you have in the bag."

Everett: "I will show it to you later."

Morissa: "Promise."

Everett: "Promise, we need to get going."

Everett and Morissa start walking away from the pawn store.


Morissa: "I like the way you surprise me when we are together."

Everett: "I never took a date where we are going. I used to walk there at least once a week as a kid."

Everett has Morissa in front of the local hospital.

Morissa: "This is really a surprise. Is there some meal being served here?"

Everett: "It is story time. The hospital reads stories to children. We are going to spend are first date listening to a story then I will take you to out."

Everett and Morissa enter the hospital. There are kids sitting in a semi-circle on the floor with a woman sitting in front of them on a chair with a book in her hand. Everett and Morissa stand behind the kids on the floor. The woman reading the book waves to Everett.

Everett: "Morissa could you please wait hear for me. I will be back in a couple of minutes."

Morissa: "Ok Everett. I will just take a seat and wait for you to come back.

Morissa is sitting in one of the seats listening to the woman in front talking to the kids. The kids are sick that are staying at the hospital. Ten minutes later She sees a clown come out of a side hall. The kids start to laugh and clap as the clown stumbles to stand by the teacher. The teacher introduces The Clown as MR Everett the clown.

Morissa gets a big smile on her face and stands and applause.

The story.

Everett reading the story. He has a clown hat and jacket on. His face is made up like a clown,

hospital

Older Brother.

My parents sit me down and tell me they want to have a talk with me. What did I do this time I wonder? What could a five-year-old keep doing that my parents keep wanting to have a talk with me. Side by side they sit and start to tell me our family is going to get bigger. Then they show me my mother's belly. She has around bump on her belly. Somehow in a couple of months I will have a baby brother. Oh boy, fun. Somebody to play with. A brother how happy I was that day. I went out and told every one of my friends. Then the day it happen. They bought my brother home to me. He was so small. All I could see was a little prune face wrapped up in a blanket. They even let me hold him for the first time. So, so small. Be careful they told me. I did learn the right way to hold him.

This little kid that was laying down in the living room. I sat there watching my parent making a fuss over my brother. I couldn't understand it. He wasn't doing anything but sleeping. Then other people started to show up and make such a fuss over this little brother of mind. So many people came and went. Some of them asked me how I felt to have a baby brother. I told them I liked him. He was too little to play with.

Over the next days and weeks, I learn what diapers were. I learned how much my baby brother did poops, Sometimes I could smell him. When I did smell him, I had to tell my mother his diaper had to be changed. Then there was feeding time. The food he would try to get in to his mouth was funny some times.

 Most of the time there was more on his face then he had eaten. My brother was doing three things at this time. He was sleeping, eating, and pooping. I didn't get to have much fun with him. All the food had helped him grow. He could now pull himself up on the rails of his crib. When I go up to him, he would start to laugh and giggle. The funny faces I would make would make him laugh harder.

My mother and father started to put him on the floor and let him crawl around. He was able to stand up when he was holding on to a table or a chair now. Then came the day when he let go of the table and started to walk across the floor. My parents were on the floor calling to him. He looked at me and then walked to me. I caught him as he got to me. Then he looked at me and started to make some funny faces that I would make.

My room got a new bed one day. I was told that it was just a temporary thing. As soon as he was bigger my brother would be put in to his own room. I like having my brother in my room.

It was nice to look over at him knowing my parent were giving me the responsibility of taking care of him. The pooping in those never-ending stinking diapers was still going on. Sometime at night I would go sleep in the living room.

I was teaching him how to play like a boy. We play all kinds of games. Sometimes he would break my toys trying to play with them the wrong way. I would find him playing with my toys more than his. There were some toys of mind I wanted to keep because I like them a lot. He broke some of my special toys. I had to understand he was much younger than me. As much as I didn't like it, I knew that I was the older brother and had to be the one to understand that he was just a baby.

My brother soon found his own room. Across from me he would sleep from now on. I would get up and go to school. My brother would be there to see me leave for the day. In the afternoon my brother would be waiting by the door looking for me to play with him. Most of the time now I would go outside and play with my friends. I like my brother but I would have more fun playing with my friends. On a rainy day when I couldn't find a friend I would play with my little brother. Sometimes I would be too rough with him. My mother would give me a lecture on he is not as strong as me so I have to be careful with him. I taught him how to tie his shoes and dress himself. I taught him the way boys go to the bathroom.

My brother is now ready to go to school. The smelly diapers are long gone. He has everything that he will need for school. I had to tell him about school and what goes on there. He was telling me that he wanted to go to school. I guess I did at that age to. I told him about the teacher he was going to have in his first year. The teacher should remember me because I was so smart.

I warned him about some rules that the school has that he would have to follow. I think he will be ok. I will be in the same school for a couple more years.

My brother has found his own friends. Some of them come over and play with him. They play the same games as I use to play with my friends. Sometimes on a rainy day he and I would find something to play together, maybe watch something on tv or get in to a fight. I think all brothers must do that sometimes. I am still watching him. Our parent go out some time and we will be by ourselves at home. Me being the oldest puts me in charge. I don't have to tell him anything. He is the best little brother to watch over.

The story ends the kids get up and go over to a table with cookies and juice. Everett the clown start to shake the kid's hands and talks to them. Morissa just stays in her seat and watches him.

A nurse name Sally comes over and talks with Everett.

Sally: "It is nice to see you again Everett. It has been awhile this time."

Everett: "Yes I know. I am ether at college or a lifeguard at work. It is nice to get back here and do a story again. There are times at school I just want to come back here and sit on the floor and do a story."

Sally: "You are welcome here anytime Everett. You know that."

Morissa walks over to Everett.

Everett: "Sally this is my friend Morissa. We go to the same college together. Her mother lives down the beech from my mother. What a small world."

Morissa: "Nice to meet you Sally."

Sally: "Hi Morissa. My friend Everett used to come in here often as a young boy. Now we don't see him as often as we use to. I guess little boys have to grow up."

Everett: "I will come by again before I go back to school again Sally."

Sally: "Morissa. My old young handsome friend here never had any girl here with him. He must like you."

Morissa: "Thank you. He surprised me. He made me a brunch and he read me a story. I like the story. Is there another part to it?"

Sally looks at Everett. Sally then looks at Morissa.

Sally: "That is the story. The person who wrote it never finished it."

Everett: "It is time for us to leave now Morissa. Thank you Sally."

Morissa: "By Sally I had a nice time."

Everett changes back in to his regular clothes. He catches back up with Morissa.

Everett and Morissa Leave the hospital and start to walk in to the town.

Morissa: "Everett thank you for bringing me there. It was nice to see all those kids listening to the story.  Why did you go there? Were you sick at one time?"

Everett: "No I was never sick. I would run away from home and I would go there. When I showed up there. The people who worked there would call my parents and tell them where I was. More often than not it was Sally there. Once in a while she would drive me home."

Morissa: "That was nice of her to take that interest in you. Why did she do that?"

Everett: "It is a long story. I will have to tell it to you one day."

Everett and Morissa leave the hospital and start the walk back to the beach.

Everett: "Do you know what I would like to do now Morissa: "

Morissa: "I can't even guess any more with you Everett."

Everett: "There is a matinee playing. I would like to take a date to see it. Do you know where I could get a date to go and see it with me."

Morissa: "Well if you ask a girl the right ways she may just say yes."

On the side walk in front of several people Everett gets on one knee and takes Morissa's hand. Morissa looks around and sees some people stop walking and look at Everett on his Knee in front of her.

Everett: "Morissa will you do me the honor of seeing a matinee with me please."

Morissa: "You know what those people looking at us are thinking?"

Everett: "As I look at them you just may want to say yes. If you don't, they are going to feel sorry for me."

Morissa: "Yes I will go to the matinee with you. Now will you please get up off your knee."

Everett gets up and kiss Morissa. The two walk away as some people say congratulations.

Everett and Morissa go down to the movie theater. Everett buys two tickets and get Morissa some candy. The two watch an old movie called A night at the Opera.

After the movie Everett and Morissa start to walk home.

Everett: "I think were done now Morissa. I am going to take you home. Later on, if we could meet somewhere?"

Morissa: "Yes that is what I was thinking. I would like to get out of these shoes. What do you think? My place or yours?"

Everett: "I was thinking somewhere in between. My father partners has a beach house for entertaining clients. We can have it to ourselves No one will be there to night. It even has a Jacuzzi on the front deck. It is all ours all night if we want it."

Morissa: "All night?"

Everett: "Yes all night or till we get evicted."

Morissa: "I can't spend all night there Everett."

Everett: "I know. I can't do it ether. I have something I have to do later to night. I'll have you back at home at ten. Is that a deal?

Morissa: "I hope you understand why I can't stay the night with you?"

Everett: "Is it because you turn in to Cinderella at midnight?"

Morissa: "No. I never been anywhere with a guy all night."

Everett: "Really Cinderella? Have a swim suit and bring some towels, and what you want to drink. I'll pick you up at six."

Morissa: "It's a date."

Everett: "I guess it is."

Everett walk Morissa to her door and kiss her good bye.

Morissa goes inside and talks to her mother about the good time she had. Then she goes to her room. After a shower she starts to think of what may happen tonight.

Morissa thoughts.

He wanted me to spend the night. Maybe this was the time I should spend the night. He let me off easy by telling me he had something else that he had to do. I will be alone with him tonight. Him and I in the Jacuzzi what could be wrong with that. I guess I'll bring the bathing suit. I guess I'll bring the two-peace bikini. I guess there's nothing wrong with that. Him and one-half naked female in a Jacuzzi together. Nothing wrong with that. Then it's how much we are going to drink tonight nothing wrong with that. I like him a lot he is such a nice guy. What he did with those kids was nothing short of amazing. This guy has me so bad right now.

This summer is turning out nothing like I thought it would. I didn't have a steady boyfriend the other day. I didn't have any boyfriend the other day. Now I have Everett tonight nothing wrong with that, I hope. I am old enough to spend the night there if I choose. I guess. I will go and just be safe with my choices and my decisions. Maybe wearing a bikini isn't the right choice for the right decision. But it will be the fun choice.

At 6:15 Everett shows up on her deck. He knocks on the glass patio door. Morissa's mother answers the door.

Miss. Brown: "Hello Everett it is nice to see you."

Everett: "Hello Miss Brown. I am here for Morissa."

Miss Brown: "I know she told me. She also told me all about the day you showed her. Thank you for being so nice to her. She doesn't know anybody else hear her age."

Everett: "I like Morissa. She is different than most of the other girls I know."

Morissa comes in. She has on blue jean short and a white halter top over her bikini.

Morissa: "Hi Everett I have a bag all packed I am ready to go."

Miss Brown: "Morissa are you going to be gone all night?"

Morissa: "Mom. No, I will be home before midnight thanks Mom. Way to embarrass me mom."

Everett: "I will have her home safe and sound. Don't worry about her Miss Brown."

Miss Brown: "I wasn't worried at all. If she wants to stay out all night, who am I to stop her."

Morissa: "By mom. Thanks a lot. I will see you later and we are going to have a talk."

Miss Brown: "You two have fun:

Everett and Morissa walk out on to the deck and down the beach. Everett takes her down to a beach house somewhere between his mothers and Morissa mother beech house. The house is just a one-story building that sits on the wood pilons. The front deck has a new jacuzzi on it. They walk on to the deck and Everett unlock the front door. He turns the lights on. There is a large room with a large tv and a couch with some chairs around the tv. A small kitchen sits to one side of the building. On the other side is a small bedroom. In the middle of those two rooms is a bathroom.

Everett: "Welcome home dear. You could put are groceries in that refrigerator. I am going to start the jacuzzi and turn the heat up in it. If you want to change you can do it in that bath room. I forgot something back at my house give me a couple of minutes and I will be right back.

Morissa: "I could go with you. I really don't want to be hear by myself."

Everett: "Morissa you will be just fine. I will not be a couple of minutes promise."

Morissa: "Ok Everett."

Everett turns and goes outside and off the deck. Morissa watches him go off. She then goes to the refrigerator with her bag. She takes a six pack of wine coolers and puts them in the refrigerator. A sport bag she brings in to the bathroom with her. Morissa comes out of the bathroom and still with her shorts over her bikini but the halter is gone. She has on a black bikini top with the straps over her shoulder. Morissa walks to the patio door looking for Everett. Waiting at the door and not seeing him coming right back makes her uneasy about being in a Strange house by herself.

Morissa turns around and goes to the refrigerator and takes out one of the wine cooler. She then takes the wine cooler on to the deck. She puts her hand in the jacuzzi checking the water temperature. Looking down toward Everett house she doesn't see Everett yet. Morissa takes a seat on the end of the deck looking toward Everett's house.

A couple of minutes later Everett could be seen walking toward Morissa. He walks on to the deck and stand beside Morissa with a box in his hand. He ask the question is this seat taken? Morissa tells him "it is his if he wants it. It is a free beach." Everett thanks her and takes his seat.

Everett: "You come here often sailor."

Morissa: "Only when I could find a guy named Everett and an empty house with a jacuzzi"

Everett: "You my kind of woman sailor. Would you like to know what I have in the box?"

Morissa: "It looks like a baker's box. Its smells like something was bake. It is familiar but I can't place it."

Everett: "How about some cannoli. Yes, some cannoli. I didn't forget them before. I just wanted them to cook just right first. I hope the water is nice and warm. Give me a minute and I will meet you in the water sailor. Morissa gives Everett a kiss on the cheek she stands up and walk to the jacuzzi. Everett stands up and watches Morissa walk to the jacuzzi.

Morissa takes her short off then looks back at Everett. She is down to a small black bikini. Everett smiles at her and watches her get in to the tub. Everett then walks to the refrigerator takes out a beer. Turning around he walks back to the jacuzzi. He stands by Morissa who is in the water.

Everett puts the cannoli's by Morissa. He undoes his shorts an drops them down to his ankles. He has on a small black swimming shorts. He then takes of his white tee shirt and gets in to the water with Morissa.

Everett: "Morissa we are here. You and me and a couple of cannoli. We have some drinks. The water is warm. I have a couple of hours before I have to get Cinderella back home. Unless Cinderella wants to be bad and stay out all night."

Morissa: "Part of me wants to spend as much time with you as I can Everett. Part of me wants to go back home and be safe and open up a book tonight. I just met you the other day and you have me in a jacuzzi half naked with you.

I look at you and I know this could be dangerous for me. The way I look at this tomorrow may be not the way I want to remember this day. I did enjoy this day. I did enjoy you, Everett."

Everett: "I am glad to hear you say that Morissa. Before we go any further, I need to tell you something first. I wish I didn't have to tell you this but I need to be honest with you."

Morissa: "Ok please tell me. I would like to think that we will be able to tell each other anything."

Everett: "Morissa I have to go away tomorrow. My father and I are going up to Canada to go fishing. We do this almost every summer about this time."

Morissa: "How long will you be gone Everett."

Everett: "Three weeks."

Morissa: "I hope you have a good time, Everett. I will be thinking about you."

Everett: "I do have a good time with my father. We get along pretty good most of the time. We like a lot of the same things. Fishing up there is one of those things we can do together."

Morissa: "It sounds nice."

Everett: "I will be back in August. That will still give us a couple of weeks before we head back to school. We could pick up where we left off."

Morissa: "Yes I guess we can. No, we can't I just remembered. I promise my father that I would spend August with him. When you come back, I will be back home. Then he will take me back to school."

Everett: "Then I will see you at school. We will be able to spend time there together."

Morissa: "I guess we can. I have my school work. I like to work on it all the time."

Everett: "We will find the time to be together. Unless you have a boyfriend back at school you didn't tell me about."

Morissa: "Everett I never had a serious boyfriend."

Everett: "I know some guys who would like to have a girl seriously.'

Morissa: "What?

Everett: "I meant to say a serious girlfriend."

Morissa: "Thank you but no thanks. I can get my own boyfriend."

Everett: "Jason at the pawn shop seems to like you. Maybe I could put in a good word for you."

Morissa: "I guess this is your I want to be funny side."

Everett: "Yes you got it."

Morissa: "How about you and girlfriends. Anything you would like to tell me."

Everett: "No. A gentle man never talks. So, I can't tell you anything."

Morissa: "I am still thinking a lot about living off campus this upcoming year with Sue. She has a lot of friends. Let me tell you. When she and her friend start talking about people and guys, they know everything. They know some much sometimes I have to leave the room because there are things I don't want to know."

Everett: "Do you remember anything about me?"

Morissa: "I don't know Everett. I never listen for any names. If they did talk about you, I can't place you with any one that they were talking about."

Everett: "Ok let's keep the conversation to us tonight."

Morissa: "Yes lets."

Everett: "Ok what would you like to talk about?"

Morissa: "The clown. Why don't you tell me more about why you do that? Why did you have to pawn that outfit?"

Everett: "Another Time please Morissa. We are both going to run in to some things that may take time. It takes more than a couple of days to have a trusting relationship. Trust me for now, it will take some time to tell you."

Morissa: "Did I just here the word relationship? What kind of relationship were you planning on having if I may be so bold to ask Mr. Everett? Let me think about that. You could be looking for a friendship type of relationship.

Like a brother and sister. You could be looking for a long-distance relationship. That is why you're going way up north to see those cold fish up there in Canada. You could be looking for girlfriend boyfriend type of relationship. You know where two people promise to date just each other. Or you could be looking for that favorite type of relationship that guys your age love to have. The physical type."

Everett: "When you showed up to that race the other day it did cross my mind. When you stepped in to the jacuzzi it crossed my mind." When I was reading that story to those kids and I saw you sitting there this morning looking at me. I was thinking of something else."

Morissa: "What were you thinking then Everett? I could understand seeing a girl in a swim suit. I don't understand what you could have been thinking looking at me. I didn't even notice it."

Everett: "You like the way I had the children's attention Morissa. It isn't easy to do. I Like doing it I wish I could do it more often. I gave you some surprises today. I treated you very nice today. I was hoping to make you feel special today. I could tell that you did like the way I treated you. I think I gave you the biggest smile when I was reading to those kids. I cannot hold their attention for long. I can't do the same thing every time because they would get bored of me. I can't teach them anything like you will be able to do. I can do a lot of things that mean nothing. I wish I could do something for them that would be a lasting gift to them. I could see that in your eyes that you wish you could do the same for them. It isn't anything easy to do. Kids have their own minds and you never know what they are thinking. They have to be the biggest challenge to anybody who wants to teach kids at that age."

Morissa: "You saw all that just from looking in my eyes when you were reading to those children?"

Everett: "Yes. You may have heard of mind readers? I am an eye reader. I had this ability since I was a little boy."

Morissa: "Oh you did. Did you. If you had this ability, what did you use it for?"

Everett: "I used it for the best reason ever. The best reason known to mankind. The best reason a man has ever had."

Morissa: "Everett please you just have to tell me what would you use that ability for. What possible greater cause to mankind could you use that for?"

Everett: "To get a kiss from a good-looking female."

Morissa: "Really Everett I never heard of a man who can do that. Could you please show me how you do it?

Everett: "Sure I could show you. First, I need a real good-looking female. Do you know where I can find one?

Morissa: "Are you kidding me. Did you happen to notice this bikini I was wearing in here?"

Everett: "Yes. I think I did. When you stepped in to the water, I think I notice you were wearing something in black."

Morissa: "That is really nice of you to say so. Now I will try to be the good-looking female here. Do you think you could use me as a good-looking female?"

Everett: "Ok Morissa. You are the only one in eyesight."

Morissa: "You just know the right way to talk to a female don't you. You must practice that a lot on your dateless Saturday nights. Let's get on now with your so-called ability to read female eyes or was that female minds."

Everett: "If you really want me to Morissa. I will."

Morissa: "Oh please Everett. Do me this one favor and show me how you do this. I may need to know how to defend myself against those guys who may use that line on me. I mean that ability on me."

Everett: "Ok if you really want me to I will. But first you have to say please Everett show me."

Morissa: "I can't believe this. Please Everett show me how you do it."

Everett: "Ok Morissa. Please just remember you ask for me to show you. The first thing I have to do is get up real close to a good-looking female.

Morissa I am going to get really close to you. I mean really close. Now I am so close I will bet you could feel me right up against you."

Morissa: "Everett yes you are now pressing your body right up against me. I can now feel your weight on me."

Everett: "That's good. I may try to get closer we will see how this goes."

Morissa: "You may be so close I don't think there is any water between us. Now what do you do?"

Everett: "I Have to put my arms around the female. I have to do this to keep her still as possible. You don't mind if I do this do you?"

Morissa: "So long as your intentions are good. I think I can see my way to trust you, Everett."

Everett: "Now that I have my arms around you. Now that I feel your body up against me, I can begin Morissa"

Morissa: "If you are just beginning, I may be in for more than I was thinking?"

Everett: "I need you to concentrate Morissa. I need you to concentrate really hard. You have to clear your thoughts. Just start thinking what you would really like to happen now Morissa. Think hard."

Morissa: "Ok I am thinking really hard. What I would like to happen now. Can you guess what that is yet Everett?"

Everett: "It will come to me. Sometimes it takes a little longer to read things I see. We may have to stay like this for a couple of minutes. If may be a sacrifice I have to make to prove I can read eyes or was that minds."

Morissa: "That is so nice of you to make this sacrifice for just me. I know having a girl in a bikini in your arms. Having her Trapped in a jacuzzi is a hard ship for you. I would bet you are having a hard time thinking."

Everett: "May be I should adjust my hands a little."

Morissa: "I would have never thought of that. I am so glad you're thinking of this important detail. Where if I may ask, will you be putting your hands: "

Everett: "I think the left one I put on the small of your back. It is so I can lift you closer to my eyes. Just above the bikini bottomed you have on. The right one I will put on the back of your head. That's so I can help you steady your head. That will help keep your eyes steady as I read them."

Morissa: "Ok. Everett I can feel your hands where you said you were going to put them. Now please tell me what my mind or was it my eyes are saying."

Everett: "Ok I am starting to read something now. It is getting clearer to me as I look deeper in those hazel eyes. Morissa, you have to stop distracting me with those sparkling eyes."

Morissa: "I am so sorry Everett to be the distraction. I didn't know my eyes were doing it. I will try to stop doing it. Maybe because you are so close, you are making them do it."

Everett: "It is just hard for me to read your eyes when I look at those sparkling hazel eyes. We may have to stay like this a little longer now."

Morissa: "I don't know how much longer do you think your arms can hold me like this? Your arms have to be getting really tired."

Everett: "I am starting to see something in those eyes. Yes, it is getting clearer to me now. I see. I see. I see you want me to do something to you."

Morissa: "I was afraid of this. I am not sure how I should ask the next question. Let me try it like this."

Morissa: "Oh please Everett you are so close. Please tell me what it is that I want you to do?

Everett: "It is a physical act that you want me to do to you."

Morissa: "Oh boy. Everett, please tell me. Tell me it is a nice act."

Everett: "I wouldn't have it any other way then something nice."

Morissa: "Everett I am starting to read something in your eyes now."

Everett: "Morissa I got it. You want me to give you a kiss. That is what I am reading in those beautiful eyes. With my arms around you Morissa. As I look in to those eyes"

Accouple of minutes later.

Everett: "Morissa we have to stop now or we may go too far. This isn't the place or time. We will have other times together. It can't be now. I have to get you back home later."

Morissa: "Thank you Everett. My head isn't mine right now. It is thinking things I haven't been thinking."

Everett: "We almost forgot about something?"

Morissa: "What?"

Everett: "Cannoli. We have to eat them before they go bad."

The next day Everett is saying good bye to Morissa. The next time they will see each other will be when school starts.

Chapter Three

School Friends.

The summer ends and Morissa father drives Morissa back to school

Morissa and her Father In his car.

Morissa: "Thank you for the ride dad."

Mr. Brown: "You are welcome Morissa. I could walk you to the front door if you want me to?"

Morissa: "No thank you dad I know the way."

Mr. Brown: "I know I was just hoping."

Morissa: "Dad you know it is something that I want to do."

Mr. Brown: "I heard that last year. Not much has changed has it."

Morissa: "No dad. I still want to do this by myself. When I did it last year, I knew I made the right decision."

Mr. Brown: "You didn't spend much money at school last year. If you want to have a good time once in a while you can. Between your mother and I we could put a couple of kids through college. Most parents talk about how much their kids' college experience is costing them. I tell my friends that my daughter is sending money back to me."

Morissa: "I will try to change my spending habits if that makes you happy. What I don't spend you can donate, is that ok?"

Mr. Brown: "May be that you are now living off campus we will see a different Morissa."

Morissa: "I would not bet on that. I may do some things different than last year. I hope to spend some time with more people my age. It should be an easier year of school for me. I hope to have some fun this year."

Dad: "Have you heard from that boy you saw this summer yet?"

Morissa: "No I haven't. Do you and mom talk about anything else but me when you two talk. I don't know why she has to tell you anything."

Mr. Brown: "We have nothing else to talk about but you when we talk. I am glad she is happy but other than you we have nothing to talk about. She has her life and I have mine. Between her life and mine is you. I talk to her about you. She talks to me about you. I hope to tell her something new about you that she doesn't know. She hopes to tell me something new about you that I, don't know. That will never change between us."

Morissa: "Lucky me. You do know that I didn't want to be the only child. I think if you two had another child I would of like that."

Mr. Brown: "Yes. It just didn't happen. Now you get to have all your mother's attention and mine."

Morissa: "I know. I am the one living with all that attention."

Mr. Brown: "To go back to your boyfriend. I would like to meet him."

Morissa: "Dad don't call him my boyfriend. We just had a couple of dates. If I get serious with someone. When the time is right. If I want you to meet him. I may let you meet him."

Mr. Brown: "Great I look forward to that day. I could just picture your boyfriend and I watching a baseball game together."

Morissa: "You are getting ridiculous now."

Mr. Brown: "Just a fathers dream."

Morissa: "Dad I should go now."

Mr. Brown: "Is there anything I can carry in for you?"

Morissa: No dad. I just have a bag. Everything I need is in the house. Anything I had at the dorm room has already been moved."

Mr. Brown: "You could help me feel better about this if you let me help. Maybe make something up for me to do."

Morissa: "You gave me a ride up here. Thank you for doing that."

Mr. Brown: "It seems like yesterday when I dropped you off for your first year of college. The ride home for me felt like the longest drive of my life. I kept thinking about things I should have said. I was thinking about the things we talked about. As the year went by it occurred to me you would be just fine."

Morissa: "I told you I would be just fine."

Mr. Brown: "You know what would make me really happy this Year Morissa?"

Morissa: "What Dad?"

Mr. Brown: "You can invite me to a football game. I could come up and watch it with you."

Morissa: "Dad I went to one football game last year. It is not a father daughter type of event."

Mr. Brown: "I guess so. I am not going to see you till Christmas this year. You will be spending thanksgiving at your mothers. I will miss you."

Morissa: "Dad maybe if I get a long weekend, I'll come down and see you."

Mr. Brown: "That will be nice. Please give me a couple of days' notice. I will be away some of the time. I am the one now doing the traveling looking at cars. It gets me out of the house. Not having you at home I can do it now."

Morissa: "You should go out and see mom with some of your time. I would like to sit at a table with you two again and have a family meal."

Mr. Brown: "I think it is time we do that. The next time I talk to her I will bring that up to her. Then it will be a discussion or a conversation. Maybe a nice disagreement over should we do it there. Or we do it back at my home."

Morissa; "If you two figure it out let me know. I don't need the details of how it was worked out. If you two could please just work it out and let me know. That would be a nice Christmas present."

Mr. Brown: "You got it."

Morissa: "I should go now dad."

Mr. Brown: "It is going to be another long ride home after I drop you off. Maybe this year you will want a car. I know someone in the used car business."

Morissa: "Dad last year there wasn't a day I needed or wanted a car. I have no place to keep it. The parking will cost more than the car. everything here is set up to get us around with a bus ride or walking. A car would be a distraction. I don't want one but thanks."

Mr. Brown: "When I was your age I couldn't live without a car."

Morissa: "I know that dad. I heard it before. Now I really have to go now Dad. You have to let me go dad. I have to leave now dad.

Morissa gets her bag and says good bye to her father. She then walks up to the house she will live in for the next school year. Her father watches her walk in to the house. Then her Dad starts the long drive back home.

Morissa has a bag in her hand as she enters her new home for the schoolyear

Morissa thoughts.

Another year ahead of me. One year behind me. Another new place to live. Maybe I should have stayed on campus like a normal student. This decision may not work out for the best for me. My friend sue and I now share a room again. No school rules for living in your rent a room, needs to be followed. I am now free to come and go as I choose. Sue freedom and lifestyle was not something that I got comfortable with last year. I always was and will always be the normal level headed person. She will make her own rules and lifestyle. I will make my own rules and my own lifestyle. Whatever problems that arise from me living here with her I cannot have it affect my school work. I cannot have it affect what I want to do after I finish school.

Everett. What to do about Everett. Sooner or later, we are going to run in to each other. We'll talk somewhere and at some time. Our relationship. Was it a relationship? Was it just a friendship? Was it just the simple attraction of two young people out for their summer break? He may have a girlfriend or several girlfriends. What to do if he wants to see me again. I did enjoy my time with him. I never had a time like that with a guy before. The way he looked at me.

The way he kissed me. The way he could talk to me. If we did see each other again, would it be the same again.

Should I be the one to set some ground rules that he may not like. Priorities are what I need to think of. What will happen will happen. I cannot go into this year anticipating or making plans for what I cannot control.

My parents I don't have to worry about them for a while. Thanksgiving maybe I will see my mother. Christmas may be my father. Spring break I will see how the year is going and who I am friends with. Next summer I will probably go back to California and be with my mother. Than what about Everett. There I go again thinking about him. I have to stop before he drives me crazy. Just stay focused on school is what I will do.

My life now as an 18-year-old who cannot say she had a steady boyfriend yet. A couple other things I can say I haven't done yet. Someday I will be able to say I graduated college I have a degree and I can teach. Isn't that what I would want to be able to say. I will be able to say I can teach kids because I have a degree. Morissa walks into her new home for the school year. Sue, Morissa last year school room mate is Inside by the front door.

Sue: "Hi Morissa. It is nice to see you made it. I mis you this summer. I tried calling you but it was like your phone was disconnected or something. It was like you fell off the face of the earth."

Morissa: "Yes I didn't even use one all summer. I just wanted to sit on a beach and read a book."

Sue: "Morissa don't you have anything you would like to tell me."

Morissa: "I put the money for the rent in that bank account and I am paid up for the year."

Sue: "No that's not what I mean. There is a rumor that you and Everett were together during the summer."

Morissa: "Where did that come from!"

Sue: "Somebody saw you two together sitting on a deck at a beech."

Morissa: "It is true. We met on a beach and we spent some time together. It is that simple. We just became friends I guess."

Sue: "You guess. Don't you know if you are just friends or something more."

Morissa: "The last I saw him he was going fishing with his father in Canada somewhere. We haven't talk since then. There can't be much going on between two people a couple of thousand miles away from each other."

Sue: "Between us girls if anything happen you could tell just me."

Morissa: "I did give him a kiss good bye."

Sue: "A kiss goodbye? This isn't junior high school."

Morissa: "Just a kiss."

Sue: "He will be back in his college dorm tomorrow. You will be able to see him tomorrow."

Morissa: "How do you know that. Did he write you and tell you that?"

Sue: "I know things. I know people. I know people who know things. I know he ask me about you last year. I didn't think you were his type. Maybe I was wrong about you. Maybe you are not as shy as you let on my pretty Morissa."

Morissa: "I have no great story of what I did during the summer. I met him we talked. I gave him a kiss good bye.

Sue, I have to start setting myself up here and making myself a home. Are the other two girls here yet?"

Sue: "They will be here tomorrow. Let the fun begin when they show up."

Morissa: "Am I missing something."

Sue: "Your in college now girl. You have three years of fun left. This is just year one for fun. Last year was just practice"

The next day the two other roommates are due to show up.

The next day

Sue: "Morissa are roommates are here. I see Clare but I don't see Noreen. I wonder where she is. Those two were always together. They even spent the summer together."

Morissa: "We still have the rest of the school year for her to show up."

Sue: "Clare will tell us where she is."

Clare walks in to the house.

Clare: "I am here. Let's let the fun began girls. Where are the guys."

Sue: "Hi Clare it is so nice to see you It has been a long summer. You are looking as good as always."

Clare: "Thank you Sue, same back to you. Hello Morissa it is going to be nice getting to know you. Two brunette and one blonde. Maybe we can enlist a redhead."

Morissa: "I will be here a lot studying. We should be able to get to know each other. Where is your friend Noreen? Sue said she would be joining us here?"

Noreen: "Sorry to say girls are friend will not be joining us this year. She will be home for the next seven months. The girl is going to have a baby. Too much fun and not enough protection. Be safe girls. Fun is fun. A bun in the oven is work."

Sue: "I hope she is being taken care of?"

Noreen: "She is. She told her family. They are giving her all the support she needs."

Morissa: "That's good to hear."

Sue: "Who is the daddy?"

Noreen: "It is some local guy she dated during high school. She told me that she started to date him again last spring break. You do the math but somewhere those two got really close again. She should be fine. Needless to say, she will not be joining us here. That leaves us with one less roommate. That leaves us with one less quarter of a payment for the rent."

Morissa: "I guess we will have to get a new roommate?"

Sue: "Maybe girls. My father owns this house, I have to tell him about Noreen and that her part of the rent will not be coming. I don't want to jump at the first girl that needs a place to stay. Let's put it out that we need another girl. If we come across the right girl that needs a place. Then we will take a vote on if we want her to join us. Is that ok with you two?"

Noreen: "That's sounds good to me. What do you say Morissa?"

Morissa: "Yes that is fine with me.  Noreen you will be in your room by yourself till then."

Noreen: "Morissa if you or Sue want the room for yourself, I have no problem with it."

Morissa: "Sue it is yours if you want it. Or if you want me to move in with Noreen I will. I will leave it up to Sue to pick what she wants."

Sue: "No Morissa I want to be your roommate again. I really got to like you last year. I had such a nice time talking to you."

Morissa: "Thank you Sue that is nice of you to say. Noreen that room is yours till we get a girl, or if we find another girl for the room. Do you two agree to that?

Noreen: "If you find me on your floor between you two don't be surprise. I may be there just looking for some company."

Sue: "Ok we have our room plan for the year. Let's get Noreen moved in."

A day later Morissa Sue and Noreen have started school. It is a mid-day in early September. Morissa is alone in the house when she here's a knock on the door. She walks to the door and opens it. Everett is at the door when she opens it up.

Morissa: "Hello Everett it is a surprise to see you. It is nice to see you again."

Everett: "Hello Morissa. I was counting the days till I saw you at school. It feels like a long time since we saw each other, doesn't it?

Morissa: "Yes Everett it does. I am glad to see you. I wasn't sure about this moment. I wasn't even sure it would happen. But here we are. Here we are you and I."

Everett: "Yes Morissa you and I at your front door. Do you think I can come in."?

Morissa: "Yes of course you can come in. Please come in Everett. I was just in the kitchen working on some school work. Why don't you come in and have a seat? You can tell me about your summer."

Morissa and Everett go in to the kitchen together. Everett has a seat at the kitchen table. The two just look at each other for a couple of minutes.

Everett: "If you want to hear about my summer, I will tell you. I went fishing in some really cold rivers with my father and some of his business partners. I have to tell you it was a good time. We ate fish that we caught during the day. At night I was the one cooking it for them. I ate to much fish. The first thing I was looking for when I came back was a pizza. It may be a while before I eat any more fish. When I got back to the beach, I went looking for you. Your mother said that you did go back home. I know you said you would be gone I was just hoping you would be there. I spent the last couple of weeks playing life guard. I came back to school yesterday and went back to the dorm."

Morissa: "I was thinking of staying there. I did promise my father that I would spend the end of summer with him. I am his only child. Being a girl, I think he likes to think of me as that little girl he knew years ago. The one he used to walk to school. I was thinking of you Everett. I had a nice time with you those couple of days we spent together. You were so nice to me. I could see you being nice to everybody. You're not as I pictured you to be. You were just being yourself to me."

Everett: "Yes I here that a lot. I am glad you enjoyed it. I was wishing it could of went on all summer. We would have spent a lot of time on those decks. It would have given us more time to get to know each other."

Morissa: "The Everett I got to know I got to like. Did you get to go back to that bar again? That was such a nice time. It was so simple and so different. You really know how to surprise a girl. There aren't many girls that can say she had a date like that. Thank you for giving it to me."

Everett: "They sold the bar. The new owner are going to turn it in to a sushi bar. My father and his partners were offer to much money to turn it down. There wasn't anything I could do. We were the last people in it. My father sold it soon after we left it. If you saw it now. You wouldn't recognize it. The new owner put a lot of money in to it."

Morissa: "That is too bad. I could see how happy you were when you were in it. Maybe someday you will have a place like it.  You can start working on that now. There are classes you can take that will help you someday if you get to do it. I can see you now at your own place. All the customers coming in on a night out. All the people with a date wanting to spend time with that other person dining out. All the young man with a pretty woman all dressed up. The people who come in there will all ask for the best table by saying they know the owner. You will probably know everybody. Wouldn't you like that?"

Everett: "It sounds nice. You have been thinking a lot about that haven't you. Maybe someday I will win enough money to do it. We will see. How do you like living off campus? Is it all the fun I hear?"

Morissa: "So far no girl fights over time in the bathroom. We lost a roommate. I don't know if you knew her. Noreen Bell is pregnant and will not be with us. Right now, it is just Sue, Clare and me. Clare has the room to herself till or if we have another girl to join us. We all have are schedules of class. Sue is in to who's who, Cheerleading, and her classes. Clare, I don't know or understand some of the things she says."

Everett: "I hope Noreen takes care of herself. Clare, I know what you mean. I talked to her a couple of time. She is always looking for the who is doing who."

Morissa: "Yes that's her."

Everett: "If you three can get along it will make the year go by faster."

Morissa: "How about you? Do you have a roommate?"

Everett: "I have the same guy as last year. I like him."

Morissa: "What classes are you taking this year Everett?"

Everett: "I have some cooking classes. I am taking a liberal arts class. Nothing too hard. It should be enough for me to pass and get thru the year with little effort."

Morissa: "Yes I understand. You told me what you get if you graduate. I understand. If you find something you like. You may want to take a chance and try it."

Everett: "Maybe. I did think about that at the end of last year. I think I could have done something else. Then the next thing I know I am unpacking in the dorm room for this year."

Morissa: "Do you have plans for this year Everett?"

Everett: "Plans? I have no plans other than getting past this year. Is that what you mean?"

Morissa: "Are you going to go to any of the football games? Sue ask me to go to all the home games this year. I told her I would."

Everett: "Yes. I will be at the games. The games are always a lot of fun. Then it is the parties after that makes the weekend."

Morissa: "I guess I will see you there."

Everett: "I was thinking maybe we can go to gather. What do you think about that?"

Morissa: "I would like that. You don't even have to make me a lunch. We could even go Dutch."

Everett: "I know the guy who runs the hotdog concession. I can promise you all the hotdogs you can eat."

Morissa: "Sounds like a date a girl can't refuse."

Everett: "The first home game is in two weeks. What do you think we could do before that?"

Morissa: "I have school work to keep me home at night."

Everett: "If you get hungry, I can come over here and cook you a meal. I could even come over here and cook a meal for you and the other two girls. I think they would enjoy that."

Morissa: "I am sure they would. Somehow I don't think Sue thinks of you as a guy who would cook a girl dinner."

Everett: "How does she think of me."

Morissa: "How can I say this, Everett. She thinks of you as a guy who would have a girl in the bed room before the kitchen."

Everett: "That is my reputation. It is undeserved. I had one girl friend last year."

Morissa: "How many are you going to have this year?"

Everett: "One I hope."

Morissa: "Lucky girl."

Everett: "How about your love life? Anything you want to tell me?"

Morissa: "Not a chance Everett. You like to bet. Don't bet me on telling you anything."

Everett: "I have my work cut out for me, don't I?"

Morissa: "You will have to imagine what you want. I will tell you my love life would be rated g."

Everett: "Let's leave it at g for good. Just good."

Morissa: "I think if people see us together that grade may change."

Everett: "Morissa. I wouldn't worry about things like that. People get jealous when they see other people having a good time with somebody else. Just try and enjoy the person you may like. Everybody has faults or a preconceived notion about somebody else. I don't try to be anybody or any person but myself."

Morissa: "Everett do you want to know who likes you?"

Everett: "I can only guess."

Morissa: "My mother likes you. I told her about the time we spent together. She said that she could tell when somebody is a nice person. She said she could tell just by looking at them. She said you are a nice person"

Everett: "Your mother is right. I am a nice person."

Morissa: "My mother still thinks of you as the paper boy who would not throw the paper against her patio door."

Everett: "A guy has to start somewhere. Why not with a girl's mother."

Morissa: "Oh yes. Please tell me now, that you were nice to my mother because you knew that you would meet me one day."

Everett: "Know I can't say that. I am just a nice guy."

Morissa: "I wonder what my father would think about you?"

Everett: "He would like me, I am sure. You said he sells cars. I like cars."

Morissa: "You make it sound so simple. A common male interest. How simple. I could see a guy talking to the father of a girl. I like cars, can I date your daughter. It is a guy's dream."

Everett: "I wish I thought of that earlier. Let me tell you about this girl I met. I have tried everything to get this girl I like to like me. I talked nice to her. I got her mother to like me. I cooked the girl a nice meal. I even have something in common with her father."

Morissa: "Everett what does that girl think about you?"

Everett: "I think I am starting to grow on her. I am even starting to think she may even like me a little."

Morissa: "How can you tell?"

Everett: "I can always tell when a girl likes me."

Morissa: "Oh you can. Can you. How can you tell when a girl likes you?"

Everett: "When she talks to me. When she can talk to me for hours without looking at the clock."

Morissa: "Oh gee what time is it. I have a lot of home work to do. I should get back to it."

Everett: "I guess I could leave now. If you want me to."

Morissa: "May be soon. I would like you to tell me the rest of that story."

Everett: "What story is that Morissa?"

Morissa: "The one you were telling those children at the hospital. You did promise me that you would tell me how it ended."

Everett: "I know what story you are talking about. This isn't the time Morissa. I will do it someday if you give me the chance."

Morissa: "Sure Everett. You know you have me on a hook with that story. I hope this isn't something that you are using to keep me interested in you."

Everett: "Not that story Morissa. Not that story Morissa."

Morissa: "Ok I trust you, Everett."

Everett: "Are you doing anything tonight Morissa?"

Morissa: "Yes. I have a date."

Everett: "A date with who."

Morissa: "It is with somebody called home work. Then I have a date with somebody called laundry."

Everett: "I do understand. I guess I will just have to wait till I can find you on the beech again."

Morissa: "I will not be on any beech anytime soon Everett."

Everett: "I think I know where I can find you."

Morissa: "I can't make it any easier for you than being right here."

Everett: "We have this year to find each other again Morissa. I hope that we can find ourselves with each other."

Morissa: "That would be nice.

Everett: "I was thinking of you a lot this summer up north Morissa. I wasn't sure if we even were something like boyfriend or girlfriend. It took me some time to come up with what we were the past summer."

Morissa: "What do you think we were last summer."

Everett: "We were friends. It was nice having you as a friend. It is that simple."

Morissa: "Thank you Everett. I did like being your friend. I never had a friend who can cook as good as you"

Everett: "I hope you are not just my friend because I can cook. I would hate to think you are using me just so I can cook for you."

Morissa: "I have to confess that thought did cross my mind. There were times the last month I was thinking about you. There were times the last month I was thinking about your cooking. My mind was a little confused about you."

Everett: "Confused about me? Can you explain that to me?"

Morissa: "I couldn't figure out what I liked more about you. Was it your cooking? Was it the way you talk to me? Or was it your looks."

Everett: "You are really not as shy as I thought Morissa. I think you may be playing with me."

Morissa: "Everett I do have to get back to my school work now."

Everett: "I take this as my time to leave Morissa. I will give you a kiss on the cheek goodbye for now. I will call you Friday to work out a time to pick you up Saturday."

Morissa: "Sounds like something a friend would do."

Everett gives Morissa a kiss good bye and leave the house. Sue, comes in a couple of minutes later.

Sue: "Guess who I just ran in to Morissa?"

Morissa: "A new roommate?"

Sue: "No. I ran in to Everett. I ran in to him as he was leaving here."

Morissa: "He stopped by. He wanted to talk to me. Wasn't that nice of him. He said he was thinking about me."

Sue: "I hope so you are a good-looking girl. You have a lot of guys thinking about you."

Morissa: "He is so nice. We were here at this table talking and the time just flew by. I love talking to him. Did you ever have a guy you can just talk to? I haven't."

Sue: "When I started dating a couple of them maybe. Then it's the same old thing. It's what can I do to you. Then it isn't enough they want more. Then they are on to the next girl."

Morissa: "I think he is different. I like him, Sue. I like him a lot Sue"

Sue: "That isn't hard to understand. He has the looks a girl would like."

Morissa: "Somehow that makes since. We are going to the next home football game together."

Sue: "That is nice. You will be able to meet his old girlfriend there."

Morissa: "I am really not his girlfriend. We only had two dates; I think. Or was it one. We just talked a lot. Did you say his old girlfriend will be there?"

Sue: "She goes to all the games. Her new boyfriend plays for the team. I am sure you two will meet."

Morissa: "Does she say anything about him."

Sue: "Not to me. She did catch him looking at you last year at a party one night. She ask me who you were."

Morissa: "Everett told me that. He told me he was looking at me and his girlfriend caught him looking at me. I don't remember ether of them being there. I wish I did. I hope I wasn't the reason they broke up. I didn't even know who he was till this past summer when we met on a beach. I hope she moved on. You said she has a new boyfriend."

Sue: "I don't know if she has a problem with you Morissa. I will try to find out if she has any problem with you."

Morissa: "Sue please don't. I don't care. Please don't I don't want any of that old girlfriend boyfriend drama. I have to get back to my school work now."

Sue: "Sure Morissa no problem."

Morissa: "Sue You do know he is from California. Nobody knew him here from before he came to this school. I think people may have prejudged him."

Sue: "Morissa. I know only he is a nice guy. If I knew anything, I would tell you."

Morissa: "I know you would Sue."

Sue: "Maybe Clare knows more about him then I do. She runs with a different crowd then I do. She will be back later. We will have a girl chat about him. Then we can compare notes."

Morissa: "You can't even say we are boyfriend girlfriend yet."

Sue: "Come on Morissa. Do you want to have some fun tonight? There isn't much else to do tonight.

The three of us in some footed warm pajamas drinking some Bailys and tea. We can light a fire and start talking about old boy friends. How much we love those losers we once dated and dropped."

Morissa: "Sounds like fun. I may be occupied by someone called laundry."

Sue: "Did you meet somebody called laundry. Strange name."

Morissa: "It is a joke. I will explain it later."

Morissa goes back to her school work. Later that night Morissa, Sue and Clare start there girl talk.

The three girls sitting around a fire place drinking Bailys and eating Milano's cookies.

Sue: "I thank you two girls for showing up to are first meeting. I have decided to call us the three hot chicks"

Morissa: "Sue you are kidding me. I did not know that this was going to be a formal meeting. I kind of thought that this was going to be just some simple girl talk. The thought of you having this in your blonde head is a little scary. How long have you been thinking about this?" Clare did you know about this?" Or were you part of this idea?"

Sue: "I think we will find are selves with each other a lot this year. We will become good friends. I am sure of that. This formal informal meeting is just fun. I think some poet said girls just want to have fun."

Morissa: "It was in a song I think a long time ago. It wasn't any poet I know. That said that."

Sue: "Didn't somebody say that girls are sugar spice and fun?"

Morissa: "It was sugar spice and everything nice."

Sue: "That to. But I am fun. That's me."

Clare: "Morissa to go back and answer your question. No, I didn't know about or have any planning for it. I do like it. I am up for it. Anytime that I can sit by a fire place in my pajamas. Having three full bottle of Bailys in front of me. I am open to anything and I mean anything. "

Morissa: "I like being here too Clare. You may want to be careful who you tell that to. You are open to anything. Some guys may take it the wrong way. You know what I mean."

Clare: "I said would. It depends who you say it to Morissa. I know who I can say things like that too. When it comes to guys, I know what I am doing. I just like to play with them. It is what you say and when you say it. That will have them thinking about you. Nobody does it better than me."

Sue: "Clare is the best at playing with them. The thing she says sometimes will have me wondering what she is thinking. Then later on when I am thinking about what and who she said it to. I wish I said what she said. Morissa you should see her work on the guys. Nobody does it better than her. Her favorite line to a guy is when she tells him that the pants, he has on are nice. No guy knows how to answer that. No other girl has ever said that to him. It takes his thinking about whatever he was thinking about right to the question in his mind of. Is she thinking of my pants or something else? The something else is always what they are thinking or thinking with. Any thought that the poor guy had in his head is gone. His little dirty mind is hoping that Clare is thinking about having sex with him. She is just the best at it."

Morissa: "That is quite the gift you have Clare. Do you stay up the night before and think of those things or does it come by you naturally?"

Clare: "It is practice. I practice it like a doctor practice medicine. I love to be talking to a guy. When they think they are doing good with making time with me I will give them a line they can't handle. I should say that most of them can't handle it. Some guys know how to handle anything that I say to them. It is just play time for me. Guys like to play, and I like to play with them."

Sue: "So do I. Most guys see me as a pretty blonde. All those movies like to make us pretty blondes look dumb sometimes. Every movie has a pretty blonde in it. Every guy wants to date a pretty blonde one time in their life. A pretty blonde never has a dateless Saturday night. Unless she wants a date less Saturday night of course. We are no smarter or dumber than any other girl. We just chose to be who and what we want to be. And that leads me back to we just want to have fun."

Morissa: "I thought about dyeing my hair blonde. I was thinking that I didn't want to be a half blonde. I had a dream that my head had blonde hair on one side and I had auburn hair on the other side. That dream just scared me too much."

Clare: "Not me I like my hair. I will never change it. I love my jet-black hair. I do think about growing it out longer. I had it long as a little girl my mother wanted me to always have it long. One day I got mad at her when I was about twelve and I cut it to get back at her."

Sue: "I guess it is that age at twelve we start looking for the person we want to grow up to be."

Morissa: "Hormones."

Clare: "Yes Hormones. God's gift to mankind."

Morissa: "How do you come up with our hormones being god's gift to mankind?"

Clare: "It is as simple as simple math. If we didn't have hormones, would we want anything to do with any guy."

Morissa: "Somehow that does make sense to me."

Sue: "Let's not dismiss them that early. We have some other use for them."

Clare: "Like what. They are just what my hormones are looking for."

Sue: "They are better at driving then most women. They can take out the garbage. They can also lift heavy things for us. Other than that, I can't think of anything can you two?"

Clare: "Not me. I think you have it covered. How about you Morissa do you have another use for them then hormones or lifting thing?"

Morissa: "Yes one word."

Sue: "No dirty words here please. This is a dirty word free environment please."

Clare: "That's so funny Sue. Morissa, I want to know what that word is?"

Morissa: "It is a word that makes all us girls very happy. It is something we have to learn to do whether we like to do it or not. That word is Cooking. Have ether of you two girls had a guy cook for you? I did and it was one of the best experiences I ever had."

Clare: "No I never had a guy cook anything for me. I had guys buy me meals. I had guys offer to buy me meals. I never had a guy cook me anything or even offer to cook me anything."

Sue: "I had a guy at a barbeque cook me a hamburger that was about it. I never thought about any guy ever cooking me anything. I did have a guy take me out to dinner and believe it or not he didn't have the money to pay for the meal."

Clare: "I had a loser like that to. If they want to go Dutch then they need to tell us beforehand."

Sue: "They have to understand the work we have to do to look good. Time and labor. We can find a lot of guys to ask us to dinner. We can't go to dinner with all of them. If they want to have us as a date, they should pay. If I ever wanted to take a guy to dinner then I would have to consider paying for the meal."

Clare: "It makes sense to me. How about you Morissa?"

Morissa: "How come neither one of you have ask me who made me a meal. I was hoping for that question. I wanted one of you to ask me that. Please one of you ask me that question."

Clare: "Morissa I am starting to think you may be drinking too much. I will take the bait. Ok Morissa whom made you a meal. Please tell us."

Sue: "Morissa. Yes, please tell us. Do we know him?"

Morissa: "Everett did. The guy can cook. The food he made for me was some of the best food I ever had. The way he did it was just as good."

Sue: "Really I would have never thought that about him."

Clare: "He doesn't strike me as a guy who would be able to cook. Tell us about it Morissa. I can see you want to tell us about it."

Sue: "Please you have my interest."

Morissa: "I met him on a beach. Then somehow, he got a date with me at my mother's house on her deck. He surprised me with a great homemade pizza. Then he took me to a bar the next day. The bar was closed but he had the keys for it. He made me a brunch of eggs benedict. He is really a good cook. The way he plan it was great. I was totally surprise by him. I didn't really want to think of it as a date at first. I have to say every time I was with him; I had a good time. When we talk it is like we can't stop talking? He is not like anything I thought he would be."

Sue: "That so nice for you."

Clare: "I didn't know that he was like that. What did you think he was like Morissa?"

Morissa: "Somebody just looking for the next girl. Some guy who is looking just to score with the girl."

Clare: "He does have that look to him. I would believe it, if that is what I heard about him. I can't say that I heard that about him. I think he just dated one girl last year. Sue, you know him better than I do. What do you know about him?"

Sue: "I can't say that I do know a lot about him. I learned he started two years before us. He came from a high school across country. Nobody knew anything about him. My friends and I just thought he was a good-looking guy who was on one of the teams here. Then we found out he was kicked off the football team. The girl he dated just said he was a real nice guy. She didn't think he was her type so she broke up with him before it got to serious. He is all yours Morissa."

Morissa: "Thank you. I don't know if he is mine or that I am his. I am a little confused as to where we are."

Clare: "Have you slept with him yet?"

Morissa: "No. We just kissed. Just some simple kissing. That was all we did, I promise."

Clare: "You don't have to promise. I believe you."

Morissa: "Really, That is all."

Sue: "We believe you Morissa. It isn't any of our business anyway."

Clare: "If you see him again, we will be thinking about it. If you start dating him, we will not ask you."

Morissa: "Ok. Thank you."

Sue: "Don't worry about us. We will give you your privacy."

Morissa: "Thank you."

Clare: "If you want some real privacy here just give us some notice. Sue and I will go to some other place for a night as you two shack up."

Morissa: "Thanks Clare. I will not be doing any shacking up as you call it here. The last thing I want is to wake up to a guy next to me and have to tell him I have to go to school. Then to tell him that my room mates will be back soon. It will take something away from the experience. If I was to have that experience with him or anybody."

Clare: "Are you a virgin Morissa?"

Morissa: "Yes. I just haven't met the right person yet."

Clare: "That is cool Morissa. Good for you Morissa. I wish I waited for a while longer. I wish I waited for somebody better. I guess I just settle for someone. Let's just say I settled and came up short of what I was looking for."

Sue: "I had the right guy at the right time. He knew what to do. I liked him even more the next day."

Morissa: "I guess that is what I can hope for."

Clare: "So many guys to choose from. What's a girl to do? We hope for that right guy at the right time. Staying with the first guy you sleep with forever isn't what a girl should do. The odds of finding mister right at the first try wasn't right a hundred years ago. It sure isn't right now for the woman of today."

Sue: "My mother told me her mother married the only man she ever had sex with. They still live happily ever after together. It is just a happy story that works for them."

Clare: "I knew I wouldn't marry any of the guys I slept with."

Sue: "It would be nice to think that would, or could happen. We all know it will probably not happen. If the guy is a jerk I want to know before I even think about it. Sometimes it is hard to judge them at first."

Clare: "I never dated a jerk. I can tell after a few minutes with them if I want to spend any more time with them."

Morissa: "You would think there would be a simpler way to find the right one."

Sue: "Could you just imagine the real old days of pre arrange marriages. I wouldn't do it. I would spend time in jail before I did that."

Clare: "I would marry him then kill him. I don't mean in a good way for him. He would die painfully. That would be the best way for him to die."

Morissa: "Sounds good to me. We should have that option."

Clare: "Morissa how many glass of Baileys have you had?"

Morissa: "To many. I just can't drink. I get drunk to easily."

Sue: "It is good for a girl to let her hair down and her guard down once in a while. The best place for them to do that is with other girls in the safety of a girl's room."

Clare: "I second it. Should we put it to a vote?"

Sue: "Maybe later. What would you two like to talk about now? Now that we got Morissa's virginity out of the way."

Morissa: "Thanks."

Clare: "I have a question. Or should I say I would like to bring something up for a discussion. Do I have the floor?"

Sue: "The floor and that chair you are in is all yours."

Clare: "I would like to bring up, do guys think we get all dressed up just for them. I never get dress up for them. I get dressed up to look as good as I can for myself."

Sue: "They do think that don't they. Sometimes I think some guys want us to dress up just to turn them on. Why would I want to add that gasoline to the fire?"

Clare: "I know what you mean. They want cleavage. The more the better for them. It's been the same with every guy I have ever known. It starts when we are young girls. Then we just keep trying different looks and types of looks. Just trying to be a pretty girl. Our hair and how we dress it is the same to them. It is all about what turns them on. I don't like that we have to spend more money for less clothes."

Sue: "I love shoes. I love the fact that I get to wear all different types of shoes. I could wear plain simple clothes. Just give me a pair of good-looking shoes. That is like a cherry on the top for me."

Clare: "I like shoes. I like a good pair of shoes."

Morissa: "Comfortable. I like a pair of comfortable shoes more then I need the fashion of it."

Sue: "I hear you."

Morissa: "Do you girls ever notice the news shows. How they have a female and a male news host. The male has to wear a suit. The female co-host can wear whatever she wants. The show wants the female to look attractive. I am glad that we can do that. We have that on them. Even in the work world the female could wear a pants suit or a dress. Every news show I see it is the same. Let the female dress up as she wants."

Clare: "I think that is because they kept the female out of the work place for years."

Sue: "We may be late to the dance but we are at the dance now. Now that we are at the dance, we are the best-looking person that any of them would like to dance with."

Morissa: "That is very good Sue. That is a very good analogy, Sue."

Clare: "You know dam well that they like having us at the dance. They love to have us to look at. School or work we are the distraction they like."

Sue: "You know what they don't like?"

Morissa: "What do they don't like."

Sue: "They do not like it when we are smarter than them. A lot of those women in the work world are smarter than the male boss or the male coworker."

Clare: "What a world we will walk in to in a couple of years. I hope we will do ok."

Morissa: "I think we were facing similar things as we passed from one school year to the next."

Clare: "About those females that went before us. When they went to school, they were told that there were in school to meet there future husband."

Morissa: "Clare did you just say females went to school to find a husband? I never heard that before."

Clare: "I am sure somebody else has said it before. It sounds strange because we are drunk."

Morissa: "Yes I second that. We are drunk."

Clare: "Do you want to know what I don't want to deal with in the work place?"

Sue: "Ugly dorky guys?"

Clare: "Worst."

Sue: "What could be worst then having to work with an ugly dorky guy?"

Clare: "A ugly dorky guy who can't get a date. Then they want to use their place at work that is close to you to try and get a date with you."

Sue: "Sounds like a creep. The work places are full of them I will bet."

Morissa: "A lot of women meet men at work then married them. There must be some good men there I think."

Clare: "Just find one. Just find a good one, what are the odds on that."

Sue: "Girls you want to know what would be good to go along with this conversation and Baileys?"

Morissa: "What?"

Clare: "A good looking guy?

Sue: "A good looking guy could go with anything that I want to be a part of. But that is not it. Brownies and whip cream is it."

Clare: "I second it. Could you go and get it please this chair has a death grip on my butt."

Sue: "Sure. Give me a moment or two. I have to use the little girls' room."

Sue leaves for a couple of minutes. Morissa and Clare have a talk.

Morissa: "That is nice of Sue to let us stay at this house with her. She could have a lot of other girls stay with her."

Clare: "Yes, it is. Her father is paying for everything you see. Her father has the money to do it. I met him and he is all business. The opposite of Sue. He is doing this to keep his daughter safe and happy at school. Her father had a back ground check on you and I."

Morissa: "How do you know that."

Clare: "I found out by accident. Then I ask Sue, she said she knew he did it. I thought you knew. I wouldn't have said anything if I knew you didn't know. I am sorry to tell you."

Morissa: "Thank you. I don't think it makes any difference."

Sue comes back in and hears the two talking about something else. She opens the box of brownies and puts the whipped cream on the table."

Morissa: "I have a question for you. I have to ask. I don't mean to be rude. Clare just told me that your father had a back ground check on me. She thought I knew about it or I don't think she would have told me."

Clare: "I am sorry Sue I thought she knew."

Sue: "It is ok Clare I understand. Morissa I am sorry that I didn't tell you. I did forget about it. My father did it when he found out who my roommates were going to be. I couldn't stop him. My father is very rich and he just wants to protect me. I don't know anything about ether of you that you haven't told me. Please understand that is something that I had to understand about having a father with so much money he could do things like that. He must think you're ok. Last year when I talked to him about living off campus, he said I could if you came with me. That is what he said. Even if he didn't ask me, I was going to ask you Morissa. Please don't be mad at me."

Morissa: "I am not mad at you. I don't understand somebody who has to do something like that. I do understand it isn't you who did it. Sue, can I tell you something."

Sue: "Sure Morissa please tell me what you want. Tell me what will make you feel better."

Morissa: "Sue I like this place. I would have to be stupid not to like this place. You are going to have a line of girls two miles long looking to join us here. Sue, I like you two. I am so happy right now I could cry."

Clare: "Somebody had too much to drink."

Morissa: "Yes I have. I like you too Clare."

Clare: "I think we need a group girl hug."

Sue: "Clare, you haven't said you like anybody. Don't you like us."

Clare: "Yes I like the both of you. I like being here with you two. I like having my own room. I hope we don't get another room mate this year."

Sue: "I did promise my father I would look for someone. I think somehow that person is going to find us. We are going to wait and see what happens."

Clare: "Do you two want to know what cross my mind a while ago when we were talking?"

Sue: "Was it a good-looking guy?"

Clare: "No. I, mean I am always thinking about them. But that is not it. It was when we were talking about the women who came before us and what they had to go through and against. My grandmother told me when she was in school girls were told to try and find a guy who may become president. Could you imagine if we never see a woman president."

Morissa: "I think we will see one. I just hope she is a real good one. The first person who ever does anything has to be a lot better than just the status quo. She is going to have the job. Then being a woman, she will have to deal with men who want her to fail because she is a female."

Sue: "The woman who wins the job will be worthy of it or she couldn't get the job."

Clare: "I like to see it. If I ever have a daughter, I would like to think that job or any job was open for her if she wanted it. I like to think that every job was open to everybody."

Sue: "I am so happy that we are getting along so well. It is harder for three females to get along then three males."

Clare: "Why."

Sue: "I will give the best answer for that that I can think of. That answer is I don't know why. It just sounded right so I thought I would say it."

Morissa: "That works for me. It does make sense, I think. But how would you prove it. Would you do a study to prove it. No, you wouldn't."

Sue: "I am glad you are on my side on that Morissa. I think we think alike sometimes."

Morissa: "Right now I can't think clearly. If you are saying you can't think Clearly. Then I clearly agree with that. Did I clearly make myself clear?"

Clare: "That works for me. I clearly understand what you just said. Sue you clearly understood what she said didn't you?"

Sue: "If she wasn't so drunk, I would think I was just clearly insulted."

Morissa: "That's not what I meant. I meant I like thinking like you because I like you."

Clare: "Morissa don't you like me? Why don't you think like me?"

Morissa: "Sure I like you. I can't think like both of you. Right now, I am having a hard time just thinking."

Sue: "Morissa I think you had too much to drink. Maybe you should turn in."

Morissa: "I would but I am not tired. What would you two like to talk about now?"

Clare: "What would you like to talk about Morissa. We will talk about whatever you want to talk about right Sue."

Sue: "I will second that."

Morissa: "I would like to talk about Everett. I think a lot about him."

Sue: "That is nice Morissa. You should think about him it is ok."

Clare: "Morissa can I ask you one question about Everett?"

Morissa: "Sure Clare ask me anything about him."

Clare: "Do you have those dirty thoughts about him. You know those thoughts about if the two of you were alone together. That Moment after he cooked you a meal that you say he cooked. Maybe you were thinking about something else you two can cook up."

Sue: "Be careful Clare. I don't think she can think clearly right now. She may say something she will regret tomorrow."

Morissa: "Promise you will never tell anybody?"

Sue: "I do promise not to tell anybody, named anybody."

Clare: "I also promise Morissa. It will never leave this room."

Morissa: "Ok I trust you two. I saw him in a wet swim suit. I was half naked in a jacuzzi."

The next morning Sue is out to an early class. Morissa and Clare are sitting down to a breakfast in the kitchen at a table. Morissa has a hangover from the Baileys.

Morissa: "Clare my head is hurting me. I have had a hangover before but this one is the worst. I had to much alcohol one time and had to have my stomach pump out. I knew I was drinking too much and I should of stop."

Clare: "You're ok Morissa. You didn't get sick just give it some time and you will be back to normal. It is good to do it once in a while. You get it out of your mind to get drunk. You don't want to go to a bar where you could get in to trouble. If you are going to do it, do it in a safe place with friends."

Morissa:" You are right. It may not be till next year if I think about drinking that much again. I don't even want to think about it."

Clare: "It is going to be a long year Morissa. You, Sue and I will be spending a lot of time here. On those night that we are snow bound in this house are drunk selves may be our own entertainment. As sad as that sounds."

Morissa: "I could live with it knowing I will wake up without this headache."

Clare: "You talk more when you drink Morissa."

Morissa: "Yes I know. I don't remember saying anything to bad. That is what I am most afraid of when I drink so much. It is the days later when you previously said something that comes back and haunts you."

Clare: "You did tell us you saw Everett in a wet bathing suit and you were half naked. Then you past out on the couch."

Morissa: "I remember saying that. I guess I been thinking about him a lot."

Clare: "You don't have any pictures do you."

Morissa: "Clare! No, I wasn't thinking of taking any pictures at the time. We were just having some innocent fun."

Clare: "He is a good-looking guy. It is ok to have some fun Morissa. We are at that age where fun is somewhere around us at all times. So have some fun Morissa."

Morissa: "I know about the fun and temptation of the fun around us. I am trying to stay focus at my time at school on school. I want to graduate and become a teacher."

Clare: "You can have both Morissa. A smart girl can have both. In a couple of years, we will be in that work world. Like we were saying last night. The guys that I see in the work world leave little to the label of fun. Most of them have a beer belly and losing their hair. They are driving their minivan and looking for the excitement of a woman younger than his wife."

Morissa: "I know Clare, I see them. Too bad we all have to grow old. Somehow we will find someone sooner or later."

Clare: "I hope I am not going to settle for the guy that comes and find me. I am looking for the guy I want. To many girl sit back and wait for the right guy to come and find them. I don't want to do that. I am always looking for the guy I want. Some of the time I have to make the first move. You should see the face on some of the guys when I make the first move. The reaction on their face tells me a lot about them. I like guys. I like everything about them. I may like them too much."

Morissa: "Clare that could be a problem. Some of them you don't know what they are thinking. Everett I was fooled bye. I saw him on a beach. The first thing I was thinking when he started to talk to me was, he was trying to pick me up. I was sitting on a beach alone in shorts and a halter top reading a book. Somehow, a couple of hours later he and I were sitting on a deck looking at the ocean. We spent that night just talking. He was the first guy I just enjoyed talking to. We could talk all night, I think. He was so nice to me every time we were together.

Every time we were together, I enjoyed being with him and talking with him. He surprised me so much. He is nothing like you think he is.

There is a innocents to him that I can't explain. There something about him If I didn't know better, I would think he was a lost little boy."

Clare: "A lost little boy? I don't understand that. Can you explain that one to me?"

Morissa: "I can't. I tried to figure it out but I can't. We only spent a couple of times together. I hope we can spend more time together this year. I would like to get to know him better."

Clare: "How much better would you like to get to know him Morissa?"

Morissa: "Better then I got to know anybody else. That scares me a little."

Clare: "Its ok Morissa. It is normal. It sounds like the other guys may fall short of how he makes you feel.

The Next day Everett and Clare run in to each other in school.

Everett: "Hi Clare long time no see. How are you and the fun group?"

Clare: "Hi Everett. If you mean my roommates. We are just us being us. We are having what other people want to be having. We are just being ourselves. Our selves are just fun people if that is what you mean. How are you and all your guy friends? Who are just looking for some fun?"

Everett: "You said that so well Clare. You said that like you been asked that before."

Clare: "That is what most of your friends are looking for Everett."

Everett: "Good point Clare. I can't lie to you can I."

Clare: "No you can't Everett. I can see right through you guys. It's the sweat on a guys for head that gives them away. I can read a guy's sweat. It's a talent I have that I never told anybody but you. Promise you will not tell any guy."

Everett: "I promise Clare no problem on one condition.

Clare: "Let me guess what condition you would like to attach to that. The answer is two words. Not interested."

Everett: "No Clare. The thought of what you are thinking is not where I am going with this. I wanted to ask you about Morissa. If she hasn't told you, we met last summer on a beach in California. We had a couple of dates and we had a really good time. Didn't she tell you?

Clare: "We talked. You are correct we are sharing a place. I have to go now."

Everett: "Clare you can't do that to me. Didn't she say anything to you about me?"

Clare: "Yes we talked. She did say she was in California last summer. That is right. Now I remember you live in California don't you. I know I heard that somewhere."

Everett: "Clare, you can't tell me she didn't say anything about meeting me out there. She had to tell you about the dates we had."

Clare: "I am so sorry Everett. Morissa said nothing about having a boyfriend and dating him."

Everett: "I didn't say I was her boyfriend. I met her there and we had a date or two I think."

Clare: "You think you had a date or two. You're not sure about that. If I had a date with someone, I would hope they remember any dates I had with them.

I am sorry you can't Everett. If you don't think of them as important. Then there is not much I can do for what you think is important."

Everett: "Clare let's keep this simple. I enjoyed going out with Morissa. I had to leave and go somewhere else. That cut my time I could have spent with her. I was hoping you would tell me that she met me and if she had a nice time with me."

Clare: "Everett, I can't tell you anything. It isn't my place to tell you what another girl may have said. I can't tell you if she said she had a good time with you. I can't even tell you that she may like you. Or If she said anything like that. Or anything that may lead you to believe that she had a nice time with you. It just isn't my place. Everett your just going to have to try harder if you want to impressed Morissa. You will have to do some really nice things for her."

Everett: "Clare that will not be a problem. I like her Clare. She is a lot different than a lot of the girls here. I could just take her for a walk and I think she would enjoy it. I made her just a simple meal and I could see how much she enjoyed the simpleness of it."

Clare: "That is so nice of you to think of her as being simple. I will make sure I do tell her that."

Everett: "Clare let's not get funny here. You know what I mean. She is as nice as any person I have known. She just looks to see who the person is. Her question of me were just to learn who I am. There weren't any question of who I may be or who she heard I may be."

Clare: "Yes that is her. That's very good Everett. I am so glad you remember something about her. You two are going to the same college this year. If you keep being nice to her you may get lucky enough to spend more time with her.

Then again you may find someone else to spend time with Everett. One can never tell about you. You have this image with us girls. You know us girls like to talk so you may want to work on that image."

Everett: "We all have an image. Some of them are not deserved. Some of those images are not the one we want to be known for Clare."

Clare: "I know where you are going with this. I am not the one interested in somebody Everett. There are a lot of people in this school I know. I do trust the ones that like wearing a skirt. Somehow when the ones who like wearing pants see or hear something the conversation start. Then it always ends up as what did you do it and when did that somebody know you did it. You know everything that happens does get around."

Everett: "I know what you are saying. You can tell her that she can trust me."

Clare: "I can't tell her Everett. I don't know what you are talking about. You will have to tell her anything that you would like to tell her."

Everett: "I can only tell her the truth. I can only tell her what and who I am. I have no fear of that Clare. My conscious is clear."

Clare: "Everett let me make this clear to you. If you and her become close let your time, here be at peace. Do something that makes her hurt. I will hurt myself ripping your time here in peace's."

Everett: "Easy with the threats. I like her. Trust me."

Clare: "As far as I can throw you dude.

Everett: "Clare please tell her I said hello."

Clare: "You can find an easier time with another girl if that is what you are looking for. You can find a lot of less complicated fun time. I know you can tell time from what I see in you."

Everett: "Ok were done."

Later that day Everett finds Morissa in school.

Everett: "Hello Morissa it is nice to see you again."

Morissa: "Hi Everett. Is this a coincidence or did you come and find me?"

Everett: "I had to find you. A friend of yours said where I may be able to find you."

Morissa: "That was nice. I will have to thank her for it."

Everett: "If you don't have another class maybe we can go for a walk together? Would you like that?"

Morissa: "I was just going to go and read a book outside. There isn't many days left up hear where the weather will be good enough to do it. Let's go."

Morissa and Everett start to walk outside the building then around the campus. Morissa has both her arms around her books in front of her.

Everett: "How was the rest of your summer in New York Morissa."

Morissa: "It was ok. Most of my friends were working during the day. At night I tried to catch some of them down by the stone wall and the water. There was only a few times when we all got to be together.

There was a time if somebody wanted to find one of us that is where you could fine one of us. I mis spending the time with them."

Everett: "You were lucky to be able to have friends you could do that with. I didn't have many friends I could do that with. There were some kids a little older than me who used to hang out on the dock. After that one kid died that ended. The police stop any body hanging out on the dock at night. The friends I had in school would go away during the summer. I spent a lot of time by myself. I learn to cook for myself and my mother. Then I went to work on getting in to shape. Somehow, I thought I may need to be in shape one day. It may sound strange but it was just a young boy trying to cope with being alone so much."

Morissa: "It did you good Everett. You are a really good cook. If they were to make a Tarzan movie you would be made to order for the part. A tall man who can swim like a fish and cook one at the same time. Men, like that are hard to find. You may have to wear a lone cloth."

Everett: "There is one thing you're missing Morissa. It is the most important part of Tarzan. You couldn't make a movie without it."

Morissa: "You can't fool me. I know what you are thinking. You would want a chimpanzee. You can't have a Tarzan without Cheetah."

Everett: "No Morissa. You're not close. I could care less about a monkey. I was thinking about Jane. You couldn't have Tarzan without a Jane. I would definitely want a Jane."

Morissa: "Your right Tarzan would want a Jane more than a monkey. You do know Janes are hard to come by in those jungles. You may have to wait a long time for a Jane to come along.

Then if you got lucky you would have to hope the right Jane came along. Not all the Jane's are the same. A Tarzan could get very lonely waiting for the right Jane."

Everett: "Maybe Tarzan would have to walk down to the local beach. He may just find a Jane reading a book while sitting in the sand."

Morissa: "I could play in to this possibility that he may find a Jane on a beach reading a book. He just couldn't go up to her and say. You Jane, Me Tarzan. Come with me now. That just wouldn't work with the women of today. Tarzan would have to use a different kind of approach."

Everett: "You may be right Jane I mean Morissa. I think he would have to look around and take stock of what was around her. May be her mother would be close by. Then he could have a chance to meet Jane."

Morissa: "Tarzan I mean Everett. You are really pulling at straws. It would be hard enough to find a Jane. Then to meet the right Jane. Then to have her mother close by would be asking too much. I don't think you would have any hope of getting a Jane in the jungle."

Everett: "Then the last hope for Tarzan to meet Jane would be to save her from a giant crocodile. We all know that would work. Any time the good-looking hero save the damsel in distress they end up walking in to the sunset together and living happily ever after."

Morissa: "I think you have me on that one Everett. I can't think of a better ending. I think Tarzan would end up with Jane. I would hope they live happily ever after."

Everett: "I think they would. That is what those movies always want people to believe."

Morissa: "Everett did you have any class yet?"

Everett: "No not yet they start tomorrow for me. I spent some time thinking about what I was going to be doing this year. Last year I spent too much money and time gambling on the football season.

By the time the season ended I was busted for the year. It wasn't till the end of July when I got out of debt. My cooking for my father up north paid back some of the money I owned him. What a waste of a year."

Morissa: "What are you going to do about it this year Everett?"

Everett: "Make better bets. Make less bets."

Morissa: "Not a very good plan if you were to ask me. You may be better off not betting at all. I know enough to know. The only people who make money. Are the people in the sport and the people who take the bets. A better only holds the money for a short time till they end up giving any money they won back with interest. It is a rigged transaction of a change of money."

Everett: "You said that all too well. Where did you here that before."

Morissa: "My father told me that. I will have to tell you about him some day."

Everett: "Why not now Morissa? You have my attention."

Morissa: "It is a long story. There isn't enough time in this month to tell you."

Everett: "I guess we both have story's we promise to tell each other."

Morissa: "You do have to tell me about that unfinish story. I thought about that a lot when I was sitting on that stone wall waiting for a friend to show up. I tried to finish it.

 I couldn't figure it out. You can only hope for the best with those people in your life."

Everett: "Morissa If you are enjoying the time with people in your life, than everything else will take care of itself. You will not have to worry about looking back and wondering about anything."

Morissa: "Did you put that under your high school picture year book.  From the short time I knew you it sounds like something you live by."

Everett: "No I didn't even take a picture for it. I just didn't care about it or what I looked like at the time. Years from now when somebody opens up the book and see a blank cube where a picture should be. They will see what I care about being remember by them. That is what I think of them."

Morissa: "Sounds like you are angry at them. Did something happen that made you angry at them."

Everett: "No My high school wasn't any different than any other high school. Years from now everybody will have more important things in their life then a picture of anybody in that book.  Maybe I am wrong. I may regret it when I get older. Someday I may have some kids and I will tell them how I was a cool kid. What could be better than that. Just imagine sitting around a fire place with your kids telling them when you were there age and cool. Then again you could fool them for a while then they will figure you out. When they figure you out your cool is gone?"

Morissa: "Everett can I ask you something."

Morissa: "Everett have you ever thought about writing those thoughts down. You may try writing a book. I have proofed read a couple of books for someone.

He was able to create stories because of the way he looked at life events. It is hard to explain you may try it sometime."

Everett: "It sounds nice. That isn't anything I want to do. You have to be a lot smarter than me to do it. I wouldn't even nowhere to begin."

Morissa: "I could help you with it if you like."

Everett: "No thank you Morissa. I like spending Time with you. I would just use it to spend more time with you."

Morissa: "Ok Everett I understand. Please think about it.

Everett: "Morissa how is it going with you and the girls in the house?

Morissa: "So far so good. No girl fights yet. We have our own schedules and that has let us each have are time in the bathroom with all the time we need. Nobody is causing any problems with any body's else things. Last night we had a girl's night. The three of us sat around the fire place. The fire was going we were in are pajamas talking all things girls."

Everett: "Could you tell me what all girl things are. I would like to know. I promise I will not tell anybody."

Morissa: "Everett, I can't tell you that. I took a girl oath never to tell any guy what we talk about when we have a girl talk."

Everett: "You do trust me don't you. In a friendship you have to be able to trust a friend. I can now say that we are friends. Don't you think we are friends?"

Morissa: "Yes Everett if anyone was to ask me, I would tell them that we are friends."

Everett: "Then you can trust me."

Morissa: "In every friendship sometimes somebody has to say no. Everett it is not going to happen any time soon."

Everett: "Can I ask if I came up in the conversation?"

Morissa: "I have to confess I may if said something about your swimming. You are a fast swimmer. But I did have too much to drink and sometimes a person may not remember everything they talked about. They may leave some of the parts out. Everett, I have another reason not to tell you what we talked about."

Everett: "I hope you told them I showed you a good time."

Morissa: "I would have nothing else to tell them but I did have a nice time being with you."

Everett: "Thank you I did enjoy being with you. I was hoping to see more of you Morissa."

Morissa: "What did you have in mind Everett?"

Everett: "Would you like to go and see a movie this weekend."

Morissa: "Thank you Everett not this week end. I check the movies and I didn't see anything that looked good. I would like to spend some time with you. Maybe we can find something else to do."

Everett: "I didn't mean a main stream movie. There is a place I know that show old movies It is free and open to anybody. If I can ask you to be my date. I would be happy to bring you to a day out on me."

Morissa: "Ok big spender you have this girl on a hook with that tempting offer of a free movie. What would be even more special if you show up at the house and I could show off my date. When I tell them about my big day out, I am sure they will be so jealous."

Everett: "It is a date. You can tell Clare that I am a nice guy. I saw her this morning and she was kind of acting like a big sister to you. I don't think she trust me."

Morissa: "I don't see why. Both my roommates seem to like you. They haven't said anything about you in a bad way. I just like to think of it as we are all looking out for each other.

 It's a girl thing. Kind of like us against you. No matter who the guy is it is us against him."

Everett: "Yes I do understand."

Morissa: "Everett can you walk me home now. It is starting to get dark and the temperature her is starting to drop."

Everett: "Sure now let me get you back home. Home to that place where the girls conspire against the male race."

Morissa: "Yes that is all we do. It is that simple."

Everett: "Morissa what do you girls do for eating there. Is there one of you who can cook?"

Morissa: "We haven't had any meals where the three of us are together. I make myself soup most of the time. Sue is spending some time with her friends. Clare, I don't think she eats. Sometimes she may be eating an apple but that is it. I haven't seen her eat any meals come to think of it. Then again we only been with each other about a couple of days now."

Everett: "If you girls let me, I could come over and cook you girls a nice meal."

Morissa: "Everett that would be like me showing you off. I would do that if they let me have you over. Sue made a rule that no guy can stay there for long. They either have to be seeing someone home or leaving. It was her parents help her set some ground rules for her to have her own place. I will float the idea with them. We will see how it goes."

Everett: "I understand. Just give me some notice and I will see what I can do."

Morissa: "Everett when the holidays come along do you have any plans? Are you going to go back to California?"

Everett: "Thanks giving I will be here. Christmas I will fly back home for that holiday. Spring break I don't know yet. How about you?"

Morissa: "Thanksgiving maybe I will go down state and spend it with my father. I may fly down there I don't know yet. It will depend if he has to see any cars up here. Christmas, I have no plans yet. I will not see my mother till the summer. She may fly up here and see me sometime this year. I hope she does. I will miss her. We did have a nice time together.  She did me a big favor last summer. I keep meaning to thank her for it."

Everett: "What favor was that she did for you."

Morissa: "She help you get a date with me."

Everett: "No she didn't. You made sure to tell me it wasn't a date. I think it took me three tries to have a date with you. Your mother just open the door for me. I thought you were trying to close the door on me."

Morissa: "I was. I did not want to be ask out on a beach wearing a pair of shorts and a halter top. Now tell me the truth. Was that the first time you notice me on the beech? Or did you see me before and was just trying to work out the right way to do it. The way you went right over to my mother you could have had it all worked out before hand."

Everett: "It was the truth. I was walking up the beech to talk to a lifeguard at the other end of the beech. Then I notice a really good-looking girl in a halter top. So, I took a little detour to make sure I could get a better look. I walked up real close to take a look.

Then when I saw your face, I recognize it from school. Then your name came back to me from Sue telling it to me. The part with your mother was a long shot. I wasn't sure if she would remember me. As soon as I told her I was her old paper boy I knew I was close.

I went home that afternoon very happy that I was going to see you again. What did you think about me after you knew that it was going to be me and you that night?"

Morissa: "I was thinking about what I was going to wear believe it or not. I didn't want you to think you could pick me up on a beach and have a date. It was one of the strangest time I spent waiting for something that was a date that I didn't want to call a date. I was over thinking something that wasn't even in my thinking before I saw you. After talking to you for a couple of minutes I was at ease with you. You were so nice just to talk to. I was never able to talk to a guy a knew so little about. Then that time on the deck went too quick for me. When I woke up the next day, I couldn't wait to see you again."

Everett: "Thank you Morissa. For whatever reason most girl think I am just looking for a score when I ask them out. It is like I have a sign on my face that says danger keep away."

Morissa: "That did cross my mind. Like I said after a few minutes with you my opinion changed."

Everett: "I am glad you trust me Morissa. You know getting back to what each of us may do or where we may go. Maybe we could fly out to California together. Then you and I could fly back together."

Morissa: "I would really like that, Everett. Thank you for thinking of it. You do know when the people at school see us do that, we will have a problem."

Everett: "What would that be?"

Morissa: "They will think we may be boyfriend and girlfriend when we do that."

Everett: "May be we will be that. You never know what may happen in four months friend."

Morissa: "Well Everett thank you for the walk home we seem to be where I live now. This is the front door so I have to say good bye and go inside now."

Everett: "I will call you Tomorrow and let you know what time I will be by to pick you up."

Morissa: "Ok. That sounds almost like a boyfriend girlfriend date."

The two-kiss good bye. Morissa walks in side and Everett walks back to his dorm.

Chapter Four

Dating Friends

The next day Morissa, Sue and Clare are sitting at a table in the house. Sue has called a meeting.

Sue: "Thank you two for being such good roommates. So far this is working out really well. I am so happy that it is you two who are the ones with me.

Morissa: "We like it too, Sue. It is working out well. No girl fights yet. What is it that you wanted to talk to us about?"

Sue: "Roommate. I found a girl that needs a new place to live. She is having a hard time with her other roommates. There are eight girls in another house across the other side of campus. This one girl just doesn't fit in at all. She has found all her clothes outside the house twice in two weeks. She needs help. We can help her. What do you two think?

Clare: "I have no problem with the idea. That other bed is in my room."

Morissa: "It is ok with me if it is ok with the both of you."

Sue: I thought that would be the reaction of you two. There is one potential problem here."

Morissa: "What could that be?"

Sue: "It wouldn't be a problem with Clare and me. It may be a problem with you Morissa and her."

Morissa: "Me and her? Why do you think that? Do I know her?"

Sue: "I don't think so. Clare and I do."

Clare: "Who is it?

Sue: "It is Becky Randle."

Clare: "Oh boy."

Morissa: "I heard the name but I can't place the face. Who is she?"

Clare: "You really don't know who she is?"

Morissa: "No I don't."

Clare: "Well you both have something in common. You both shear something. "You both have the same taste."

Morissa: "I am more lost now. Clare what is she talking about."

Sue: "Everett. She was the one who dated Everett last year. She was the one who caught Everett looking at you."

Morissa: "Wow. Of all the girls here, she has to be the one who needs the room. I can't even tell you what she looks like."

Clare: "It may not matter. She knows what you look like. I am sure by now she knows that you and Everett are boyfriend girlfriend. This could be a problem."

Morissa: "Boyfriend girlfriend may be getting ahead of ourselves here. We are friends. We went out a couple of times. They broke up last school year, from what I was told. People move on."

Sue: "I told her about you and Everett, when she ask me about the open bed we have. She said that she wouldn't be any problem about Everett. The relationship ended and she ended it. She did say that he is a nice guy. Morissa and Clare, we are going to take a vote on this. I want all three of us to agree on this. If we don't agree on her as the other roommate then we will have to let her find some other place to live. She does need another place to live. My vote is to let her come here. I like her and I don't think she will be a problem."

Clare: "I like her to. I am the one who has to share the room. I rather have her then a lot of other girls."

Sue: "That leaves her fate in your hands Morissa."

Morissa: "I have no reason not to let her stay here. I vote to let her live here. People move on. We all dated guys who had other girlfriends. I can't be so scared to let another girl live with us because she dated some guy I like and have been out with."

Sue: "Thank you Morissa and Clare. I will let her know that the bed Is hers. It may be a little awkward at first but you two will get past it."

Clare: "It is going to be awkward at first. It will be awkward every time he is here. It will be awkward every time Morissa talks about him. Yes, it will be awkward for you two. Sue and I are going to have a hard time controlling are laughter some times. Those priceless awkward moments are sure to be at hand from time to time."

Sue: "Morissa there isn't anything reassuring I can tell you. Clare and I will not purposely try to make any problems between you to. Right Clare."

Clare: "Sure."

Sue: "I hope that you two girls can both do what is best for the house."

Morissa: "I understand. I don't think this will be anything that will be a problem. I am sure it has happened before. By the time we finish this year, or are time here. Who knows who will have dated who? Or who will have been friends with who.

Clare: "Oh the fun we are going to have this year. Fun is who is dating who?"

Sue: "Ok Clare. Let's just try, having a let's just get along time."

Morissa: "When will she be moving in Sue?"

Sue: "Sunday night. Her first rent check is do then."

Morissa: "Everett and I are going to be spending Sunday together. I will have to tell him."

Clare: "Can I be there when you tell him. I could just see the look on a guy's face when he is told his old girlfriend and his new girlfriend are friends and that they are living to gather. I could just see what will be going on in his mind or any guy's mind. The thought of having both girls in the same bed with him."

Sue: "Yes I could see that. I think you are correct on that Clare. A little creepy but that is what they would hope for. Two girls in the bed with him."

Morissa: "Stop the male fantasy. Not in my life time will I be in any three some."

Clare: "Don't knock it till you tried it."

Sue: "Clare. Please not here. What you want to do else where I don't care. But not here."

Clare: "Don't worry you two are not my type."

Morissa: "I hope this works. I want to think about my school work. Not what a female may be thinking about an old boy friend of hers."

Sue: "Ok girls I think we are done here. Our next meeting will be Sunday night. The four of us will be together then."

Clare: "What if, Morissa and Everett decide to shack up. Those two just may start living together in Everett's room."

Morissa: "I will be here. I will not be living with any guy any time soon Clare. Thank you."

The meeting ends the girls go on with the rest of their night.

Early Sunday morning. Everett shows up at Sues house to take Morissa out for the day. Sue and Clare are still in bed on this early Sunday.

Everett: "Hello Morissa. Thank you for taking time away from your school work to join me."

Morissa: "I like spending time with you Everett. You are such a nice person to be with. Every time I was with you, we have done something different. I was trying to think of what you had plan for us today."

Everett: "I don't think I have to try and plan to much out when we go out together. I think I could take you for a bus ride and you may like it. Just think of the last time you were on a bus Morissa.  Because that is what we are going to do today."

Morissa: "Oh boy a bus ride. You are right. It has been a while since I was on a bus ride. What a lucky girl I am."

Everett and Morissa get on a bus that takes them to the local town.

Everett: "I wanted to give you a day on the local small town on me. I heard that is what every woman wants once in her life."

Morissa: "Your close. But I think it is a night on the big town that we want once in our lives. An expensive restaurant with two waiters, waiting on you. An old private label of wine.  That hard-to-get little private table that is in a secluded corner away from everybody else.

My date would have to be a good-looking man who knows how to dress up for a date. May be a little gambling where we could walk away with some of their money. Then at the end of the night my date takes me dancing.

Everett: "That is a tall wish there Morissa. The average guy would have a hard time getting all those little detail right. You may just have to settle for some good food. Some kind of drink and a crowded dance floor at a casino."

Morissa: "If I have the right man with me, it would be just as good, I am sure."

Everett: "I will work on it for you Morissa."

Morissa: "Everett what is in this town we are going too? You don't find many people are age in the local town on a Sunday morning."

Everett: "It is just a local town. Just like all the other small towns in the world. No different. There are some shops and some small mom and pop stores not much else."

Morissa: "At first it sounds like a cheap date. From what I have seen of you and what I have learn from you. This is a way for two people to spend time with just each other. Two people can talk and get to know each other doing this. Every time I am with you Everett, I get to know you. It is like getting to know you for the first time. Everett, I do enjoy being with you."

Everett: "Thank you Morissa I like you to. I will show you a real good time if you let me. At this time, I can just say I am in a cash crunch. I have a budget for school, cars, insurance, food, clothes and fun. I took the car and insurance money and gambled it away. That is why we are on a bus. The food money is still food money. I have new clothes so I am down to the fun money. My parents are millionaires.

Some girls I have gone out with want me to spend all kinds of money on them. Those girl friends don't last long when they find out I am broke. I am no different than a million other college kids Morissa.'

Morissa: "Thank you for being so honest with me."

Everett: "Morissa are bus ride is done, let's get off the bus and go get ourselves some breakfast. I am sorry to tell you I will not be the one cooking it for you.

There is an old restaurant along the main street that has some table set on the side walk. If we are lucky, we will be able to sit outside and eat."

Morissa: "sounds nice Everett. I don't think I will ever find a man who could match up to your breakfast."

Everett and Morissa find an empty table out in front of the small stone building. The front of the building has two big glass windows with the front door between them. In front of the windows are two tables with white wooden chairs. Everett pulls out a chair for Morissa. Everett and Morissa are talking when a waiter walks up to them. The waiter's name is Pete. Pete is in his fifties.

Pete: "Hello Everett it has been a long time since I saw you last. I think it was last fall if I remember right. How are you?"

Everett: "Hello Pete. Yes, it was last fall when I saw you. You are still in the best shape I ever seen a man your age Pete."

Pete: "It is all the walking back and forth. Inside, then outside when the weather is good."

Everett: "How are your parents. I heard your mother was sick last December. I hope she is doing better now?"

Pete: "Yes she is fine now. Those two will live forever. I would like to see them again Everett."

Everett: "Maybe they will come up and see me. My parents often talk about coming back here and seeing this place and your family"

Pete: "My family would like that. Please tell me who this beautiful young lady is, that sitting across from you."

Everett: "This is my friend Morissa. We go to the same school. You may not believe this, I used to deliver the paper to her mother's house when I was a paper boy."

Pete: "I believe it. It is a small world. You must have a very lovely mother Morissa, because you are very lovely. It is my pleasure to meet a young lady who is a friend of Everett."

Morissa: "Thank You Pete. You are very nice. I will tell my mother about the compliment thank you."

Pete: "What can I serve you Morissa. Tell me anything and I will bring it to you. Any friend of Everett is a friend of me and my family."

Morissa: "Please just a cup of green tea and I will have the number three with wheat bread toasted."

Pete: "Wheat toast, green tea. A smart girl I can tell. Very health conscience. A smart beauty. Everett I would not let this one go."

Everett: "You should see what I had to do too get a meeting with her. I had to go and ask her mother if I could have a date with Morissa. Then Morissa told me it wasn't going to be a date. She put me thru a lot. I have no plans to give up what I work so hard for."

Pete: "Good. You need to settle down a little and enjoy life pleasures.

Everett: "Ok Pete I will have the same as Morissa with a cup of coffee please. If your wife is hear please tell me and I will go in and see her."

Pete: "It is Sunday. She went to church and will be working at home. She will be sad that she missed you. I will go and get the tea For this nice lady and the coffee for you."

Pete goes off to the kitchen.

Morissa: "I am amazed Everett. How do you know him and his family?"

Everett: "My father used to work here when he went to college. My father had to work his way thru college before he join the navy and became a lawyer. Pete and my father worked to gather here. Pete looked after my father let's say. When my father became a lawyer, he came back here and found Pete still working here. To make a long story short. My father with the help of his partners bought the place. My father made a deal with Pete for him to buy the place from my father. Now Pete is the owner of the place. He still likes to wait the tables."

Morissa: "What a nice story. How often does your father come out here and see him?"

Everett: "Every year my father makes two donation to the college. One is my tuition. The other one is to keep me in our school."

Morissa: "Is this where you learned to cook?"

Everett: "No I learn it from my father and on my own. I just enjoy cooking. I enjoy people liking what I cook"

Morissa: "Maybe you could get a job here cooking."

Everett: "No I couldn't do that. I would have to start off being a bus boy and washing dishes first.

I will be done with my time at school before I could get a chance at the kitchen. You need something from a culinary school to get in to a good kitchen.

Any other place that is what I would have to do.

 I wouldn't use my father's friendship to ask Pete to give me any special favors."

Morissa: "I understand."

Pete: "Here is a fresh pot of green tea for the young lady. Coffee for You Everett and some orange juice. Your meals will be along shortly."

Everett: "Please don't rush for us Pete. Morissa and I are going to walk the town today then head back to school later in the day."

Pete: "That so nice of you to enjoy the town during the day. I wish the other kids did that. The town could use the business. Those kids like the big city on the other side of the college. The only time the kids come down here at nigh is to visit the bars."

Everett: "I know that is what us college kids like to do."

Pete: "Live and let live. I will be back."

Morissa: "Does he get any business from the kids at college?"

Everett: "No not much. He close his doors at eight pm Tuesday thru Saturday. Sunday he will close at Two and go home. He makes enough to support his wife and his kids. The restaurant will bring him enough money to retire when he wants."

Morissa: "Please tell me about his wife.?

Everett: "I met her but I don't know that much about her. Pete and her met here. They were both working then started to see each other after work. They got married and then bought the place from my father. They have kids and now live happily ever after."

Morissa: "Sounds nice. That makes things easier when you met somebody then get to know them before you start dating. You don't have to wait to see if you can get along with them. It is kind of like a test run with somebody. You can say it is like a trial period."

Everett: "Would you like to do that with me. Give me a test run? Give me a trial period? You could even write me a review after each time we go out."

Morissa: "I can give you a review right now."

Morissa reaches over and gives Everett a kiss.

Everett: "That is better than a review or one of those stars a teacher gives you as a kid. Do you do that to all your dates?"

Morissa: "No just the one I like."

Pete: "Here is your meal kids. Let me know if there is anything else, I can get you please. I will leave you two alone for now."

Everett: "Thank you Pete."

Morissa: "Thank you."

Everett: "I hope he doesn't give us so much attention. That is why I don't come here to often. I feel bad that I think he owes me something for something my father did for him. He will give us a check when we are done for a dollar. He thinks of it as paying my father back. It makes me uneasy when he does it. I try to figure what the bill is and leave that money and a tip."

Morissa: "He gave me way to much food on my plate. I can't eat all this. I hope I am not insulting him if I don't eat it all."

Everett: "No just the opposite. If you eat it all he will think he didn't give you enough. Please don't eat it all."

Morissa: "It is a deal. The food taste good Everett. The tables inside look to be filled. He must do a pretty good business for morning breakfast."

Everett: "Breakfast and lunch are what keeps this place going."

Morissa: "Could you see yourself owning this place, Everett? It is like that other place you made me breakfast at.

Everett: "That Thought did cross my mind. My mother would like the idea of it. My father wants to start downsizing what he owns and wants to spend more time up north fishing. It may be a hard sell to him. I rather live in California any way. There isn't much to keep me up here in snow and cold for the rest of my life."

Morissa: "What if you met the right girl who lived up here. Then you wanted to marry her. What if she had a job here that she loved and she wanted to live here."

Everett: "I don't know. I would have a hard time talking myself in to staying up here after college."

Morissa: "What if you two were married."

Everett: "There are enough what ifs in life. I try not to think of the what ifs. There are too many things that are left to the what ifs."

Morissa: "People make plans. People work to avoid the what ifs. People set goals and try to achieve their goals.

Sometimes people have to work harder than they thought just to get to a point in their life where a goal is in reach."

Everett: "I know I heard it before Morissa. Right now, let's keep it just you and I enjoying being with each other. I do like being with you Morissa. We are just at that trial period now. Let's not make those complicated life plans and goals for a while."

Morissa: "Ok Everett. I understand. I do like who you are. There is something about you that I wish I had. Everett you are freer then anybody I know. That must be nice to be like that."

Everett: "Free? I don't think of myself as free. I am just trying to avoid being any trouble to anybody."

Morissa: "I don't think I understand that. What trouble are you talking about?"

Everett: "Any time I got in to trouble my father bailed me out of it. If I could just go a year without needing his help, I would have had a good year. If I look free right now that is because I am not in trouble or in his need today. May be tomorrow I will not be so free."

Morissa: "I am done with what I can eat Everett. How about you?"

Everett: "Yes I am done. I am going to have another coffee and watch the people go by for a little while longer if you don't mind."

Morissa: "Ok Everett I would like to do that after I go to the lady's room. I will be right back.

Morissa goes off to the lady's room. Pete comes out and collects the dishes then he brings out a fresh pot of coffee. Morissa comes back to the table.

Morissa: "I see that the table has been clean off and we have a new pot of coffee. I hope he didn't say anything about the food I ate or didn't eat. I was thinking about that. There is no right answer for that is there."

Everett: "No there isn't any answer for that because you are the only one thinking about it. The people in the kitchen is just looking at your plate like any other plate.

Morissa: "I see you moved your chair so you could watch the people go bye.

Everett: "Yes I like to do it. I am one of those people who like to do it."

Morissa: "You could have told me you moved your chair so you could be closer to me. That would have been nice."

Everett: "You know when I first saw you on the beach, I wanted to pull up a chair right by you."

Morissa: "You did now? Why would you have wanted to do that."

Everett: "It was that book you were reading. I read it before and I wanted to talk to you about it."

Morissa: "You have put yourself in to a corner Everett. If that is true. Then you are saying you didn't find me attractive enough to try and meet me. Now you have to tell me the name of the book I was reading. If you can't then you didn't read that book and you are lying. If you are saying you just wanted to meet some chick in a halter top, I would believe that but then you are lying. So, what is it, Everett? Was it the book? Or was it a chick on a beach"

Everett: "I see chicks in bikinis all day. I do enjoy the sites that a warm California beach has to offer. Sometimes you can look at something that catches your eye like a pretty face. A pair of hazel eyes that are sparkling in the sun.

The light breezes flowing thru an auburn hair as it lifts the hair. Then you notice those curves that are in shapes that are so appealing to the male eye. That the loveliness that is in front of you to be hold is some beautiful woman that you have seen before. Then it comes to you where you have seen her before. Yes, it was the same face the same shining eyes. The same deep color of the hair. This one is different than any other female that you wanted to approach. You have to be careful not to scare her off.

You look around for something that may help you in your approach to this beautiful female. Anything your hoping for. Then you see it. A chair on that deck behind her. On the deck is a similar chair she is sitting in. There is a woman sitting in that similar chair. The woman. You have met the woman. You used to deliver papers to her. She may remember you for it. That's it you have the information you need to meet the lovely lady in that chair. I walked up to her knowing I have read the book. Knowing I was nice to her mother. Knowing I seen her before. Knowing what school, she goes to. Morissa our meeting on the beech could of happen about a half a dozen ways. Morissa it was going to happen. There was even a chance, if you saw me first that we would have met. I didn't lie the book was call Stay Till Dawn. You are a real good-looking woman Morissa. When I first saw you in the bar that night, I wanted to meet you. I was on a date and couldn't do that to my date."

Morissa: "Everett you know I was just trying to have some fun with you and the way I met you. I am sorry that I suggested that you were a liar. It doesn't matter to me now how we met or how are meeting came about. I am so happy that you did ask me. That answer was one for the ages. Were you thinking of that answer before or did it come to you as fast as you said it? You are right that was the title.

I am amazed you had all those detail so fast Everett. What you just told me was the best words any guy has ever told me. I don't know what to say next."

Everett: "You don't have to say anything Morissa. Sometimes people meet. Boys have been meeting girls forever. We just had our meeting the way we had it. Years from now we may say that was just a nice way to meet."

Morissa: "I am so glad I don't ever have to tell somebody. He was looking at me in a halter top and liked my boobs, enough to ask me out."

Everett: "So long as are stories are the same nobody will ever know Morissa."

Morissa: "Good we just have to agree on which one of the half a dozen ways the story could be told."

Everett: "You pick it and I will agree to it."

Morissa: "It will have to be the one I told my father of course. I can't give my father a different story, now, can I?"

Everett: "Good you tell me what you said to him and that's what I will say."

Morissa: "I don't remember exactly what I said to him. Let me think about it for a while."

Everett: "You do that Morissa. The pot of coffee is done. I see some people looking for a table so let's go. I am going inside to pay for this. He isn't going to ask us to leave or bring us a check. I will be back in a minute.

Morissa: "Ok there is a clothing store across the street. I will meet you there."

Everett: "Ok it is a date."

Everett goes inside to pay the tab. It takes him about ten minutes to do it. When he comes out, he can see Morissa across the street looking inside a clothing store. The left window by the door has men suits on mannequins. The right side has women dresses on mannequins. Everett walks up to the right window and gives her the line.

Everett: "Hello good looking don't I know you from somewhere?"

Morissa: "Yes you do mister. I was the one you took to breakfast don't you remember? Or do you take so many lady friends to breakfast?"

Everett: "It is only the pretty ones I remember."

Morissa: "I am flattered mister. I am sure. Mister what is that bag in your hand?"

Everett: "Maybe lunch. You look like you are trying to make up your mind on what you want to buy. Is there something in there you like?"

Morissa: "It isn't what is in the window. It is the store. When I was a little girl, before I wanted to teach, I wanted to own a clothing store. I would want to create the latest fashion. It is a dream; a lot of other girls have had as they grow up. We love having the latest fashions. I do like that hazel green jewelry the mannequin is wearing"

Everett: "I don't know if you know this but on behalf of all the boys, we are glad that girls like to wear the most stylist clothes. It may be just as important to us as to all of you how you look."

Morissa: "Really. That thought would of never cross my mind."

Everett: "Morissa do you see those two women in there. What do you think there doing in there?

Morissa: "They are working. They are changing some of the outfits that are on display."

Everett: "It is a Sunday morning. This store has a close sign up in the door window. The sign is right by the sign that says it is closed on Sundays. It is strange Morissa. Why are they working on their day off? Whatever they have to do could wait till Monday, when the sign says the store will open."

Morissa: "I think you have something Everett. What may look like the average woman's clothing store may be just a front. The question I have for you is what this women's store is a front for?"

Everett: "Maybe it is a group of underworld spies. They are here to find the greatest minds of the college student. Then they would have to convert them to whatever side they are on."

Morissa: "I think they found the wrong college.

Everett: "I agree with that. Morissa maybe someday you will own your own store like this one."

Morissa: "When I was younger I would of like that dream. Now that I am older, I want to be a teacher. I am going to this school because they have the classes, I would need to be credited to do it. I worked in a deli for a while in high school. To run a small business, it takes a lot of time from your life. It is a twenty-four hour a day life. The people who own the deli I worked at is hoping that they can make enough so there son could find something else to do with his life. He is a teenager and doesn't have much of a drive to do anything."

Everett: "It sounds like what it takes to own and run a restaurant. I may be like that boy. I may not have the drive to do it. There is a lot more than just being able to cook a simple meal."

Morissa: "Everett I want to believe you could do it. You're not like somebody who would fail. I think if you want something bad enough you would get it. If you wanted to do something you would find a way to do it. I don't know if you know it Everett you are something special."

Everett: "I have never been called special Morissa. I hope you mean that in a good way."

Morissa: "I do. I found what I wanted to do and that is to become a teacher. You will find what you want to do Everett. When you do, it is going to be something very special."

Everett: "We need to start walking away from the store window. I think they noticed us looking at them. If those two old ladies are under world spy's, we should leave before they come out and get us."

Morissa: "Ok Everett. I think they may have a use for you. The old one is looking at you and licking her lips. As for me I think I am safe. Let me take your hand and take you to safety."

Everett: "We have a little time left before we have to be at the matinee. There is a park up ahead do you want to take a walk in the park with me to day Morissa."

Morissa: "I would love to take a walk in the park with such a nice guy."

Everett: "You think you could trust me to take you in to a secluded place?"

Morissa: "I hope I can trust you. When I was a little girl, my mother told me not to talk to strange men in the park. Everett that means you can take me in to the park but I can't talk to you."

Everett: "If we don't talk, we are going to have to find something else to do. What do you thing two young adults could do. A male and a female in a secluded park. The possibility are endless don't you agree."

Morissa: "Everett I hate to dash your dream. I can see the park from here and it is a small park that is full of people."

Everett: "Maybe we have the wrong park. Maybe we can find that secluded park elsewhere. What do you say we by pass this one and try to find another one somewhere else?"

Morissa: "I think this is a one park kind of town, if you ask me. We may have to walk a long way to find another park."

Everett: "Ok Morissa. We have to settle for this one."

Morissa: "Look Everett there is a duck pond in the middle of it. Let's go and see the ducks. I love ducks. I think they are one of the smartest animals in the world. Just think they could fly in the air; They could swim in the water and walk on land. How many other wild animals can do that."

Everett: "Not many Morissa not many. When we get up there make sure you don't fall in to the water. I may not be able to be a life guard here."

Morissa: "I see some old man over there playing bocce ball. I am sure they would love to pull me out of the water. They may fight over who would be the hero."

Everett: "Those are the old men your mother warn you about when you were a little girl. You may not want to even smile at them. They may get the wrong idea."

Morissa: "I am not a little girl any more Everett. You never know one of them may come over to me and give me that line they saw me somewhere else. That would be a great pick-up line. They could do that line so good that I may just be swept off my feet by them. A girl never knows when mister right is standing right in front of her."

Everett: "If that happens my walk home will be a long lonely one. I will miss you."

Morissa: "You may be safe. I don't think any of them can cook as good as you. I think you are safe for today. But one never knows about tomorrow."

Everett: "My work is never done with you is it. I just have to keep working at it don't I?"

Morissa: "You are very good at its Everett. I think you are really good at impressing a girl without even trying. It is just the way you are. I think you even treat your guy friends in a nice way. It is just your nature."

Everett: "That's funny. Please don't ever tell any of my guy friends that."

Morissa: "I know it is a guy code. Don't worry your secret is safe with me.

Everett: "Morissa why don't we take a seat on the bench by the water for a while we have some time yet."

Morissa: "Ok Everett let's see if we can fine one free of duck poop."

Everett: "I see an old paper in a waste paper basket over there. I will go and get it. That will give you a safe place to park your butt."

Morissa: "Thank you for thinking about it."

Everett: "My pleasure."

Everett goes and fines a paper in the waste paper basket. He brings the paper back and puts it down on the bench. Morissa and him have a seat looking at the ducks.

Everett. Morissa, would you like to know what I have in this paper bag? I bet you can't guess."

Morissa: "You said it was are lunch."

Everett: "No I said it was lunch. It is something called duck lunch. Here you go I will give you the bag. Open it up and see what is in it."

Morissa: "Oh Everett it is just simple bread. We can feed the ducks with it. Everett, I can't believe you. You think of everything. You planned this out didn't you. You did this just for me. I don't know how you knew I liked ducks."

Everett: "I didn't. I was just thinking of the ducks. It's getting cold at night now and less people are coming here. I got some left-over bread from the restaurant."

Morissa: "Everett can I ask you a question."

Everett: "Yes you can Morissa. You are allowed to ask me a question. Please don't make it a hard one. It is a Sunday and it is a day off."

Morissa: "I will make it simple. Did you ever bring another girl here before? Please tell me the truth."

Everett: "That is an easy one Morissa. I haven't done this before with a girl. I came here one-time last year when I was feeling down one day. I was alone when I did it. You are the first person or girl I have taken here. My father told me he used to come here sometimes and tell himself that all the work he was doing at the restaurant and school will be worth it.

Morissa: "From what you told me about him it was."

Everett: "Yes it was. My father is still working. Like I said before he likes it up north and is starting to think of spending more time up there."

Morissa: "You like your father, don't you? A lot of people our age find reason not to appreciate their parents. They don't appreciate what they did for their kids."

Everett: "Sorry Morissa I am no different than anybody else. Let's talk about something else Morissa."

Morissa: "What would you like to talk about."

Everett: "Let's talk about the ducks."

Morissa: "The ducks? What could we possibly find to talk about the ducks?"

Everett: "There is a world of things that we could talk about the ducks. The easiest thing we could talk about is how a boy duck meets a girl duck. I don't know if you know that the way a boy duck meet a girl duck is exactly like the way a human boy would meet a human girl. Not many people know that fact."

Morissa: "I never heard that before. Please tell me about that fact. You did say it was a fact. So please tell me. It isn't like I have to leave anytime soon. It seems my date wants to spend his time with me helping me understand the dating ritual of dating ducks."

Everett: "Ok Morissa. If you really want me to."

Morissa: "Yes. Please Everett do it for me."

Everett: "Ok. I don't know if you ever notice that the boy ducks have more color to their feathers. That is to make them more attractive than the females. That is only one of the ability they have to win the affection of a female duck. Another ability they have is to use duck talk. It just so happen I am an expert at duck talk.

See those two ducks by the center of the lake. I have been listening to those two ducks over by the center of the lake."

Morissa: "Wow Everett, that is amazing you can hear those two ducks all the way over there."

Everett: "Morissa let's just play along with this ok."

Morissa: "Ok Everett you have the stage make it good."

Everett: "Ducks speak in word groups of three. If you listen to his inflection in his voice. It is every third sound that is the more important sound. The first two sounds are just the sounds to get the attention of the female. That third sound is the sound the female use to determine the male's intentions. The male cannot make the third sound, too hard. If he does, he may scare the female off to another male duck. If he's says it to softly, she may leave him for a more promising male duck.

Then and if, he has the attention of the female duck. The next group of three words, he uses will be the words the female duck will most remember about their first meeting. He would have to be careful not to tell the female duck something that he will not remember at a later time. Those words may come back to haunt him. The male duck would not take the chance to lose the opportunity with the female duck. The next step is to keep the female duck interested. The male duck would have to make those next group of words relate to the female duck. He could tell her he has seen her at another duck pond. That works more often then you may realize. There are a lot of duck ponds and the chance of that happening are going to be pretty good. Another line he could tell the female duck is that he knows her mother. Now he would have to be careful on how he does that. Then he would have to keep the dialoged going with the female duck. The way to do this would be something that the female duck was interested in.

The most common thing female ducks are interested in are themselves or what the male duck may be thinking about them."

Morissa: "Oh I didn't know that. I guess that we as females are just interested in our selves aren't we. I didn't know that."

Everett: "Morissa Please I have more."

Morissa: "You go on. If you dare."

Everett: "That would just to keep the conversation going as I just said. Then the male duck would have to listen to the female duck. How she return his words would determine if he had any chance with her. If she did answer any question that would tell the male duck that she was giving him a chance to talk to her. It is telling the male duck that the female duck may have some interest in him. Then the male duck would have to work on a way for him to have another meeting with the female duck somewhere else. He would have to be smart enough to have the next meeting in a duck pond that the female duck would consider a home pond. Something like a house with a deck on it. If you get the picture Morissa."

Morissa: "I can picture it. Please don't stop I think all the male ducks in the duck pond are listening to you for pointers on how to have a chance with a female duck."

Everett: "He can tell the female duck that he knows this great duck pond where a very pretty girl will feed the ducks with bread from a very nice restaurant. There some special male ducks that will go one step further and make some special bread for the female duck and maybe call it a pizza. This could be his big chance. The male duck may not know if the female duck even like pizza.

Then again, he may have seen the female duck eating pizza somewhere else. I mean to say the male duck may have seen the female duck eating the bread crumbs at another pond.

After a while the male duck would have to know it was time to end the first meeting. He will hope for a good outcome of to meet her again at another duck their first meeting. If the male duck couldn't get the female duck to meet the male duck at another duck pond. He would have to hope pond somewhere.

If the male duck was lucky enough to have the female duck agree to have another meeting at another duck pond, he would have to find a way to have her think about how she was going to prepare for it. The male duck would have to not tell her it was a date. The female would not know how to be prepared. She would be used to having her feather dress a certain way for every meeting. To leave her with questions in her mind on how to have her feathers ready will help him learn about the female duck. When she showed up to the next meeting at the next duck pond. The male duck with one look at her casual feathers could tell she is a casual type of female duck. That she takes things as they come.  If the female duck had her feathers all dressed up then the male duck could tell the female duck is an event kind of female duck. That everything in the female duck's life will be an event.

After the first meeting he will know how to approach the female duck. He will ether keep the next couple of duck meeting as casual or formal. This is a talent I have Morissa. You have to promise me that you will never tell anybody. If this gets out, I could see my face on the national inquirer. One other thing you can never tell any male duck about my talent because they would never talk there duck language around me again. They may have to make another duck language if it got out."

Morissa: "Thank you Everett. I never had anybody tell me a story like that. To know you were thinking of me as you told it was nice of you. I think I am out of bread now."

Everett: "We need to go now the matinee is about to start."

Everett walks Morissa down the street to the local church. The last mass for the day has ended.

Morissa: "Everett there is a sign out front of that church that say there is a movie today. Is this where you are taking me?"

Everett: "This is it. Just think about it Morissa. You are eighteen and somebody you just met is going to walk you down a church aisle. I bet when you woke up this morning that thought didn't cross your mind."

Morissa: "You are correct about that. This wasn't someplace where I thought you would be taking me. I wish I known. I would of ask my father to walk me down the aisle. I could just see my mother in the front seat crying. I think Sue and Clare are going to be upset I didn't invite them."

Everett: "Just think of the money you saved on a wedding dress."

Morissa: "That's it I have to call this off. There is no way I am going to marry you or any other man with me not having a wedding dress. It has been a dream of mine to wear that white dress when I get married. Sorry Everett I can't get married today."

Everett: "Morissa you just broke my heart. You think I can ask you to stay for the movie? It is an old Marks brother movie. You just may like it."

Morissa: "What is the movie called?"

Everett: "The name of the movie is called A day at the races. Those guys are still funny all these years later. The church is having a hard time getting enough people to come in on Sundays. Somebody came up with the idea to show movies. There will be a short talk from the preacher before and after the movie. When we go in there, we will see a place for us to leave some money as a donation. Then there will be some local kids and their parents selling some popcorn and candy."

Morissa: "Everett you are just a big-time spender aren't you."

Everett: "I do what I can."

Morissa: "I like this church. Look at all that stone work. I hope to get married in a church that is as beauty full like this."

Everett: "There is a Granite quarry accouple mile from here. They used to take the granite from there and send it down to the city back when they were building new York city. The people who lived and worked at the quarry back then took some of the granite and built this church with it. The better pieces are out front for the face of the church. In back are the low-grade pieces. You will also see a lot of the granite back at the college we go to. After a while the quarry ran out of any usable granite. The quarry closed and a lot of people left this town. The only thing this town has now is the college."

Morissa: "I wonder how many people were married at this church. It makes you think about if they stayed married. If they did live happy ever after. Then how many of these kids were born here and came through this church."

Everett: "Come on Morissa we need to go inside and get a seat."

Everett and Morissa go inside to watch the movie called a day at the races. Everett buys Morissa some candy. The two-take seats in the middle of all the chairs. All around them are kids running around not watching the movie. Their two ten-year-old girls sitting in front of Everett and Morissa. The two girls keep looking back AT Everett and Morissa. The two girls will exchange whispers after they look back at the two. Everett and Morissa leave the church after the movie finishes. They start the walk back thou the town.

Everett: "Did you like the movie Morissa?"

Morissa: "It was very funny. The one who doesn't say anything is the funniest one. Without saying anything he is so funny. He is so likeable. I am going to have to watch some there other movies."

Everett: "They have a couple classics. That one we just watch was ok but they do have some better ones. We have to watch them together.

Morissa: "Is that an offer of another date."

Everett: "Yes Morissa it is. I thought you wouldn't notice it. It just another way for me to get another date with you."

Morissa: "It worked. Is that what a male duck would do to have another date with a female duck."

Everett: "It is. That is where I got it from. It never fails."

Morissa; "You need to work on your asking girls for dates Everett. You may want to go back and talk to some of those other ducks."

Everett: "Really what have I done wrong? I thought we were having a good time. I thought you were enjoying yourself."

Morissa: "I was Everett. I was thinking what a nice guy you are. I was thinking of how much I was liking you. Then it hit me. You did something wrong and you made two girls unhappy."

Everett: "Two girls un happy. You will have to explain that to me."

Morissa: "Did you notice those two girl that were sitting in front of us."

Everett: "The ones that kept turning around and looking at us."

Morissa: "Yes those two. Did you notice that they kept whispering to each other every time that they looked at us?"

Everett: "Yes I did. That is just what girls at that age do."

Morissa: "It is what they do. Being a ten-year-old girl at one time I had an idea what they may have been whispering about. They were whispering about us. They had a bet on whether you were going to kiss me. When you got up and went to the rest room, I had a girl talk with them. They ask me if you were my boyfriend. I told them that we just started dating and we were friends. Then they asked me would you be kissing me. I told them I didn't know if you were going to kiss me or not. They had a bet on if you were going to kiss me. They kept looking back to see you kiss me. Everett, you didn't kiss me. One of those girls lost a bet. That means you disappointed two girls. That isn't good for a guy to do that."

Everett: "If one of the girls lost the bet and one of the girl won the bet. That leaves only one girl I disappointed."

Morissa: "Everett do I have to draw you a picture. If you kiss me, I would have liked it. You didn't kiss me. It is basic math. One girl lost a bet. One girl didn't get kissed.

That makes two girls you disappointed. You sure are slow Everett."

Everett reaches over and kiss Morissa.

Morissa: "It is too late to help the other girl who lost the bet. You did make me feel better. Can I ask you where you are taking me next?"

Everett: "Morissa why don't you pick a place you would like to go."

Morissa: "I don't know this town."

Everett: "Just think of this town like any other town anywhere else. It has everything else any other town has."

Morissa: "I am at a lost. I have no idea what we could do next. I think you have played out everything. Even if I thought of something you have something else in mind, don't you?"

Everett: "I do Morissa. We are going to go for a little walk now. The place I am taking you is a little farther away. Are you up for it?"

Morissa: "I am all yours Everett. You have this girl by the hand. I could do this all day."

Everett: "Don't you have some school work you have to do today?"

Morissa: "I did it yesterday. There is a paper I have to go over before I hand it in tomorrow. It should take me about an hour."

Everett: "Morissa there is a difference with us any time I have to spend an hour on any work. It turns in to an all-day affair for me to do it. I will be happier when I am done with school. I never did like what school was."

Morissa: "I like the idea of school. It is where we grow up as kids. We need to learn how to live with other people. We just can't turn eighteen and be pushed out in to the world without the basic skills we learn at school. The teacher is so important to the kids. They are the center of what the learning Experience is. There are classes of different kids with different lives. The kids are all at different learning ability. The teacher has to be able to move all the kids forward the same. The teacher has to teach all the kids the same material. The ability of a teacher to do it is something special. Teachers are so underappreciated."

Everett: "Morissa I have to kind of disagree with you. I could have been home school and ended up just like I am. I can't tell you I ever had a teacher that I think made a difference.

It is up to the kid and the effort they put in to school that will be how they learn in school. If a kid doesn't get anything out of school it is because they did not want it. Or there was nothing they needed."

Morissa: "I think we just have had our first disagreement Everett. I hope that we can overcome this difference in what we think."

Everett: Morissa when we have nothing to talk about, we can always talk about what we disagree on."

Morissa: "I hope that one day I can pull you over to my side of the disagreement."

Everett: "You do know there may be a lot of things we are going to disagree on. We are two different types of people."

Morissa: "I know Everett the more I talk to you I find that I do look at things in life differently then you. I always heard that opposite attract. That is why we are attracted to each other. I wish I could have been more like you sometimes. I am always second guessing myself. Guessing did I make the right decision. Was there another decision that would have been a better decision? Sometimes it is just the simplest thing that I second guess my self. I think you are more likely to make a decision and just live with it. I wish I could do that more often."

Everett: "The time I would of second guess my self was if you didn't agree to meet me when I asked you on the beach. I think I would have been still second guessing myself if you turn me down."

Morissa: "You have to remember that it was my mother who gave you the yes answer not me."

Everett: "Ok Morissa you have to tell me. If your mother didn't give her ok, would you of still saw me that night?"

Morissa: "I don't know if I want to give you that answer. I don't want to give you too much confidence. You may get a big head. It is a girl's privilege to keep a guy guessing on what she thinks of him. I may never tell you Everett."

Everett: "From that last kiss I think I have my answer that you are happy that you did see me that night. A guy can tell when a girl likes him from a kiss."

Morissa: "I may have let you kiss me so one of the girls could win there bet. You may have not notice they were watching us from their car."

Everett: "How could I be sure of that. I didn't see them in a car. I have to believe you that that is what they told you."

Morissa: "That is right. You need to be careful Everett you never know what may be happening around you."

Everett: "I guess I should thank you for looking out for me."

Morissa: "Everett you do know that this is a dead-end road we are on. That the only thing on this road is a small old grave yard."

Everett: "That is right we are on a small road. A dead-end road that has a small grave yard at the end of it."

Morissa: "What are we doing here. It is a little creepy you know."

Everett: "Morissa you do trust me don't you."

Morissa: "I do Everett. Could you tell me why we are here please?"

Everett: "I promised somebody I would do something. That is why we are here. You will understand when you see it."

Morissa: "You are a mystery sometimes Everett."

Everett: "Some girls like mystery Morissa."

Morissa: "I will hold judgment on this one till I know the ending."

Everett: "Just a little longer now. Like I said you will know it when you see it."

Morissa: "I don't know what I am expected to see in here. Oh my god! I see it I can't believe it. It can't be. It isn't you. You are right next to me. Your alive. But there it is. There is your name on that granite head stone. Who is it?"

Everett: "It is my father's brother. My father's older brother. My father named me after him. I promised my father I would come by here from time to time and check on him, I should have told you first. It was easier for me to do it this way. I wasn't sure if I could of explain it better."

Morissa: "It is ok. I understand how hard it must be. No question from me. I will be here for you Everett."

Everett gets on his knees and says a few words not heard by Morissa. He gets up and says "good bye for now." He gives Morissa a hug and thank her for understanding. He takes her hand and starts to walk back out of the grave yard. It is not till they have left when Everett starts to talk."

Everett: "He was my father's older brother. My father and him were down at the granite quarry playing around being kids. His older brother was always looking out for his younger brother at the time. Both of their parent were working that day. My father said his brother took a wrong step to close to the edge and he slipped and fell of the edge. My father watch his brother fall to his death. Then my father looked over the edge of the cliff where he fell. He saw his brother laying on some broken stones. It took him an hour to get to his brother.

Then my father had to run in to the town for help. My father had to show the sheriff where is brother was."

Morissa: "That's so sad. I can't imagine how hard that would be to a child."

Everett: "If you have any luck in your life you will never know. It has to mess up a child to see his dead brother just lying there."

Morissa: "From what you tell me, he did well for himself. I guess he manage to be strong enough to overcome it. Not everybody could do it."

Everett: "You are right you would have to be strong to overcome it. If he didn't, he would be considered weak. Morissa thank you for being here, but I don't want to talk about it anymore. May be another day."

Morissa: "Sure Everett I understand."

Everett and Morissa walk awhile hand in hand before Everett starts to talk.

Everett: "We are going to start to head back to the school now. I have accouple of guys coming over to watch a football game. We don't want to be out here late with no car. It will get cold by the time we get back. It is back to the bus for us. Next spring when the weather gets warmer, we will come back out here. Does that sound like a date to you?"

Morissa: "Yes and you will not need my mother for me to say yes to it."

Everett: "I guess I am getting better at asking you out."

Morissa: "What would you and your friends do if there wasn't a football game on. Would you and your friends still hang out together?"

Everett: "Sometimes we will play poker on a Sunday night. Friday and Saturday night, we like to go to the parties. You know we go to those parties to meet the girls. Its date night for people are age. It is boy meets girl. Girl meets boy."

Morissa: "Everett I am not interested to meet any other boys right now. I am happy I met you. I do like you."

Everett: "Morissa I understand what you are telling me. Right now, I consider us friends.  If I was to be ask what are relationship was. I would tell them we are friends. I would tell them I don't have any other friend I like better. Morissa, I like you a lot there is nobody else I rather be with."

Morissa: "Thank you Everett, I needed you to say something like that. It is important to me to know that."

Everett: "Are bus is here at that stop let's get on it before it leaves."

Everett and Morissa get on the bus going back to their school.

Morissa: "Everett I have something that I have to tell you."

Everett: "Go ahead Morissa tell me what you would like to tell me."

Morissa: "The girl you dated last year. Becky is going to come and live in the house I am living in."

Everett: I know I heard Morissa. What do you think about it.?"

Morissa: "I don't know what to think about it. I don't know what to think about it.  I don't know what you two men to each other. I don't know her. I know you. I know it may be complicated when you come over to see me. I was asked what I thought about her living with us. I didn't want to be the bad guy in this. Sue and Clare left it up to me. I hope I don't have any problems with you or her."

Everett: "We did date for a while. It didn't last. The best way I can explain it. We just didn't have what it takes to be a couple. Did you ever date a guy and know that you just didn't want to spend any more time on a relationship that wasn't working? She was the one who called it off first. I knew it was going to happen sooner or later. I have seen her several time since. We do say hi and ask each other how we are doing. I don't wish anything bad for her. I hope she says the same about me. I don't think this is going to be complicated."

Morissa: "How come you didn't say anything before about it, if you knew she was going to be living in the same place as me?"

Everett: "I wanted to see how you would handle it. I thought you may bring it up today. I wasn't going to say anything that may be a reason to give you a problem.

Or ruin our day together. Morissa I am not out for drama. If I cause any problem coming over there let me know and we can work something else out."

Morissa: "She is going to be there when I get back. I haven't met her yet. I am a little nervous about its Everett."

Everett: "Morissa why?"

Morissa: "Everett, I like you. I don't want to lose you."

Everett: "Morissa do you know what a male duck would say to a female duck when he was told what you just said. "

Morissa: "What would the male duck tell the female duck to reinsure her?"

Everett: "He would tell her the next time your father comes to the school I would like to meet him."

Morissa: "He would like you, Everett. There are parts of you that are like him. Maybe that is why I like you because I like my father."

Everett: "We are here Morissa; Let's get off the bus and I will walk you to your house. Then I will walk back to my room.

Everett and Morissa get off the bus. Everett doesn't go inside. He kiss Morissa good night then starts his walk back to his dorm room. Morissa Goes inside and finds Sue, Clare and Becky in the kitchen talking with an open bottle of white wine. When they see Morissa, they stop talking. Morissa stops in mid step and looks at the three. Then Morissa walks in to the kitchen.

Sue: "Hi Morissa how was your day?"

Morissa: "I had a nice time. Thank you."

Sue: "Morissa this is Becky our new roommate. I don't think you two know each other."

Morissa: "Hi Becky it is nice to meet you. Welcome to the house."

Becky: "I thanked the girls for letting me fine a new home here. Now I would like to thank you."

Morissa: "It is Sues place you should thank her."

Becky: "I did. Now I am thanking you for not voting against me staying here."

Clare: "This is going well. I don't feel the tension."

Morissa: "There is no tension. I am glad that we found somebody who needs a place to live."


Becky: "I didn't need this place. I had other places to live. The other places there was going to be some drama with one of the girls. I hope I don't find any drama here. For any reason that somebody may find."

Morissa: "You will not find any drama with me. I have no drama now. I will not have anybody giving me any drama."

Sue: "Morissa please have a seat at the table. We need to talk. It will be better to clear the air now then to have any problems later."

Clare: "Problems can be constructive. Problems can be good for the cardiovascular system."

Morissa: "My cardiovascular system is just fine. I don't want to hear about anybody's problems, with anything that is none of their business."

Becky: "Problems are only what a person wants to deal with. Sometimes you just have to kick a problem to the curve because he isn't what you want. Then you let somebody else come along and pick up your old unwanted problem."

Clare: "Could you explain that better Becky. I don't think I have the full picture. May be you have a picture of you kicking a problem or an old boyfriend to a curb. Sometime those old boy friends and problems are one of the same."

Sue: "Clare please you're not helping here. Morissa and Becky, we need to clear the air with both of you. The only thing I think that will be something that is an issue with you two is that you both dated the same guy."

Becky: "I used to date a couple of guys. Which one of them are you referring to."

Clare: "A guy named Everett. Unless Morissa has a story, she would like to let us in on? How about it Morissa maybe you dated one of Sues old boy friends too?"

Morissa: "No I didn't. And I didn't date any of your old boy friends Clare. Clare, I don't have a score card of old boyfriends. Some girls may have been with more guys then me."

Becky: "What is that supposed to mean. Was that directed at me. If it was, I don't like the sound of it."

Sue: "Girls. I want all of us to get along here. I need to have trust between us. Morissa and Becky, you two are going to have to deal with you both dated the same person. It isn't any of my business of the who what and where. I don't care."

Clare: "I do. I am hoping for all the facts of who did who and for how long and was it any good. And are there any pictures?"

Morissa: "There isn't any of who did who here. There isn't anything to talk about here."

Becky: "I dumped him. They only talk after they get dumped. Then they start with the recovery of their ego. Trust me sometimes the talk is just a cover for their short comings."

Clare: "That is another one of those things, that I need a picture of what you mean. You didn't have any pictures to prove it do you?"

Sue: "Clare, I think you had a little too much to drink."

Clare: "There goes that word little again. Poor Morissa I feel so sorry for you."

Morissa: "Clare I wouldn't know."

Sue: "Girls. Let us please keep this to how we are all going to get along."

Becky: "I have no problem getting along with anybody. So long as they stay out of my life and out of my things. It is when people want to judge me, it creates a problem for me."

Clare: "What thing was yours that somebody has now. May be you have a picture of him I could see."

Sue: "Clare enough with the pictures please."

Clare: "Becky did you ever see Everett in a wet tight swim suit."

Becky: "No. I didn't even know he could swim."

Clare: "Morissa did."

Becky: "I don't care. It is over between us. I am better off without him."

Morissa: "Becky I am sure that he had a girlfriend before you. He may have another girl friend after me. Right now, I like him. Right now, I think he likes me. You said you dumped him. I didn't know him when he was dating you."

Clare: "He knew who you were. He asked Sue about you."

Becky: "I saw him looking at you one night at a bar. Now tell me you didn't see him."

Morissa: "I don't have to tell you anything. I didn't notice him. I wasn't looking for him."

Sue: "Becky that is the truth."

Clare: "I could believe that. It could happen. It may of happen that way. Then again, a year later here we are. Morissa is dating Becky's old dumped to the curb boyfriend."

Morissa: "Clare you have a real nice way of looking at things."

Clare: "He is nice to look at. That is why you were looking at him that night."

Becky: "I don't care if she was looking at him that night. I didn't care if she and him were seeing each other after I dumped him. I just don't care If she and him were seeing each other behind my back."

Sue: "Clare you are not helping here. Please help me."

Clare: "Ok I had enough fun with you two. Becky Morissa is telling you the truth. She didn't know who he was or you were last year. Everett saw Morissa on a beach last summer and that is how those two met."

Sue: "That is how they met. Morissa was my roommate last year back in the dorm. She didn't date anybody last year. She seldom even went out."

Becky: "I know I sounded like I have a problem of getting over him. If I am wrong then I am sorry Morissa. I want to believe you three. The last group of girls I lived with was talking a lot of crap about you and Everett. They found a lot of other things to gang up on me about. I think they were just trying to get under my skin and they did. Moving on from him wasn't hard Morissa. Our relationship never got far."

Morissa: "I understand. I will ask him to stay away from the house. We could see each other elsewhere."

Becky: "Please don't do that. Just do what you would if we didn't date. If you start doing that then you will be thinking about me. What you could do is invite him over so we can get it out of the way. I will not be any problem between you two. He is a nice guy, There wasn't anything with us that kept us together."

Morissa: "Thank you.

Clare: "This could have been more fun than how this turned out. You two ruin my night."

Sue: "Oh poor Clare. How about we get a bottle of Bailys and all meet at the fire place, Then we can get more alcohol in you. Then we can hear about your love life."

Clare: "The boy girl love life, or the girl, girl love life?"

Morissa: "Sounds like a plan to me."

An hour later the four girls are on a couch and a pair of oversize chairs. The fire place is roaring. In front of them on a table are two bottle Bailly's an empty bottle of white wine, and four boxes of cookies. On the tv is an old movie.

Becky: "This is so nice girls. This is so much better than the last place I was at. The house was always cold and a mess. Somebody was always fighting with someone. How do you keep the place so clean?"

Sue: "I have a cleaning company come in twice a week and clean the place."

Becky: "Is that something I have to pay for?"

Sue: "No not out right. It is coming out of your rent money. My father set this up for me. So long as I don't get in to any trouble here, we are safe. My father has enough money and he is picking up most the cost for us to live here this way. I gave you the rules we have to follow before. Please don't do anything that I will have to explain to my father."

Becky: "I will become a nun to live like this. I will do anything to keep your father happy with us."

Clare: "Did you just say you will do anything to keep her father happy. I could draw you a picture of what you could do to make her father happy."

Sue: "Let's not go down that road. Never go down that road. Never go down that road with anything with my father. I don't want to think about anything like that."

Morissa: "Clare where do you come up with those things, that come out of your head."

Clare: "I have the same things in my head that you three have in your head. I am just free enough and comfortable enough with myself to say it."

Morissa: "You mean you are drunk enough to say what is in your mind."

Sue: "Clare doesn't need alcohol to say what is in her mind. She needs a sensor to stop her from saying it."

Clare: "I want to say this is the way every female should live. If the guy we are with can't afford it we should be able to kill them."

Becky: "I agree with that or dump them to the curb."

Sue: "You could still dump them if they have money. Then you take them for as much as a good sleazy lawyer could get from them. That is what my mother did with her first husband. A sleazy lawyer and a state that has a divorce law that has to protect a wife."

Morissa: "I want to be able not to need a lawyer or the state. We should be able to make as much as them."

Sue: "I don't need to worry about that. My father will be my bank account. I want to be smart enough not to screw it up. I know I am not dumb enough to let some guy take it from me."

Becky: "What is this movie you have on?

Sue: "It is one of those old movies. My home work for a class I am taking has me watching old movies. They want us to be able to analyze the movie then write a review of it and have a class discussion. Really easy class. Would you believe that there are some people who will show up with nothing written?"

Clare: "I believe it because I have done it. There is a risk reward to doing homework. You could just do enough home work to pass. That would be the reward. Not doing enough home work is a risk of failing."

Morissa: "I think I saw this movie before. They are on the same small boat from the start till the end of the movie."

Sue: "Don't ruin the movie Morissa. I want them to get rescued."

Becky: "I haven't seen this movie before. I don't think this movie is about them getting rescued. I think it is going to be about a good guy and a bad guy. How two of them are in a boat?"

Sue: "The good guy has to be the worker type better looking guy. We have to figure out who is going to be the bad guy here."

Clare: "It is going to be the rich old guy. I could see it coming. He is older than who we want to be the good guy. That will make him a better good guy."

Sue: "I wonder witch female is going to be the one the good guy gets at the end."

Clare: "I want to see a movie where the female doesn't end up with the guy. I want to see a movie where she tells him that he isn't what she wants. After he saves her and is almost killed. The movie end she walks in to the sunset without him. Or better yet she walks off with another female."

Morissa: "It wouldn't sell. Especially back then. Back then the audience wanted the good-looking guy to end up with the good-looking good girl. Everybody wanted the girl to be good. I mean virgin at the alter good."

Clare: "Fat chance of that happening in real life."

Sue: "Back then virginity happen at weddings a lot. Now it would not happen as much."

Morissa: "That is the same difference."

Becky: "I think what Sue is saying. People are more interested in the female love life then the males love life."

Clare: "Not me. I don't want no virgin at any alter that I am sharing with him. He better have an idea of what he is doing. I would have to kill him if he ruin my honeymoon."

Becky: "I agree with you Clare. I would have to kill him to."

Sue: "I wouldn't kill him. I would just call that divorce lawyer I was talking about."

Becky: "How about you Morissa. What would you do if the man you married was a flop on your wedding night?"

Morissa: "I don't know. It wouldn't be the first time that I would have slept with him. I would know if it was just a one-night thing or not. I hope that the rest of our love life would be better."

Clare: "Morissa you are just not much fun sometimes. I wanted to hear you say you would kill him. I guess that isn't you is it."

Sue: "I don't know. Sometimes it is the quiet and shy ones that go to the extreme. I could picture Morissa hiring a hit man to kill him. Then running off with the hit man."

Clare: "I could see that. Then I could see those two end up as lovers and international killers for hire."

Becky: "I'll be sure to stay on your good side Morissa."

Morissa: "They are just having some fun with me."

Clare: "What is up with that woman voice in the movie. Is that part of an act. Or did she really talk like that."

Becky: "Nobody ever really talks like that in real life. Way back then or any time anywhere. I think we missed the part where she gets shot in the throat."

Sue: "I think that is her real voice. I heard it somewhere else. I just don't remember where."

Becky: "I think we just found the bad guy. They fished a German out of the water. He has to be the bad guy."

Sue: "I would agree with you on that."

Clare: "I still don't see a good-looking hero type."

Morissa: "You can see the right type of guy. He is right there. The younger guy. The muscular guy with the tattoo. The guy with the hurt leg is not the smart one, so he is not going to get the girl and be the hero."

Sue: "We have three women to choose from. I wonder who is going to be the one who is the female lead."

Clare: "If somebody had to choose one of us three as a female lead who would get the job."

Sue: That is a good question, Clare. We are all good-looking girls. We all are the same age. Who would get the part? It may depend on what role is being offered. We are all different looking girls with different color hair. We have a red head that is Becky. Morissa auburn. I am a natural blond. Clare is jet black."

Becky: "It could be if they want a good girl or bad girl. It could be if they want a smart girl or a girl with an attitude.

Morissa: "It could be who is the best actress. It could be who they can trust to be dependable enough to show up to work every day. It could be who would bring in the most male audience."

Clare: "It could be who would do a nude seen."

Sue: "Not me I don't need the money enough to do it. I think my father would cut me off if I did it."

Becky: "I don't know. It would have to be that I was comfortable with doing it. I would hate to look back on what I did and consider it pawn."

Morissa: "I don't think that I have anything more than any other female. It would have to be for something I could believe in."

Clare: "No pawn. No real sex. I would do it. It would have to be harmless then I could see myself doing it."

Becky: "What if a fat ugly looking producer told you. You had to have sex with him for a good part in a movie."

Sue: "No way."

Clare: "I would tell him to get naked first then take a picture of him and run away. Then send the picture to his wife or boss or somebody that would humiliate him."

Morissa: "Not me no way."

Becky: "I like what Clare would do."

Morissa: "Oh no the woman in the movie knows the baby is gone."

Clare: "That has to be the worst."

Morissa: "The writer had to show that what is going on in the boat is life and death. Tough way to do it, It does work."

Sue: "I think we are going to see accouple of more people die by the time this movie ends."

Becky: "I like the one they call spark. I don't know why but I do like him."

Clare: "I like the one with the bad leg. I bet he is, or was a lot of fun. I could see him keeping a girl up all night just going from one bar to another. Then he finds a place to dance with her. He would be more interested to party all night than anything else."

Sue: "Not good looking enough for me. He looks too much like my father for me. I like the one who was in the men's room when the ship was hit. He is lead male in this movie."

Clare: "I could see the German kill everybody in their sleep and rowing the boat back to Germany.

Morissa: "They couldn't do that back then. The good guys always won back then."

Clare: "Maybe it is the radio operator that will save them at the end?"

Morissa: "I think we now know witch female is the lead female. The British nurse is the costar female. I wonder who she will end up with? I like her the best."

Sue: "I think just the German is going to be the bad guy here. It would be good if one of the other people were a hidden spy. That person was under cover and no one knew it. Maybe the radio operator. He may have been giving out the boat's location to all the German subs. He would know when to get ready to be by a life boat. He would have done this before. Every time he was saved, he would just get on another ship and do the same thing over and over. I wonder if that was thought of."

Becky: "Is this what you girls do on a Sunday night? At the other place I lived we would be at war with each other. Somebody would be mad at somebody. Most of the time they were all mad at me. This is a nice change."

Clare: "This is what we do. We tend to drink too much. Somehow, we find a lot of nothing to talk about. Somehow, we have managed to get along. We are just some boring chicks that drink too much. We could have some fun again if you and Morissa would really go after each other."

Becky: "Morissa I'm sorry if I accused you of anything. I have no proof of anything. It was the other girls over there that wouldn't let it go."

Morissa: "It is ok. We cleared the air. He hasn't said anything about anybody else he has dated. I don't think he would, unless I asked him about that person."

Becky: "He doesn't say much about anything sometimes. You will find that out about him. The tall quiet type."

Sue: "What do you girls think of the tattoo on the lead guy chest?"

Clare: "His chest wouldn't work today. To plain. The tattoo would be a bad tattoo today."

Becky: "I agree with that. Give me a guy with a nice chest and some muscles."

Clare: "Morissa I think she means Everett."

Morissa: "He could, Clare. He would qualify. So would a lot of other guys right Becky."

Becky: "You are right Morissa."

Clare: "You two took the fun right out of that."

Sue: "Did anybody catch the voting question to George. I think the writer wanted to say something between the lines there."

Morissa: "The writer did. There are a couple of other things being said between the lines here."

Clare: "I think the nurse and the other guy there are starting to get close. What a way to meet a guy. I could think of a lot of better ways to meet a guy. Becky why don't you tell us how you met Everett."

Sue: "Clare maybe you should turn in. I think you had too much to drink. There are some things that we don't need to know."

Becky: "I will tell you. So, we could put some things to rest. He was in one of my classes. We sat next to each other. I ask him out. At first, we got along good. Then we just did the same things. We went to the same simple places.

He had no money to do anything. He would gamble any money he had. You can't have any relationship like that. He is ok, I guess. He just wasn't what I wanted. Morissa, I do wish you luck with him. Clare it is over with him and I. Please understand that you're not being funny here."

Clare: "Ok I'll stop. I was hoping for a cat fight, I guess. I promise I will stop. I think you two did clear the air to night. You never know you two may become best of friends. Then what would Everett do."

Morissa: "I don't think you should worry anything about him. You are going to have to find your fun elsewhere."

Sue: "I think we just had our first kiss. It wasn't a very good one at that."

Clare: "I kissed girls better than that."

Morissa: "Clare could you draw me a picture of it."

Sue: "Come on Clare you are done for tonight."

Sue takes Clare to their bed room. Morissa and Becky have a talk.

Becky: "Morissa I do hope you understand that it is over between us. It didn't last long between us. I think he is a nice guy. But he is not my type of guy. It is that simple."

Morissa: "I do understand and thank you for being so honest with me."

Becky: "You really like him don't you Morissa?"

Morissa: "I am afraid I do. I enjoy being with him more than being with anybody. He is so nice to me. We have done just some of the simplest thing but I loved doing them with him. Did you know he could cook? He made me a couple of meals and they were some of the best food I ever had."

Becky: "Know I didn't know that about him. Morissa if you are happy with him good for you. I would appreciate it if you didn't tell me a lot about him."

Morissa: "It is a deal."

Sue comes back in to the room without Clare.

Sue: "I think she had too much to drink tonight. I hope you understand she was trying to have some fun with you two. She wasn't trying to be mean."

Morissa: "I think we understand. It did help us clear the air with both of us. It was a good thing we had this night."

Becky: "You missed the guy with one leg was pushed off the boat by the German. Then the rest of them throw the German over board. That bring the girl to boy ratio a little closer.

We can tell who will end up with whom. It is going to go as we thought it would."

Sue: "That woman has lost some jewelry. I think she lost everything she had when she got on the lifeboat. I would have dived in to the water for the jewelry if it was something I didn't want to lose."

Becky: "I think they purposely had her lose everything she had. It was a symbolism for life is more important than any material things. She learned that life lesson as she saw people who had fewer material things here die. It was about the struggle of right and wrong. In war time we still need to find where right and wrong are. The two big things in this movie to me is about George voting. The remark about all the people in China waking up. Somebody back then had a great insight of what was going on and what may go on in the future."

Sue: "Can I use that for the paper I have to write on about its Becky."

Becky: "I will do better than that let me write the paper for you. That is my major. I want to be a writer. Morissa thank you for being so nice to me before. Some girls would have been possessive and scared of an old girlfriend of a guy she likes."

Becky: "Sue this movie is like that movie called the breakfast club."

Morissa: "It is nice to have you here. I am glad it was you Sue found."

In the room with Everett and His roommate Herbert. The same night.

Everett: "Herbert do you have any plans next weekend?"

Herbert: "No big plans. No big date. No date at all."

Everett: "Are you going to the game Sunday? May be you can find a girl there."

Herbert: "I am on a losing streak lately and could use a big win. I was so close on a big trifecta. So close to getting ahead again with that bet."

Everett: "Yes been there done that. I spent today with that girl Morissa. I was thinking of betting on something but I didn't have the money. I needed it for my big date with her. It was a tough choice but I chose the girl over a bet. My ten-dollar choice. A girl or a bet. A simple ten dollars. I manage to get a nice breakfast real cheap. Then we saw a movie for a couple dollar donation and had some candy. Then a big-time bus ride back to the campus."

Herbert: "You are the best at that. Take a girl out and spend as little as possible. I wish I could do that. I take girls out and spend too much on them and go home with just a kiss good night. My dating life isn't much."

Everett: "You will find the right girl Herbert. It doesn't take a lot of money with the right girl. The right girl you will be thinking more about her and the fun you will be having with her."

Herbert: "Do you have a date with Morissa next week end?"

Everett: "I do. I am taking her out Saturday night. I am trying to work out what we are going to be doing. If I had a car, we could go out in to the local city. I am going to look for something cheap to do."

Herbert: "You could bring her back here. Just let me know and I could stay somewhere else any night."

Everett: "I don't think she would do that. It is too early to bring her back here. I will keep that in mind for another time but not yet. The library is open you may find us there."

Herbert: "You can't bring a girl to the library on a Saturday date. There has to be a movie you can take her to. You could get some fast food and make a night of it."

Everett: "I am trying to save that for another night when I need to bring her somewhere when she gets tired of this really cheap dates. That girl I dated last year got tired of the cheap dates real fast. Then she started to look for her fun with other people and things I couldn't do. I just couldn't take her to the places that she wanted to go to. I spent a lot of Saturday night without a date."

Herbert: "What do you think is going to happen with the new girl? If she wants to do the same things. You are going to have the same problem. Girls that age like to be entertained. Now a days us guys need that cash to keep them entertained."

Everett: "Yes I know. It is my life as a debtor. I even owe you a hundred. Till I leave school that is what my life is going to be. A debtor. I think Morissa is different. I enjoy just being with her. We can do the simplest thing together. She hasn't complained once about not going to some fun more expensive places. The girl and I can just talk. I never was able to talk to a girl as much. Any conversation is the conversation I can have with her. I hope that doesn't change. I really like this one. I hope I don't screw it up."

Herbert: "There are a lot of girls here Everett. You know the girls think you're a good-looking guy. You will have no problem getting another one."

Everett: "Herbert I like this one. I may have to give up on making any bets to have just some simple cash for some fun. I think this girl is worth it."

Herbert: "If you can do that you will be a lot smarter than me. I spend so much money on gambling. When I win, I just give it all back? It isn't like when I win, I will have all the money I will ever need. Sometimes I wonder why I do it. Let me rephrase that. I am always wondering why I do it."

Everett: "I know why we do it. It is the high of the win. Then the cash from the win to get that high again. When we leave school and go out in to the world, we become more responsible gamblers. We hope."

Herbert: "If you want, I could loan you some more money to have a good date with her."

Everett: "No thank you Herbert. I have to pay back what I owe you. If I ever have an emergency, I may ask again. But I do thank you for the offer. It may help for one night then what. I will be in the same place the next day. I know how I have to live and what I have to live with. I haven't promised a girl anything that I couldn't do.

## Chapter Five

### Relationship

A couple of months later. Morissa and Everett have had been spending more time together. Most of their dates are around the school. Date night Saturday. Everett walks up to Sues house to pick up Morissa. He knocks on the door. Morissa opens the door and greets him with a kiss.

Morissa: "Hello Everett. Thank you for coming tonight why don't you come in."

Everett: "I was going to take you out tonight. I was hoping you were ready."

Morissa: "I know that is what we were going to do. The girls here have gone out together. We have this place to ourselves till ten. Everett it is just you and I here. I made you some food this time. I have a fire going. There are just two glasses some wine and us alone Everett."

Everett: "Sounds good to me. I will follow you in."

Morissa: "You told me there is a Rule that Sues father had that no boys were to be in here. Everett you can't tell anybody that we were alone here. And you have to be out of here before the other girls come back. They know you are here. It was Becky who came up with the idea to give us a date night here."

Everett: "That was nice of her to do that. Morissa you could tell her I said thank you for suggesting it."

Morissa: "I will."

Morissa and Everett take a seat in front of the fire place with candles on the floor and some bottles of wine.

Everett: "This is nice Morissa. Living in a house like this has to be so much better then living in a dorm on campus."

Morissa: "This is great. You don't know how much better this is till you have done it."

Everett: "Morissa can I ask you something?"

Morissa: "Sure Everett."

Everett: How are you and Becky getting along?"

Morissa: "I knew that question was going to be asked sooner or later. We had a talk when we first met. All four of us girls were at the kitchen table. Becky and I cleared the air and had a good talk. We have been getting along very well.  Like I said she was the one suggested that you and I have this night alone in the house, Sue gave her ok. Sue Becky or Clare haven't done this with any guy. Everett you are the first guy who got to enter our female layer. That should make you proud."

Everett: "It kind of does. But I will not tell anybody."

Morissa: "Ok Everett here we are. It has been a couple of months since we met on the beach. People have been married and divorce in less time. We can get close with each other. The wine and the fire place and the candles are my idea."

Everett: "We could find your bed room. I am sure it isn't that far away."

Morissa: "Everett, I like you a lot. I like you more than anybody else I have dated or known. It will not be tonight when we get that close. I don't want it to be here or in some guy's dorm room. When you and I take that next step. I need it to be something special for me. Everett, I need you to understand and do that for me."

Everett: "I understand Morissa. I will make it special for you."

Morissa and Everett get in to a heavy kissing and making out. Morissa stops Everett from taking that next step."

Morissa: "Everett we need to stop. I haven't been farther than this."

Everett: "Ok. I understand Morissa. I will keep my word."

Morissa: "I am still a virgin Everett."

Everett: "It is ok Morissa. You are not the last one. You don't need to explain it. It will happen for you sooner or later. If you let me be the first, I will make you happy you waited. I had an idea you still haven't had intercourse. Morissa, I like you a lot. I will wait till you are ready."

Morissa: "Thank you Everett. I knew I could talk to you about it."

Everett: "Ok Morissa lets change the subject and get our minds on to something else."

Morissa: "I heard when guys think of baseball it helps."

Everett: "I think you are a little confused about that. I will explain it to you at another time.

Morissa: "Ok Everett let's talk about you. What do you do on your week nights? You do know we could still see each other during the week. I could come to your dorm room."

Everett: "Morissa maybe the library would be better. My roommate doesn't go out much. He likes to hang out in are dorm room. There are always some guys there talking about what games they are going to be betting on. That is their idea of a good time."

Morissa: "I thought all guys thought of a pretty girl as a good time."

Everett: "He likes girls. He is just a little shy. He will meet the right one and that will change him. He will find himself spending more time with her then his gambling friends."

Morissa: "Do you get along with him."

Everett: "Yes I like him he is a good guy. He goes to extremes some times to make sure I like him. He is always wanting to let me borrow money from him. I owe him one hundred dollars and he is still willing to let me borrow more. Most other guys would be wanting to beat on me for the money."

Morissa: "He likes you, Everett. What is he studying?"

Everett: "Math and accounting. All the math he can take. He is a math prodigy. He could go to a lot of better schools for as smart as he is. His family lives not far from here. Here is where he wants to be."

Morissa: "How about we do a double date. I could have one of the girls I live with go on a date with us. It would have to be Sue or Clare. Becky may be a little awkward. What do you think about that idea?"

Everett: "Yes Becky would be a little awkward. He like Sue. He would really like Sue as a date. Clare would just play with him. She wouldn't take the date seriously. She would do it then just play with him. I like him so Clare is not going to be the one. May be Sue but I would want to talk to her first before the date."

Morissa: "You knew Sue before I knew you. Sue likes you Everett she never has a bad word to say about you."

Everett: "We had the same class and seat next to each other. We got along really well. She was dating someone else.

Within a month I was dating Becky. We did go out on a double date once. I think Sue and I did more talking then our dates did with us. We are almost two of a kind. Kindred spirts you can say.

If you put all the boys and girls in to one of those match making computer that go to this school, I think Sue and I would come out as a perfect match."

Morissa: "Everett I don't think I like that. I would like you to think you and I are a perfect match. That is the way I want to think about you and me."

Everett: "Morissa have you ever heard that opposite attract. Morissa I am more attracted to you then anybody. I like you more than anybody Morissa. The first time I saw you I was attracted to you. I was thinking about you a lot last year. I was hoping to see you at a game or out at night. I was just hoping to run in to you somewhere. Then I got in to a big gambling debt. Even if I did see you again, I didn't have enough money to take you out on a date. If I had the chance to ask you."

Morissa: "You got yourself out of that one. I like that answer. I don't need a computer to be a match for you. I just need a beach deck and some homemade pizza. Somebody I could talk to. I was just hoping for a good tan that day then you came along and block the sun from me."

Everett: "I am glad it wasn't your father on the deck that day. I may have been by myself that night."

Morissa: "Everett that is so funny. I could see you going up to my father and asking him if you could have a date with me. Let me have some fun. I will tell you how you would have asked him for a date with me. You would walk up to the deck and say. I saw that hot girl in a halter top on the beach. I was hoping that you would let me take a crack at her. Oh, by the way.

I was the paper boy who used to give you the wet daily paper way back when. So, what do you say bud how about it? Do I get to take that babe out?"

Everett: "That isn't anywhere the way I would have done that. You are not even close how I would have done that."

Morissa: "Ok Romeo, break it down for me how you would have done it."

Everett: 'Sir

I come to you now in this life that I am living. At this life occasion. I have seen the person that was meant for me to find. Man have walked the ground on this planet in search of the things he has look for. Man have sales the seven-sea looking for new grounds for him to walk on. Man have found the knowledge to fly across all the sea and ground on this earth.

My last few steps in this life I am living has taken me to be in front of you. In front of you I stand with some fear in my mind and these words in my heart. I stand here with the want of a young man. A young man who wants to travel in to the unknown of the future. I hope to find my future with your daughter. Your daughter has given me a mystery that this young man will want to solve

Is it her beauty that I, see? Is it her care free smile that has me wearing this new smile I wear? Is it her eyes that has me looking to see what she sees?

I don't take the responsibility of asking for your daughters' hand with any care free thinking. I don't come to you looking for a pass to do some wrong by her. I mean to be the good that has the want of a father for his daughter. A writer knows that they are a writer. A singer know that they are a singer. A person of god knows that they are a person who has been called on to deliver his message.

I have a call to take your daughter and give her the story of the rest of her life. I am here to give her the words that she will use to talk of her memories. I am hearing my heart sing for her. I am here by some greater power that is not understood by me to deliver my message of wanting to care for her.

Morissa: "That is very nice of you to think of me like that Everett. Do you really look at me like that? Or is this just a clever way to tell me something that a girl would like to hear?

Everett: "If I say it. It is in my head. If it is in my head. I am thinking it. Morissa I am thinking of you. I am thinking of you a lot."

Morissa: "I don't think you should tell that to my father. He may think you are asking to marry me. Or he may think you are just a crazy person."

Everett: "Morissa what would you like to do next week end?"

Morissa: "Everett I have a couple of papers I have to do. I am sorry but next week end I will be here just doing school work. I am sorry. Maybe we can meet for lunch during the week. Just us and all the other people at our school just having a quiet lunch to gather."

Everett: "Ok sounds good. How about Wednesday."

Morissa: "It is a date."

Everett: "I think I should go now. It is getting to be that time."

Morissa: "Yes Everett I was just thinking the same thing. Thank you for having patience with me. Some day we will have more time together and the right place."

Everett: "That is something we are going to have to plan and make the time together."

Morissa kiss Everett good night. Everett walks back to his room. Sue, Becky and Clare come back to the house. They have some fun with Morissa being alone with Everett. Next Wednesday Everett and Morissa are sitting in a school cafeteria having lunch and talking.

Morissa and Everett are sitting at a lunch table at school talking about where and when they are going to spend some time alone. There are other people at other tables around the room. Some people doing school work. Some tables have boy and girl couples. The room is filled with people talking. Nobody is listening to anybody's else conversation.

Everett: "How are you and the girls doing."

Morissa: "We have been getting along just great. No cat fights. It has been much better than any of us thought it would be. Sunday night it is just the four of us and we just sit by the fire and drink. We just talk and drink. Four girls talking and drinking what could be better."

Everett: "What do you four talk about if I can ask?"

Morissa: "Everett, I would tell you but then I would have to kill you. It is one of those girl secrets I can't tell any guy. Sorry Everett."

Everett: "If I had a guess. My guess would be the four of you talk about that race of people known as the male race. That race that is always looking for that race of the female type."

Morissa: "You are the betting type Everett. You would be smart to take that bet."

Everett: "It is ok. Our side is always talking about your side."

Morissa: "Everett that talk is for when we are with those other people. We need to talk about us. We need to plan out some time when we can just be alone. Just you and me. Every time we are together there are too many people around. Or we have to be somewhere else to soon."

Everett: "I know Morissa. I want to spend more time with you too. If I had some money, I could really show you a good time. You been so good to understand the cheap dates. There isn't many girls who would understand it like you."

Morissa: "I understand I like you, Everett. I like just being with you. We could be in the same class and I would say it was the best time I had that day. When I am having a good time with the girls, I am thinking I rather be with you. Even if it is a deli sandwich on a bench. I enjoy the meal because it is with you Everett."

Everett: "Thank you Morissa. You make it so easy for me to be with you. I haven't had a girl stay with me long lately. In high school you can take a girl out for a simple meal and have a good time. It got a little more complicated the last year or so. I guess it is just the way it goes."

Morissa: "We all grow up and look for different entertainment. We all grow up and look for different ways to spend our time."

Everett: "We have thanksgiving break coming up. If we are going to spend it together it is time, we figure it out. Where would you like to spend it together?"

Morissa: "Everett we could go to Atlantic city for a couple of days. What do you think about that?"

Everett: "I would like to do that Morissa. But I have the fact I don't have the money to take you there."

Morissa: "Everett we are a couple. Me and you. You and I. We are not married but we are accouple. I have some money. I have a credit card with a zero balance on it. I could pay for all of it."

Everett: "I can't let you do that. I can't let a girl pay for something that I should pay for."

Morissa: "Everett you know how dumb that sounds. If you were paying for it just to have sex with me, I would have a problem with that. You want to be with me. I want to be with you. Everett, I want to do this. I already planned it out. I told my father I am going to Atlantic city with some girlfriends. He gave me some coupons that he was given from some of the casinos. He gave me enough to pay for a room for four nights. We have food coupons to feed us for a week. I have this planned Everett. Please put a male ego a side and lets just be a normal couple and enjoy some time together. Please Everett do this for me. Please."

Everett: "Morissa. Ok. It does sound nice. I do want to spend that time with you. I guess I will have to put my male ego aside and just think of the beautiful woman who I am falling in love with."

Morissa: "Everett do you know what you just said?"

Everett: "I love you Morissa. I know how I feel about you. I know how I am changing who I am for you. Have patience for me Morissa. From the day I found you on the beech my life has changed Morissa. It has changed for the better. You are the first person who never gave me a lecture on how I should be. You just except me for being me."

Morissa: "That's because I love you, Everett. I never ever loved anybody before. I would look at couples who were together and I would wonder what it was like to find that person you fall in love with. I found that person Everett. It is you.

I think of you all the time. When I think of me, I think of you. There is no plans that I am making that I don't think of you."

Everett: "Morissa. We do need to spend more time together to get to know each other. Nobody's perfect. We are going to find things that will take patience with each other. You are going to learn things about me that you may not like. There are things about you that I don't know yet. When I find those things out you will want me to have some patience with you. Just keep that in mind

Morissa: "I know that. I am not a child. You are not the first guy I kissed you know. I had friends before. I have an ability you will never have. It gives me a license to have an insight on people and how to compromise with them that you will never have.

Everett: "Ok please tell me what gives you a license to have an insight on people and how to compromise with them that I will never have.

Morissa: "I live with three other females. You will never do that."

Everett: "What if I get married and have two daughters."

Morissa: "Then I will be the one who issues that license."

Everett: "It is a deal.

Morissa: "Everett now let me tell you what I have planned so far. We could take a couple of days around thanksgiving. Spend thanksgiving day and night there. Then leave the next day."

Everett: "How do you think we can get there and back."

Morissa: "There is a bus in the next city that goes to the casinos. We can take that bus there and back. That's the way honey moon couple used to go up to Niagara falls. Some people will think we are on are Honey moon. How romantic."

Everett: "I will try and get a car to go there. I don't like long bus rides. Have you ever had to use a bus rest room? There isn't anything romantic about it. Let's leave the transportation part to me."

Morissa: "You are not going to steal a car, are you?"

Everett: "No. Just leave it to me."

Morissa: "Ok transportation is your department."

Everett: "We have to talk about us having sex. We need to talk about contraceptives."

Morissa: "Bring some condoms. I don't want to talk about that yet. We will have a talk later about it. Is that ok."

Everett: "Yes I understand."

Morissa: "Are you going to tell your parents that you will not be there thanksgiving? I am going to tell my mother the truth about me and you. My father I have to lie to him. I don't want to but this one of those things a girl can't tell her father."

Everett: "My parents are starting to wonder about me. Last year at this time I was calling them up for money. When I tell my parents, I am going to a casino they will be thinking about how much money it is going to cost them."

Morissa: "Everett all you ever told me is that you lose money when you gamble. Did you ever win anything?"

Everett: "When I did, I gave it right back on another bet. It is the life of a gambler. A suit case and a trunk. Some people can walk away and never worry about losing a bet. I just look for that next bet to get even. I can never get even. My life is now about not making that next sports bet. The football games with the money lines. The over and under. The points spreads have taken a toll on me and kicked my ass."

Morissa: "Everett we all have to learn those things in life. Most people are age they start to learn about drinking too much. Or drugs. As far as I know you don't have that problem"

Everett: "No I don't. I have a beer when I have pizza or at a baseball game. I don't have that baggage too."

Morissa: "Your kind of like my father. Maybe that's why I like you so much."

Everett: "Does your father cook and gamble?"

Morissa: "I have to tell you about him some day. I like my father, Everett. I think you would like him to."

Everett: "You said that before."

Morissa: "I met your mother. Can you tell me about your father"?

Everett: "My father is all about the business of work. That is all he ever did. He made enough money years ago to retire and go fishing anywhere in the world.

He rather work. He feels like if he doesn't work enough, he can't enjoy his time off fishing. After a couple days of fishing a clock goes off in his had that he has to get back to work. I don't have that clock in my head for anything."

Morissa: "I wish you told me, that you had a clock in your mind for me. That when you don't see me you want to see me. That would have been nice to hear Everett. It is things like that girls like to hear once in a while."

Everett: "Do you remember that Sunday when we went in the church to see an old movie. I was thinking what it would be like to be at that alter with you. I was thinking if I could take care of you. I was thinking how proud I would be that I was lucky enough to have you believe in me to have you. I look at you and I see a beautiful woman. Then I have to think am I just looking at a beauty. Or am I looking at a person who cares for me. Then I think why am I lucky enough to have her like me. What did I ever do to be given this person who cares for me? I like just sitting across a table from you and talking. I never enjoyed that as much with anybody like I do with you. If you want to know the best time, I ever had with anybody. It was the morning back in California when we went to a bar and I made you breakfast. When I was making plans to do it, I was looking just to save some money. That is where the idea came from. Seeing you enjoy it so much was good for me. I enjoyed it because you enjoyed it."

When I was in the kitchen, I looked out from the kitchen so you couldn't see me. I just looked at this woman who was giving me her time. I had the privilege of being with her. It may have been a simple date but it change the way I think about things. I look at you and I want to be with you. I want to care for you. I want you to care for me Morissa.

Morissa and Everett have been seeing more of each other as the school year goes on. They would find time being together in the library and the dining hall. If the weather permitted, they would sit outside and have a good time being with each other. More plans were being made for their thanks given vacation away with just each other.

One day to save some money Everett had Morissa come to one of his cooking classes for lunch. The teacher knew something was going on. She let Everett make lunch for Morissa and all the other people in the class. Sue and Clare would some time join Morissa and Everett on the side line at a football game. The four of them would have a good time watching the game and being together. Becky would not be part of that group. Becky would be in another part of the stadium. When she ran in to Morissa and Everett, she just gave a friendly hello and go to her friends.

Morissa and Everett are in the audience of a rehearsal of a school play. It is another one of Everett low-cost dates. It is a dry rehearsal for a Sherlock Homes type of play. They are in the back-row seats. There are about twenty people in an auditorium that holds about five hundred people.

Morissa: "Everett how did you find this. I never been to a dress rehearsal of any show."

Everett: "I have a friend who is in this. She was asking me to come. They don't get enough people at these dress rehearsal. The actor and actress like to think that there are enough people out here to give them the feel of a real show."

Morissa: "You are really just a good guy to have this date with me, just to help them out. Not to mention the low cost of free seats."

Everett: "You may just like this Morissa. They do a pretty good show. Tonight, they are doing a mystery. It isn't any mystery you may know. They use the sherlock character then somebody writes a new mystery. It is going to be a who done it. I took you in these back seat so we could be alone and talk about the who did it."

Morissa: "I thought you got me back here so we could make out. I guess I was wrong."

Everett: "If I guess the who did it, we still may have time to do it."

Morissa: "What if I guess it before you Everett?"

Everett: "Then you get the prize."

Morissa: "Let me try to guess what that prize is."

Everett: "I am pretty good at figuring out who did it. In the who done it."

Morissa: "What makes you so good at doing it?"

Everett: "I look at it like a writer would write it. They know who is going to do it.  The writers know how and when it is going to happen. You have to look for the things in the story that are put in the story. Like those things that are being told to you that don't need to be told. Look for information. See how that information is being told. It could be in words. It could be in what place they are in. Somewhere in the story you will be able to look back at the story and see what the writer was telling you."

Morissa: "Everett you do know even if you figure it out early, we still have to watch the show to see if you are right. I don't think we will be able to make out."

Everett: "We will have more than enough time alone just you and I soon."

The play is about a female who seduce rich men then kill them. The actress who plays the seductress is on stage in several cleavage revealing outfits to entice her next male victim.

Everett figured out who did it half way thru the play. The play ends. The lights come on. Some people stand up give some applause then the audience start to leave.

Morissa: "Very good Everett, you figured it out faster than I did. You win. Too bad the lights are on now. I would give you the prize. I think I heard that old man down there had it before you. You think I should go down there and tell him he won the surprise?"

Everett: "You tell him something like that looking as good as you look. He may get the wrong idea what the prize is Morissa."

Morissa: "Don't worry Everett, I like them much younger like you."

Everett: "Lucky me."

Morissa: "So Lucky Everett what should we do now?"

Everett: "We have to go in the back stage for a couple minutes and see the person who wrote the mystery."

Morissa: "You know the person who wrote it."

Everett: "Yes. Do you mind us going back there?"

Morissa: "No."

Back stage Everett brings Morissa to meet a female student friend. There are three people talking when Everett brings Morissa to them.

The lead actress see Everett walking toward her, she smiles at him. She breaks off from the people she is talking to then runs up to Everett. She throws her arms around him and gives him a long kiss on the lips. Everett returns the kiss. Morissa stands to the side just looking at the two in a lip lock. When the kiss runs its course the two step back from each other breathing heavy. Morissa looks at Everett.

Everett: "Hello Stacy you put on a good show tonight. I really enjoyed trying to figure it out."

Stacy: "It would have been better if you and I did it like last year. I really missed you."

Everett: "No you are being nice. You were just carrying me last year."

Stacy: "I do like that visual. Everett any time I could get my hands on you I would."

Everett: "You look great up on that stage. You will be the first leading lady who can write her own movie. Move over Hollywood legends here comes the new queen. She will be the best-looking lady on the big screen."

Stacy: "I was looking for you out in the seats and I didn't see you."

Everett: "Stacy this is my friend Morissa. We were in the back seats watching the play. Morissa this is my friend Stacy."

Morissa: "Hi Stacy it is nice to meet you. I like the show."

Stacy: "Hello Morissa. It was a play Morissa not a show. But I am glad you liked it. Everett, I heard you have a new girlfriend why didn't you bring her?"

Everett: "Stacy. I did Morissa is my girlfriend."

Stacy: "Oh that's so sweet of you to date her. I am sure she is a real nice girl if you like her. How rude of me. The cast is going out to dinner tonight why don't you and your nice little friend join us."

Everett: "What do you say Morissa. Would you like to join them? Last time I went out with them it was a lot of fun. All the actors and actress do a lot of acting with the people in the bar. The actors make up a bunch of fake life crisis and see how far they can go before somebody walks away. Stacy likes to do the I just lost my last boyfriend act. All the other girls try to get other guys to go over to her thinking they have a chance with a girl looking for a rebound. They call it the rebound act."

Stacy" "Come on Morissa, you will have a ball with us. You can watch us and get some pointers for the next time you get dumped."

Morissa: "You are really something aren't you."

Stacy: "Thank you. Did Everett tell you I wrote this play I did star in?"

Morissa: "He did."

Stacy: "I hope he didn't tell you anything else about us. Some of the love scene I write, I do think of this tall good-looking fantasy of mine. Sometimes an actress has to think of another man when they are in a love scene on stage. It helps us fake it. Do you know what I mean? I am sure it works the other way sometimes. Like the man you are with is thinking of a past lover. Because the one he is with is just some plain Jane he is just trying to get off on. But I am sure that will never happen to you. Please come with us tonight. Maybe you could impress me in some acting ability you may or may not have. I may just ask you to do some little part for us."

Everett: "Sorry Stacy. We will not be making that show. Morissa and I are going to go where we don't have to put on a show for anybody. We don't need the applause of anybody who may be watching us. The words that we say to each other are from the heart not some written words that are used to cheapen are time together. When you talk to people Stacy you are writing the words that you have said on some stage in your mind. I find the words that Morissa says to me something new and different every time she tells them to me. I sit by myself sometimes and think of this beautiful woman and wonder why she thinks of things she does think of. I want to be a part of her thoughts more then I want to be a part of anything else. Every time I hear her voice, I am glad that she likes me. Her words are from the feeling she has for me. She isn't about any show for anybody that may be watching us.

I like her Stacy. I like her a lot. Someday you will walk off that stage in your mind. I don't think you will know how to walk when you do. I don't think you know how to talk to people without thinking people are stage characters in your head. All the people on the stage with you are not your friends. They are just the people who you tell them what to say and how to act. I didn't want to be a part of your act. I didn't want to be in your show with your hand pick character.

I was hoping that you would be nice to my new girlfriend. You had to put on an act for your friends. It was just a one-night mistake. You need to find somebody else to have a second act with. This one has been played out. Come on Morissa we have to leave now."

Stacy: "Boy I hurt you didn't I. It's too bad you had to find this one for your entertainment. But I guess it is all you want to pay for."

Morissa: "You have no idea who he is do you."

Stacy: "Let's just say I saw a part of him you haven't dreamed of. Now I have to go and leave the sad dreamers of I can't be anything else then what I am."

Everett and Morissa start to head back to her house.

Morissa: "What was that all about Everett? Did you know all that was going to go on?"

Everett: "No. Not all that. I heard she was looking for you. We had a one-night stand after Becky and I broke up." We were in the bar together with some other people. It just ended up with us sleeping to gather, The next day I told her I didn't want to be in that kind of relationship with her. She had a boyfriend and told him that I used her as a rebound from Becky. She was all about making it a soap opera.

Sooner or later, you would have heard about it. I was going to tell you after you met her. I wanted you to see who she was. I didn't think she would be such a bitch about it. I thought that we had become friends. I think when she saw you with me it just set her off."

Morissa" "Everett I didn't like that. It is not anything I want to be a part of. Everett, I have to tell you I don't want to be a part of any old girl friends of yours. Becky, and I come to be at ease with each other. We are not best friends. I feel secure that you and I like each other. I don't like being judge by an old girlfriend of yours. It is unfair."

Everett: "What I told her about you was true.

Morissa: "It was nice to hear those words from you Everett. Right now, I am not happy with you. I don't have anything in my closet to hurt you with. I am not going to ask you to tell me everything about you. There are somethings I am better off not knowing. I want you to know enough about me so you know how you can hurt me.

Everett, you hurt me tonight. This was the first thing that happen with us I didn't like."

Everett: "Morissa. There are some things we haven't told each other. I will try to be sensitive how I tell you. There isn't any relationships I had here in college that you don't know about now."

Morissa: "As for me I don't have anything to tell."

Everett walks Morissa home they don't have any other words. Everett gives her a good night. Morissa just says good bye. With a tear in her eye, she kiss him on the cheek and walks in to the house and shuts the door behind herself. Everett stand looking at the door in front of his face then turns and walks home.

   Two weeks before the thanksgiving break. Morissa is having a date with Everett. She walks in to Everett's campus room to meet him. Morissa and Everett are going to see a basketball game. Morissa knocks on Everett dorm room. A teenage boy answers the door who is about one hundred and twenty pound and about five foot five inches tall. His name is Herbert and he is Everett's roommate. Herbert has on a pair of thick reading glasses. He has a number ten NY jet football jersey on. Morissa looks at Herbert.

Morissa: "Hi I am Morissa. I am here to meet Everett. Is he here?"

Herbert: "No he will be right back. He said you would be coming by and ask me to tell you he would be right back. Would you like to come in and wait for him? I will keep the door open is that ok? My name is Herbert."

Morissa: "Yes please. Nice to meet you Herbert Everett told me you were his roommate. I guess he told you I was his girlfriend."

Herbert: "Yes he did. It is nice to meet you."

Morissa walks in two the room. The room has two beds on opposite side of the room. One bed has pictures of wrestlers and comic book super heroes. The bed has some school books and note pads. On the other side of the room is a bed that is made up very neat with hospital corners. There are some shoes lined up under the bed in some kind of order. At the head board is a picture of a younger Everett. In the picture is another boy a little older then Everett. There is a desk next to the bed with nothing on it. Herbert takes up a position standing up against a wall looking at Morissa.

Morissa: "I guess this is Everett's bed and desk. Do you mind if I sit at his desk and wait for him?"

Herbert: "Sure no problem. I don't think he will be much longer. He left about five minutes ago. There is a person he had to see. He is getting the tickets for the game you two are going to see."

Morissa: "Let me guess he is getting free tickets for the game tonight."

Herbert: "Yes."

Morissa: "That is my Everett."

Herbert: "He should be right back."

Morissa: "I know you said that before."

Herbert: "Sorry."

Morissa: "It is ok. How long have you known Everett?"

Herbert: "Not long"

Morissa: "He said you were his roommate the last three years. I guess you have known him since his first year of college. Is that right."

Herbert: "Yes."

Morissa: "Everett Keeps a very nicely made bed. I would have thought that about him."

Herbert: "Yes."

Morissa: "Where are you from Herbert? I am from lower New York. Not too far from here. Just far enough to keep any parents from coming up and seeing me. You know what I mean."

Herbert: "I live a couple of miles away."

Morissa: "That is nice. I like it up here. It's the small streets You can walk the street and have a meal outside on a table on the Sidewalk.

Herbert: "Yes. I never did it."

Morissa: "To bad. It is a nice thing to do. Everett took me to a restaurant off campus. We had a breakfast there on the side walk.

Herbert: "Sounds nice."

Morissa: "Yes it was nice."

Herbert: "He should be back any minute now."

Morissa: "It is ok Herbert. We still have time before the game starts. You don't mind me waiting here for him do you."

Herbert: "No."

Morissa: "Good Herbert. I see you like wrestling by the pictures on the wall."

Herbert: "Yes."

Morissa: "I met that guy in the pink outfit. My father sells cars and he sold him a car. My father knows a lot of those wrestlers. I just happen to be with my father that day. That guy gave me an autograph picture. He told me who he was. Then I had to tell him I didn't know who he was. I think I insulted him. Then again I was just a ten-year old girl at the time with no interest in wrestling."

Herbert: "Really he is one of my favorites. I would have loved that sign autograph poster."

Morissa: "I still have it somewhere at my father's place. My father knows a lot of those guys. I will ask him to send me that picture. I will give it to you if you would like that."

Herbert" "Wow, that would be great. How much money would you like for it?"

Morissa: "Nothing. I have no use for it. I think if my father had a boy, he would have gotten more stuff like that. I had no interest in it."

Herbert: "Thanks. If you need any money let me know."

Morissa: "Herbert I don't need any money it is ok."

Herbert: "Thank you."

Morissa: "What is your major Herbert. I want to be a teacher."

Herbert: "Math."

Morissa: "Math?"

Herbert: "I like math. They say I am good at it."

Morissa: "There are better schools then this one for people who are good at math. Boston has two of the best."

Herbert: "Yes I know." Morissa did you ever go and see a wrestling match?"

Morissa: "No it wasn't anything that I wanted to do."

Herbert: "I watch it whenever I can. If I was bigger, I would try to be a wrestler. I have this idea for a wrestler. It is all about what kind of character they are. I would be the invisible man. No one has thought of that character ever. See I would tell people that I will become invisible just when I need to be. I would sit in the audience with those white bandages around my face like you see in the movies. See I would be invisible. Nobody could say I wasn't. Isn't that great."

Morissa: "Sounds good, I guess. I don't know much about it.

Herbert: "I sent the idea to the wrestling company but I haven't heard back from them."

Morissa: "They probably get a lot of letters.

Herbert: "You think it is dumb don't you."

Morissa: "No I didn't say that. I said I don't know much about it."

Herbert: "The comic book already have that hero. It wouldn't be new."

Morissa: "I saw a movie with the invisible man."

Herbert: "I saw it to. I saw all the good sci fi movies."

Morissa: "Are you going to the game tonight Herbert? You could go with Everett and I if you want."

Herbert: "No."

Morissa: "My first year of college I stood in my dorm room a lot. I look back on it now and think I should of went out more than I did."

Herbert: "I don't have a girlfriend."

Morissa: "You don't need a girl friend to go out. There are a lot of girls who go out who don't have a boyfriend. That is the way it works. You could go with me and Everett maybe meet another girl."

Herbert: "I don't think I could do that to night. I think I have something to do."

Morissa: "May be another night"

Herbert: "Yes. Maybe. I don't know. We will see."

Morissa: "Do you and Everett go out."

Herbert: "No."

Morissa: "He likes you, Herbert. You know you and I have something in common."

Herbert: "You and me. What?"

Morissa: "We are both shy."

Herbert: "You are so pretty. You're not shy."

Morissa: "Thank you Herbert. Trust me I am as shy as you."

Herbert: "Do you want me to go and find Everett?"

Morissa: "No. He will be back soon. He hasn't stood me up yet. I can't see him doing that to me when he ask me to meet him in his room."

Herbert: "Ok."

Morissa: "What are you going to be doing at thanksgiving break Herbert. Are you going to go home?"

Herbert: "No."

Morissa: "Everett and I are going to the casinos for the break. Did he tell you that?"

Herbert: "Yes."

Morissa: "Do you plan on going home any time this school year."

Herbert: "No"

Morissa: "Don't you want to see your family? Do you have any brothers or sisters?"

Herbert: Two younger sisters and two older brothers."

Morissa: "Middle child. Everett and I are the only child. That is something we have in common.

Herbert: "Yes. He told me about you."

Morissa: "You say yes a lot."

Herbert: "Yes."

Morissa: "Yes, what else did he tell you about me."

Herbert: "I have to go next store for a minute and get a book. I almost forgot. I will be right back."

Morissa: "Ok I will just sit here is that alright?"

Herbert leaves. Morissa gets up out of the chair and looks around. Never having any brothers or being in a boy's room Morissa start to become curious about how they live in a room.

Morissa walks up to the posters by Herbert bed and looks at them. A childless kind of entertainment is her thought.

The absence of a poster or calendar with some half dressed up, dolled up, airbrushed chick seems odd. Both beds being made up was different then her old dorm room. On any given day one bed or both would not be made. No open bags of any food could be seen in the open. The carpet looked like it was recently vacuumed by the vacuum lines. No dirty laundry bags laying on the floor.

Then she looks at Everett's bed. The size of the bed was just long enough for his height. The bed would just be wide enough for her and Everett to sleep in. Then a look at the picture of a young Everett on the head board. The picture starts to look familiar to her. She remembers seeing it at Everett's mother house. The same curiosity of how the two boys in the picture look alike.

Morissa walks over to Everett's stand-up closet and opens the door and looks inside. All the clothes are neatly place on the same type of hangers. The clothes are facing the same way with all the buttons button. Some toilet supplies arranged on the lower shelves. Polished shoes on the closet bottom. Morissa close the door and goes to Everett desk.

She opens the draws and see some envelopes and writing paper. The second draw down she opens and see some school books. Morissa close that draw and opens the bottom draw. In side she sees a journal. She freezes at the sight of it. A thought of opening it up and reading it is her first thought. Getting caught and having to explain it is her second thought. What is in it about her crosses her mind. What could be in it about any other girls. "I know I can trust him. He has told me a lot already. Maybe I will read or just look at one page." Morissa says in a low voice.

Looking back over her shoulder at the open door has her thinking about Everett walking in.

She close the draw. Morissa takes a seat back on the chair at Everett's desk.

Morissa thinking to herself. I never had a guy who I was so close to. I could see what he really thinks about me in that journal. I could see if there was any other girls that he was involve with that I don't know about. I may get to know who he really is. May be I am the only girl he was this serious with. May be I do know who he really is. It has to be trust. I do trust him. He hasn't given me anything not to trust about him. Maybe it is empty. Why keep a journal if it is going to be empty? Just a quick look may be is all I need. I am his girlfriend. What would be the harm of that? If he does catch me. He would forgive me.

What if Herbert caught me? That may not be good. That would put him in to a difficult place. My guess he would tell Everett. That would be worse than if Everett caught me. Everett said his roommate was a smart quite person. He is almost childes like. I should be happy with Everett not having one of those guys who bring the girls back to their room. I could keep my mind to rest that there are not any girls coming in here at night for a party. This room isn't anywhere near anything that a party would be a part of.

This room looks like something you would find in a marine boot camp. The bath room let me see what is in the bathroom.

The bathroom is clean the toilet seat is down. Whites' clean towels folded and stacked on some carts. Electric toothbrush and a flossing machine next to it. The mirror with no dust or lint on it. Let's see what's on the shelves behind the glass mirror. Aspirin nail clippers tweezers ear cleaners.

All guys can't be like this. It looks like something out of good housekeeping. I wonder if they have somebody come in and cleans the place for them.

Sue and my room was clean but not like this. I better get back to the chair before someone catches me in here.

Morissa's back at the chair when Herbert comes back in to the room without any books.

Herbert: "Sorry it took so long. I see Everett hasn't come back yet."

Morissa: "No not yet. I am a patient girl. We still have some time. Herbert, can I ask you something if you don't mind."

Herbert: "Yes."

Morissa: "I lived on campus last year with another girl. Are room being not as clean as this one is. Do you have someone come in and clean it?"

Herbert: "No."

Morissa: "Do you keep it like this."

Herbert: "No."

Morissa: "Then you're telling me Everett keeps this place this clean."

Herbert: "I do help."

Morissa: "He has another surprise for me. He always has something about him I don't expect."

Herbert: "I know what you were thinking. You are thinking because I am kind of small and geeky, I was the one who kept this place so clean. That is what everybody who comes in here says or thinks. It is the same thing. Everett is only my friend because I clean for him. Or I do his homework or give him money. Or I'm Everett house keeper. Do you know what Becky called me last year? She had a really good time with me calling me his live-in boyfriend.

It is all about perception and judgment isn't it. You don't have to say It. I could hear it in your question. Everett bounce a guy out of here on his head because the guy made fun of me. I couldn't do it. Everett had to do it for me. Do know what that feels like to a guy. I can't fight my own battles so Everett has to do it for me. I have one good friend. I know a lot of other people but I can't be friends with any of them because of the way they judge me.

Those two colleges you asked about before in Boston for people who are good in math. That is where you think I belonged don't you. I was offered a full scholarship to go to both of them. My parents look at me as a future bank account because I am so smart. I just want to be in a normal school and be a normal person here. You walk in to are room and start to theorize that I am his roommate who cleans does his homework and gives him money. He likes you Morissa. He likes you a lot. The next time you come over I will leave like I am going to do now. I won't tell him anything about this. I will just tell him that you are very pretty and nice. If I, was you, I wouldn't mention this? If he ask me, I will not tell him anything."

Morissa" "I am sorry if I judge you, Herbert. You can tell him anything. I like to think I have no secrets from Everett. If I hurt you then I was wrong. I was wrong because I don't know you. I know Everett well enough to know he likes you a lot.

Please let me get to know you. I will like to be your friend too. Do know what friends do Herbert?

Herbert: "What?"

Morissa: "They get to know each other. Then they accept each other for who they are. Once you get to know somebody and start accepting who they are it the start of a relationship. Herbert we both have a common friend. I am not looking to take his friend ship from you.

We could both be friends of his in a different way and we could be friends if we work on it. Let's be friends."

Herbert: "Thank you Morissa. I would like you as a friend.

Chapter Six

US

Thanksgiving. The time Everett and Morissa have been planning for. They made plans and reservations. They both wanted to bring their relationship to one of lovers.

Everett borrows Herbert's car. Everett has one gym bag of clothes and bath supplies. Morissa had two bags pack with a couple change of clothes. She also had a green, white and a black dress in a dress bag. The two had two hundred dollars in cash. Morissa has her credit card and some comp coupons from her father. Plans were made to have a limit on how much money they would spend. They talk on the drive down to Atlantic city.

Everett: "Well Morissa we are off. You and me. Me and you. What do you think about that Morissa?"

Morissa: "I been thinking a lot about you and us. I been thinking about this couple of days that wait for us. I been thinking about the first time that I would be alone with you. For a longer time, I was thinking of the first time I would be with a man, the first time. The thinking or over thinking us young females do. The thinking who would be are first. The thinking of how long should we wait. The thinking of what we want him to look like. The thinking of what the experience would be like for the first time. The thinking of hoping for an enjoyable experience. The thinking of the next day. Hoping that day would give us the enjoyment of knowing the man and the experience made everything better then what we were thinking."

Everett: "That is a lot of thinking. Us guys don't think like that. We don't need the same feeling as you females do."

Morissa: "That is nice of you to tell me that. That is nice of you to tell me that, when we are about ready to take our relationship to that next level."

Everett: "Morissa. Trust me you are different than any other female that I have been with. You are more to me, then any other female I have known. It is hard to explain. I have been looking at you females as long as I notice the difference. Sometimes that difference is all I can think about."

Morissa: "I am quite aware of the difference. I know what the male race has on their mind most of the time Everett. Me being of the female race, I have had my moments with your race of people. Most of the time I think you guys are crazy. Sometimes I think you guys are so funny the way you go after us females. Sometimes a few of you guys did scare me. Everett. I don't want to think about most guys. It's you Everett I want to think about. I understand you find me attractive. I need more than that from you Everett. I need to know how you feel for me. No, I need to feel how you feel toward me. Everett, you have a lot of pressure on you the next couple of days. The next couple of days I will be thinking of you the rest of my life."

Everett: "I haven't thought of us going away together like that. I know how important this next step to you and to us is. Morissa I will do my best to keep your feelings in mind. I don't want you to be hurt by a careless word or act. I don't want you to tell me everything is ok when it isn't." You may have to tell me things you never have told anybody else. You may have to tell me things that you think may be embarrassing. What we are and what we are going to become is us. Just us. Nobody will ever know us like we are going to know each other. I know I am taking your hand and leading you to the place you have been thinking of. I will take your thoughts and feelings then keep them in a safe place in side of me.

Morissa, I want to be able to talk about us years later. We will have conversation about us.

It will be us because it was meant to be just us. We will always be two different people with different wants and needs. Two people who know and understand each other wants and needs. Two people that can be giving without the fear of not having someone understanding them. It is something that most people want to find with another person and never do. Do you ever look at an old black and white picture of two people? Two people who are man and wife. I do and I want to think about what their lives were that lead up to that picture. Then what their lives were after that picture. Those two people were on to the next picture. In that next picture there would be a change. Maybe so small. Ever so small there would be a change. We are going to change after are first picture. Someday our last picture together will happen. In that last picture it will be us. Just us. There something about you Morissa that I like. Something about you that tells me it will be us for a long time to come."

Morissa: "That was nice to hear you say that. I like to think I didn't need you to say it. I look at you looking at me sometimes. I look at your eyes and try to read what you are thinking. There are times when you are talking to me and I see those words for me. Everett us females are looking for those guys they like. They try to interpret words from men in to something that they can believe. Sometimes those words our mis interpret into something that is the furthest from the truth. We say we want the truth from somebody that means something to us. What we do is convince ourself that what is said, is the truth. We want the right person. We all want the words with the right meaning with the right person."

Somewhere on the new York thruway Everett gets pulled over by an New York State trooper. Everett looks at Morissa and says "this could be a problem".

Morissa: "Everett you were not going too fast. I think. It will just be a ticket."

Everett pulls over to the shoulder turns the flashers on and rolls down the driver side window. A state trooper gets out of his car and walks over to the driver's side.

Trooper Simon: "Do you know why I pulled you over."

Everett: "No sir"

Trooper Simon: "You were doing Eighty in a sixty-five. License and registration please."

Everett: "This isn't my car. It is a friend's car and he let me use it. I am sorry I don't have a license on me."

Trooper Simon: "Really. Do you have any identification on you? And if you do, can I see it."

Everett: "Yes sir I will show you my school ID."

Everett nervously pulls his wallet out of his back pants pocket. He opens his wallet and looks for his ID. A couple of condoms fall from his wallet. Everett looks over to Morissa and mouths the words he was sorry. Morissa turns a shade of red and shakes her head. The state trooper looks at Morissa and ask her if she was ok. Morissa looks at the trooper and tells him that "Everett is my boyfriend".

Trooper Simon: "Where were you two heading young lady?"

Morissa: "We are on our way to spend some time together at Atlantic city."

Trooper Simon: "We have a problem here. This young man doesn't have a license. You two are in a car and the owner is not here. Do you have a license young lady and can I see it? Then can you see if you can find a registration and an insurance card."

Morissa finds Herbert's car registration and insurance cards in the glove compartment. She hands the trooper the cards and her New York state driver's license. Trooper Simon takes Everett ID. He also takes Morissa license and the registration and insurance cards back to his police car. He tells the two to stay in the car that he would be right back. Morissa looks at Everett as her anger builds. Everett keeps looking back to the trooper car then he would look at Morissa. Morissa breaks the uneasy silence first

Morissa: "Nice job mister. I don't have a simple drivers' license. You would think somebody who say that they are going to do the driving would have a simple drivers' license. What were you thinking? All you had to tell me was that you don't have a license. Why don't you have a license may I ask. No please don't tell me. I know You can walk everywhere you have to go. If you can't walk there, you could take a bus. How about I am taking my girl out and I want to show her a nice time. Were you thinking? No don't tell me what you were thinking. I know what you were thinking. Everett you were just thinking I am finally going to get the girl. All the time you were thinking about getting the girl. Thank you, Everett you are going to get the girl. You may have to wait till we are out of jail. Maybe we can spend the next couple of days together in a cell together. How romantic for a girl to have her first lover. It just couldn't of work out any better. I can tell all my friends how romantic you were in our cell. Everett, I love you so much. I am going to cry."

Morissa starts to gets tears in her eyes. Everett reaches out to Morissa. Morissa pulls away from him. The two say nothing for a couple of minutes as the trooper is back in his car checking the ID and the registration and insurance card. Then Everett talks.

Everett: "Morissa I am sorry. This isn't what I planned. I don't know what is going to happen. I will make it up to you I promise."

Morissa: "You could never make this up. This was going to be something special for me. This was going to be something special for the both of us. This was going to be something I would remember my whole life. I wanted this. I waited for this. Do you want to know how many times I almost gave in and just settle for someone I kind of like? Everett you are more than kind of like to me. Everett, I love you and want you more than any other guy I have ever known. You just broke me. You just broke my heart. I could have seen you with another girl and understood that more then I understand this. Thank you, prince, charming."

Everett: "We will be ok."

They spend a couple more minutes waiting for the trooper to come back to the car. Morissa just looks out her window not looking At Everett. Everett keeps looking back at the trooper's car in the rearview mirror. About one half hour after the trooper pulled the car over, he leaves his car with all the documents in his hand and walks up to the driver's side window to Everett. He hands Everett his ID and the registration and insurance card. He looks at a tear-filled eye Morissa holding her license.

Trooper Simon: "Morissa can you please get out of the car and meet me behind the car. I would like to ask you a few questions."

Morissa looks at Everett with a look asking for approval. Everett looking at Morissa then the trooper.

Trooper Simon: "It is ok Everett. I just want to talk to her for a minute. She will be ok."

Everett: "I guess."

Morissa opens her door and walks to the back of the car. It is her and the trooper looking at each other. Then the trooper says her name.

Trooper Simon: "Morissa Brown."

Morissa: "Yes."

Trooper Simon: "Are you ok?"

Morissa: "Yes I am. Like I said he is my boyfriend. I didn't know he didn't have a license."

Trooper Simon: "I could understand that. Morissa Brown, I know your father. We met along time a go when you were just a baby."

Morissa: "I don't understand how do you know my father?"

Trooper Simon: "Your father and I served in the army together. Then we became state troopers together. Your father had to resign because of some other things in his life. I even was at his wedding to your mother. Then as the years went by, we lost touch. I have an old picture of him and me when we were in the service to gather. It is nice to see what a lovely young lady you turned out to be."

Morissa: "Thank you. I am sorry to say I don't remember you."

Trooper Simon: "I do not expect you to remember me. You were just a baby. Please tell me how your father and mother are.?"

Morissa: "My parents are divorced. My father still lives in the same house that I was born in. My mother lives in California. I am going to college at a school up state. Everett is my boyfriend we were just looking to spend some time alone together. We are really sorry about this."

Trooper Simon: "It is ok. I called this in to the state police office to check out the car. They were able to talk too Herbert and said he did lend Everett the car. The registration and insurance are up to date so it isn't any problem. Everett not having a license is a problem. He cannot drive anywhere till he gets a valid license. Your license is valid so you will have to drive the car."

Morissa: "Are you telling me we can go if I drive?"

Trooper Simon: "Yes you could go on your way as long as you drive."

Morissa: "Thank you I will drive the speed limit."

Trooper Simon: "It is kind of a coincidence I should run in to you now. I am about to retire in a couple of weeks. It has been a long time since I saw your father. I think of him from time to time. He was a good man and a friend. I hope you tell him about this. I wouldn't have done this for anybody else. You being his daughter that is enough to think you are just in the wrong place at the wrong time. "

Morissa: "I will tell him thank you."

Trooper Simon: "Let me have you wait here for a minute. I will ask your boyfriend to get in to the passenger seat. Then I will get you in to the driver seat safely."

Morissa: "Thank you again. I will tell my father about meeting you, thank you."

Trooper Simon walks up to the driver window and ask Everett to get in to the passenger seat. Everett does as he is asked without saying anything. Trooper Stewart then tells Everett he and the other troopers will be looking for this car. If they see him driving it, they will arrest him. Everett nods his head.

Then the trooper tells Everett not to do anything to Morissa that may get him in a real bad situation. Everett replies that she is safe with him. The trooper laugh and says. "Your off to a good start. She been crying and you have her standing in front of a police car. There is more to taking care of her then telling me she is safe with you. Grow up and be responsible to someone who may love you". Everett answers the trooper with a simple ok."

Trooper Simon goes and get Morissa from the front of his car. He walks her to the driver side of the car. Morissa gets in the driver's seat and thanks the trooper again. Trooper Simon then tells her "you are free to leave and drive safely." Morissa looks at Everett then back at the trooper. She puts the car in gear thanks the trooper and tells him she will tell her father she met him. Then she pulls safely away from the side of the road and back in to moving traffic. The trooper watches her pull away and goes back to his car.

Everett and Morissa continue their drive to Atlantic city. Morissa is driving below the speed limit as Everett looks out the passenger window with an occasional look at Morissa. A half hour later Morissa breaks the silence.

Morissa: "I am sorry Everett. I over reacted. I know you are trying to be good to me. I know you didn't want this to happen. I try to be so careful not to have problems like what just happen. I plan things so I don't have any unexpected problems. I know you are different. You just handle whatever comes along.

You never break a sweat or panic do you. You have no fear of what may happen to you. Is it that you know your parents will bail you out? Or is it you have no fear of what may happen to you. There are things that are out there that can hurt you. You may not be able to get yourself out of trouble one day Everett. It is like you don't think about tomorrow and the price you have to pay for what you may have done today"

Everett: "Thank you Morissa. I didn't want there to be any problems with are time together. There is some truth in what you say about me. I never had to worry about the price of the payment of tomorrow for today. If I can't pay for it tomorrow then I pay it the next day. I think people are destined to travel a road that they can't change."

Morissa: "Be careful Everett you may lose that ability to do that. You are a young healthy strong man. My life is happier thinking about you not worrying about you. Do you understand I need you to think of yourself as part of us? It is you and me. Your problems are mind. My problems are yours. That means us Everett.

Everett: "I understand Morissa."

Morissa: "Thank you Everett."

Everett and Morissa stop talking. Morissa turns the radio up. Everett recline his seat and close his eyes.

At the casino.  They park the car, grab their bags and walk-in side to the check in counter. Everett checks in then he and Morissa walk up to their room. Everett opens the door and Morissa follows him in. Morissa drops her bags at the foot of the bed. Everett turns around and see Morissa standing by the bed. Morissa standing by the bed with a scared look on her face. Everett walks up to her then puts a hand on each shoulder.

He gives Morissa a long kiss.

Everett: "It is ok Morissa. You will be ok. I will be here. It is just you and I now. We have plenty of time to enjoy ourselves."

Morissa: "I know Everett. We will have time to enjoy ourselves. I want to be here with you. There isn't anybody I rather be with. Be patient with me I never been alone in a hotel with any man. I am not sure what to do now."

Everett: "Relax. Relax and try to enjoy your time as a young woman. Do You know what time it is?"

Morissa: "No I don't. Why don't you tell me what time it is?"

Everett: "It is time for us to get ready for tonight. We are going to have some drinks some dinner some dancing and some gambling. Then we will see what the night brings us. Whatever happens tonight it will be just you and me. How does that sound to you? Do you think you may enjoy being here with me?"

Morissa: "It does sound like a nice time. We could have a real nice time together. Just think of how much time alone we will have together Everett."

Everett: "I have been thinking of that a lot. I been thinking of how nice I would make this for you Morissa. Leave it to me and I will be the person you can trust."

Morissa: "I love you, Everett."

Everett: "Morissa do you want to know the first thing we need to do?"

Morissa: "I don't know. I am afraid to ask. I do think you are going to tell me."

Everett: "It is simple. It is what every couple has done since the beginning of time Morissa. Morissa, we have to get ready for tonight. I am going to take my bag and go on down to the gym and get ready. You can have this room the shower and anything else you need. At seven tonight I want to find you at the bar looking as good as I can imagine you can."

Morissa: "A simple woman can't imagine what a man may be imagining about her. Sometimes it is better not to know everything that they may be thinking."

Everett: "I am going to take my bag and leave you with a kiss. I hope to see you at the bar tonight. Morissa there will be a lot of other men there like all the other bars. Please look my way when I bump it to you tonight. Not like that first night I saw you after that football game."

Morissa: "I really didn't see you. I promise, like I said before I didn't see you. I will be alone and looking for you tonight Everett. I promise. There is only one man I want to be with tonight and that is you."

Everett: "I believe you Morissa. I am going to leave you now. In a couple of hours, it will be just you and me."

Everett grabs his bags and goes on down to one of the casino exclusive man's clothing store. He walks in and finds a man at the counter. Everett gives him his name. The man at the counter tells him he is the owner. He tells Everett his father called and that everything was ready for him. Everett and the owner walks to the back of the store. The owner call his best tailor over to measure Everett. After he is fitted Everett walks to a barber and gets a haircut and a shave.  Then he walks back to the tailor. He is able to get a shower in the back. Then Everett puts on his tailor tuxedo.

In the meantime, Morissa unpacks her bags and gets ready for her night with Everett. Two hours later a beautiful young woman, dress in a long green dress is looking at a beauty in a mirror. Her long auburn hair flows with waves to her shoulders. Her face is a soft pallet of colors that highlights her god given looks. Each ear has a small white diamond in it. Around her neck is her communion gold neckless that her father purchase for her. A step back from the mirror is enough to capture the shape that is of a young woman.

A spin around in a small circle lets her hair and dress spin in an upward lift that floats on the rush of air. A look at the small gold watch tells her it is time to be the princess that every girl grows in to being.

Morissa takes her black purse and walks to the door. She turns around at the door then looks at the large bed on the other side of the room. The next couple of days of being with a man she loves. The pleasure of just the time a man and a woman can enjoy to gather. This was a well-rehearsed play that she had done before in her dreams. The thought of the events that will happen in just a few hours after the romance. The time has come to cross that next step of life was in store for her. Out the door she walks to the elevator.

On the elevator are two older couples. The two couples are dressed up for a night out. The four people look at the young lady in green that walks on to the elevator and smile at her. One of the man push the close button and ask Morissa what floor. Morissa answers him back with one word casino. Both man take turns steeling looks at Morissa. The two woman look at each other with the smile of their thoughts of their younger days. Out of the elevator Morissa walks with a thank you to the man holding the door for her. The two-man steel one last look as Morissa walks away.

Morissa makes her way to the bar trying to find Everett. As she looks around Everett is not to be found. She sees an open seat at the crowded bar and makes her way there. The bar tender comes over to her and ask her what she would like. Morissa orders a seven up.

She looks straight ahead and see herself in the mirror behind the bartender. Her face is looking like it could be a vogue cover. A confident smile comes to her face. The bartender brings her the drink with a coaster.

Morissa takes a drink and looks around for Everett. A voice from the seat next to her gets her attention. There is a thirty something year old guy next to her asking her a question. The guy's name next to her is Bob. Bob is wearing a sports jacket with a tie that has been retied to many times in the last couple of days. Half of Bobs front shirt is hanging out under his stomach.

Bob: "Hello there babe My name is Bob can I freshen up that drink for you?"

Morissa: "No thank you I am waiting for a friend."

Bob: "Maybe your girlfriend will be late. Maybe you want a different drink babe"

Morissa: "My name is Morissa, please don't call me babe"

Bob: "Ok Morissa. I don't mind calling you anything you like. You can call me Bob. I am here on business so I have a credit card to entertain VIP. VIP, Very impressive princess. Or is that very impressive person. I think you qualify for both.

Morissa: "That's nice."

Bob: "It is a big weekend down here for us. I sell restaurant supply's you know. If they make it, I can sell it. I even sold supplies that don't even exist.

You have to be really good at selling. To sell something that doesn't even exist. I have sold supplies to people they didn't even need. I had a sale today to a restaurant chain. That means all there sixty-two restaurants will be buying the supplies from me all year long. That commission can buy drinks for everybody in this bar for an hour."

Morissa: "That's nice."

Bob: "If you like I can get a table and we can get away from this noisy crowded bar. Like I said I had a good day today. A small table with champagne would be no problem. You look like you would like some champagne. Maybe we could have some food with the champagne. Wouldn't you like that."

Morissa: "No thank you. I am still looking for my friend"

Bob: "Morissa I will tell you something. I have a friend coming down later with his wife. You know what it is like being a third wheel. His wife and him are just trying to keep me company because I am here alone. If I was with you, they would probably leave and enjoy themselves more. And not worried about me being alone. Just think of the good you would be doing for an older couple. What do you say? A Little champagne. Some dinner. You will probably have a good time."

Morissa: "No thank you."

Bob: "Let me have the bartender get you a new drink. Don't worry like I said I will take care of the drinks. Why don't you tell me something about you? I told you I was in to sales? From the looks of you I would say you are a model. Am I right? I have to have a nose for figuring people. When you are in sales you have to figure people out fast if you want to sell them something. Am I right you are a model? It is that dress you have on. I have seen a lot of sponsorship models.

You know those girls who pose alongside a product. Like at an auto car show. That's where you can find the high price girls to stand along one of those high-end price cars. The last couple of days I have looked around at all the booths. I saw a few models that some of the bigger merchants had because they can afford them. I don't recall seeing you. I am sure I would have remembered you. May be you are going to be in the next show. It is going to be an electronics show. I got it that is where you are going to be modeling. I bet you get top dollar, for your time don't you."

Morissa: "No I still go to school. I don't model. I wonder where my friend is. He said to meet him here."

Bob: "I am sorry I didn't know you were waiting on a guy friend. I guess you are on a date. That is nice. I am sure he is a good guy. Guys sometime have something else on their mind. He could just have forgotten about you. Maybe something came up and he couldn't make it. You want to think about why any guy would make you wait. A babe like you should have guys waiting for you. That is the way I think it should be. You have to teach those younger guys how important you are. You have to teach them how to appreciate you. If I had a looker like you, I would know how to treat her. That offer of champagne and dinner still stands. The tables look like there all filled. But you leave it to me. I know how to talk too these people. A little cash, hand to hand gets you a table for two. Unless your friend told you, he had reservations you are not going to be able to get a table. I saw my friend and his wife just sit down at a table. I am sure that cost him. Better him then me. That table and the food in this expensive restaurant is about a month's pay. You and I can go over there now if you like. It would not be any problem. You would be doing them a big favor. Then if your friend did show up you can teach him a lesson about leaving such an attractive babe alone.

You may want to waste a night with some free drinks and a free meal. The road stories my friend and I will talk about will have you laughing the whole time you are with us. Don't worry about being out with strangers. There will be another female at the table. I am sure she will be happy to talk to you."

Morissa: "No thank you."

Bob: "Morissa. Ok we will just stay here. Can you excuse me for a minute? I have to go over to my friend and tell them that we may be joining them later. Please don't let any other guy take my seat by you.

Most guys see a good-looking babe at a bar alone and they think it is an open invitation to start a conversation. I am going to leave a twenty-dollar bill at the counter. Just order anything you want and a beer for me."

Morissa: "Right."

Bob gets up and goes over to his friends at the table. Bob talks to his friends for a couple of minutes. He keeps looking back at Morissa and his empty chair at the bar. Bob sees a good-looking young man dressed in a tuxedo take his seat at the bar. Bob goes right back to the bar and his seat.

Bob: "Hi Morissa I am back. I told you I wouldn't be long. That is my twenty still on the bar by my seat. Did you tell this guy in my seat that you were saving it for me? Guy, I don't want to be rude to you but I was talking to this babe If you don't mind, please get up and fine another place to sit.

Everett: "I am sorry sir. I saw this good-looking woman alone here and I just couldn't resist. I told her I know how to make a good pizza and she offered to go home with me. It was that easy."

Morissa: "It's true. I am a sexual freak for a guy who can make a pizza. Sorry babe"

Bob: "What? Dam."

Everett: "Here is your twenty dollars Bob. Say good bye Bob."

Bob walks off and leaves the bar. Everett and Morissa start to talk.

Morissa: "That was funny. Where were you, Everett?"

Everett: "I was back a couple of chairs listening to the conversation you were having with Bob. I was hoping you would notice me this time."

Morissa: "I would of notice you if I saw you. You are a good-looking man in that tuxedo, who knows how to show up for a date. You gave me a nice surprise dressing like that for me."

Everett: "It isn't about how I look. It is the woman I am looking at. It is about the woman who is talking to me. It is about you and the way I look at you. It is about the special way I think of you Morissa."

Morissa: "Thank you Everett. I think we waited too long to get a table."

Everett: "Not a chance Morissa, like Bob said cash in the hand or something like that. Come with me very impressive princess, and we will find ourselves a table."

Morissa: "Ok Everett. I am all yours please take me anywhere."

Everett takes Morissa to a secluded table behind some plants. There is a sign that says reserve on it.

Everett picks the sign up and puts it in the plant's pots that are around them. He pulls a chair out for Morissa. Morissa takes her seat and thanks Everett. The two start to talk.

Morissa: "I think we are taking a chance sitting here at this table. I don't want them, asking us to leave this casino. The people who own this place do not play games Everett."

Everett: "Morissa I think you may be right. Here come a maître d and a waiter. Get ready to go."

Maître d: "Hello Mr. Everett and Mis Morissa. It will be a pleasure to serve you to night. This is are best waiter. His name is Sal. Anything you want tonight just ask him and he will get it for you. If there is anything I can do please just ask. You two are our special guest tonight. All of your bags are being moved to the sweet just as it was a ranged."

Sal: "We will have a wine Stuart bring out a private label of wine. A different waiter will bring out the drinks. Everett has already order dinner for you two. I will be back with the meal."

The maître d and Sal the waiter leave.

Morissa: "Ok Everett what's going on here. You can't afford a tuxedo no matter how good it looks on you. You can't afford a reserved table with your own waiter."

Everett: "I have another surprise for you Morissa. I think you are really going to like this."

Morissa: "You won the lotto and you are going to give me half."

Everett: "No sorry. No lotto. When I went up north this summer with my father, he had a couple of clients. One of them was a part owner of this casino. I made him the best fish pizza he ever had. His name is Gerald, he told me he would take care of me if I was to come here.

It is that simple. I ask my father to call him after we made are plans."

Morissa: "That is a nice surprise, Everett."

Everett: "That isn't the surprise I have for you. It is something you saw and like."

Morissa: "I don't know what you mean Everett. You know you did enough. You don't have to do anything more."

Everett: "Morissa see this little black box I just pulled out of my pocket. It is for you."

Morissa: "Everett, I can't marry you. We are still in school.

Everett: "Morissa it is not a wedding ring."

Morissa: "I am so sorry you have my head so confused."

Everett: "Please open it. It will explain it self to you."

Morissa opens the little black box and starts to cry.

Morissa: "It is the hazel green neckless and earing we saw at that shop. That shop across from that small restaurant by are school. And it matches my dress and eyes. I just love it. I am going to wear them now. I hope you don't mind do you."

Everett: "I was hoping you would. Please do.

Morissa spend a couple of minutes taking off the diamond earing and gold cross neckless and putting on her gift from Everett.

Morissa: "How did you know I was going to wear this green dress?"

Everett: "Sue told me and you can fill in the pieces."

Morissa: "I will have to thank Sue."

Everett: "That green goes with your eyes better than I could have hope for."

Morissa Reaches over the table and give Everett a teary eye kiss.

Morissa: "Thank you for thinking of me. You must have been thinking a lot about me. The planning you have been doing for this moment in our lives together. Thank you for every moment you planned it. Every time I remember this night, I will be thinking of the special time between us. There was no guarantee that you or I would be here to have this moment. A person could never really know if they will ever find that other person. You could have found someone else in the time you were planning this. You could have been thinking I may have found someone else. Sometimes it does work like that. There are no sure things when it comes to the way people feel. This tells me a lot about you.

It tells me everything I thought or dream about you was true. The time I was alone thinking about you. I do think about you a lot. Sometimes a girl has a fantasy about the way we want to be romance. Everett, you have gone beyond the dream I could have dreamed of. There aren't many of us girls get what you just have given me. I will always remember you being the dream that came true.

As young girls we ask our mother how they met our fathers. We want to hear the story of Cinderella and a prince. We watch movies or it could be in a book looking for that moment when the man come along to fall in love with the woman. After the man has met the woman of his dream, he tries to sweep her off her feet. The woman knows she may play hard to get in hopes to make him want her more. The way you treat me is better than any dream. I could of dream to come my way.

Everett you are meant to be mine. You are meant to be mine forever. We are meant to be together forever."

Everett: "I love you Morissa it is that simple. Thank you. When we tell each other, we love each other it will be simpler now."

Morissa: "It will be."

Everett: "I do love you. We are here to be together."

Morissa: "I do love you."

Everett: "Here comes dinner."

Everett and Morissa eat dinner and enjoy the time together talking and the good food. After dinner Everett ask Morissa to dance. There is a small band playing some Benny Goodman and Glenn Miller soft dance music. Everett takes Morissa and escorts her on the dance floor. On the floor are the last married couples of the world war two generation. The last of them who survived together.

Surviving the good and the bad that life has to give. The time that they get when the kids are gone. When their last occasions of health lets them live there life endings. Everett and Morissa are the youngest people dancing on the floor.

Everett: "Morissa maybe you notice we are the youngest people out on this dance floor. The people around us were probably dancing to the same music years ago. They were probably dancing the same way years ago. I don't think they change the way they dance over the years."

Morissa: "I hope they are dancing with the same person, that they were dancing with back then. That is so romantic to think that about them. I hope someday when we are old, we are together doing this Everett. Me and you together still in love as we are today.

Our looks will have change by then. Our lives will be very different. I think are love still have the same want for each other. We will still want each other as much as we do tonight. Having you so close to me now means more than I can explain to you or myself. I dance with other guys before. This is different Everett. I want you to hold me. I want you to look at me and want me. I want you to think of me like no other woman you have ever looked at. I need you to be the man I have been dreaming of. I am going to close my eyes now and concentrate on this time we are having. I want to remember you. I want to remember you holding me as you are holding me. I want to remember the scent of the man who has me in his strong arms. Everett, please talk to me softly and tell me what you are thinking."

Everett: "I am thinking of you Morissa. I am thinking of this lovely woman that I am holding. This beautiful female that I have a desire for. A young woman that is so mature in her thinking. A woman that holds the value of herself not cheapen by a false promise or a current want or need. She is holding strong for her wants of her life.

The wants that are so important to her life. The woman who cares for me. The only woman whose thinking is what I hope to learn from. Yes, Morissa I love talking to you. I think you are so smart. The way you look at things we talk about. I find myself thinking about the things we have talked about. Sometimes it is the simplest things you say. Sometimes I think you purposely say certain words in certain ways to have me think about them or you. Weather you purposely do it as a cat playing with its toy. Or you are just trying to communicate with me to reach me. You are the conversation that is over thought about. Even after the conversation is over, I am still thinking about you and what you said."

Your face. The face that is in a portrait I will always remember. The portrait of a beauty that eludes most man in their life. The beauty that they will only dream of. The portrait that hold the face of a woman who is looking at me with those eyes of a dreamy hazel green. Those eyes that are looking for the understanding of the person they belong to. I love your green eyes. Especially when I know they are looking just at me. I want those eyes just looking at me. I will always be jealous if I see those eyes are looking at any one but me.

Your hair. Your soft auburn hair that is a frame for the portrait of your face. It is a gift for me to behold. It is a gift for me to hold.  It is the fabric of a master peace. The different shades that flow with the waves of light that shine on every layer. The years it had taken to grow. This night is for me to enjoy and appreciate the care you had given it.

The green dress that is holding the shape of a woman. Those shapes that have men thinking about the desires that those shape can give. Those desires that are not easily explain by a man. Those desires that are felt from the part of us that are uncontrollable. We can only hope that we as man can controlled those desires that comes from those shapes. Morissa, I have to confess of my desire for you. There isn't a time when I don't have to control my desire for you. The first night when I saw you in the bar was the first moment of desire, I had for you. You may think the next one was when I saw you on the beach for the first time. Or the night I was in the hot tub with you. It was that morning we had breakfast together. I made breakfast for you. I was dreaming in my mind that we spent the night together. Then I woke up looking at your face. I wanted to hold you and have you right then. Something told me that I would always have that desire for you.

Somehow, I learned to have just enough control over that desire for you. Morissa thank you for giving me that desire."

Everett and Morissa finish their eating, dancing and talking.

The next morning after they consummate their relationship.

Morissa wakes up in the center of a super wide bed. The light of the early morning is shining past the open curtains. She has the cover pulled up under her chin. Her head is resting on a large soft pillow. She looks at the light and a smile comes to her face. She looks at the morning light and squeeze her eyes to shield them from the brightness. She looks to her left the to the right. The thought of last night comes back to her. The smile of a gambler who won all the chips she had put on the table."

Then a look past the cover and at the foot board. The bottom of two male feet are on the foot board with the toes facing down. She see the feet going forward and back. Then the strains sounds of breathing is in timing with their movement.

Morissa: "Everett is that you? Please tell me what you are doing there."

Everett: "Yes, it is me. Fifty pushups is what I do every morning and night before I wake up and turn it. I would have done it last night but you know what happen."

Morissa: "I didn't know that about you. I was wondering how you kept in such good shape. You do have the body of an athlete. Let me tell you as a woman you have a nice body. You could be a poster boy for what men should look like without a shirt. You may not believe this but the bottom of your feet are all so sexy. You are genetically gifted."

Everett: "I don't think I heard the feet comment before thank you."

Morissa: "Your welcome. It is my pleasure."

Everett: "I hoped you enjoyed last night?"

Morissa: "Like I said it was my pleasure."

Everett switches his feet so that this toes are face toward the ceiling.

Morissa: "What are you doing now may I ask?"

Everett: "Fifty sit ups with my feet on the foot board."

Morissa: "Really. Fifty you say. You are such a man. You really know how to turn a woman on don't you. I'll bet that is a trick you use on unsuspected females so you can take advantage of them Mr. Everett. if you think that trick is going to work on me. You are right. When you are done down there you could come back up here and I will try to tire you out in another way."

Everett: "Anything I could do for you princess. Please let me know. This man is now under your spell. The spell of a young female. You have given this man a taste of a princess and all of her attributes, to leave a man week and powerless forever."

Morissa: "Shut up and get in this bed now or there will be hell to pay my prince charming."

Three hours later Everett and Morissa are at a breakfast table eating breakfast.

Morissa: "Everett you were really good to me last night. You did everything just the right way. You were kind, gentle and caring. Thank you for making it better than anything I could have dreamed."

Everett: "You are welcome Morissa. You mean a lot to me. I never loved anybody like you. If you couldn't tell I enjoyed last night to."

Morissa: "I wasn't born yesterday. I could tell you had your fun. For the athlete you are.  There were times I heard you breathing heavy."

Everett: "I think you turn the tables on me this morning."

Morissa" "Everett what would you like to do today? What do couples do when there not in there room making a mess out of the bed?"

Everett: "They enjoy their time together doing other things. Like shopping, eating and dancing. In a place like this gambling."

Morissa: "Gambling. Oh my. Are you trying to be a bad boy?  Maybe feeling your oats after last night. Maybe You know that would be dangerous for you. You been so good at not making those sport bets. Why do you have to do that now?"

Everett: "I was thinking we are in a place like this and it would be some fun. We only have so much money. We just need to set a limit and follow it."

Morissa: "Ok a limit sounds good but what else could we do?"

Everett: "There is a Franchise convention for restaurant owners in this casino. I am going to visit some of the booths and see if I can learn anything from them.

 It is that dream I have to have my own restaurant one day. There are some people selling franchise to a chain of restaurants. I don't have to worry about buying anything because I have no money. You can join me or visit some of the shops here. You did say you have your credit card. We also have some comp gift certificate. You could use them while we are here. Morissa try and have some fun outside the bedroom door.

Put your hair up and be free of what you think you should be and have been. It is fun time, have some fun. Let's have some free time."

Morissa: "The term is let your hair down and have some fun. I will have some fun. Somehow, I think the most fun is, and only can be found with you Everett. After I finish this breakfast, I want to get a little sleep and a long hot bath. Maybe I will go and get my hair done. I may get it done in a way that may surprise you. May be I will dye it. May be I will get it cut short. Real short what do you think about that my love Everett. May be you will be holding a different looking woman tonight. Isn't that what every man wants. A different woman every night.?"

Everett: "I think you mean a sailor and a woman in every port. Morissa, I like the way you are. You don't have to do anything to have me infatuated with you. Please keep yourself the same just for me. What we did last night did not change you. Don't worry about changing anything about yourself. You are the same person as you were yesterday. The woman I knew yesterday I want to know her today."

Morissa: "Ok I will not make any changes to myself. I will try to make myself somewhat attractive to you. We do need to make plans on where we can meet for lunch. Do you think you could make plans to meet me somewhere and we could have a lunch?"

Everett "There is a fast-food burger place on the other side of the casino. We can meet there about three. What do you think?"

Morissa: "Last night I had a man treat me to a fancy dinner at a private table. He talked so nice to me and told me what I meant to him. Then he took me up to his room and did things to me I never had done to me. Now that same man wants to take me to some fast-food burger joint.

I can't imagine what he is going to have in mind for me after that. My mother warn me about men like you."

Everett: "Morissa I am starting to see a different kind of humor from you. Or are you trying to be playful with me?"

Morissa: "You know all of us women like to keep you men guessing. I learn that man are more worthy when you can keep them guessing. It is when they think they have a sure thing is when you can't trust them."

Everett: "Did you learn that from experience or your mother.?

Morissa: "No I was watching some old chick flick movie. There was these two old women talking about their younger life and all the men they knew. You know how old women are."

Everett: "I like to watch that movie with you one late night."

Morissa: "Sure Everett, we will make it a date. A date? Are we now daters after last night or are we consider lovers? Oh my, it just occurred to me. I am in un chartered waters. I dated other guys before but I never had a lover. Do I consider you a lover and not somebody I am dating? How do I introduce you to people? Do I tell them you are my boyfriend? Do I tell them you are my lover? Then it is the worst case would be my father, Everett. I can just here myself. Hi dad meet my lover his name is Everett. He has the body of an athlete."

Everett: "Don't worry about it Morissa. It will all work itself out. Whatever makes you comfortable just go with that and you live with it. What we are is important to us. That is all we have to think about."

Morissa: "I am curious what you are going to tell people what we are. Are you going to tell your guy friend's one thing and other people other things?"

Everett: "I am just going to tell people the same as always. That you are my friend."

Morissa: "I would like it if you tell people that I am your girlfriend, Everett. I would like to hear that from you. It would make me comfortable. I do feel that we are more than boyfriend and girlfriend. When I think of you, I know we are more than that. I know how special you are to me."

Everett: "We are going to go back to school and be the same as we were. We are going back to living the same way. I am going back to the dorm and you are going back to the house with the girls."

Morissa: "I didn't even think about that. This means we could get together anytime and have sex. Isn't that great. I think. I don't want everybody thinking about us when I am not in the house. I want to be with you but this is going to be a problem. I am going to want to be with you. But where are we going to be together and when. What's going to happen this summer and when you graduate? I didn't think further then these couple of days."

Everett: "Don't worry about it Morissa. We will have our time together. Males and females have been getting together for ever. Let's just let it happen."

Morissa: "I love your confidence. You always have that don't you. You had it your whole life. Most normal people don't have that kind of confidence. Everett was there ever a time you weren't the Everett I have fell in love with. There must have been a time in your life that you second guess yourself. I know people who can't leave well enough alone. You never look to change anything do you. You just take it as It comes. I would like to see you second guess yourself one day."

Everett: "No that isn't true. I have second guessed myself. There was a time when I should have done things different. There was a time when an event could of turn out different. We all have those times in our life that we wish we did things different. I learned to live with what I did. Morissa I am a flawed person. The more time you spend with me you will see the flaws."

Morissa: "We all have them."

Everett: "I hope you will still like me when you see them. I may not even be thinking about them when you see or notice them. Please have some patience when you see them. I am just a normal person."

Morissa: "I have flaws Everett. Have you seen any of my flaws? You can tell me I can handle it."

Everett: "Yes you have one big flaw that may be the biggest problem in your life. Sometimes I see you having this flaw and I like it. Sometimes I even think it is cute. I will bet you nobody has ever told you about this big flaw you have. And I hope you never lose it."

Morissa: "You have to tell me what flaw I have and why you waited to now to tell me Everett. I don't recall you saying anything yesterday about any flaw you may think I have. I want you to know I am the level headed one here. I think we can both agree to that can't we.

 I don't recall my mother or father telling me of this great flaw you think I have. I don't recall the girls I live with telling me I have this great flaw. The guys I dated before didn't think I had this great flaw. Tell me is it something about my looks. Is it the way I talk? Is it the way I eat? Is it about something I did or didn't do last night?"

Everett: "Stop. I was going to tell you your biggest flaw is that you like me. Morissa I am truly in love with everything about you. I love you and the way you are. I wouldn't change anything that I have come to love about you. Morissa I am sorry if I made you un easy. You should never feel that way."

Morissa: "I knew what you were going to say. I just made you sorry for saying something that you do regret saying. You should take care I am always thinking about you."

Everett: "Very good Morissa. You got me. I think it is time that we leave this breakfast and start our day before we find ourselves here at dinner.

A kiss good bye and the two go their separate ways. Morissa goes back to their room and takes a bubble bath in a large tub. Everett goes down to a convention for restaurant franchise. This is a place where a company sell the opportunity to purchase an independent business franchise.

Everett walks from booth to booth listening to the people behind a table filled of brochures and opportunities. These in formal business meeting start with Everett listening to a sales pitch from a seller that promises huge profits and low overhead for a small start of fee. A clear track from a successful independence franchise owner who have found the fast track to financial independence. They were all men in white shirts and ties of color. Some of the larger table were adorn with a charming young lady who knew how to make small talk to the man with a Walter Mitty dream.

Everett hears the startup price and knows that much cash is possible from his father. His father and all his partners would be his partners. A payment to his father would have to be paid from his free time. His independence would be found only in his hours of work.

Everett walks up to a table for a pastry franchise. The table is small with two small black and white pamphlets. Everett starts a conversation with the owner of this small company selling franchises. The owner looks at Everett and takes note of his young age. Then he starts the conversation with the same opening lines "I am looking for young men, who have those same dreams I had." The sales man's name is Philip Ponzu.

Philip: "Are you looking for the day when you don't have a boss because you are the boss. I bet a sharp guy like you had enough of the low pay and meaningless jobs. Could you think about this young company that is ready to explode with opportunity for the right smart person.

Everett: "That sounds nice. It may not be what I want. I am trying to learn something about a business like yours and how it got its start. Then what it took to make it work for a day. Every table here has a sales pitch and a buy in option. Then the freedom of financial independence after the debt were paid. Then the monthly franchise fees are paid. Then you have to buy from the company vendors. True independence are not in any plan of the parent company if you do succeed."

Philip: "I may go home right now. You have us all figured out don't you. Can I ask you for your name Young man? My name is Philip Ponzu. I am the real owner of my company. I started this company on my own from a small shop next to a police station. Police station are a twenty-four-hour business. To keep my business going for the first year I slept, ate, and lived there. I did have a lot of headaches that year. A lot of unknown surprises.

 I learned a lot. I can save a young person like you a lot of unnecessary expenses. The money I can save you will more then cover any cost you will pay."

Everett: "If you didn't open up by the police station could you have survived."

Philip: "On sure will and the want to do it. I wanted to succeed more than anything. I gave up on visiting any family members. I gave up on everything that took my time away from me not working on my business. To save money I would turn the heat down in the shop at night and froze in those cold Boston nights. I learn new tricks on saving cost for material and not sacrificing taste on anything I sold."

Everett: "Why are you selling franchise? If you could start a pastry shop why can't somebody do it without you."

Philip: "I can make it easier for the right person. I can save the right person time and money like I said. If you are interested, I could help. To the right person I could even lend the startup money."

Everett: "Startup money I could get from my father. He is a lawyer. The money would be tied to his business. It is a little complicated to explain. It is there if I need it. Getting the money from elsewhere may be less complicated but cost more. The problem I would have is where and what to make and sell. I like baking and cooking. Some people have told me that is what I should do. I am in college at this time. When I graduate, I get some money? I don't know if it would be enough to start a small shop.

Philip: "A small shop of what. You said you like baking and cooking. You say people have told you that is something you should do. Do what may I ask. Cook, bake, or what. What you haven't said is what you want to do.

You can bake and cook for other people and have them pay you by the hour. Is that what you want to do. You will be baking and cooking what they tell you to do. Then they will tell you how to do it."

Everett: "Some chefs make a lot of money without any risk."

Philip: "Any real good chef wants to have their own place. Then they can do what they want to do. They take a great pride in being able to do it. When you get to that level it is a different type of revenue."

Everett: "I have been in some of the best. My father businesses have taken him to some of these places. He knows I like them. He will invite me when he can. I would like to have something of my own smaller and in a small town."

Philip: "All places from a deli to the most exclusive restaurant are local. You may see a franchise in New York and one in Alabama. They may have the same name but they are a local establishment. Every place that is a place for some kind of food service has one major goal in their business plan. Do you know what that goal is Everett?"

Everett: "Good food?"

Philip: That is a bragging right. The most important goal is to make a profit. If you can't do that nothing else matters. I will help anybody who signs up with me to make a profit."

Everett: "There are times when I go in to a place and think, if I could make the place better than the current owners. Sometimes I think it is the food that needs to be better. Sometimes it is the inside of the place I would change. I know making a place better may not make more of a profit. I am going to do something in some way I just haven't figured it out yet."

Philip: "Everett, I will give you some free advice. When I was your age, I had the same thoughts. I was in a pastry shop one day. I saw the customers at the counter enjoying the experience of the small shop.

The counter people with the pride of selling their products. That day in that shop I knew what I wanted to do. I worked in six different pastry shops to learn what I could. Then I had my own shop. I told you what I had to do my first year just to survive. It sounds like to me you have the want to do it. I have the opportunity. The first part you will have to do is find a place that you can sell a product that you can make. Find a product with a low cost that you can sell. Pay yourself first. At first when you do that, you will have to be working the most hours and doing most of the work. Find a way to keep your over head down. I have that all worked out for my partners who buy one or more of my franchise."

Everett: "I know I am going to have my own business one day. I have thought about it as long as I could remember. I learn how to cook. I learned how to make food that people like. I saw a place I would of like to own. My father company owned it then had to sell it. I wanted to own it and have my owned place. The dream I have. The want to do it I have. I didn't have the money or the knowledge to make a dream work at that time. I will have my own place and I will have my own type of food service."

Philip: "Ok Everett I have another person here. If you want to contact me you can find the information in the perspective. Good luck"

Everett: "Thank you."

Everett walks around the convention for a while and talks to different people offering endless opportunities. The opportunities of life time payments and life time partners.

Morissa is enjoying her day. Her morning is spent having a long bubble bath. She then goes down to the beauty salon. Her mind is now free of the right place and right time. The place and the time had come and passed. It was the right time and place with the right man. The enjoyment of a woman in love.

The enjoyment of a woman who found a man who gave her the freedom. The experience that she now has.  The experience to be a confident woman who can enjoy her new freedom.

Morissa is sitting at a seat having her hair washed and cut. The hair dresser is a middle-aged woman named Ruth.

Ruth: "Ok dear what would you like me to do for you? Maybe I can cut it really short for you? No maybe not. You are one of the few young ladies I have seen that have not dyed her hair. Auburn hair and probably just at the right length for your face. You have to excuse me for looking at your hair and noticing that. It is just what I do. I have seen so many heads of hair in all the years of doing this. It is seldom that I see women who have hair like yours that is as beautiful as yours.  Just a shampoo and a trim I am to guess."

Morissa: "Thank you I love my hair. I had it like this for such a long time. I would hate to change it and not like the change. I do have a boyfriend to think of. He likes my hair. I would hate to change it and not have him like it. I could be daring one time and have you cut it short. What a surprise that would be for him."

Ruth: "Have you known him long?"

Morissa: "Yes about five months. We go to the same school."

Ruth: "I guess that is where you met him."

Morissa: "No I met him on a beach in California. I was visiting my mother. Then one day on a beach there is this tall good-looking guy in front of me. He was blocking the sun when I was reading a book. Then the rest is history."

Ruth: "Sounds like a meeting I would like to have. I met my husband so long ago. A couple of children a go. The dream of a middle age woman who likes to read those romance books. To be young like you. I bet you have the guys lined up to have a date with you."

Morissa: "No more than any other girl my age I guess."

Ruth: "Do you and your boyfriend come to places like this a lot. Places like this are not cheap. We don't see many young couples here. People your age are just looking for a day or two with some privacy."

Morissa: "No we don't go out to places like this. This is are first time being alone together by ourselves. We are hoping to make it something special. Just him and me."

Ruth: "You said you met him five months ago. I could see why this is something special for you two. I have seen many couples your age doing the shacking up thing. Then the I'll see you later maybe thing. I hope you two do well together."

Morissa: "Thank you I hope so to. He so different then a lot of other guys I have known. He has this independence to himself. He has a confidence that shows no fear of any decision he will make. It is like he knows what happens can't be second guess. He has no fear of anything. I haven't met anybody who doesn't like him. He is gifted athletically yet he doesn't use the ability to prove or gain anything. He just wants to be himself. The way he talks to me. It is like I been waiting for those words my whole life. He is something special. I think they broke the mold when he was born"

Ruth: "I guess they made that mold after my husband was born. I mean he is the father of my kids. I mean, I still love him. I guess, or I say it or something, I guess. I guess I felt that way about him at one time I thought. Is he good looking? I hope."

Morissa: "He looks like a good-looking man. Long or short? What should I do? What is a girl to do? I think I will keep my hair the same. I could always change my mind. I have that option to choose.  If I choose. Please keep it the same. I have no need to change it now. I can still enjoy my hair as I choose to have it. I will keep it with the same color. I choose to be me. I choose to stay the same. I am still me inside and outside."

Ruth: "I understand. We will keep you the same way. You will leave here with just a little change. You will know a change was made. The people who knew you before, may notice just a difference. You will be the one to know what changed."

Morissa: "Thank you."

Ruth: "You sound like a girl with her feet on the ground. When I was your age girls like me were told to find a guy, who would take care of the money part of life after the school years were over. Girls now a days seem to have a plan for themselves. Do you have such a plan?"

Morissa: "Teacher. I want to become a teacher. I want to teach children. I am going to school to learn how to teach."

Ruth: "That sounds nice. I think some teachers are really good at it and some just go thru the motions of teaching. Some of the teachers I had were just tired of teaching. I could still see them in front of a class of student talking. I think if they turned around and talked to the black board, we would not of notice anything different. There words would have been the same.

There tone would have been the same. The black board and the kids would be the same.

Some teachers have the ability to reach and teach the kids. Other should have found something else to do with their lives. There wasting the kids time there trying to teach. Those teachers may have thought that they were given a god given ability to teach. Teaching is a learn profession. Every year you do it you should try and get better then you were the year before. The students you are currently teaching are going to be taught better than the students you taught before them."

Morissa: "I will be good at it. I want to do it."

Ruth: "What does your boyfriend want to do."

Morissa: "He wants to cook for a living. He hopes to own his own place. He has a father that could help him with that end of it if he needs it. After he graduates this spring, he will have to make some decisions on what he will be doing. I am two years behind him."

Ruth: "If you two stay together you will have to make some hard decisions."

Morissa: "If we stay together? We will be together."

Later that day Morissa finds Everett at a black jack table. The table has four middle age man at it. All the man and the female dealer look up at her."

Morissa: "Hello sailor is this seat taken?"

Everett: "Hello Morissa. I see that you have found me. I am afraid I lost the mortgage and the baby's milk money."

Morissa: "You do this every time dear. Every time we have a kid you lose the mortgage and milk money. I just don't know what to do with you anymore. What do you think I should do with you Everett?"

Everett: "I guess we will just have to keep on having more kids till I start winning. What do you say about to night? You are looking good today. I see you just had your hair done. I hope you did it just for me."

Morissa: "Last night Everett, Had me thinking of you all morning. I will be thinking of you for the rest of the day. I will be thinking about how many kids you and I will have."

Everett: "Sounds like a plan to me. I think I am done here. I am down to about fifty dollars."

Morissa: "Let's go Everett. We will have some time before it is show time for you."

Everett gets up as the men at the table look at Morissa and think about what a lovely young lady they see. The dealer clears her throat to get the men's attention back to the table.

Everett and Morissa star to walk around the casino. Morissa take Everett's Elbow with her hands. The two start to talk."

Morissa: "Everett you know what this feels like to me. Me walking with you holding your arm."

Everett: "No Morissa. I hope it is something good."

Morissa: "Yes, it is. I never felt like this before. I feel so free. If I was doing this with anybody else, I would not feel the same. I feel so free. I feel like we are on a honeymoon together just you and me. I don't have any guilt about being in love with you. I want the way we are. I want you being in love with me. I love the way you want me. The way I know we are a couple in love. I hope we will always be like we are today."

Everett: "I think we will be Morissa. Some day if it works out right.  If we do things right, we will be able to do a lot together.

We have a lot of time to work on those life occasions together."

Morissa: "What did you just say? Life what?"

Everett: "Life occasions. It is something my mother told me years ago. I was going thru a hard time when I was really young. My mother sat me down when I told her I didn't want to live anymore. She told me you have to live all of life occasions. It is the occasions that you live with other people that gives you your life."

Morissa: "Everett what made you not want to live back then."

Everett: "I promise I will tell you some day. This isn't the time to tell you."

Morissa: "Everett please do that. I don't want us to have any secrets. I am not going to ask you to tell me. I will be waiting for you to tell me."

Everett: "Promise. Morissa why don't you try your luck on one of these slot machine. You could hit it big then we could skip school and go right to retirement."

Morissa: "Not a chance bud. I hit it big I will be going back to school."

Everett: "What about me. What would you do with me?"

Morissa: "Well. I have some ideas what I could do with you.

Everett: "I hope you still would want me like last night."

Morissa: "I can't tell you that right now. But I promise someday I will tell you por boy Everett."

Everett: "Too shay Morissa. Morissa this is one of the mega jack pot machine. For a dollar you can win a million dollars. Then you can have your way with me."

Morissa: "I don't know if you realize this. I have had my way with you already Everett."

Twenty minutes later Morissa is down eighty dollars and calls it quits. Everett and Morissa start walking around again arm in arm. Morissa stops Everett in front of a roulette wheel. She watches the ball being spun around. Then the dealer calling out a number and color."

Morissa: "Everett do you know how to play this game. I want you to play it."

Everett: "Yes I do. It is just another game of chance. Black or red it will double what you bet. Pick the number and you win more."

Morissa: "What is the green. What do you win if you pick the green?"

Everett: "If you pick the green, you will win thirty-five times what you bet. It is just dumb luck to play that color."

Morissa: "I want you to play that for me. It is the color. It is a different color then the green of that jewelry you bought me. But it is green. Please just do it for me."

Everett: "Why don't you play it. I am not that lucky on gambling. Maybe you still can be lucky."

Morissa: "Please Everett play it for me. I want you to do it for me. It would mean a lot to me. Just do it. I have two hundred dollar. It is that color. It is the color. You gave me that color. Please."

Everett: "Ok. Morissa I will do it. Let me have the money and I will put it on green. It will be the only bet I will make that I don't need to win. I realize that I have already won.

I have those green eyes of yours looking at me. I am a man who has won haven't I.

Everett and Morissa holding the one hundred dollars together put it down on green. The dealer takes the ball. He spins the wheel then drops the ball. Everett watches the ball drop then looks in to Morissa eyes. Morissa is watching the ball. The wheel spins. Around and around the ball rolls. Then the wheel starts to slow down. The ball jumps from number to number. It hits the different colors over and over. Everett eyes never leaves Morissa eyes. Morissa facial expressions change with ever different change of the ball position. The ball is now slowly riding the upper rail. It falls down to a number then another color. When the ball has its last movement. The dealer calls out something. It is not heard over Morissa yell of: "Green it is green. We did it we did its Everett, we hit it. It is green. We just hit the mother boat load." With eyes still on Morissa eyes in a soft voice Everett says "Yes I have you. I am happy to have you." Unheard by Morissa. Morissa takes the coins and puts them in her pockets. Morissa jumps in to Everett armed and jumps up and down.

Morissa: "Oh my god we won did you see that. Did you ever see anything better?"

Everett: "No I never seen anything better then what I was watching. Thank you."

Morissa: "That was such a rush of fun."

Everett: "What do you want to do next mis big time?"

Morissa: "I don't know. Could we do it again. What could we bet on next?"

Everett: "How about we stop and get some lunch Mis lucky."

Morissa: "I don't know. I may be on a winning streak now. I don't want to cool off."

Everett: "You will be alright for a while. I am getting hungry lets go get some lunch and we can come up with a plan to take this place down. How about it. We will be doing them a favor letting them stay open for another hour or so. Then we will come back and brake them."

Morissa: "Ok. Let us go out in the sun and walk the board walk and talk about the things we could buy. We could eat some fast food and sit on the beach."

Everett: "Ok let's go."

On the beech Everett and Morissa are eating some deli sandwich and drinking bottles of coke.

Everett: "Ok Mis big time winner what are you going to do with that money you won. Just think of all the things you could do with it. You could buy a new wardrobe. You could buy a car. There are a lot of things you could do with that money?"

Morissa: "It isn't just mine Everett, it is ours. Yours and mine. I want both of us to have it. I will give you half win we cash it in. I want us both to enjoy it."

Everett: "Morissa I have what I want. I have you. I don't need the money. If you gave me the money, I would just gamble it a way."

Morissa: "Come on Everett have some fun. You could come up with something fun. I could give it all to you and you could by a car.

Then get your license. We could have normal boy girl dates. You can pick me up and drive me to dinner. Then we could make out like normal people do on boy girl dates."

Everett: "Sounds like fun to me. A car is just a problem I don't need. My life is working just fine. I have my restrictions. If I change, I could go back to spending more than I have. Let's keep me simple. The best way to do that is for you to have the money."

Morissa: "That is sweet of you. What would you do if you could do something with the money? Think about it Everett."

Everett: "If I had that money when that bar was being sold. It would have help to put a down payment on it. I think that would have been fun. Morissa if I did that, we would have been on different sides of the country. Who knows how are relationship would have worked out?"

Morissa: "Everett I would like to think that we would still be in the same relationship. Everett, you graduate this spring. We haven't talked much on what is going to happen. Do you plan on going back to California?"

Everett: "Yes Morissa. If I use the money, I will get from my father to live at school with you after I graduate. I may not be able to open my own place."

Morissa: "You could take the money we won to day and start your own place back in California."

Everett: "I think I would have a better chance to succeed there. My father and mother would help to get people there. I will have my father closer for his advice. He knows how to make money."

Morissa: "I want to finish school where I started. I would mis you Everett."

Everett: "You can come and see me on your breaks."

Morissa: "You could come and see me. I would like that a lot Everett."

Everett: "I would if I could. We will have to see what I will be doing."

Morissa: "Plans. I wish we could make some real plans. It would be nice to have that peace of mind on what are future would be together."

Everett: "let's keep it simple for the next couple of days. It is just you and me and the love we have for each other."

Morissa: "You mean you and me. You and me and the love we have for each other with the money we have. You could never forget the money."

Everett: "Your right the money. You know most people have to worry about money coming between them. You want to give it to me, and I want you to keep it. So young are we and we have the problem of too much money. What would the old folks say?"

Morissa: "Our old folks. I could tell you what my father would say. First, I should tell you something about my father. Or something about what my father was at one time. Everett if you're wondering why, I never said much about my father. I will tell you now if you would like to hear it."

Everett: "Yes. Please Morissa tell me."

Morissa: "My father was the best. I loved my father so much. I can't imagine how hard it was raising a girl. All the things' fathers have to worry about raising and protecting girls. It was puberty for me and hell for him, I am sure. As far as the girls my age I was a good kid. I never had any school problems. I never had any really steady boyfriends.

My few dates had me home early by my choice. The only bad boy I dated was you, Everett. When you told me, you gamble I instantly thought of my father. Everett you may not believe this my father was a bookie at one time. He also took numbers for a group of people. Yes, a bookie and number taker. He made a nice living off of young men gamblers like you. He had to leave the state troopers when they found out. When I see him again and tell him I have fallen for one of those young male gamblers. Then I will tell him about the money we just won. I can't wait to see the look on his face."

Everett: "I would have never guessed that. Your father a bookie. Those guys did make a lot of money off of me. Now I am dating one of their daughters. How nice."

Morissa: "Everett I am not any consolation prize for you. It is just the way it worked out."

Everett: "I know. It is funny at some level. I will try not to sink to that level."

Morissa: "Yes you would be smart not to go too that level of your male ego Everett."

Everett: "Right."

Morissa: "These sandwiches are pretty good don't you think so."

Everett: "They are. They are fresh. They are not mass produce. The meat on them is all meat with no artificial ingredients. The muster isn't left over condiment from a past day when they couldn't sell it. The bread was baked last night. I am very impressed with this sandwich. How is yours?"

Morissa: "Are you kidding me. It is a deli sandwich. To me it just another sandwich. How could you even start to think of those things? How do you even know you are correct? It could just be a simple good sandwich."

Everett: "It is something I do. Everything I eat I analyze. I been doing it my whole life. When I was young, my mother ask me to stop doing it. I was doing it so much she got tired of it. I used to do it with my friends. Then they got tired of it. I been trying really hard not to do it around you. Some will analyze a movie. I just do it with food."

Morissa: "That is a flaw I never heard of. If I dated someone who over analyze a movie, I may think of it as cute at first. After a while I would be asking them to shut up and let me enjoy the movie. Everett if you told me that when I met you. I would have thought of you as weird. Now that I know you, I understand it. It is just the way you are. I like the way you are."

Everett: "Morissa when do you think we get to the point. Where we can say we know everything about each other. There must come a time in a relationship when that happens. Every time we talk there is something new, we tell each other. Or we find out even more about each other."

Morissa: "I like that, Everett. The more I find out about you the more I like you."

Everett: "What do you want to do with the rest of the day Morissa? Then we have to make plans for tonight."

Morissa: "I was thinking we just stay in are room and mess up the bed again. What did you have on your mind?"

Everett: "The bed part I was thinking of. I think we should have a nice dinner and see a movie. We should do those things that we couldn't do at school.

Let's be a couple and enjoy this time together. It could be a while before; we get to do this again."

Morissa: "Ok sounds good to me. I finish my sandwich. Let us do some window shopping together then come up with a plan of how to spend the money you won."

Everett and Morissa start there slow walk up the board walk and the shops in the different casinos. They talk about what they would like to buy. They talk about what they need to buy. There some talk about what movie they should see. They talk about where and what they would like to have for dinner. Accouple of hours later they are in an elevator going back up to their room. Morissa has a small shopping bag with some sea shells a local kid was selling. The two saw nothing that they wanted to buy. On the elevator Everett and Morissa are joined by a man in his fifties in a black and white suit. He starts a conversation with Everett. His name is Tony Perri.

Mr. Perri: "Hello Everett and Morissa it is nice to meet you. Let me introduce myself to you. My name is Tony Perri. I am the part owner and manager to this casino. I hope you two are enjoying our casino and the hospitality we are showing you two."

Everett: "It is nice to meet you sir. We are having a nice time. Mr. Perri"

Mr. Perri: "How about you Morissa. I hope you have found everything up to your standers."

Morissa: Yes, everything is so nice and the people here have been so nice to us. When we arrive here, they changed our room to a sweet. Like Everett said everybody has been so nice. We even won a lot of money. Thank you very much."

Mr. Perri: "Yes I heard. I was told how much you won. I am very happy to see such a young couple win so much. It made me and the other people of management very happy. I hope you give us a chance to win some of it back. We would like to pay for some of those upgrades and perks given to you. There is a cost to run a place like this."

Morissa: "Yes Everett and I were talking about some of what we were going to do with the money. We may not do much gambling. We think we won enough."

Mr. Perri: "That is sad to here. We would like to see you have some more fun. Oh, by the way Everett I was the one who received the call from your father asking for the comp and perks we have given you. You can tell him that we are pleased to help out him and his partners."

Everett: "Yes sir. I understand. I will tell him. Thank you for everything."

Mr. Perri: "We are at my floor. This is where I get off. I will say good bye for now. I will be by when you check out. Please have fun and good bye for now."

Everett and Morissa say good bye to Mr. Perri as he gets off the elevator. The two go up to their room and Everett and Morissa start to talk.

Morissa: "That man Mr. Perri was so nice to us."

Everett: "We have a problem here Morissa."

Morissa: "What problem Everett."

Everett: "It is what that manager Mr. Perri said."

Morissa: "He said have a nice time."

Everett: "It is the money we won. We won way too much."

Morissa: We won too much, what is too much. We could have lost too much. That is the game that is played here. We could win or lose. Win or lose you got it. We won I hope that works for him. It works for me."

Everett: "We have to give it back. We need to do that before we leave."

Morissa: "Give it back are you crazy. Give it back. No problem I will just go down there and hand the chips back to them and say thank you for being so nice. I didn't realize that we had to pay for their niceness."

Everett: "Please do not get upset. Let me explain it to you. My father. His company use this casino to entertain customers. There is some work my father does for this place. That is why we got the meal and sweet. They know that people our age don't have enough money to pay for our room. People our age don't have enough money to spend on gambling here. They are going to lose enough money on us staying here and not paying for the room."

Morissa: "What do you think we should do?"

Everett: "Morissa I think we should go back to the casino and lose almost what we won. Then over tip the people who are so nice to us. We can't leave here with any more than we had when we walked in here."

Morissa: "I don't believe this. We won it fair and square. Now we have to give it all back. This is crazy."

Everett: "It isn't anything that I would have dreamed of doing. Tonight, we will have a nice dinner together. Then we will go in to the casino and play with all the money we won. If we get lucky by tomorrow morning we will be back to even."

Morissa: "Sounds like fun. Sounds like we are throwing in the towel before we even take to the ring."

Everett: "We are going to take one for the team. I think it is something we should do. My father's connection gave us this couple of days. What the casino would charge a normal guest for what we are getting for free would be more then we could pay. Someday we may be glad we did this."

Morissa: "It makes sense. I don't want you to do something that you don't want to do. I understand that it is your father and his business relationship that is paying for are time here. How do you suggest we give the money back? I don't think they get many people who want to give the money they won back. It will look strange if we walk up to the cashier cage and give them back all the chips, we won Everett."

Everett: "We are going to give it back the old fashion way. We are just going down to the floor and lose it."

Morissa: "Lose it. Are you kidding me?"

Everett: "Let me think about this. When we have dinner, I will tell you how we are going to do it."

Morissa: "Dinner. What should we do till then?"

Everett: "Give me that do not disturbed sign and I will make sure the door is locked."

Dinner. Everett and Morissa. They are at a table eating at a steak house. It is about eight at night. Everett is in dress black pants and a white button-down shirt. Morissa is dressed in mid-thigh high white dress with white pumps. She is not wearing the hazel green jewelry that Everett bought her.

Everett: "I like this steak it is very good. Some times when I ask for my steak to be well done it comes back with some red in it. Places like this who specialize in steak know how to cook a steak the way people ask for it."

Morissa: "I am starting to learn more about you Everett. You did do what you said you do."

Everett: "I am glad you're starting to learn about me. I hope you like what you are learning about me. I do have to ask you what is it that you are learning about me that you like."

Morissa: "You just analyze the food you are eating."

Everett: "One day you may want to sit at a different table from me. Then you won't have to hear me. My parent ask me to do that a couple of times."

Morissa: "Your kidding me. How could your parent ask you to sit at a different table? That is awful."

Everett: "You're right I am kidding you. They did threaten me if I didn't stop analyzing what we were eating, they would do it. They never did it."

Morissa: "Oh you poor boy. I could just see your sad little face. The only child. The only child who was so mis understood. I wish I could have been there. I would give you a nice hug and maybe a kiss to make you feel better."

Everett: "Depending on what age I was, that would have worked."

Morissa: "Yes I think it would of."

Everett: "What was it like for you being an only child. Did you wish for another brother or sister?"

Morissa: "It couldn't have been any different then what it was like when you were a kid."

Everett: "Morissa we have to talk about what we are going to be doing tonight. Back in the room I was thinking how we are going to walk out of here with the same money we came in with."

Morissa: "I am sorry to hear I didn't have your full and undivided attention back it our room. The whole time I thought you were just thinking of me."

Everett: "I am still thinking about you. I will be thinking about you for the foreseeable future. Let's get back to business."

Morissa: "Ok business first. We play later poor boy."

Everett: "I was thinking of playing blackjack. I understand the game enough to lose at it without making it like I want to lose."

Morissa: "I am sure that make sense on some kind of sherlock level. But can you please explain it to me and make it somewhere simple so I can understand it."

Everett: "We cannot go up to the casher cage and just give the money back. If we play the slot or roulette there is that chance, we could win even more money by sure unlucky luck. Blackjack a person can lose a lot more real fast. I will find a table with a couple of people who know what they are doing, so I don't draw any attention. In a couple of hours, I could be poor again."

Morissa: "It sounds ok to me. It make sense to me. What will I be doing in the mean time?"

Everett: "You will go back to the same bar as the one last night where you met Bob. Maybe Bob will sweep you off your feet this time."

Morissa: "Your kidding me right. I am Eighteen and I have seen enough of Bobs in my life. There is always a Bob around the corner. If he isn't telling you how smart he is. He is telling me how much money he has. Or those great stories of some over exaggerated made-up event.

I am waiting for the days when the Bobs are telling me there wife don't understand them. I will know that I have reach the time when I heard it all.

Everett: "I guess it just comes with being a good-looking female in a world of us Bobs. Your life is so hard being so good looking."

Morissa: "Don't play that with me poor, poor boy Everett. You know you are a real good-looking guy. I am sure you reached a point in your young life when you found out how much the girls liked you. I am sure that put a smile across those ultra-bight whites of yours. I could see you the day after you found out about the facts of life. A young Everett in a candy store of girls with his pocket full of money. You just looking around at all the candy. What is a pretty boy to do? What did you do when you found out your looks were like a pocket full of money at a candy store? Please tell me."

Everett: "It didn't happen like that. When I was young a little before puberty it wasn't easy for me. I was small for my age. I just went thru a hard time in my life. I just wanted to be left alone. I didn't want to talk to anybody. Everything I try to do was so hard for me. When I turned fifteen it change for me. I grew in to this body. Everything started to get easier. I could talk to anybody. I saw the kids my age now having a hard time. I learned that we are all the same. I am glad if you like the way I look. I am more often thinking about doing the right things at the right time. Morissa, I think everybody has a calling in their life. Most people hope that they can recognize it when it happen. We all hope we react the right way or do the best we can do. We don't think about the consequences of failing in that one moment of a life's calling. If you fail to do or react the right way in your life's calling. The payment for the wrong choices will have you thinking the rest of your life about being wrong.

You could do anything after that. You could achieve anything after that. It will never mean what it should."

Morissa: "Come back to me Everett. I think we were talking about something else. I was just trying to have some fun with you. You started talking about life's calling. I missed that. Could you go pass go and start that again for me please."

Everett: "I guess. I guessed I just got carried away. I was enjoying my time with you. I didn't think I could be as happy as I am with you. Simple as I am just happy, I can be with you."

Morissa: "I think there was something in their someday you can explain it to me."

Everett: "Let's just say there are things we will find out about each other that we don't know now. Over time we will come to learn more about each other and still be surprised that we didn't know those new things."

Morissa: "See that middle age couple over there. Do you think they know everything about each other at this point in their life?"

Everett: "No I don't think so. People grow and change as they live their lives. There are times you are surprise at some of your thinking. Or maybe some of the new things that you find yourself doing."

Morissa: "Let's have some fun Everett. I want to play a game."

Everett: "We will be back up in the room before you know it."

Morissa: "That isn't what I was thinking about. I want to play a different game. It is a game where you look at the people at a table near our table.

You have to come up with the best story of the two people. You have to give them names then why they are here. What are they doing here? The couple has to be a man and a woman."

Everett: "What kind of game is that. I never heard of it."

Morissa: "I made it up as a kid. Being the only child, I would be bored when I went out with my father. I came up with this game. I had a couple of girl friends who used to play it with me. The stories we would come up with."

Everett: "So sweet so shy. I could only imagine what you could come up with. Sounds like fun. I never played this game before so I will pick the couple out. Then you have to go first with who you think they are and what you think they are doing. Then I will take a turn."

Morissa: "It doesn't work like that. The rule is we flip a coin over who gets to go first."

Everett: "I don't have any coins on me. And my mother has always told me that ladies go first. I would hate to tell my mother I didn't let a lady go first. If I didn't tell you my mother does like you. My father will like you I am sure"

Morissa: "You think you are so clever don't you. You came up with that really fast didn't you. Ok you win the line up; I will go first mister chivalry. I will go first. I will give you a couple of minutes to look around and pick a couple.

Everett looks around at the different people sitting around the place. There are older couples, middle age people and some younger couple a little older than them. Some of the people looked married. Some people look like they had financial security. Most of the people looked like they would like to win some financial security. Then he sees a young couple about ten years older than himself and Morissa.

The man is about thirty and the woman is about twenty-eight with just average good looks. The man is dressed up in his cleanest low-cost daily clothing. The woman has red hair and the look of someone who has been shy her whole life. He found the subject of the game.

Morissa: "I see two people out on their first date. The young man ask the young woman out to the date. There is a story on how he did it. There is a story on where he first met her. He couldn't ask her out the first time he saw her.

The first time he saw her there was something about her that he liked. He found something about her being attractive that he wanted to be her boyfriend. There is the better story in what he saw in her. He has been looking for that special person. Something more than those exotic face that cover those girls that cover a skin magazine. He doesn't date much. He wants her to be the love of his life.

He is a single guy that lives alone. His work is that of a manual type a truck driver I would say. Makes enough money to show the young woman a nice date. I think he is so shy he had to come up with a way to ask her out. He probably had asked other females out without much success. He may even scare a few of them off. He had to be careful with this one. This one could be scared off really easy. He finds the place where she works. I put her in a place where different people come and go. Once he found the place where he could approach her, a plan would have to be made on the method to meet her.

The easiest thing for him to do is sit outside the place where she worked and see if he could find her schedule of her coming and going. When he has the information of her times at work, he would plan the timing of going in to her place of work to be notice. Then the days of him going in and just happen to be in the place she is at the right time.

His name is Richard

The Female

Eventually she notice this guy coming in at the same times she is working.

The occasional hi from a man who taken care to notice her, with a smile and a nice greeting of a hello. Not to many man come in here and have given her the attention shown by him. The first day she notice him is just a lost day with no real date to be remembered. Then the realization by her that he is interested in her. Could there be something with this guy. Could he find me attractive? Is he planning to ask me out? How is he going to do it? When is he going to do it? What will I say when, and if he does?

The Man

To many times I have gone in to this place. Everybody in there must know my face by now. Somebody must have caught on to my timing of always coming in there when she is there. What day to make that move. The place where it could be done. The place can't have anybody else around. Every time I go in it is the hope to find that place where the best chance for an easy right time. The hi and hellos are now coming easier.

 A smile back from her. A hello how are you today are the long conversation of two people who really don't know each other.

One day he finds the young woman alone in a place with nobody around. He walks up to her and says hello. The hello comes back to him. The timing is now or never for him.  Then the line to her "did I see you at an event." She tells him "it wasn't her." Then the line "could I have your phone number maybe we can go out?"

She will run and get a yellow piece of paper to write her phone number down. He goes home with a smile on his face. A major life accomplishment.

He calls her a day later and the two work out a date. They are here on their first date. They hit it off and find that they really like each other. They like being with each other more than anybody else. Fun times and lots of dating. They met each other families and become a romantic couple.

Then the realization there are some parts of their life they do not want to share with the other person. There life forward with the other may not be the best path. The difficult decision to stay together. Maybe there is another love that a waits. Is there more. Is there something out there that makes a person wonder if they found the right person.

The break up. The two will go there different ways. The dates will stop. The just you and me will end. Then the tale of the break up.

Accouple of years later the female who remembers the relationship will give her first lover the call. Before long the two are back to being a couple. They both have mature and learn patience. The engagement. The budget that has them making decision for the next ten years of their life. The marriage with the families from both side are at hand. It is all about them. The best day of their life is over. The next years of their life starts.

Goods days are far more than any bad days. The years of work and the lack of any production of children will be a price to be paid later. The lack of support for the other one has begun. Its two people living there life together a part. The days of work for the companies that supply the pay check go on.

The interest he has found in any kind of entertainment has taken its payment on her patience and sense of being desired. Sleeping in separate beds has come between them. The tale they have to tell the relatives will be a sad tale. The lawyer and who is to be the one holding the legal payment. Then the life of I wonder how the other person is getting along.

They may run into each other years later. It will be how's the family doing. It was nice to see you take care. The conversation, The plans that were once made. Have past to that long ago occasion of life. Then the news from a former family member that the other love of their life has passed away. They had their romance that was everything to them. He found the love of his life. He couldn't find the freedom of the distraction that means for sakes all others. All others are not only people. All other is anything that will be a temptation in a bond between two people.

It is a sad story. As I look at them that is what I see. Not everybody can have happy for ever after. We all want that happy ever after. We all want that right person. We want that person to be there when we need them. There are so many things that happen in relationship that can end it.

 Right now, today I am thinking she is trying to get to know about him. She will need the information for her family. I would bet she goes to college looking for a degree. She is safe with him. He doesn't look like someone who will try and have sex on the first date.

He is trying to be as nice as he can be for her. He will ask her about her family. He knows what she does for a living. That is where he asked her out. The question she will have for him will be what he does for a living. A good living, she hopes. The clothes have already told her no such luck. Then where he lives. Not at home is her guess. No girl likes to meet a guy who lives at home with his mother.

I was happy to see you live with your mother Everett. It put me at ease with you.

After they leave here, he will take her home. Then the promise of another date. They make plans for a more fun date. He gives her a kiss good night in the car. He gets out of the car and walks her to her door. Then a longer good night kiss."

In side she will tell her mother what a nice date she had. She will see him again. Then the break down to her mother of what she learned about him. He goes home alone to his small rented place. It was a date for him. A long time between dates for him. He falls asleep thinking about the female that he will now have a second date with. The questions of the people at work asking him what his life is like will now have an answer. An answer of a date with a female. That is all that needs to be said. The times of telling people he didn't have a date was over. He will not be sitting outside her place of work looking for the chance to meet her and ask her out again.

Her name is Jean

That is my story of those two. You will have to beat that story about those two. If you can't make it as long you lose. If you tell me something that can't be possible you lose. Tell me something I said you lose."

Everett: "I can't even try to do that. You won. Would you let me concede victory to you? I could tell you the second part to that story I read to those kids at the hospital."

Everett tells Morissa the second part to the story from the hospital.

## Chapter Seven

Fun

Later that night Everett is at a blackjack table. Morissa is at the bar drinking seven up soda and talking to a couple of business man.

At the blackjack table. A female dealer name Jan. A man in his early forties wearing a white button-down dress shirt and blue jeans. On his left side sits a blonde woman in her early-twenties wearing a blue tube dress. Everett looks around at all the other black jack tables. He picks that table because there were only two people sitting at the table. He takes the chair next to the young lady. He says hello to the young lady and the man next to her. They return the hello. Everett puts a couple of hundred dollars of chips in front of him. The man on the other side of the young woman introduce himself as Kurt to Everett. Then Kurt introduce the young woman as his daughter Alice.

Everett: "Nice to meet you and your daughter. My name is Everett. I hope you don't mind me having a seat at your table."

Kurt: "No I don't mind. May be you will bring us some luck. This wonder woman whose name is Jan is taking all are money. May be you can distract her so we can win back some of the money she has been taking from us. Do not let her looks fool you she has the heart of a lawyer at a contract signing. It is those young females with those pretty smiles that will be the down fall of mankind."

Alice: "Stop dad. She is just doing her job. It is all you guys of mankind, that want those pretty smiles to be your down fall. Don't you agree Jan."

Jan: "This young man Everett. is what we want man kinds face to look like. If you ask me."

Alice: "I am glad I asked you Jan. I was thinking something like that."

The dealer starts the games of blackjack. The conversation among the four start.

Kurt: "Everett can I ask you what you do for a living."

Everett: "I do school for a living. Full time student. I graduate in June I will have to find a job then."

Alice: "Same here I graduate in June. I hope to find myself in the movies someday. What do you think of that dad?"

Kurt: "I hope you do find yourself in the movies. Then when you make a small fortune, you can pay me back the big fortune your school cost me."

Alice: "No chance dad. I make it I keep it. You may have better luck here at this table then me paying you back. Don't get me wrong dad I will always love you. You are my most favorite guy."

Kurt: "Thank you dear. You were always my favorite, only child."

Everett: "Alice if you do not get in the movies what would you like to do when you finish school."

Alice: "I will become a lawyer. I will be an agent for a movie star or athlete. With the right connection I will be the agent for a talented person that signs the next big contract. Then I can make my living off someone who is more talented than me."

Everett: "You do have the looks of somebody in the movies. You may want to think about modeling. I hear some of those models make more than most athlete".

Alice: "Thank you Everett. I do appreciate that complement. Believe it or not. I have done some modeling. Most of the work I have had, was the back ground person in the picture. I even had one no lines extra part in a tv show. No call backs yet."

Everett: "It could happen for you. You just may have to be in the right place at the right time. You just may have to meet the right person who has some connections."

Alice: "Thank you for that cheerful outlook. What do you think about that dad? I may just have to meet someone with a connection. Do you think I could find someone with the right connection?

Kurt: "I would like to meet some connection with the right cards. I am losing my shirt. Everett don't worry about my daughter. She is set to inherit a small fortune from her grandfather. My father will leave her a nice check. She will be looking fill her time with whatever career she will fall into."

Alice: "Thanks dad. My biggest fan."

Kurt: "Everett have you thought about going out west and trying to get in to the business. You could find a part in something doing something?"

Everett: "No. I am from California that is not what I want. I saw a lot of want to be come and go. I haven't met anybody who made it. I Lived there my whole life and don't even have one autograph from anybody. You think I would have seen anybody who has something to do in Hollywood. I can't give you a name of anybody I have seen. Acting is not a job for me. No interest in it."

Alice: "What do you think Jan. Do you think this good-looking man here on my left could be a leading man?"

Jan: "I do. I am sorry he isn't very lucky at this game tonight."

Alice: "I think Everett can get lucky any time he wants. I could see Everett as a batman super hero. Quiet and shy on the outside. Then when his talents are needed the cape goes on and the man of steel goes into action. Mister hero I call him. He can rescue the beautiful leading female from the clutches of any evil producer. What do you think about that dad? Sounds like something to me."

Kurt: "Alice you have your heroes cross. Batman and the man of steel are two different people."

Alice: "Not in my heroes. You know what I mean Jan."

Jan: "I do. I see him as the next secret agent."

Alice: "I would like to find a secret agent. Then have him work on my secrets"

Kurt: "Everett, I think you found two fans."

Everett: "The dealer is smiling at me, and winning more than I am."

Kurt: "What do you plan on doing after you finish school Everett."

Alice: "Dad may be Everett does not know what he wants to do. You can't ask him that."

Everett: "I want to cook. Someday open up my own place. I am going to school to learn about the business."

Alice: "What do you think about are super hero now Jan. A man who can cook."

Jan: "I like him."

Kurt: "Everett I don't think the dealer likes you enough."

Everett: "Yes I think you are right. The night is still young. Maybe my luck will change before I leave."

Looking at Alice then Everett."

Jan: "I think the cards or love may find Everett by the end of this night."

Kurt: "Alice I think Everett wants the cards more."

Alice: "We all have are wants when it comes to luck. Everett what else can you tell me about you."

Everett: "Not much else. I like to bet more then I should. I have been doing good this year on not betting. I don't win enough at betting on sports. I was hoping to change my luck here."

Kurt: "Everett if I didn't know better, I would think you are trying to lose as much money as fast as you can."

Everett: "Wouldn't that be funny. If I was trying to do that."

Jan: "You never know when somebody's luck will change at this game. Everett, I seen people lose more then you and come back and win a lot more."

Alice: "That is right Everett you could end up winning it all back. Then have more then what you came in with. You could leave this table with your hands full.

Kurt: "Where do you live in California Everett.?

Everett: "I live with my mother on a beach in Los Angeles. I have a summer job as a life guard during the summer."

Alice: "Do you hear that Jan we were right about him. He is shy and honest enough to tell us he lives with his mother at night. Then at day light he trans forms in to a hero. He is a hero in a pair a swimming trunks. Please tell me Everett how many females do you get to rescue a day."

Everett: "It is a good day when I don't have to rescue anybody."

Kurt: "Did you ever lose somebody?"

Everett: "I been a life guard for six years. I been lucky. I need a drink anybody see a waitress.

Kurt: "Let me buy. I am back to even since you started to play. Alice is holding her own."

Kurt calls for a waitress and buys Everett and Alice a drink.

Everett: "Thank you for the drink. I am not down as much like it looks. I won a lot before. I am just killing some time."

Alice: "killing time? Killing time for what. Are you meeting somebody later?"

Everett: "Yes. I am meeting my girlfriend later."

Kurt: "You have an expensive way of killing time Everett. You could go play the slots and slow the cash hemorrhage a bit."

Alice: "Girlfriend. You and a girlfriend, great. I am sure she is a doll. Let me guess is she a model. Maybe I have met her. Jan too bad, he has a girlfriend."

Jan: "I am engaged."

Alice: "A course you are. The ring on your finger. I didn't notice. I don't look to see if females are wearing rings. It is just the men. Good for you. I never had the honor of being ask. Everett, are you engage to your girlfriend? Or is it my business."

Everett: "No. just friends still."

Alice: "I hope to meet her before the night is over. You will introduce her to me."

Everett: "We are to meet here later."

Kurt: "You may want to slow up on the betting. When, or if you tell her how much you lost. That could be a problem."

Everett: "I will be ok. Like I said before. We are up for the day."

Alice: "Your lucky to have a girlfriend so understanding. If my boyfriend lost as much as you do, I don't think I would be so understanding. She must be a princes."

Everett: "I like her. Alice is your boyfriend here."

Alice: "I am currently boyfriend less. Somewhere in that place I live. Somewhere in that place I reside. In between the last one and the next one. That lucky place of spending my time as available to the next person who will be the temporary current one. No ring just those short time space with that thought of who is next."

Kurt: "Everett please excuse my now twenty-one-year-old daughter. The twenty-one-year-old who still a preteen drama queen. She has had a little too much to drink today. She and her last boyfriend broke up last week. I took her here hoping she would move on. She will be back to her self tomorrow with any luck."

Alice: "Thank you daddy. Anything else you would like to tell him about me daddy."

Kurt: "Sorry about this Everett. I think my daughter is the greatest kid a father could have."

Everett: "I am enjoying sitting and talking with you two. It is making the time go by."

Alice: "If you two will excuse me. I have to go to the drama queen room and powder my drama queen nose."

Everett stands up as Alice gets up. Alice pauses for a moment as Everett does this. Everett and Alice are face to face.

Alice kiss her finger tips then plants the kissed finger tips on the side of Everett's cheek. Everett watches the twenty-one-year-old single woman in a blue tube dress seductively walk away. Everett is caught staring at the walk of Alice. The voice from Alice father brings him back to the present."

Kurt: "It is your turn. I could see you have to make that decision of to hold what you have or risk it for the thought of something that you hope is better. By The way. The cards are in front of you."

Everett: "Yes the card game. I will hold my hand. I will keep what I have."

Kurt: "Good move. Not every female is the queen of hearts."

Everett: "You are lucky to have a daughter who will still go out with their father. The girls I know wouldn't want to do it. If they didn't have a date. They would be out with their girlfriends."

Kurt: "We have a great relationship. I always give her anything she wants. I just can't give her what she wants now. She wants to meet the right guy. That is out of my hands. If I could do it, she wouldn't like him."

Everett: "If you don't mind me saying. Your daughter has nothing wrong with her looks."

Kurt: "As her father I appreciate the way you phrase that. I know my daughter is an attractive woman. She is enough to keep a father up at night. Do you have any sisters?"

Everett: "No I wasn't lucky enough to have a sister. Just a brother. My mother would have loved a daughter. Somehow she endured me."

Kurt: "From what I see of you your mother did a nice job of raising you."

Everett: "Thank you. The next time I see her I will tell her."

Kurt: "What will you do if your plan of cooking after college doesn't work out?"

Everett: "I don't know what I will do. I am not qualified to do anything else. I could play some sport well enough to know. I am not good enough to be a pro and make money that way. As you could see I can't win at a life of gambling. Life guard is a seasonal job at best. My opportunities are limited."

Kurt: "My daughter dream is to become an actress as you can tell. She has been told to start training on an off-Broadway play. She doesn't want to do the work unless there is a big enough stage for her ego. Have you thought about acting?"

Everett: "No. I have no interest in it. I am sure my mother would love to tell her friends that I was in a movie. Like I said no interest."

Kurt: "Everett I know something about people who make it in the business. If you want to act you have to want to be an actor. There those exemption in life. Those exemption have something us mere mortals don't have. They have a personality and a presence about them. Everett, you have that about you. You may not realize that about yourself. I bet that you never a had somebody hate you. You make lifelong friends with just a hello. There are people who come up to you and remember you from years ago.

I would say they have a smile on their face when they see you. You may not remember them. I would guess every female teacher thought of you as their personal pet student."

Everett: "Your close. I can't explain it. It is uncomfortable sometimes. I don't try to be anybody but me. When I was fifteen things change for me."

Kurt: "Why do you think you are the way you are."

Everett: "My parents have material things. I don't want what other guys my age want. I don't want more money then I will spend that day. I don't want much. I lost somebody close to me. There is no material thing that can replace that person."

Kurt: "How about the females."

Everett: "I just try to be nice to them. Then I let nature take its course."

Kurt: "Nature has been good to you, hasn't it?

Everett: "We all have are problems. We all have had bad days. We all have some regrets."

Kurt: "Everett can I ask you if something happen to you. I am very good at reading people. It is like you know your own destiny in life. It is part of what I do for a living."

Everett: "Sir I don't want to be rude. What is it that you do for a living?"

Kurt: "I am a lawyer slash adviser for some well-connected people in the sports and entertainment business. I have to be able to figure people out. Then come up with a game plan for them. A plan for their career in there career. Once a person gets some success they want to reach out and do other things. I help them find a market for what they want to do. That is what I do."

Everett: "That is how your daughter gets her non speaking parts. She has the looks but she lack the talent to do what she wants to do."

Kurt: "You are correct. She has to start near the bottom and work her way up. One day she will want it bad enough to put the work in."

Everett: "I am sure you will help her if you can."

Kurt: "Sure like any father. Everett, I don't tell people exactly what I do. I just tell people I am a lawyer. That is enough to keep them from asking me any other questions. Everett, I think you are a person who has those traits that everybody wish they have. I can help you, Everett. That music channel has a new show that puts people in a house. A couple of single girls and guys your age in a house. They are going to video tape it. They are looking for people to be in it. I can get you a screen test and an interview. I would bet my nineteen sixty-seven. Four hundred cubic inch engine. Triple black convertible firebird with only fifty thousand miles on it, that you would get the part. I love that car. I love that car so much I wouldn't let my only daughter drive it. That is how sure I am you would get a part."

Everett: "Thank you sir. It isn't anything I would want to do. I will graduate in June. I will have to make those decisions I been putting off till I had to make them. I want my own restaurant. I will start at the bottom and work my way up. I know what I want. I just have to make it happen."

Kurt: "You are different Everett. People would give up college to do a tv show. I think that show is going to be something big. That music show is an phenomena and it is just getting bigger."

Everett: "No thank you sir. I am sure. Here comes your daughter."

Alice joins the table. She looks like she had to many drinks. Everett gets up pulls her chair out for her. Alice puts her arms around Everett's neck. She looks in to his eyes. Then she gives Everett a lip kiss on this other cheek. Then Alice looks at his eyes again and takes her seat.

Alice: "What have you two loves been talking about when I was gone."

Kurt: "We were talking about you. What else would we be talking about Alice."

Alice: "Talking about me, oh goody. I hope it was good Daddy. I hope you didn't tell him any stories about me when I was younger."

Kurt: "No Alice I was just telling him that I was looking forward to the day when I walk you down that aisle. Maybe I will get a son-in-law as good as you Everett."

Everett: "Thank you sir. I think Alice will do better than me."

Alice: "A course you would say that. That is almost the perfect response to that awkward question. Very good for you. Everett I been thinking about you since I first saw you. I liked everything about you. I tried to figure you out. I think I did. I can't tell you what I came up with."

Kurt: "Alice I am up enough for tonight. What do you say we go back to our rooms?"

Alice: "Daddy you can call it for the night. I am now just over twenty-one. I will call it a night when my super hero calls it a night. Or when that girlfriend he says he has, shows up to carry prince charming away."

Everett: "Prince charming. I am just the average guy here. I have no castle to carry any princess away to. I don't even have a car to do it with. Like I said I live with my mother."

Kurt: "Well I am done. Jan, I played my last hand here. Here is something for you putting up with us tonight.

Kurt gets up he shakes Everett's hand and tells him to think of his offer. Then he ask Everett to get his daughter back to her room safely. Everett tells Kurt he would do it. Kurt gives Alice a kiss on her head and starts his walk back to his room.

Alice: "I see you and my father have become friends. He trusted you to safely get me back to my room. I would be a little wary of most men to get me safely anywhere. I do think I am looking pretty good in this tight little blue dress. Don't you think this dress is a little tight Everett."

Everett: "You are a sight to see in that dress. I think you are safe as long as you don't leave the cassino. There are enough cameras around. I have a girlfriend somewhere. I am sure she will find me sooner or later."

Alice: "What do you think she will think about me sitting so close to you. I am a little close to you. Then again, we are just playing games here. I don't mean black jack. I was playing first with you. You are playing like you may like me. It is just a game you do around girls. It so people don't catch on to you. Isn't it?"

Everett: "Catch on to me. What is there to catch on to?"

Alice: "Could you tell me about your girlfriend. Please I will bet she is just the most perfect girl in the world. Somebody like you would tell people nothing less?"

Everett: "Perfect no. I like her. I am lucky to have her."

Alice: "That is the perfect answer. I would expect that answer from you."

Everett: "Any time you want to leave let me know and I will walk you to your room. I lost enough for tonight."

Alice: "Everett I have my own room. My father has his own room. You could make me safer if you came in to my room with me later on."

Everett: "If my girlfriend shows up that will not be a good idea for me. You would feel the same way if you were my girlfriend."

Alice: "Everett, you didn't tell me what your girlfriends name was. Please tell me her name."

Everett: "Morissa. Morissa is her name."

Alice: "Nice sounding girl name. It works well. Could you tell me how you two met? Us girls like those kind of things. Maybe someday I will meet someone like you."

Everett: "It may have been in a bar when I saw her. Or it could have been at the beach where I asked her mother if I could have a date with her. I am not sure. She may have a different story."

Alice: "Are you kidding me. You ask her mother. You don't expect me to believe that. You could come up with something better than that."

Everett: "I could understand why you doubt what I am telling you. It does sound like something made up. I guess you would have to be there to understand it."

Alice: "I think I understand why you tell that story."

Everett: "I would like to know where she is. She was supposed to meet me here."

Alice: "I guess I will just have to keep an eye on you till she shows up. I am sure she would want somebody to keep an eye on her good-looking boyfriend."

Morissa is sitting at a bar seat drinking seven up. She is talking to a man in his early twenties. His name is Earl Miller and he is a backup rookie quarterback for the local professional football team.

Earl: "It is nice to meet you Morissa. What brings you in to this place of win something or lose more then something.

Morissa: "I am here with my boyfriend. We came down here together for a couple of days to spend some time away from school."

Earl: "Is it just you two or did you come down with some friends."

Morissa: "Just us two. Me and him. Him and I. We are having such a nice time here. We even won some of their money."

Earl: "I can't remember any body telling me that they won some of the casino money and didn't give it back before they left. You may want to quit while you two are a head. As somebody said take the money and run."

Morissa: "Yes we talked about doing that. There are some other things we have to consider before we leave. It is a little complicated and will not make much sense if I told you. Let's just say we will be happy to leave with what we came in with."

Earl: "It sounds like you have a plan. It is always good to stay with a plan. I made a plan about eight years ago. Last April that plan I made for myself came to a successful payoff. All the work, patience its up and downs worked out for me. As I look back on all the decision I made. There are just a few I would have done differently."

Morissa: "Please tell me what plans you made that worked out for yourself."

Earl: "Let me start by giving you, my name. Then tell me if you ever heard of me. My name is Earl Miller. Every once in a while, my name has made the local paper."

Morissa: "Sorry that name doesn't sound familiar. I don't get a chance to read any of the local papers. If I did maybe your name would sound familiar."

Earl: "My name was even mention on tv and radio from time to time. If you watch the local news, you may have heard of it."

Morissa: "Sorry. No luck Earl. Please tell me what you do or what you did that makes you think I heard your name before."

Earl: "I was drafted last April for the local football team. I was the last player taken in the draft. That made me MR Irrelevant. That is the name attached to the last player taken in the draft. I was working and planning to be an NFL quarterback. I was a backup in college for the number one pick.

Morissa: "Good for you. I have to say I don't follow football at all. My boyfriend and his friends do. I will ask him if he had heard of you. Can I ask you what plans do you have to make to be a quarterback for a football team? I would think that either you are good enough to do it or not. The guys who played for the school I went to were just good enough to play. All they had to do was be better than the back up."

Earl: "There is a little more than just being good enough to make it where I made it. There has to be a commitment to the process. Everything around my life was about me getting to that next level. I had some coaches that gave me some good advice on how to get to that next level. I took there advise and did the work and made the commitment. There are so few professional quarter backs. I am lucky to make it."

Morissa: Do you think you will be the starter one day?"

Earl: "I don't know right now. The starter has been around a long time. Next year is his last year of a contract. The team will have to decide on which way they want to go. You will have to check the news out to see what happens to me."

Morissa: "My boyfriend did play football. He got suspended because of betting. He has the looks of a very good athlete. He told me that he just didn't want to play enough."

Earl: "That is too bad to hear. A lot of guys like to bet on football. You can't play any sport and bet on it. There is no second chance for doing it. What is your boyfriend going to do when he leave school?"

Morissa: "Don't laugh. He wants to cook. What I should say. is he wants his own restaurant? He is making plans for it. He is a very good cook. I think you will be good at anything he does."

Earl: "What about you Morissa what are you going to do when you finish school."

Morissa: "What do you think I am going to do, when I finish school Earl."

Earl: "Without making this a pickup line. A model. You have the look of a successful model. You have the looks."

Morissa: "Thank you. What do you mean successful? I never knew there was a line between a model being successful or not."

Earl: "It is like the pros. We get paid to play. There are people who play some sports and have to pay to play. I get paid. There are good looking women, who are looking to be a model that can't get any work?

They will call themselves a model because that is what they want to do. They have to pay to go from job interview to job interview. A professional model gets paid to go and do her job. I dated both. A professional has a better bank account."

Morissa: "I thank you again. I am not a model. I never model for anything. You are way off. I will give you one more chance to guess what I want to do. I will give you a clue. Like you I have been planning it for a long time.

I have a commitment and a plan. I have listened to some people who gave me some good advice."

Earl: "That game plan sounds familiar. Are you planning to be a backup quarter back for a pro team?"

Morissa: "That is a bad guess. Sorry to say your still not even close. I will give you one more chance. I will give you one more clue. You know at least one person who does what I want to do."

Earl: "You don't give a guy much of a hope to guess anything about you. If I am to guess what you want to do with my last guess. Let me put some facts together for this. You are going to college. You say you are not a model. You have a boyfriend. Your name is Morissa. When all those facts are put together what do I get. Morissa my last guess is a teacher. Morissa, I guess you are going to be a teacher."

Morissa: "You are right. I didn't want you to guess it. You are right how did you guess it. I gave you know real cluse."

Earl: "Morissa there is a term in sports called a Heal Mary play. I will keep the explanation short. A quarter back in a game was down to his last play of a game with no time on the clock. The quarter back had one chance to complete a pass in to the endzone for a touchdown.

Morissa the quarter back threw the ball in to the end zone as the time ran out. As he threw, he said a Heal Mary prayer. The ball was caught by his receiver and he won the game. When the press asked him the question after the game about the throw, the quarter back explain by saying he said a heal Mary prayer when he threw it. Morissa I just threw a Heal Mary to guess it. My mother is a teacher and that was the only career I could come up with."

Morissa: "Earl. I like that, Earl. Yes, that is what I want to do. It isn't like a professional quarter back. I don't need to have your talent. I just need the right classes to get a degree"

Earl: "What do you mean by that."

Morissa: "There are so many teachers out there. Like you said there are so few professional quarter backs. It is easier to be a teacher then a quarter back."

Earl: "Don't sell that job short. You will be doing it a lot longer than any quarter back will be playing. You are going to help shape a lot of young children. My mother has had a lot of kids come her way. There is no sat sheet for what she does. There are kids she will never forget. There are parent she would like to forget. I think she puts in more time in what she does then any player or coach.

Morissa: "I don't sell the job short. I know what it takes. I saw some teachers have a hard time. I think I can do it."

Earl: "That is a good attitude to have. I hope it works out for you.  Maybe you will be a teacher near where I am playing. One never knows what may happen."

Morissa: "May be someday you will call your own heal merry and win that big game. Then when I see your name and face in the papers, I could say I know you. Then I could even tell the kids in my class that I know you."

Earl: "What else can you tell me about yourself Morissa."

Morissa: "Can I ask about You Earl. I would bet you have a girlfriend somewhere. Can I ask you if she is here with you? What would she think about you talking to me?"

Earl: "I am here to meet with my agent. He is trying to land me a commercial. My girlfriend is at her parents' house. If she saw me with you. I think she would trust me. What would your boyfriend think if he saw me with you?"

Morissa: "He would think you were hitting on me. I think he would trust me. What else can you tell me about yourself Earl."

Earl: "There isn't much else I think I can tell you about me, that would be of any interest."

Morissa: "Come on Earl you can't be so one dimensional, to tell me you only play football. You can tell me how you met your girlfriend."

Earl: "That is funny you ask. I met her at a bar."

Morissa: "A bar. Please tell me how you approached her."

Earl: You see that piano over there. I can play the piano. I was playing the piano at a bar one night and she just happen to be there. The rest is history."

Morissa: "That is so nice to hear. That is a nice story a girl could tell her girlfriends on how she met a guy."

Earl: "She told her parents that story when she told them about me. You can relate I would think. How does a girl tell her parent she met a piano player at a bar? Then tell them the guy she meets plays football and wants to be a pro.?"

Morissa: "I understand Earl. Earl, can you do something for me. Can you play the piano for me? Please.

Earl: "I can but first you have to do something for me."

Morissa: "Oh my. Should I be afraid of what you may be asking me to do."

Earl: "No Morissa. Just tell me about your boyfriend. First is your boyfriend the jealous type. The second one is he bigger than me."

Morissa: "I hope he is the jealous type. He is about your size. I think your safe, so long as I don't lay across the piano. Please play it for me. My boyfriend may be at the blackjack table for a while still."

Earl: "Sure. If you promise me, I am safe from him if he finds me playing the piano for you."

Morissa: "Your safe. I promise you are safe."

Earl: "Good. Let's get some new drinks and if you take my arm, we make are way to that Steinway.

Morissa and Earl walk arm in arm to the piano. Earl takes the chair in front of the piano. Morissa stand to the side and looks at the good-looking man about to play a piano for her. Earl starts to go thru some notes.

Morissa thinking to herself. He is a nice guy to do this for me. He is a nice-looking guy. He is like Everett. I never had a guy do anything like this for me. I like him doing this for me. I hope he doesn't think I am trying to find him as a date. I hope he doesn't think that he could have a date with me. He did say he had a girlfriend. I guess I am safe. This is just two people out at a bar. It is harmless. Who am I kidding? I am having a good time with him. I wouldn't be here with him if I wasn't?

When I get back with the other girls. When they start asking me about this trip with Everett do I tell them about Earl. I guess right now it is still a safe story to tell. I am sure it will end as a safe story. I could see why a girl would fall for this guy. I wonder if I met him before Everett what would of happen. I love Everett and he loves me.

I don't get many chances to have some fun like this. This is just fun. I know he will understand. I wonder if he is having fun. Her thoughts are broken up by Earl.

Earl: "Morissa don't stand up there you could have a seat by me. This seat is made for two. I promise I will not bite you."

Morissa: "Ok I can watch you better there. I can see if it is really you playing. Or is it a paper punch playing the piano."

Earl: "What type of music do you liked Morissa?"

Morissa: "Earl surprise me. Did you ask your girlfriend what music she liked? I want you to surprise me."

Earl: "Your right I didn't ask. Let me play something then you can guess what I am playing.

Earl plays some songs on the piano and Morissa does guess them."

Earl: "Nice job Morissa you got them all. You have an ear for music. Do you play any instruments?"

Morissa: "Yes can you guess what instrument I can play."

Earl: "That is not fair if you can play the piano to. Why didn't you tell me?"

Morissa: "You didn't ask. I can get by. You are really good, that is a nice talent you have. Did your mother ever show you off as a kid?"

Earl: "Yes all the time. The other boys being boys used to make fun of me. When I started to play football, my father would show me off. Then I got bigger than those boys who used to make fun of me. I guess it was the shoe being on the other foot or something like that. I loved playing the game of football. I was a very good athlete in college.

I was a good piano player, but I was never better then somebody who loved it more than me."

Morissa and Earl are joined by three middle age guys. Their names are Pat, Jim and Steve.

Jim: "Can we make request here. I guess you are the casino piano player. If you play a song for us, we will appreciate it."

Earl looks at Morissa and winks his eye.

Earl: Sure thing. My name is Earl and I am the new piano player here. It is my first night working here so be kind to me please. This beautiful woman to my side is my friend. Her name is Morissa. She is sitting with me to take the edge off."

Jim: "She looks like she could take the edge off a sharp knife. You are quite the looker there Morissa."

Earl: "Be nice to my friend. You should see her boyfriend. He is the backup quarterback for a Football team. He is as jealous as you can imagine."

Steve: "He is being nice to her. You play for tips, don't you? How come I don't see a tip jar on the piano."

Earl: "Like I said I am new to this. May be one of you two can get me a glass from the bar. Put a buck in it and I will play you a song."

Pat: "I will be right back. I will get you that glass."

Pat goes and gets a glass. He puts a dollar in it and goes back to the piano. He puts the glass on the piano. Pat and Steve are standing on opposite sides of the piano. Earl starts to play the piano and take request.

Steve: "Morissa you really don't have a boyfriend in the next room, do you?"

Morissa: "I really do. And he is a very jealous guy."

Pat: "I don't believe it Steve, or she wouldn't be sitting with the guy playing the piano. Why would a dish like that sit by a guy playing a piano in a bar with a jealous boyfriend?"

Steve: "You have a good point. I think he is her boyfriend."

Earl: "No guys. I am not the lucky guy to be able to call her a girlfriend."

Jim: "Still girls like her will have a guy somewhere."

Morissa: "You sound like you're sure of that. Just because you find me attractive, I must have a boyfriend somewhere. You make it sound so easy for someone who is perceived to be attractive. That does mean that everyone who is attractive has a boyfriend or girlfriend. To have someone you like isn't easy for anybody. To find that right person isn't easy. You could be blessed being attractive. Then be curse not finding someone that likes you as you like them. It isn't that easy guys."

Earl: "I think you guys made her a little mad."

Steve: "Tell me the truth Morissa do you have just one boy friend?"

Morissa: "Yes. Just one really nice guy."

Pat: "Lucky guy."

Morissa: "Yes he is lucky. But not for the reason you may have in that head. If he likes the way I look then I am the lucky one that he finds me attractive."

Pat: "I am lucky then because I find you attractive."

Steve: "I find her freaking hotter than hell."

Morissa: "You are kidding me. Hotter then hell. What does that mean. I don't think I understand that. I know I don't like it."

Pat: "It is just his way to tell you he likes the way you look."

Earl: "You guys would be better to just change the subject."

Steve: "Like what. I don't want to talk about what you're playing."

Morissa: "If you don't like it you could move on. Maybe you can find something that is even hotter than hell elsewhere."

Steve: "I like the side show here thank you."

Morissa: "I hope you don't mean me. I am not the side show for you."

Steve: "Then we are the side show for you. You can just sit there and we can be your entertainment."

Morissa: "How in the world do you think that you two are my entertainment."

Steve: "We are interested in you. That is what I find women like. They like it when guys show interest in them. You are all the same."

Morissa: "What rock did you guys crawl out from under."

Pat: "I think she just said we live under a rock."

Earl: "I warn you two. For as long as I have known her, she hasn't changed. You just don't understand an intelligent woman. They are free to be the owner of how they want to be perceived. The days of a female having her looks valued by us men is over. They are now free to set their own value to judge themselves by. The old days of us lining them up in a line, to give them our top prize of are value is over."

Steve: "I think he just insulted us."

Pat: "What do you want from a bar piano player. This guy will be playing the piano for years to come."

Earl: "Yes you are probably correct about that. I did want to play high school football. But I just couldn't keep up with guys like you three. I will bet you three played all the sports in school. I will even bet you had all the school cheerleaders didn't you."

Steve: "You are right about me. I made the football team. I blew out my knee and was told to stop playing. I could have been good enough to make some college team somewhere."

Jim: "I played golf."

Earl: "How about you Pat. What manly endeavors have you done."

Pat: "Little league baseball. I was the best pitcher. A couple of bad coaches ruin my elbow."

Earl: "That is too bad. I am glad to hear the three of you had the potential of a sports career. Maybe you can tell This young lady what you guys do for a living. In the old days a good job could impress a female. As you said entertain her with what you do. A real man could."

Pat: Not that I need to impress anybody. I am a store manager in a chain of hardware stores. Steve sells cars. Jim sells insurance. We all make a good living. We make more money than a piano player can make here."

Earl: "What do you think about that Morissa. How would you like to be married to a guy with those careers?"

Morissa: "I don't think those careers are hotter than hell. If their wives like them, who am I to judge them."

Earl: "What type of guy would you like to find Morissa. Why don't you tell us?"

Morissa: "Since I was a little girl all I wanted was to marry a quarter back I saw on tv. Those pro quarter back with those broad shoulders is what I hoped to find. That is why my boyfriend is a quarter back."

Steve: "And you criticize us for finding you attractive. I think you just put the shoe on the other foot."

The three guys leave some money in the glass jar and walk away.

A woman in her thirties goes over to the piano and puts a couple of dollars in the jar. Her name is Bell.

Bell: Hello mister piano man. My name is Bell can I ask you to play a real sad song. I just had a break up with a guy I was married with."

Morissa: "I am sorry to hear that. I hope you are ok."

Earl: "Sure no problem how about this one."

Bell: "I am fine now. It is the breaking up that is the hard part. When the divorce is final it gets easier. Once the money is agreed to. Once the kids are put through the ringer and come out the other side. Then when the lawyers are paid you can say it is over.

Then you go out and try to find that freedom that comes with being free. The person you once were before the divorce is gone. It is a new experience no married person should once in their life have. I am here with a couple of other female divorcees having a good time. We are not as young as you Morissa. You may look at me as being a silly older sad woman. I am just looking to enjoy being a single female again."

Morissa: "I understand."

Bell: "Not yet you do. I was once as young as you. I was in love with this guy. The best guy I ever knew. The future was ours. Those fun times we had. The dreams then turned to plans. The wedding and the marriage that we both wanted. The kids we both wanted. We took each other and forsaken everybody else. A happy home we both had. Then the change of who we became. Our wants and needs change. It wasn't his fault his lawyer said. It wasn't my fault my lawyer said. Our kids had it right when they said it was both our fault and not there's. There wasn't anything we could have done we just changed. Some people say change is good. Change in what a person wants after they are married isn't good. Finding an interest in another person isn't good. Finding yourself confiding in other people isn't good. Spending those time feeling sorry for your voids in your life is just the start. Finding that other person to help in feeling sorry for your self is easy. It could be someone to drink with. It could be someone to have sex with. That is just as easy. It is easy to change.

I can't tell you win it first happen. There was one day when his father died. I called him at work to tell him. When he got home, we just had a few words, and he was out the door. He wasn't looking for me to understand or some closeness. A couple of hours later that man just wanted to be left alone. I left him alone and gave him his space.

I think an investigator from the FBI would say that was the start. Any person could see that was a sign. There was other signs that things have changed. I was just looking at those signs along that ever-widening road between us as we drove down that rough road of time.

It was those nights of not feeling like having sex. It was those days then weeks of not having sex. It was thoughts of the last time we have had sex. Then we just started to agree on anything. There was no argument on anything anymore.

When asked about anything from dinner to major family decision was answer by anything you want.

Those family activities had stop. We were just a show of two people who were once in a relationship with each other. Now we were both in a relationship with someone we wish would move on with their life. Then one meaningless simple disagreement, ended up with the words of you are not going to be around here much longer.

The relief of being able to see it was over. Thank god it was going to be over. It was once said let this two be join in gods' eyes. Now I was thanking god that it would end. That one day it would be over. One day we wouldn't have to be together from now and forever.

The guilt of not being able to work out a relationship, that you wish ended earlier. You hoped that the anger you now have was a past memory. The long time it takes for your people and his people to work it out. Why we just couldn't part as close friends. The lawyers had to have a winner and a loser. Both sides had the numbers that would make their side a winner and the other side a loser. The only winners were the lawyers and the banks. One bank gets more money the other bank loses money. Then when you think there isn't anything else to put on a table.

The lawyers will find that last crumb that even a mouse doesn't want.

The money gets worked out. The kids time with whom gets worked out. The freedom get to be real. The real freedom that was never felt before. Feeling young enough to be with other men. The independence to come and go as you please. The ability to have a relationship with a man that has an interest in you. The fun of new people and new places to go. The planning to fill all your free time. Fun at hand is fun to be free of that marriage to that other person you knew so well at one time.

You go out some times and see that older couple. That couple that had children and was able to stay to gather. They stayed committed to each other over all those years. They found each other at family weddings to family funerals. Together they found each other everywhere. What did they do right? How comfortable they are with each other. The second guessing of how much effort should have been given to make it work. Those times when you look in the mirror you know you are alone. No matter what you do for the rest of your life. You know that you failed in a marriage.

The ring that you don't wear. That date that was all about the two of you. That date that used to be called a wedding anniversary. It is just a date that reminds you that of a failure to something that was so important once in your life. The failure of a promise to another person for the rest of your life. The status of being in a number of other people who failed. The thought you had at one time it wouldn't happen to you."

Bell leave some money in the glass and walks off.

Morissa: "All that was interesting. I never thought I would be at a bar in a casino and hear something like that. I think she had a lot to drink. I wonder how often she goes through that in her head. Could you just imagine what is going on in side of that head? The second guessing of anything she is doing is always at hand. I hope that I never get the walk in those shoes. I have a boyfriend and someday that might happen to us that we get married. I often think about it the longer we are dating. I guess that's just what people our age who are dating do. That is the next step in any progression of a relationship. We date to find out if we are compatible with somebody in the hope that we find that person we can marry. I don't want to get ahead of myself too fast sometimes. I just want to enjoy myself with him. I told him I just want to finish school. Then we will have to figure things out when I graduate. He's going to graduate first this June. He doesn't know if he's going back home or if he's going to stay around the school. Long distance relationships are hard. You must be away from your girlfriend from time to time. How hard is it for you?"

Earl: "It isn't easy. You have to be careful of what you do when you are away from that other person. There are places the people I play with go that I can't go. Even though I'm a single guy making a decent living I just stay away from them. I try to find other things to occupy my time away. I do work on my career. I spend a lot of time in the gym. I spend time watching film. There are other players like me who are single. Some of them I think have a girl or two in every other city. I haven't cheated on her. The temptation is always there."

Morissa: "That is nice to hear you say that. My boyfriend is a good-looking guy like you. The girls I know think he is a good-looking guy. He is the kind of guy a lot of girls would like to have. I think I am very lucky to have him. He acts and treats me in a way that makes me like him even more. I have only known him for a short time, but the time has been the best time I have had with anybody. He met my mother, and she likes him. Someday I will have to introduce him to my father. I often wondered what my father would do when I brought home the guy that I love. He has a lot in common with my father. I think my father would like him, but you never know do you.

Earl: "I think about the same things with my girlfriend. I think we will get married one day and be living with my NFL career. For as long as I have one anyway. I have an accounting degree. If I'm lucky I will get a job somewhere where I can make a decent living. Right now, in the short-term future of an NFL player who is making more money than I will ever make in such a short time. I will give a lot of it to my father to invest. That's what he does. With any luck and if he doesn't runoff to Tahiti, I will be all right with money Marissa.

 I have a question for you. Are you going to tell your boyfriend about sitting here with me for so long? I think you should. If you explain to him some of the people we talk to. Then tell him we were pretending to be piano players for the bar he might get a kick out of it. I must leave tomorrow early in the morning and go back home. I would have liked to meet your boyfriend. If you want to see a game this weekend. Just contact the team and give them your name, I will know who you are, and I will get you a couple good seats for you and your boyfriend. Then I will take you two out to a dinner if we could arrange it."

Morissa: "I will tell him about tonight and the other guys who were here.  Maybe not tonight maybe on the ride back to our school. The conversation we just had with Bell. I think he'll get a kick out of that. I will tell my mother. She's a divorced woman and she might have some of the same thoughts that Bell had. If she had those thought she never mentioned them to me. Bell may have had too much alcohol tonight. It could be your sad piano playing just got that woman too emotional. Did you know you had that talent to make those women so emotional with your piano playing? Maybe you missed your calling in life. You could be a piano player that gets all the middle-age women to go to your concert so they can cry over their life and their past lives. If you like I would like to be your agent. Maybe we can clean up with some record money. I could be sitting on the side of you while you're playing. If we can entertain her and those other guys, we may have an act."

Earl: "I could think of all the people we can make a buck off of with you sitting with me. We could be an idea for a movie. A piano player and his charming partner."

Morissa: "I really enjoyed being here with you tonight earl. You are a lot of fun Earl. if I do meet your girlfriend, I will tell her that you are a good man. If I didn't have a boyfriend, I would give you a kiss good night. If you don't mind, I would like to give you a hug."

Earl: "If we ever do run in to each other remember this. I am going to play a song. The name of the song is Every passing heartbeat. Just say the name of the song and I will remember this time with you."

Morissa listens to the sad song then gives Earl a hug and a kiss on the cheek. She thanks him and walks to the casino. Morissa sees Everett sitting at a bar. Next to Everett is an attractive young woman about Morissa age, she is wearing a tight tube dress. She is sitting closer to Everett seat then the other seat on her other side. Morissa walks to Everett's back side. She looks down at Alice then gives her a harmless smile. Morissa walks around to the other side of Everett.

Morissa: "Hello. I hope you don't mind if I take this empty seat by this good-looking man."

Alice: "It is a free world help yourself to any seat. You wouldn't bother me. I could see a lot of other empty chairs around. You could consider going to one of the other chairs. We have this little private conversation going on."

Morissa: "Bartender? What do you say?"

Bartender: "The chair is open. Unless you are over twenty-one, I can't serve you alcohol."

Morissa: "I will not order any alcohol. Could I just take a seat and watch? I see something that I am interested in."

Bartender: "It's a free world. Somebody once said. If the gentlemen and the lady do not mind."

Everett: "My Name is Everett. This lady to my side is Alice. It is nice to meet you what is your name."

Morissa: "It is nice to meet you Everett and your girlfriend Alice. My name is Penny. Alice, you have a nice-looking boyfriend here If you don't mind me saying."

Alice: "We are just friends. If he plays the cards right, you never know."

Morissa: "You two look like you belong together. What do you have to say about that? That lady on your side there is one very good-looking girl."

Everett smiles at Morissa then takes a good look at Alice from head to toe. Then he looks back at Morissa.

Everett: "Yes she is. I think she is way out of my league. I am sure that she has enough guys wanting to be her boyfriend."

Alice: "I am sure Penny can tell you all about the guys that she has calling on her. I don't need quantity. I am the kind of girl looking for quality like Everett. Let me tell you my friend Everett is all about quality. I think that is why we are getting along so well. Everett, don't you think we are getting along."

Everett: "We are. I think you and I are like old friends now."

Morissa: "From where I sit, I can see Everett is just stuff with an overabundance of quality that we as young women would like to have some of. Don't you agree Alice. I bet you can tell me all kinds of stories about all of his qualities."

Alice: "Penny I am surprise at you. You know good girls never talk about such things about the men we know."

Morissa: "Oh please. You know how guys like to have their ego pumped up. I am sure Everett would not mind you telling all those little secrets you two have shared. If Everett was my boyfriend, I would like to show him off."

Alice: "Sorry Penny. What I know about him is all mine. Don't you have a boyfriend here. I find it hard to believe that somebody like you can't find some guy here to entertain you. With all the men here just looking for any female to buy a drink for. They can make you so easy. I am sorry Penny I meant to say it is so easy to find a guy here. You don't want to be here wasting your time with us."

Morissa: "Everett please tell me that I can spend some time with you two. I like being with you two. I think you two make such a nice couple. I can't say the last time I seen a nicer couple."

Everett: "Alice. I think we can let her stay a while. She seems like a nice person."

Morissa: "Thank you Everett. Alice maybe you can tell me how you two met. I hope to meet someone someday and be like you two. The perfect couple."

Alice: "We like to consider ourselves just friends. You may not believe this. I just met him at a blackjack table. I was with my father. Then the next thing I know I was here with him. Maybe you can tell me about your last boyfriend. You have such a nice figure. I could see all the guys who can't find a date drooling all over you like a centerfold. You know what I mean. Why don't you tell me how you met your last boyfriend?"

Morissa: "I don't think Everett would care to hear about that. Would you Everett. I am sure all he wants to hear is what you have planned for him tonight. The way you look in that dress is all he has on his mind. Doesn't she look nice in that dress Everett."

Everett: "Yes she does look nice. I will be thinking of the female next to me tonight. I would like to hear about you and your boyfriend. Alice and I would like to hear about him."

Morissa: "You may not believe it. He met me first. He bumps in to me at a bar. I don't recall him doing it. A couple of months later. Three thousand mile away from that bar he finds me on a beach. Then he swept me off my feet."

Alice: "Really. I think it really did happen like that. That is just too good to be true. You did such a good job explaining it. What do you think about that Everett?"

Everett: "Nice. I would like to think he fell for you when he first saw you Morissa. If he was with another date that night, he went home thinking about you. Every time he saw you at school was hard for him not going up to you and meeting you. Before he knew it you were gone before the school year ended. Seeing you at the beach was his chance to meet you. He found you at the beach. A treasure on the sand. His life was at that opportunity to meet you. He met you and lived that opportunity of his life. I would think he put a x on the sand to mark the spot he met you."

Alice: "Hello Everett what about me. Remember me. I don't recall her saying she went to any school. I had so many guys who wanted to meet me. Just put a skirt on and they will find you. I can't imagine what would happen if I was in a bikini on a beach. Everett, can't you picture me on a beach in a bikini. I will bet you would like that."

Everett: "You are putting a nice picture to it."

Morissa: "Thank you Everett that was very nice of you."

Everett: "You are welcome more, I mean Penny. What do you think about your boyfriend?"

Morissa: "I think he is the best person I ever known. He is kind, nice and so gentle with me. I look into his eyes and I see the person who cares for me. In his voice I hear the music that makes my heartbeat just for him. When he holds me, I know it is him that I love."

Alice: "That is very nice. I hope you find that guy you are talking about."

Morissa: "I did."

Alice: "It is too bad you lost him. Maybe better luck next time. Everett, don't you think we should get back to the blackjack table. That table is for people over twenty-one. Morissa it is too bad you will not be joining us. My friend Everett is behind with a little bad luck. I think his luck is about to change tonight. Everett let's get back to that table. Tell me, Everett do you want to get lucky tonight."

Morissa: "Everett I am sorry you are down on your luck. How much more time will you need to get back to what you walked in with."

Everett: "I am almost there. Another hour may be two at the most."

Morissa: "Then you should go back to the table with Alice. I think she will keep you safe from us desperate females that are looking to find a nice guy like you. Good luck with him Alice, I hope you find what you're looking for."

Alice: "Thank you Penny. Let's go Everett. Let me be your lady of luck."

Everett: "By Penny. You will be the one your boyfriend will want to night."

Everett gets up and takes Penny hand. He kisses it. Alice grabs Everett hand and pulls him toward the blackjack tables."

At the blackjack table. Alice puts her chair right next to Everett. They are the only people at the table.

Alice: Everett what did you think of Penny. I think she was getting too friendly with you."

Everett: "I think that is her just trying to be nice."

Alice: "Nice. You don't know us females do you. I could see she wanted you a lot."

Everett: "Let's talk about you Alice. Can I ask you what is the longest relationship you have had?"

Alice: "Two years. I met him when I turned nineteen. We had lots of fun. I thought he was the guy for me. Then I caught him with a girl friend of mine. They went camping and they hooked up. I didn't think she was his type. They didn't stay together. I think she did it because she could. That is sad to think she would, and he did. I have had guys come on to me when I was dating him. I never cheated on him. There were guys I liked. There were guys I was attracted to. I guess we are just out there trying to find that right person. That person we hope is just ours. To be shared with no one else."

Everett: "You will find that person Alice. I wish you luck with it."

Alice: "Maybe I did Everett. Maybe it is you, Everett. One can never tell."

Everett: "I don't think I am your type, Alice. I am dating someone I do like. I wouldn't do to her, like your old boyfriend did to you."

Alice: "Everett I hate to say this. It is going to make me sound easy. Maybe if you get to know me you will like me. I like being with a good-looking man."

Everett: "Don't sell yourself short Alice. He is out there. The guy who is looking for you is out there. He is some were right now. I can't tell you what he looks like. I can't tell you, his name. He wants to find you. He can't find you if you're with somebody that is not him. Trust yourself to make the right decisions for yourself. I am not the right decision to night."

Alice: "I don't believe what I am hearing. I am being rejected. I must be losing it."

Everett: "You haven't lost anything by the looks of you. You just haven't found that person who is looking for you. It will happen Alice."

Alice: "Thank you Everett. I would like to meet your girlfriend and tell her what a great man she has found. Everett, I think I would tell her what a great person she has. Whoever she is I am sure I would like her."

Everett: "Yes I am sure you two would get along just wonderful. I think you two are different. Sometimes different people do like each other."

Alice: "Can you tell me about her."

Everett: "I like her. I like who she is."

Alice: "Tell me what she looks like. Tell me what she is like."

Everett: "She looks kind. She looks like she cares for me. She has a beautiful heart. Her demeanor is as soft as a rose. Her arms are always warm when she is holding me. She is what I have found because we were looking for each other."

Alice: "Everett my father offered me this trip because I just broke up with that boyfriend, I just told you about. He said I will have some fun and it will get my mind off of him. My father was right I just got over him. Now I must get over you. I am going up to my room tonight. I am going to go up there and have a cry I didn't meet you first. Tomorrow I will pick myself up again and hope what you say will happen for me. I will always remember you, Everett. Good night Everett."

Everett: "I did promise your father I would get you to your room."

Everett walks Alice to her room. Alice gave Everett a kiss good night then walks in to her room alone. Everett walks back down to the blackjack table.

Everett stays at the table till he loses all but two hundred dollars. He tips the dealer with the two hundred and thanks her. On his way back to the bar to meet Morissa he plays a slot machine and wins the two hundred dollars back. Back at the bar Morissa is talking to a woman named Valerie. Valerie is a researcher for a major food brand distributer.

Valerie: "Are you here by yourself Morissa?"

Morissa: "I am here with my boyfriend. We are spending a couple of days here."

Valerie: "Were is your boyfriend If I can ask?"

Morissa: "He is in the casino room trying to lose enough so we can leave here even. It sounds strange doesn't it. That is what he is trying to do?"

Valerie: "You will have to explain that to me. Most people want to leave this place with more than they came in with."

Morissa: "Valerie it is a long story. We did nothing illegal. We are just trying to keep some people who know my boyfriend's family not interested in him. They gave us some comps. We don't want to go to the well and be ungrateful."

Valerie: "I guess you want to leave here not owing anybody anything is what you are saying."

Morissa: "That is what we are doing."

Valerie: "Good for you. You may live to regret it later. You may live to know you did the right thing. When is the boyfriend going to join you?"

Morissa: "When he gets back to even. He has been in there for several hours. I been here waiting for him."

Valerie: "I guess you two are down here away from school. What is your major."

Morissa: "I want to teach. What do you do for a living?"

Valerie: I am a researcher of a major food brand distributer. The pay is good and I get to travel a lot."

Morissa: "What about your husband and children. Don't they mis you?"

Valerie: No husband. No kids. I never been married. I am what you call a career girl. I have done things that only man have had the chance to do."

Morissa: "I am sorry. I shouldn't of ask."

Valerie: "That is ok. Most of the time I have to explain it to the men I meet. It is nice to find another woman to talk to."

Morissa: "I never had so many so-called single guys offering to buy me drinks. Then the offers of lets find a quiet place so they can buy me a dinner. Then those offers that I didn't want to hear."

Valerie: "When you are an attractive female the offers will just keep coming. If your just a female the offers just keep coming. Don't believe that all the offers are from single men. Single or married they are just trying to bed you. It is safer to sit with another female."

Morissa: "Not much different than a college bar. At those college bars I don't have to look out for the married ones. It is hard to tell them apart here. All the married ones should have a sign on their head. The sign should say married keep away."

Valerie: "After I finish school and started this career of mine. I thought the same thing. After a while you see things that will tell you if they are married, single, or just a man who is just looking for someone to talk to. I like those men. They don't want to cheat at that time. They will tell you all about their home life good or bad. Some of them will show you pictures of their kids. I get a little envious of them. They can have a career and kids. I just have a career no kids. I did find some men I really liked. I was with some of them for a couple of years. At the end it was the same ending. You go your way and I will go my way back to work. Bye for now. It does turn it to, I wonder what happen to him. I wonder if he was the right one. I wonder if I should have slowed down enough to be caught long enough for them to put a ring on my finger. I did have some men ask the question. I felt like I would be settling if I said yes to them. There was this one guy I wanted to marry more than any other. I was so in love with him. He was in school with me. It was my last year of college. We were so much in love. When we graduated, he join the air force and became a pilot in the war. We lost track of each other.

I often wonder if I should of went with him. He told me he would come back to me. He never did. Some old friend of ours who I ran in to said he was flying international flights. Maybe it was for the best. I could be here drinking with you talking about what a lousy husband I have. Morissa, can I ask you if you love your boyfriend. Or is he just some guy you like enough."

Morissa: "I love him a lot. I never loved another guy. I had some boyfriends. Nobody like him."

Valarie: "That guy I told you that I love in my last year of college was my first love. He was the first one I had sex with. Sometimes when I look back on him, I think he was something special. If I met him later in my life my thoughts of him may have been different."

Morissa: "What was he like. Can you please tell me?"

Valarie: "I can't remember the last time I talked about him. How strange."

Morissa: "If you don't want to don't worry about it."

Valerie: "Sure I will tell you about him if you tell me about that guy, you love so much. Deal?"

Morissa: "Deal."

Valerie: "Deal. I will go first if you don't mind."

Morissa: "Deal."

Valerie: "He was a good-looking nerd kind of guy. Not very athletic. On the skinny side. Black coke bottle glasses. Very smart. A good guy. He wanted to be a great guitar player. When all of us kids back then got together, he would play the guitar and entertain everybody for hours. I think that is what made me fall for him. The guitar player. I don't think he was good enough to make a living from it.

For us at that age he was good enough. Our lives were just about each other. I took him home to meet my parents. My father liked him enough to tell me to marry him. I think my father thought of him as safe. It was the sixties. My mother liked him. She said we made a nice couple.

When I met his parent if was strange. I think they were just glad there boy found a real girl. They were nice to me. The last time I saw him was when we graduated. Then a week later he was gone. I started to date some guys when I started working that fall. I never found that same feeling like I had for him. I am now in my fifty's sitting here missing a life that could of, maybe have been. Now it is your turn."

Morissa: "He is an athlete that doesn't play any sports. He is smart enough to get by. He is kind and understanding. Good looking tall and strong.  Everybody likes him. Could you believe he can cook to?"

Valerie: "Could be the best man I ever heard of. I hope he has some money."

Morissa: "Yes enough. His parent own some expensive property. He has taken me out on some dates that didn't cost him five dollars. He has spent too much on gambling. He has a budget for school. Since we have started dating, he has been keeping to his budget and hasn't borrowed any money. He tells me when he graduate, he get some money. I don't know how much."

Valerie: "In my experience gamblers are a red flag. I haven't found any that can make a living on it. I hope he is different."

Morissa: "Yes I know. I think he can stop."

Valerie: "What is he doing now. Why are you here in this place? There are other places a young couple could go to be alone."

Morissa: "It does look bad. We got are room and some free meals by his father. That is why we have to be careful on what we want to leave with. I trust him. I know enough about him that I know I can trust him."

Valerie: "It sounds like you want to take the chance with him."

Morissa: "I do."

Valerie: "Are you two graduating the same year?

Morissa: "No he is going to graduate this June, Me in two years. We don't know what he is going to do after he graduate. As soon as I graduate, I want to find a job teaching somewhere."

Valerie: "Are you going to try and find a job where your boyfriend will be. Or are you going to take a job where you want to teach?"

Morissa: "We haven't talk much about it. I hope we will be together. It would be nice to start off like that."

Valerie: "Maybe If I started off with my first love, we would have made it work. Sooner or later, you will have to make that decision to stay with him or go on without him. If I can give you some advice. Be able to support yourself all the time any time. There are a lot of women out there who stay in a bad relationship for financial reasons. It is easier to talk about woman's lib or independence when you are financially secure."

Morissa: "I understand Valerie. Thank you."

Valerie: "I think your mother did a good job with you. You are a young woman with her feet on the ground and able to take some advice."

Morissa: "Thank you. Valerie my father raised me. My parents separated when I was really young. They left the decision to me where I wanted to live. I chose my father because I would stay at the same school and have the same friends. I learned things from my father my mother couldn't have taught me."

Valerie: "Then he did a good job helping you becoming you."

Morissa: "Thank you. I will tell him that I met a woman in a bar and she said you did a good job."

Valerie: "If he is good looking, I could tell him. I guess he is about my age."

Morissa: "A little younger may be. If you give me your number maybe we could double date."

Valerie: "Oh the fun. A double date. The old days. Morissa you could do this woman a favor. Just a small favor."

Morissa: "Sure. If I, can I will. What favor can I do for you."

Valerie: "If you are with your prince charming and you see me. Let me meet him. The athlete that doesn't play any sports. He is smart enough to get by. He is kind and understanding. Good looking tall and strong. Everybody likes him. Could you believe he can cook to?"

Morissa: "I wish he was here now. I thought he would be back by now. I do trust him. He hasn't done anything crazy. How much trouble could he get into. He doesn't have a life changing amount of money with him."

Valerie: "Morissa it has been nice talking to you. I see a little of myself in you. When I was your age, I wanted a career a husband and children. What you want now may be what you will have in your life. However, or whatever happens in your life I hope you are happy with how and what you end up with.

 It is going to be what opportunities a wait for you. I hope you find happiness in your life time."

Valerie pays for the drinks and leaves Morissa at the bar. Morissa is at the bar for a half hour talking to the bartender. When Everett shows up. Morissa gets a big smile on her face. Everett walks up to her and gives Morissa a long kiss.

Everett: "I did it. It took longer than I thought. You would think it was easier to lose at that table then it turn out to be. I am just getting unlucky at losing. After I lost it all. I put a couple of coins in a slot machine and walked away with two hundred dollars.  I wonder how much money I could have won if I was trying to win."

Morissa: "I am so happy to have you back with me. Everett, I trusted you to walk back to me as a winner. You won a battle that has me free of thinking In fear of living with your gambling. Thank you."

Everett: "You are welcome Morissa. I am not sure where you are going with that. I will think about it later, I think. What do you want to do now?"

Morissa: "Something that will put me in your arms Everett. I am so in love with you."

Everett: "How about a movie. There is a mob type movie playing. Maybe we could fine some back row seat with some dim light. Then I could put my arms around you."

Morissa: "Not what I was thinking. It does sound like fun so let's go."

Everett and Morissa watch the movie in the back row of seats. There are just a few other couple watching the movie.

After the movie they walk out of the theater and go to get an early breakfast. It is four o'clock in the morning. The two are sitting at a table eating there breakfast.

Everett: Are you tired yet Morissa."

Morissa: "Yes I am. This has been a lot of fun for me. That was a pretty good mob movie. It is all about who kills who first. If you are in the mob, it is about when you get it. Not if you are going to get it."

Everett: "That isn't the way it really works. That movie was more of a comedy then a real mob movie."

Morissa: "I didn't know you were an expert on the mob. How come you didn't tell me this earlier. Are you in the mob Everett? May be you are a hit man for them. I would love to tell the girls when they ask me about you, that you are in the mob. Then I would tell them you're a hit man. How exciting for me."

Everett: "The term mob could stand for Men Of Business. My father is a lawyer for a business that will buy a business. Sometime they make an offer that someone can't refuse. It is my father job to help make the offer legal and best for his clients."

Morissa: "I thought you said your father is a maritime lawyer."

Everett: "He is. When they need him to work on a business venture, he will take the legal lead. Sometimes my father is asked just to give advice. That is how he makes his living. We were able to use his connections."

Morissa: "I am glad you lost what we won Everett. It would be too bad if you ended up with an ice pick in your back."

Everett: "Me why me."

Morissa: "I am the pretty love interest. Hollywood would never let that happen to the lead female."

Everett: "You may want to think about your female costar. The one who is a little older. The one who still wants to be the female lead with the best out fits."

Morissa: "Your right. It is those older females trying to still be the lead. In Hollywood those females have a shorter time to be the lead. The males can be the lead for years. Most of the actress will lose the roles that are an attractive young female."

Everett: "After we finish breakfast what would you like to do Morissa?"

Morissa: "A shower and some sleep. This girl is dead on her feet Everett. You must be tired?"

Everett: "No I feel find. It is just the way I am wired. I don't get tired like most people. Eventually I will need to sleep a couple of hours. Then I will be good again."

Morissa: "Let's get back to the room. You could do your pushups and sit ups. I am done."

Everett: "Ok sleeping beauty. Let me take you back to the castle. Maybe your prince charming will wake you up with a kiss."

Morissa: "I would like that, Everett. Please wake me up like that."

Everett: "I am yours."

Everett and Morissa go back to the room. Morissa takes a quick shower. Everett tells Morissa he has some things he has to do and he will be back later. Everett goes out for a run.

A couple of hours later he goes back to the room and finds Morissa asleep. He does his daily sit ups and pushups. Then he takes a shower. After the shower he gets in to the bed with Morissa.

Chapter Eight

Memorable

Three hours later Morissa wakes Everett up with a kiss.

Morissa: "Good morning prince charming. You didn't wake me up this morning as you promise. You were supposed to wake me up with a kiss."

Everett: "Sorry Morissa. I guess I owe you one."

Morissa: "Yes you do. You are going to have to be especially nice to me today. I want you to treat me to a nice day with you."

Everett: "What would you like to do today. This is our last full day here. We will have to get back to school and our regular lives."

Morissa: "I know. This has been a nice time being here with you. I am going to look back at this time together for the rest of my life with my heart."

Everett: "Morissa I do have a surprise for you today."

Morissa: "Please tell me. I want to know how I should dress for it."

Everett: "I can't tell you yet. How you are dressed will not be anything for you to be worried about."

Morissa: "Ok Everett you have the advantage of me. You have the advantages of a naked female under these sheet to. I am going to let you treat me to a nice surprise."

Everett and Morissa leave there room later that day in the afternoon. The two are sitting outside at a deli eating there late lunch."

Morissa: "Everett where are we going today. You can tell me now."

Everett: "No not yet. We have some time to go yet. You don't have to rush your meal we still have some time."

Morissa: "What time do we have to be there. I could go back and put a dress on."

Everett: "Don't worry about it I have it covered."

Morissa: "Ok Everett you are in charge of tonight entertainment. Can I expect a date like the dates we have had? Those five-dollar dates. We do have a couple of hundred dollars to play with. We could go back into the casino and win more money. Then you can give it all back again."

Everett: "No I don't want to do that again. I think my gambling days are over. When I was sitting at the table last night, I was looking at all the people trying to beat the house. There are some things in life you can't beat. I don't want to waste the time trying to beat something I can't beat. It was fun at one time for me. It was a way to past time and have some fun with the guys. Then it became a factor on everything else I did. There are other things in life I want."

Morissa: "I like to think I am what you want."

Everett: "You are Morissa. That you are."

Morissa: "Everett thank you."

Everett: "See all those boats out on the water. Have you ever wanted to own a boat?"

Morissa: "No Everett. Coming from a place by the water some of my friends had boats. They cost too much. There is too much maintenance to them. It was nice to go out on them some times with some friends. Boats are not anything I want."

Everett: "Do you see that cruise ship out there. Have you ever wanted to go on a cruise ship? They have everything you could think of. All the people are there just to wait on you."

Morissa: "Someday Everett maybe."

Everett points to a large cruise ship a quarter mile off shore.

Everett: "That one you are looking at is the newest cruise ship made. The name of that ship Is Arwen. It is out there having a shake down of it crew and some of the ship entertainment. They will be out there all night then come back in tomorrow. In two days, they will set sale for its maiden voyage. We will be back at school and that boat will be on the ocean heading to Florida."

Morissa: "Why are you so interested in that ship. How come you know so much about that ship?"

Everett: "I will give you one guess. One guess what your surprise is."

Morissa: "Oh no. Your father a maritime lawyer. That ship just happen to be here when we are. Everett, we don't have time to take a cruise. I have to get back to school. Maybe some other time. Maybe."

Everett: "Don't worry we are not going on that ship on its maiden voyage. We are going to have one of those five-dollar dates."

Morissa: "Good you had me scared. Now please tell me what we are going to do tonight."

Everett: "Let's go for a walk on that boat dock down there."

Everett and Morissa finish their lunch and start the walk down to the dock. They walk to the end of the dock. At the end of the dock is a shuttle boat with a couple of dozen people waiting to be taken out to the big cruise ship.

Everett: "Ok Morissa this is your surprise. We are going out to that cruise ship called Arwen."

Morissa: "Everett we can't do this. I am sorry we can't do this. Don't you understand we have to be back at school in a couple of days."

Everett: "I will tell you the truth now. Like I said before it is just a shake down for the ship crew tonight. They need people to be passengers for a night of entertainment. We are going to have a fun time tonight and we will not have to spend a five-dollar bill. Tomorrow morning, we will catch one of the shuttle boats going back to the dock. We will have some time to get some sleep and head back to school."

Morissa: "That sounds great Everett. I don't want to be the person who keeps bring up any negatives with anything. I am going to be very tired tomorrow to drive back to school. You can't drive you don't have a license do you remember."

Everett: "I do remember. One other thing we don't have Herbert's car any more. It is back with Herbert."

Morissa: Everett how in hell do you think we are getting back. Can you please answer me that?"

Everett: "I have it taken care of. You will not have to drive us home."

Morissa: "Please put my mind at ease and tell me."

Everett: "Morissa trust me it will be another surprise for you. We need to get on the shuttle boat now."

Morissa: "I believe in you Everett. I trust Everett. I am in awe of you."

Everett and Morissa get on the shuttle and go to the cruise ship. The two of them and the other people are greeted by the captain of the cruise ship on the ship. The captain tells them his Name is captain Smith. Then captain Smith gives the people a few words about the ship and some safe rules they have to follow. Then the captain breaks the people down in to two groups. The captain has one officer take one group to the stern of the ship. Another officer takes the rest to the bow of the ship. Everett holds Morissa hand till the other people were taken away. "Morissa just stays in the same spot." The captain, Everett and Morissa are now by themselves.

Captain Smith: "Hello Everett how are you."

Everett: "Fine Mr. Smith. This is my girlfriend Morissa."

Captain Smith: "It is nice to meet you. The last time I saw Everett he was making us a fish breakfast up in Canada somewhere. All he could talk about was this girl he met. From looking at you I can see why he talked so much about meeting you."

Morissa: "This is a little embarrassing. Thank you. This is a really big boat you have sir."

Captain Smith: "No sir needed. Just captain is enough for my ego thank you. We like to refer to this boat as a ship."

Everett: "She has no idea. I kept it a surprise."

Captain Smith: "You're a brave sole. Some women would not like it. Morissa and Everett I am going to take you on a tour of the ship. The captain takes the two on his exclusive tour of the new ship. In the wheel house the captain Lets Morissa hold the controls as the ship was moving out to sea."

In the galley Everett talks to the head chef. The captain has to cut Everett off from the chef from all the question he has on food, food prep, and service. The captain then takes Everett and Morissa to watch a Broadway show. The show that will be part of the entertainment for the first-class passenger. The captain leaves the two alone. Everett and Morissa watch the show rehearsal from the second row of seats. In front of them are the director, writer and producer watching and talking about last minute changes. It is a seat that few people have ever had. Everett and Morissa sit arm in arm.

After the show a deck officer is waiting for the two. The officer takes Everett and Morissa to a high-end dress shop. Everett ask Morissa to pick out a black dress and some shoes. He explain that there is a black-tie dinner dance. Morissa ask Everett "why just for me."   Everett kiss her on the cheek and tells her somebody will take her to meet him later. After Morissa picks out a black dress and a pair of black pumps, a ship officer brings her up to a first class sweet. She walks in side with a dress bag and a new pair of shoes. Inside the room Everett is dressed in a black suit with a white shirt and a black tie. Morissa looks at Everett for a moment. She drops the dress bag to her side.

Morissa: "Everett, again why all this for me. You didn't need to do this for me. I don't understand any of this. This is way too much just for me. I am not comfortable with this. What do you owe for all this? Please help me understand all this."

Everett gets up and puts his arms around a teary eye Morissa.

Everett: "Like I said before the ship and the fun is free. I will have to pay for that dress and shoes. That invoice will go across my father desk next month. Everything else is just us free loading off the cruise line for their shake down.

The captain told you the truth. He is just paying me back for the food I cooked him. That is all.

Why don't you take that dress and shoes then go in to the bathroom and freshen up? You can get dressed for some dinner and moonlight dancing. There are some other things you may need in there."

Morissa: "You think of everything don't you."

Everett: I will explain later. Time for you to get ready Morissa."

Morissa: "Ok. It is hard for a woman to get ready as fast as a man can."

Everett: "Why?"

Morissa: "It is the results. That's why."

Everett: "I will be right here."

Morissa picks up her dress bag and shoes and goes in to the bathroom."

Everett and Morissa are having a moon lite dinner on the deck of the ship.

Morissa: "Everett I never had anybody do what you are doing for me. I thought I knew you. I thought I found somebody who can just enjoy the simple things in life. I only saw this kind of datetime with a man in the movies. No girl thinks she will ever have a man do this for her. You haven't answer me why you are doing this for me."

Everett: "You have been very good about the dates we have had. Most girls get tired of those five-dollar dates. I couldn't have taken you out to those places that girls like to be taken to. I have to live with a budget. This wasn't hard to put together. A little help from my father made it easy."

Morissa: "I will have to thank him when I see him. Everett when will I meet him."

Everett: "This June when I graduate. He and my mother will come up and see me. It will be nice of them to come back and see the place where they met. My father wants to see that restaurant he worked at and his brother's grave. He will be there next June. My mother wants to see me graduate.  Then she will leave and get back home as fast as she can. Morissa, will you do me the pleasure of a slow dance. we will talk about something else."

Morissa: "Thank you Everett I would like that."

Everett takes Morissa hand and brings her on the dance floor. Dancing body to body slowly around the floor. Just a few people are there. The band are in there street clothes.

Morissa: "Everett, you have made me very happy. I do appreciate the attention you are showing me. I am not used to it. I am wondering how I can show you how much I do appreciate it."

Everett: "Morissa when I had pizza with you that first night was all you had to do. I wanted that time with you. I wanted to get too know you. I wanted to spend time with you. Sometimes people will find that other person. I think it is that simple. We have found each other. What we have been doing during the last couple of days can't last. Us being together can last for as long as we live."

Morissa: "I am going to cry Everett. The people around us are going to think you said or did something to me."

Everett: "I better be careful or they may make me walk the plank. Then you will have to go back to the school and tell them you lost me."

Morissa: "Those girls I live with are not going to believe all this Everett. I should have taken some pictures. Everett, we have no pictures of our time here to gather. What is wrong with us. One of us should have brought a camera."

Everett: "We will remember this time to gather. You can tell your friends if you like. I don't think there is a camera to show them how much I love you Morissa."

Morissa: "In between the surprises you have had for me. I was thinking about are relationship when we get back to school. Are we going back to exactly the same relationship? I was thinking you may want to get your own place. Then I could come and spend some private time with you. Or were you thinking I could live with you. Then when you leave in June, I could go back with the girls."

Everett: "I have. I was thinking that you would stay with the girls till you graduate. I am going to stay in the same room with Herbert. When this June comes, we will have to make some hard decisions. Us spending time together in an intimate relationship? We don't need to change our lives. We will live and do what makes both of us comfortable. Us living where we live is the way we should keep it for now."

Morissa: "Thank you Everett for understanding."

Everett: "What will happen after I graduate is what we have to work on. I will need to get a job in New York or California. If I get a job here then I can see you during the school year. I will then have to get my own place. I could even rent you out a half room. How does that sound."

Morissa: "It sounds like an opportunity for me to take advantage of you."

Everett: "I could live with that."

Morissa: "Everett can you now tell me how we are getting home. We don't have a car and you don't have a license."

Everett: "Not yet Morissa. Tomorrow I will let you know."

Morissa: "My watch says it is tomorrow the day we have to leave. You can tell me now."

Everett: "You are right it is tomorrow here today. I still cannot tell you. Just let me sweep you off your feet."

Morissa: "Ok."

Everett: "I was talking to Captain Smith last summer. He liked my cooking well enough to get me a job on a cruise line. The job would be just the basic bus boy at first. He said I could work my way up. The school cooking degree would help me. What do you think about that?"

Morissa: "I think you would be gone to long for me. Last night I was talking to a woman at the bar. She told me when she was my age her boyfriend went away to the war. They never got back to gather. She never found anybody she wanted to married. I don't want to lose you Everett."

Everett: "Don't worry there is no war for me to go off to. I don't want to work on a ship. I want to own the place I work at."

Morissa: "If your father helped you do all this could he help you do that."

Everett: "The simple answer is yes. Then he and his business partners will own a bigger part of my place. Somehow, I will have my own place wit out him and his partners. I hope it comes to me sooner than later."

Morissa: "If I can help you, I will Everett. I will give you any money I can. After I graduate, I can teach. After that I will need to get my masters. My parents have given me a lot."

Everett: "Thank you Morissa. I think for now we just keep planning for are lives together. Then live those occasions that our are lives."

Morissa: "Everett this is a little embarrassing please don't laugh. I have to tell you something. Promise me you will not laugh."

Everett: "Your safe Morissa I will try not to laugh."

Morissa: "That is not what I ask for. I guess I will have to take it. When you gave me that box and I told you I couldn't marry you I felt really bad about that. I jump the gun. I feel like we are on a honey moon right now. I love being in love with you. I love being in love with you. I don't want to be married right now. If you ask me then I would have said I could not do it. If you were to ask me when we get back, I would still say the same thing. I hope we are together when we both get what we want. That would make us very happy don't you think so."

Everett: "If we end up. When we end up with each other I know we will be very happy together Morissa."

Morissa: "How did I find you Everett."

Everett: "We have about an hour left on this ship. I did not think we would be on this ship for so long. Let's get back to the room to get our other clothes and things. Then we need to get to the shuttle and get back to the casino and check out."

Everett and Morissa finish there dancing and collect there belonging. Captain Stewart says good bye to them and tells them To let him know any time they want to go on a cruise. Everett and Morissa take the shuttle back. The two walk back to their room as the morning sun comes up.

Three hours later Everett and Morissa are on the elevator going down to check out. Tony Perri the casino manager just happen to get on the elevator with them.

Tony: "It is nice to see you two before you leave. I hope you two had a nice time with us."

Everett: "We did thank you for everything."

Morissa: "This was more than I expected. Thank you."

Tony: "You are welcome. It is nice to see such young people enjoy our place. I am sorry to hear you gave us back all that money you won your first night with us. We plan on opening a place up state by your college. It would be nice of you to come by and bring some friends from time to time. Everett tell your father thank you for that work he did for us please. I have to go now you two take care and I hope to see you two in our new place."

Everett and Morissa say good bye to Toni. Everett check the two out. Everett and Morissa our outside the casino with their bags by their side."

Morissa: "Ok Everett we our here with no car. We are a long way from where we want to be. I am really tired."

Everett: "There will be a taxied here to pick us up and take us to where we want to go."

Morissa: "We can't take a taxied back. A bus or train maybe. Is that what we are going to be doing?"

Everett: "No I have one more surprise for you."

Everett and Morissa get in two a taxied. Everett tells the man "You know where." Ten minutes later they are at an airport. In twenty minutes, Everett and Morissa are in a small airplane. The plane is a private training plane to teach new pilots. The plane flies the two back to the local airport by their college. Morissa being so tired doesn't ask Everett to explain it. She falls asleep and is woken up when the plane lands.

Everett takes the bags from the plane. Everett and Morissa find a taxied back to Sues place. Everett carries Morissa in to the house and puts her on her bed. Then he brings her bags in side and kisses her good bye. Morissa just crashes on her bed without talking to anybody. Everett takes the taxi back to his dorm. Herbert is in the room to greet Everett. Everett thanks Herbert for taking a bus down to the casino to get the car. Everett then lays down on his bed. He goes over the last couple of days with Morissa till he falls asleep.

I have just started the relationship with her. I have found a love we all want to find. I love her I love her a lot. I had a good time with her she is a lot of fun. It was nice having such a lovely female. I may never be able to repeat this past weekend. If I can't get a job when I graduate, I won't have the money even to ask her to marry me. If it wasn't for my father, I would've had her at some cheap place promising her a better time in the future. I reversed it. I showed her a good time and promised her not much for our future. There has to be a way I can find what I need to make it work with her. The answer is out there, I hope I can find it before too long. When we finish school this year, I'm afraid we're going to be going in separate directions. I want to stay with her. I have to be able to earn enough in a place close to her so I could live near her. My father won't just give me the money to do it. He will give me the money if I could find a way that makes business sense to him and his partners. His partners it is always his partners it is not the one son he has left. It could have been different if the other son had lived. I will never know. I am just the one left now having to live with what is left for me. Someday I am going to tell her all about me. Someday I am going to tell her about are family the four of us. She is going to think I cannot be trusted. I saw him drown. I should have told her before we left. If I have told her already, I would not have to worry about it. Before I graduate this June, I will tell her.

I hope she had a nice time. I would like to be a fly on her wall when she gets those questions on her vacation with me. I think most women would like to be able to tell of a vacation like that. She may not say much about it. I have to start thinking about what we are going to be to each other going forward. We are going to want to have sex. Where and when, is going to be our challenge. I am tired. I will think about it later.

Everett goes to sleep.

The next day Morissa walks out from her room and goes in to the kitchen. She is still in the clothes that was on her from yesterday. In the kitchen sitting at the table is Sue, Clare and Becky. The Three of them watch as Morissa walks up to a pot of coffee. Morissa pours herself a cup of coffee then takes a seat at the table. The three girls just watch Morissa pour the cup of coffee then takes a seat. Morissa drinks some of her coffee then looks over her cup at the three girls. The three girls' eyes are on Morissa as they exchange looks with her.

Morissa: "What is new girls."

Sue: "Hi Morissa. Not much new here, Clare, Becky anything new with you?"

Clare: "Not here. Nothing new here."

Becky: "Nothing new here. Not here. Not me. How about you Sue. Anything new with you Morissa."

Morissa: "Tired."

Sue: "Tired she says. Really. Could you fill us in on why you are tired? What made you so tired Morissa."

Morissa: "Not enough sleep."

Clare: "Really. I don't remember our girl ever looking so tired."

Sue: "Your right Clare. This young well-structured woman has never looked so tired."

Becky: "I wonder why she so tired."

Sue: "Please Morissa can you let us in on why you are so tired."

Morissa taking a drink of her coffee and looking over the cup at each of the three girls again.

Morissa: "I need a shower. I can't believe I am in the same clothes I wore yesterday."

Clare: "I can't believe you came back here with your clothes still on."

Becky: "I can't believe she had her clothes on yesterday at all."

Sue: "I can't believe you two girls are suggesting are girl here may have had her clothes off. Not are Morissa. Not the good little girl we have come to know."

Clare: "We are assuming that our Morissa is still a good girl."

Sue: "Do you want to tell us anything Morissa. Are you still a good girl?"

Morissa taking a drink of her coffee and looking over the cup at each of the three girls again.

Morissa: "I had a nice time."

Clare: "Morissa I would have hoped you had a nice time. We were hoping that you tell us about your nice time."

Sue: "We were hoping that you told us all about everything nice that has happened to you."

Clare: "I was hoping that you tell us about everything that happen to you. Please tell us all the dirty parts."

Becky: "Inquiring minds want to know."

Sue: "How about it Morissa."

Morissa taking a drink of her coffee and looking over the cup at each of the three girls again.

Morissa: "We got pulled over on the way down there. We won some money and we lost some money. I saw a good movie about mob guys. I met somebody who is a backup quarter back. Mister Irrelevant he called himself. He was so nice. He played the piano for me. I think I was on a ship or a boat. I think I was in an airplane."

Sue: "Do you remember Everett carrying you in here yesterday?"

Morissa: "Everett. I need to call him. He has to be so tired."

Clare: "What did you do to him to make him so tired?"

Morissa taking a drink of her coffee and looking over the cup at each of the three girls again.

Morissa: "I really like him. He was so nice to me."

Sue: "I am sure he was nice to you Morissa. Can you fill us in on some of the details?"

Clare: "The dirty details."

Becky: "We are over eighteen."

Morissa taking a drink of her coffee and looking over the cup at each of the three girls again.

Morissa: "Did he say anything."

Sue: "He put you on the bed then dropped the bags on the floor. I ask him if he had a nice time. He just said you were tired."

Clare: "What did he do to you Morissa?"

Morissa: "He is better than advertised. He was so nice to me. Excuse me I have to take a shower and change my clothes."

Clare: "Excuse me? Are you kidding me? I want to know how many times he was nice to you."

Becky: "We know he was nice to you."

Sue: "It is not so much that he was nice to you. It is not so much how many times he was nice to you. How nice was it when he was nice to you?"

Becky: "Are you two going to start living together?"

Morissa: "I just remember I have a lot of homework to do. I am going to take a shower now girls. I had a nice time with him. We will talk later. Maybe."

Morissa goes to take a shower. After the shower she starts on her homework. Morissa Goes back and forth from her room to the kitchen all day. She manages not to say anything that the girls want to hear from the questions they ask her.

Back on campus Everett wakes up in his room. He goes to the end of his bed and starts his pushups and sit up. Herbert wakes up and starts to talk to Everett.

Herbert: "Hello Everett it is nice to have you back. Did you have a good time?"

Everett: "Yes we had a nice time together. Thank you for the car. Thank you for going down there for the car."

Herbert: "You are welcome Everett. Did everything you planned work out."

Everett: "Yes it did. She didn't suspect anything. It worked out real nice. We won a big jackpot the first day. Then we gave it all back. It isn't as big a deal as it sounds. Over all we had a nice time together."

Herbert: "I am glad you two had a nice time. I like her. I hope you two can spend more time together."

Everett: "We had such a good time. I don't know if we can have the same kind of time together again any time soon. We will have to find a way to be together."

Herbert: "Are you two going to start living together?"

Everett: "No Herbert. I have to finish school living here with you.

Thanksgiving holiday ends. Everett and Morissa go back to their life at school. They spend time together on Everett low-cost dates. On several occasions they find time and a place to be intimate with each other. Sometimes it is in Everett dorm room when Herbert could find another place to sleep. Sometimes they find time at sues place when the girls are out for the day. Christmas break comes Everett goes out to Californian. Morissa goes down state to see her father. After they come back to school, they go back to their familiar relationship

Spring break come and Morissa goes out to California. Everett's father fly's in from New York to see Everett. Everett's father brings out some of his business partners. Everett his father and his father partners spend a week in the local town. Everett and his father spend time together at the stone quarry and the old restaurant his father used to work at. Morissa talks to her mother about how far her relationship has gone with Everett.

Morissa and Her Mother are on her deck one spring night overlooking the ocean. The two are on the deck with some drinks.

Morissa: "Mom I am in love with him. I want to marry him when I am done with school. I don't want to meet any other guy."

Miss Brown: "I could understand that at your age. You may want to date some other men before you walk down any aisle with him."

Morissa: "I don't want to do that. I have who I want. He wants only me. I know that."

Miss Brown: "When was the last time you dated someone else Morissa. Can you even remember who you last dated before you met him?"

Morissa: "No I haven't thought about that. I am sure there wasn't much to remember. The last guy I talked to that I had any interest in was a guy I met last fall. I met him when Everett and I went to Atlantic city. The guy was a backup quarter back for a football team. There was something about him I liked. If I wasn't with Everett, it would have been nice to get to know him."

Miss Brown: "That is good to hear Morissa. You have been smart enough for me not to worry about what man you would end up with. As a mother having you as my daughter help me sleep at night."

Morissa: "Everett and I have talked about are future together. We don't know what we are going to be doing this summer. I will be doing some volunteer work at a local elementary school. I am planning to spend most of the summer there. It will help me become a teacher. It is part of the work that I have to do to get my degree. Everett isn't sure what he wants to do or could do.

He wants to own his own place. He has not worked in any place. He has no experience at even washing dishes. The only job I know he can do is be a life guard. Once he finish school this year he will have to move out of the school. We have talked about living together. The problem is money. He has no hope of making enough money to support us. I don't have any idea how we can make us staying together work."

Miss Brown: "Every relationship will come across some obstacles. You two will learn to work them out, If you can't the relationship will end. When you don't want to be together the simplest problems will be what you will use to end the relationship."

Morissa: "I think Dad will like him. I Wish Everett had a plan that I could tell dad. I don't want to tell him Everett doesn't have a job; I don't want to tell him that Everett is a college grad and his job is a life guard."

Miss Brown: "Your dad had a great job as a state trooper when we were married. Then we found that simple problem to break us up. We wanted to do different things with our lives. We both became happier living apart."

Morissa: "I wish I can see the future. I just don't know what the answer I need is. For the first time. I don't have a plan to get what I want. I want to stay with him. I want to stay there and work on my degree. A couple of summers ago I just wanted to go to college. Mom tell me what I need to do to get what I want."

Miss Brown: "My daughter who at such a young age knew she wanted to live with her father. How much I wanted you to come and live with me. Do you know how much I did mis you? I would often want you to call me and ask me any question that showed me that you needed me. The days and nights I wanted to go and see you. Other mothers who had their daughter with them.

They had the fun of dressing their daughter up. Doing their daughters' hair. Seeing them going out on their first date. My daughter going to her prom you couldn't give that to me. Asking me to mend your broken hart on your first crush. Now you come to me and ask for my help."

Morissa: "Mom how long have you held that inside of you?"

Miss Brown: "Since the first night I didn't have you with me. I been waiting a long time to get that off my chest. Morissa, it feels good to tell you that."

Morissa: "You could have said something years ago mom. I thought you understood. Now I feel bad about staying with dad."

Miss Brown: "Good. Morissa back to your question. I can't help you. You and Everett will figure out it somehow. If I could give you the answer I would."

Morissa: "I know you would mom."

Miss Brown: "What does his family want Everett to do."

Morissa: "I don't know. He calls his father and mother just to tell them how he is doing. I think they are waiting for him to tell them what he is going to do."

Miss Brown: "Morissa I have a confession. Everett's mother and I have become friends. We have had talks about you two. We just share information on you two. We meet once a month and compare notes on you two. The last I heard she said Everett doesn't know what he is going to do after he finish school."

Morissa: "That is ok Mom. I understand. I think Everett's father may help him. Everett's father has a lot of connections. His father used some of them so we would have a nice time last November. It wasn't like he gave Everett all the money he needed.

He just made some phone calls to some of the people he knows. I don't know if he plans on helping Everett. His father may want Everett to figure it out himself."

Miss Brown: "Have you met Everett father?"

Morissa: "No mom have you."

Miss Brown: "No I haven't. When I ask Everett's mother about him, She doesn't say much about him. I feel bad telling you this. Miss Stewart drinks a lot."

Morissa: "I notice that when I first met her. Everett told me she has a problem."

Morissa: "When he graduate this spring, I will get to meet Everett's father. Everett says his father and mother will be there. I hope we have some kind of plan to tell his parent what we are doing."

Miss Brown: "You two will have one, you are so young. There are endless opportunities for the young. In a couple of years, you two can be very happy.

Spring break ends Everett and Morissa go back to their now very familiar relationship. Everett now has apart time job in his father's old restaurant. He tells Morissa he wants to learn about the real logistics of running a restaurant. Everett gets a driver license and is able to use the restaurant van for some of his dates with Morissa.

A week before Everett graduate his father fly's in to spend time with him. Everett has spent little time with Morissa while his father is in town. Morissa is spending her time doing volunteer teaching. Everett has a range Morissa to meet his father the night before he graduate. The three of them will have a dinner together at the old restaurant. Everett's mother is Flying in late that night before his graduation.

It is the night before Everett graduation. Everett picks Morissa up in the restaurant van. He brings her to the restaurant to meet his father. As Morissa gets out of the van, she remembers the last time she and Everett were at this place to gather. The outside is the same as she remembers. There is a closed sign on the front door. Everett opens the door and walks in. Everett walks her to a table were a man in a black suit is sitting. The man in the black suit stands up when he see the two walk thru the door. The man is about fifty years old and about the same size as Everett. Morissa can tell the man is Everett's father by their similar athletic looks. Everett's father name is Carman Stewart. Everett and Morissa walk right up to the table that Mr. Stewart is sitting at.

Everett: "Hi dad this is my girlfriend Morissa."

Mr. Stewart: "It is nice to meet you at last Morissa. My son has fallen for the prettiest girl I have ever seen him with. My wife who described you to me was right. I am sorry she is not here right now. Her flight was delayed. I am going to be picking her up later tonight. This will give us a chance to talk."

Morissa: "Thank you it is nice to meet you to. I can see where Everett gets his looks from. You could be his older brother. I am sorry Miss Stewart can't be here. I would like to say thank you for that great time we had at the casino the cruise and everything. When I told my girlfriends, they were green with envy.

Mr. Stewart: "You are welcome. Just a phone call sometimes is all it takes."

Everett: "Mom would have loved this dad. You would think she would like this more than me graduating tomorrow."

Mr. Stewart: "She was telling me the same thing yesterday. When they delayed her flight, I had to hear about it. She wanted me to do something about it. Like that would happen. Morissa, would you like something to drink. Everett is are waiter to night. He is are cook to night. He is are bus boy tonight. And the best part he is even going to pay the check tonight. Right Everett."

Mr. Stewart: "That is right Morissa. This place is closed for tonight. If you haven't notice we are the only ones here. The owner let me have this place to night. I had to promise him that we would leave it the way I found it. Right dad."

Mr. Stewart: "I am just glad you are paying the check to night."

Morissa: "I thought it was Strange that there was a close sign on the door. Then when we walked in here there was only one person at a table. Everett that was nice of your boss to do that."

Everett: "It was. He suggested it to me."

Morissa: "Really."

Everett: "Morissa can you guess what we are having tonight for dinner."

Morissa: "I can't. Why don't you tell me and your father?"

Everett: "He knows. He suggested that I cook what we are going to have. He wanted to see if you would like it."

Morissa: "Mr. Stewart your son is really good at cooking. If he ever gets his own place, I am sure that it would be a real nice place. He talks about it a lot."

Mr. Stewart: "We think the same way Morissa. I have heard him talk about it more then you have. I am sure I have eaten more of his cooking then you have. His mother would have him cooking any chance she could get.

When I go away, I would try and get him to go with me so I could have some of what he can cook. Most of the time I would hire a cook for myself and I had a lot of restaurant food. During the summer it was nice to have him cook for us on those fishing and hunting trips."

Everett goes in the kitchen and starts getting the food he has already cook for their meal. He comes back with a large plate of chicken wings then places it in the center of the table. He looks at Morissa and tells her he will be right back. Everett comes back out with some bread loaves. He smiles at Morissa again and goes off in the kitchen and gets some wine.

On the table in front of Morissa and Mr. Becker is a table filled with enough food for six or more people. Everett takes a seat at the table. He looks at his father first and smile at him. He then looks at Morissa and ask her what does she think."

Everett: "What do you think Morissa."

Morissa: "You made to much food. There is no way we are going to eat all this food. Why did you make so much? Were you expecting more people here tonight? Why chicken wings and bread. It looks like bar food. I didn't know this place did that kind of food."

Everett: "You are right. It didn't. I thought I would try something new. I would like to know what you thought about it."

Morissa: "If you are asking me if I like the food. I am sure that I am going to like it. If you are asking me if you want the restaurant to make this food. You may want to ask the owner what they think about it."

Everett: "You are right Morissa. I was planning on it. I was thinking that this place could make more money if it made more food like bar food. That school we go to have a lot of kids who like bar food."

Mr. Stewart: "Everett she is right you should talk to the owner about any changes. Somehow it managed to stay in business all these years without you and your changes. What makes you think you could do better than the people who used to own it."

Morissa: "Used to own it? You didn't tell me Everett somebody else now owns it."

Everett: "I am sorry that I didn't tell you. It change hands to day. The new owner made an offer to the old owners last winter. The last paper work was done today. When this place opens up again late August it will have knew food. A new inside. A new name outside."

Morissa: "That is nice. I think you should tell the new owner. Have you met them yet? If you did have you talk to them about the food. Everett, we have talked about what you are going to do after you graduate. The last time we talk you did not know if you would stay here with me or go back home and get a job. Do you plan on asking the new owner for a job and staying here? I would like to know."

Mr. Stewart: "She is right Everett; I hope you have asked the owner for a job first. Then you could tell them about any changes you would think that may help this business."

Morissa: "The food is good Everett. You never made me wings before. What do you think about the food Mr. Stewart?"

Mr. Stewart: "It is good enough for your young college kids or us old working people. The challenge for this place would be finding a market to sell products during those school days. Morissa I am glad you like the food. Can you ask the new owner if he likes the food?"

Morissa: "I thought it was just the three of us. What do you mean Mr. Stewart?"

Mr. Stewart: "My son and I are having some fun. He has talked to the new owner about changing the food here. The new owner has told him he can work here for as long as he can keep this place in the black."

Morissa: "That is good Everett that means you are going to be here next year with me. If you knew this, why didn't you tell me. I have asked you to let me know when you knew what you will be doing."

Everett: "I know you did. I wasn't sure until several weeks ago. Now you me and the new owner are here."

Morissa: "There you go again. What are you telling me it is just the three of us here? It is you me and your father."

Everett: "Morissa I am the new owner. Last spring break we made the old owner an offer. He accepted it. My father and his partners have bought this place and they hold the mortgage. I am going to run it.  I will have to pay them back."

Morissa: "That is great for you Everett. I am so happy for you. Thank You Mr. Stewart. I am sure Everett will be a success."

Mr. Becker: "I hope so. It isn't only me who invested in him. I have partners. If he cannot turn a profit by next June, they will want to sell this place. I have talked to some people who know about food places close to colleges. They all say to make any money you have to serve alcohol. The drinking age changing accouple of years ago will make it harder to make any money on just food. We have some plans in the works to help this place make money."

Everett: "I didn't want to tell you any of this till, I was sure. That did happen and I have my chance. Morissa you can now ask my father what he thinks about the food."

Morissa: "Mr. Stewart What do you think about the food?"

Mr. Stewart: "I think the food is ok. It taste like other bar food. I have told him that. There are some other surprises he has for you. I have to leave and go pick up Miss. Stewart. I want you to know that my son has found a very nice young lady to fall in love with. I am hoping you two can make it work here."

Morissa: "Thank you. This isn't mine. It is his not mine. I will help him if I can. I still have two more years of college still. I want to be a teacher."

Mr. Stewart: "I will leave now you two have a lot to talk about."

Mr. Stewart says good bye to Morissa. Everett walks his father out to his waiting limousine. They have a few words about Morissa. Mr. Stewart Limousine heads out to the local airport. Everett goes back in side to Morissa. Everett gives her a tour of the place. He tells her of the changes that are going to be made over the summer. The upper top third floor is where he will live.

The floor has a large living room and bed room. One full bathroom and a kitchenette. The floor above the restaurant has three small bedrooms a Full bathroom and one small bathroom.

Everett has shown her the place. They go back in to the restaurant and clean the food up. They talk about their parents and tomorrow graduation. After they clean up the place Morissa goes and uses the restroom. When she comes out Everett has the lights down low. He is sitting at a table. The table has some candle burning on it. There are two plates of cheese cake. Everett pulls a chair out and ask Morissa to have a seat. Morissa walks to the chair does a bow then takes a seat, Everett takes a knee and pulls out a small black box. Morissa looks at it and laughs.

Morissa: "You're not going to fool me this time. You are going to give me a necklace or some kind of jewelry.

Everett opens the box. The box has an engagement ring in it.

Everett: "Morissa will you marry me."

Morissa cries.

Morissa: "Everett I can't. I want to. I can't. I want to finish college first. I love you so much. I can't. Not yet. Everett, please give me time to think about it. We are so young."

Everett: "Morissa I love you. I want us to be engaged for now. We can wait till you finish school. Morissa, will you marry me after you finish school."

Morissa: "Everett trust me. I am not going anywhere we can wait."

Everett: "Ok Morissa I do understand would you like to wear the ring till we cross this bridge again. A lot of girls would like to."

Morissa: "It is a beautiful ring. Please not yet. Ask me again in the future I will say yes. I just can't do it yet Everett. Please understand."

Everett: "I will ask you again and again in the future till you say yes.

Morissa give Everett a kiss and thanks him for understanding.

Everett talks to Morissa about the changes that the restaurant is going to make over the summer. He is going to have a twenty-seven-year-old female French chef to help him with the menu. She has a five-year-old boy. The woman and boy will live upstairs on the second floor. Herbert will live on the second floor some times. Herbert has found a bookkeeping job at the prison.

Everett takes Morissa back to Sue house that night. Everett goes back to his dorm room for the last time. The next day Everett Graduates. Everett his mother, father and Morissa are sitting to gather as they watch Everett walk across the podium. Later that day Everett his parents and Morissa are at the restaurant celebrating, Sue, Clare, Herbert and some of their friends show up to join the party. That night the party ends Everett's parents leave and fly back to their separate homes. That night Everett and Morissa spend the night there in Everett's new apartment.

The next day Everett and a working crew get to work changing the Restaurant. Morissa starts her volunteer teaching for credits. Morissa has moved out of Sues house for the Summer. She has told Everett she was not sure on where she would live during the next two school years. Morissa teaches for three weeks. After those week she leaves for her mother's place. Sometime in August she will go to her father's place. Then her father will drive her back to school.

The next day after Morissa is gone Everett drives out to the airport to pick up the new French chef. Her name is Cyd, her five-year-old boy name Is John.

Back at the restaurant Everett gives Cyd and her son John take a tour of the place. Cyd ask Everett to make some changes to the floor that she is going to be shearing with Herbert. The changes are to give her more privacy. Everett and Cyd get to work on the chicken wings and bread they are going to be making. Cyd tells Everett that her specialty is bread and pastry. Her suggestion to Everett is let her make the dough for everything. The bread and the breading for the wings. Everett likes the idea. He thinks that would give him something different. Cyd also tell Everett she would like to make pastries. Everett tells her that there isn't a market for it. The college kids will not be looking for pastries at night.

Everett and Cyd work to get the place open for the next school year. Cyd's son is enrolled at a local summer camp. During the day. John spends a lot of time out back behind the restaurant. Everett see the boy playing outside one day by himself. Everett goes tells Cyd that he has to go out and pick up some supplies. Two hours later Everett returns with some baseball equipment a football and a soccer ball. An hour later Cyd is by the window watching Everett and her son John having a catch.

Herbert has started his job at the prison as a bookkeeper. He comes by one day asking Everett when he can move in. Everett introduce Herbert to Cyd and her boy. He tells Cyd that Herbert is the company book keeper. Cyd hears Herbert and Everett talking about Herbert new job at the prison. Cyd makes a suggestion that Herbert take some of the bread and chicken wings to the prison guards. Cyd wants to test some of the different way that she and Everett were making bread and wings.

Herbert would come back and tell the two what they liked and what they didn't. On one of those days Cyd sent the guards some of her French pastries to say thank you. Herbert came back the next day telling Everett and Cyd that the prison guards want Herbert to bring pastry and bread every day. The guards offered to pay for the pastry and bread. Everett and Cyd look at each other and knew that they have stumble on a cash opportunity. A week later Herbert pick up about twenty dollars of bread and pastry product. That night Herbert bought back two hundred dollars in cash.

Accouple of days later Everett Cyd and Herbert are at a table talking about the business.

Herbert: Everett and Cyd you can't keep on selling pastries for cash at the prison. The IRS will come in and want a closer look at the books. I suggest we come up with a contract with the prison. You two come up with a plan on how much of your pastries you want to make. I will figure out what you can make on it."

Everett: "I think you are right Herbert. What do you think Cyd? You have a better idea on what could be made and how fast it could be made."

Cyd: "I understand that Herbert works at the prison and doesn't want Everett to go to prison. I think Herbert is right. I think Herbert should go to some other place and ask them if they would like some pastries also. We can make a lot more then you may be thinking."

Herbert: "I was thinking the same thing. We should try the hospital and the college for some business. I think we may get some orders from them. As book keeper of this small business, we could use the cash. The new machines. The renovation and my and Cyd salaries are draining the restaurants bank account.

That account is also yours Everett. Not to mention the taxes, insurance, and supplies that are going to be billing us soon."

Everett: "If we could start making some money before school starts. Why not. I need to ask your opinion Cyd. You are the only person here with any experience."

Cyd: "It would be nice to have something that is familiar to me. The wings of a chicken are a funny idea to cook. The people I worked with would be making jokes at me if they saw me making those little wings of a chicken. A lot of what we will have to do will be prep of the flour and the dough. Everett you and I will have to find what we want to do and who is best at what we do. What we are going to create and sell will take us being good at what we do. I know what has to be done. I know how to do it. I know how to create the dough that will be the base of our products. Everett and Herbert should work on selling what we create. Everett I am here because I need a place for me and my son. If I am happy here with my son. I will be happy with what I make.

I want you to know Herbert I am here because my son father is a married man. Everett knows who the father is. My son thinks his father is in the army. Please be careful what you say around him. Please be kind to him. You will have your side of the floor and I have my side of the floor. Respect our boundaries and we will get along. I asked Everett about you he said I can trust you.

Herbert: "Cyd yes you can trust me. I get that a lot from women for whatever reason. I never did anything wrong. I knew that question was going to be asked. I am going to spend most of my time elsewhere. I will not be here a lot."

Everett: "If you two have any problems with each other let me know. I will need both of you to be in this building to gather. I need Herbert to be here and pay me some rent so I can pay his bookkeeping salary. I need you Cyd more than Herbert. I told you when we first met that I lived with him for four years. You can trust him. I can trust him with my girlfriend. I can trust him with my mother. I can trust him with you and your son.

My father told me you were the best person at what you did. I didn't think that a pastry chef from France was what I needed to make chicken wings. Like he always does. My father knows what a deal needs, to make a deal work. Cyd, we haven't even open and you are going to be the important ingredient to make this business work. I would like to be selling those pastry to those places as soon as we can. Cyd, we need to start working the hours that will need to be worked to make those pastries and specialty bread. Please tell me what time do we have to get up. Herbert you can go if you want to. Cyd and I will work out a schedule between us."

Herbert: "Ok Everett good bye. Cyd I am ok."

Everett: "Talk to you later Buddy."

Cyd: "Thank you Herbert good bye."

Herbert leaves. Everett and Cyd start to work on their work schedule.

The first week of August Herbert signs a contract with the local hospital for pastry and bread. The second week of August Herbert is delivering pastries and bread to the prison. Herbert has to wait till the first of each month to send out an invoice. The restaurant will not have any money coming in till September."

The last week of August Cyd gets up at four AM as her son is asleep. She goes down to the new kitchen and starts to finish off the dough that was prep for the daily pastries and bread. Six AM Everett comes down after his sit ups and pushups. Everett will start his work day. Cyd will leave with her son and take him to school in the company van.

Cyd comes back with the van at eight thirty. Everett loads the van up with pastries and bread then heads out to the hospital. Cyd goes on with working on new dough. Everett comes back at eleven. Twelve o'clock Everett and Cyd sit down at a table and have a lunch that Everett makes her. The two will talk about supply's first. Then Cyd stars to break down what she knows about dough, flower, yeast and everything else she knows and Everett doesn't. At one o'clock the two go back to work. At two o'clock Cyd is done for the day she takes the van and picks her son up. Cyd and her son will spend the rest of the day together. Everett works on making product and cleaning. At five o'clock he makes Himself Cyd and John dinner. Six o'clock Cyd and her son go up stair for the night. Saturday and Sundays Everett does everything and gives Cyd time with her son John. Everett works till Eleven at night before he turns in. Most of the time Herbert will sleep elsewhere. Sometimes he will sleep at the restaurant. Cyd and Herbert start to feel at ease with each other.

Morissa has spent the last weeks of August with her Father. Her old friends were off living their lives. She spent most of her time by her self-waiting to go back and join Everett.

Morissa talking to her father on the drive-up to school for her Third year

Mr. Brown: "Here we are again Morissa. Here we are again and we are just a little older and wiser."

Morissa: "You will only have to do this one more time dad."

Mr. Brown: "I do look forward to are talk. I think about everything that I did not say, for the six months after I drop you off. Then for the next six months I am thinking of what I will say to my daughter when I bring her back to college. The last time I drop you off I heard you had a boyfriend.

Your mother has told me he is a nice young man and that I would like him. She says he used to deliver the paper to her. What a small world. I am sure when I do meet him, I will like him. If you like him, he has to be a good person."

Morissa: "Stop Dad. When you meet him then you can have your opinion on him. I don't want you to think you have to like him because he is my boyfriend. I want you to like him because you like him. It is important to me that you meet him and see who he is. Dad he cares for me in a way I cannot explain. Sometimes I can't explain how I like him. I like who he is. I love him dad like I never loved anybody."

Mr. Brown: "That is the way it usually works. I am glad for you Morissa. I cannot wait to meet him."

Morissa: "You will dad, just a little longer."

Mr. Brown: "I remember meeting your mothers' father. The man liked me because I was a state trooper. Good job. A reliable person who can take care of his not married pregnant daughter. Lucky for me her father was a realist. He had a daughter who could been impregnated by somebody who he didn't like. We got married and try to make a go of it. He did thank me for marrying her before he died. Somehow your mother and I did live happily ever after. We did it living on different sides of the country. Every father wants what is best for his daughter. I think he knew I gave your mother her freedom. He gave her his money. Your mother won all around."

Morissa: "Dad I want more than that. I want him. I want the way he cares for me and about me. He is who I have been waiting for. I spent his summer with you knowing I wasn't going to live with you anymore. I will be living my life with him. I didn't want to be away from him. This was the first summer I did not mis seeing my old friends.

Dad: "I understand it. You will never be able to spend time with them like you used to. You have changed enough to live as a different person. You are not that same person that your friends are familiar with."

Morissa: "I wonder what my old friends and I will be talking about years from now when we get back together. I guess it will be about the good old days."

Mr. Brown: "That is the way it works for everybody.

Morissa: "Dad I had to make that decision where I would live for the next two years at school. I could go and live with Everett if I wanted to. I have decided to go back to Sues house and live there. I want to work at school like I did the first two years. When you first drop me off at school. I got used to living away from you really quick. It was nice. Not that I didn't mis you. The next year living at a house with those girls was great. I enjoyed being with them. I enjoyed having my life with Everett. I liked having a place close to him and still have time being away from him. I told him that I am going to live with Sue till I finish school. He supported me on my decision."

Mr. Brown: "My daughter who is always so level headed. I can't give you any rules to follow any more. I can only give you some advice now. When I figure out what advice I should give you I will."

Morissa: "I will be waiting for it when you figure it out."

Mr. Brown: "Sometimes I think about you and I can't believe what a good job I did. I see and hear about all the problem some parents have with their kids. I was never able to relate to any problems about kids. If someone was to ask me what my secret was. I would have to tell them to ask you what my secret was. Some day you will have a kid. I hope you have a kid as good as you."

Morissa: "Thank you dad. You told me that before."

Mr. Brown: "Are you going to be working with Everett.?"

Morissa: "No. He has hired a female French chef. I haven't met her yet. Everett told me she has a five-year-old boy. Her name is Cyd and the boy's name is John. Back in France she would make pastries. Her family owns a bakery in Paris."

Mr. Brown: "How did he find her?"

Morissa: "He didn't find her. Everett's father found her. I think there is more to this. I don't want to ask him about something that may be something to do with his father. I will have to be careful on what I say to her. Everett says she knows more about everything then he does. He is just doing what she is asking him to do."

Mr. Brown: "When you told me that he is opening a place that will sell chicken wings. It sounded like a funny idea. From what you told me about his father. I would think that there is something else going on here."

Morissa: "Like what. What else can be going on."

Mr. Brown: "Maybe he is using the place to laundry money."

Morissa: "Are you kidding me. Why would they use a little place like that? Everett would have nothing to do with anything like that. You haven't even met him. I can't believe you would think that about him."

Mr. Brown: "May be it is his father?"

Morissa: "His father has the kind of money he doesn't need to do something like that. His father wants Everett to be independent from his father's money. If he wanted Everett to have a crooked business, he would have bought Everett a used car lot."

Mr. Brown: "Good point Morissa.

Morissa: "Dad Everett doesn't want to gamble any more. He hasn't made a sport bet since last November."

Mr. Brown: "Good for him. I see more people who have quit gambling then you may think. It is the people who hide what they are doing that are the ones with the problem. From a far I don't think you have to worry about him."

Morissa: "I do worry about him. Not in any way you think. I just want what is best for him."

Mr. Brown: "I understand. I once was in love with your mother. I was once young like you. I have a good idea on what you may be thinking."

Morissa: "I don't think about that part of your and mom's life. I haven't ever talk to you about it. I know what happen and what decision you two made. You two were about Everett and my age when you two met."

Mr. Brown: "We were. I fell for your mother and she fell for me. Looking back on it we were two different people. I now think we were bound to break up."

Morissa: "Dad neither one of you found somebody else. You and mom dated other people but you two never remarried. What does that tell you about you two?"

Mr. Brown: "You are right. I never looked at it like that. I wonder what your mother thinks about that. Have you asked her the same question? Morissa: "No I haven't. I just gave you two, something else to talk about beside me."

Mr. Brown: "Won't that be strange. The only thing we have talked about was you."

Morissa: "Sounds like a trip down memory lane for you two. May be this can be the start of a new beginning for you two. I may even be able to give you two advice this time. I could see Everett and I sitting in an aisle watching you two walking down an aisle."

Mr. Brown: "Are you kidding me. We are happy just the way we are. Don't get any ideas in your head. You are still the one who is the product of us two. Say something like that again and I will ground you for life."

Morissa: "You can't ever do that can you. All you can do is from now on is just cope with me. If you do something I don't like there will be hell to pay. When you meet Everett, I want you on your best behavior. Do you understand dad?"

Mr. Brown: "I can't believe this. Where did that come from."

Morissa: "I don't know. I haven't thought about it. I do like it. I think it was going to happen sooner or later. I am going to have a talk with mom come to think of it. She should get a job or do some volunteering somewhere. She just spends too much time at that house by herself."

Mr. Brown: "I would like to see that. Could you wait till you graduated so I can see it. It would mean a lot to me."

Morissa: "I will see how you act when you meet Everett, dear dad."

A couple of hours later Morissa and her Father Mr. Brown pull up to Everett's bakery.

Mr. Brown looks at the name of the bakery above the door. He ask Morissa what does the bakery name mean. "Noble princes" she replies. The place is closed for the last Sunday of summer. Morissa walks up to the mail box. She opens the box and looks for some mail. Seeing no mail Morissa walks up to the front door. The front door is locked as she pulls on the handle. Mr. Brown suggest that they go get something to eat and come back later.

Morissa looks back at her father then pulls some keys out of her pocket book. She looks back to her father again and reminds him to be good. Morissa unlocks the door. She and her father walk in to the building. They walk behind a new counter and enter the kitchen. There is some loud music playing. A couple of mixing machines are on are just as loud.

The back of Everett is seen by Morissa. She ask her father to stay by the door. Morissa walks up to a baking flower covered Everett. She taps Everett on the shoulder. A startled Everett turns around and see Morissa. He grabs on her butt cheeks and pulls her up to him and places a long kiss on her lips. Everett kissing her, notice a man standing by the door. He lets go of her butt and Morissa feet land back on the floor. Morissa father see a pair of baking flower hand prints on the bottom his daughters' jeans.

Everett: "Hi Morissa. It is so good to see you. I mis you so much. Oh, by the way who is that guy by the door? Is he the taxi driver looking to get paid?"

Morissa: Everett meet my father Mr. Brown. Dad meet my boyfriend, Everett."

Everett: "Hi Mr. Brown it is nice to finally meet you. I thought Morissa was coming up next week end. I would have been ready to meet you. I been working on these machines all day."

Mr. Brown: "It is nice to meet you, Everett. Can I come over there and shake your hand?"

Everett: "I am sorry let me come over there and shake your hand. First let me clean my hands off. I have flower all over myself."

Mr. Brown: "You even have some of it in a pair of hand prints on the back of my daughter young man."

Everett looks down to Morissa back side. Then he looks back up to Morissa.

Morissa: "Nice job Buddy. Why don't you turn down the racket in here? Then go upstairs and clean your self-up. I will be down here with my father waiting for you."

Everett: "Ok Morissa I will be right back. Mr. Brown I will be right back. Don't go away."

Mr. Brown: "Right. Right here."

Everett gives Morissa a kiss. He then turns all the machines off. On his way up the stairs he flips the switch off for the music. The kitchen becomes quiet as Everett runs up the stairs. Morissa and her father look at each other. Morissa starts to brush the flower of her butt with her hand.

Fifteen minutes later a showered Everett comes back down in to the kitchen. He is wearing grey shorts and a LA dodger tee shirt. On his feet are a pair of beach flippers. Morissa and her father are sitting at a table waiting for him. Everett goes up to Mr. Brown and shakes his hand. The three of them are sitting at the table.

Everett: "I am so sorry Morissa. I thought you were coming up next Sunday. I wanted to give everything in the kitchen a last run. Then clean the kitchen up for are first week of real business."

Morissa: "It is ok Everett. We will have a talk later about it. Let me try this again. Dad this is my boyfriend, Everett. Everett and his father own this bakery."

Mr. Brown: "Nice to meet you again Everett. I didn't know this was a bakery. Morissa told me you bought a restaurant."

Everett: "We did by a restaurant. My father and I came up with a business plan to sell chicken wing to the college students".

My father arrange for a French pastry chef to come and join me here. Over the summer we were able to get a contract to sell bread and pastry. We have a contract with a prison and a hospital to supply them with some of those products. It was nice to know we have another revenue stream. When school opens again for the year, we are going to be selling breaded chicken wings to those students. I would have had something ready if I didn't get the date Morissa was due wrong."

Mr. Brown: "That is ok. I do have to leave soon. Morissa has told me you are a good cook."

Morissa: "Dad you have some time. You have not eaten since this morning. Everett, please fix my father something to eat. Just make it simple."

Mr. Brown: "Everett please don't bother. I can get a hamburger on the way back."

Everett: "Ok I understand."

Morissa: "Ok Everett you don't understand. I want you to find something for him. Please get him something for me. You know what this means to me dear."

Everett: "I will be back in a few. I think I have something in the freezer upstairs. It will be reheated something. Just stay here. I will give you a tour after we are done. Morissa, could you get your father something to drink. You know where all the drinks are. I even got some wine coolers and Bailys for you. Right back guys."

Everett goes back upstairs to come up with something for Morissa and Mr. Brown to eat. Morissa goes in to the back room. She returns with two beers in one hand. In her other hand is a wine cooler. Morissa takes her seat and opens her drink. Mr. Brown watches his daughter drink alcohol for the first time straight from the bottle.

Mr. Brown: "I didn't know you started to drink. I never seen you drink anything. You are not even twenty-one yet. When did you start to drink?"

Morissa: "Daddy you may not believe this. I even kissed a man."

Mr. Brown: "Does your mother know about this behavior?"

Morissa: "Don't be so naïve. I have talks with my mother you don't want to know about. How come you are not drinking the beer?"

Mr. Brown: "You are right I don't want to know. About the beer can you get me some water. I have a long way to drive. I have a beer I will be looking for a rest room every hour. It comes with age."

Morissa: "Poor old man daddy. I will be right back."

Twenty minutes later Morissa, Everett and Mr. Brown are sitting at a table. Everett had reheated test runs of different breaded chicken wings.

Mr. Brown: "Wow Everett you have something here. These are absolutely the best wings I have ever had. I have been eating fast food for the last three years. Nothing has been as good as this meal. How did you get that taste? This is something different then some simple wings."

Everett: "Thank you. It is something that Cyd has cooked up. I had a little part of the final product. Her specialty is pastry and bread. She has come up with a mixture of bread crumbs that give those wing something different than any other wings."

Morissa: "Where is Cyd and her son John."

Everett: "Cyd took John to see a movie. They should be back later."

Morissa: "How are you two getting along?"

Everett: "Great I just do as she ask. Cyd has been working more hours on just trying to get the taste right for everything we want to sell. We must of went thru several hundred wings. After we got tired of testing them. Cyd and I went to our local neighbor shop owners and used them as guinea pigs. The wings you are eating is what Cyd and I have considered not worth selling."

Mr." Brown: "Young man you will make a killing with these wings."

Everett: "I hope so. I am in debt right up to my ears. Most of the bills haven't started to come in yet."

Morissa: "You will make it work Everett. I believe in you. You will get some cash right after the school opens. After the first month you will get your first check from the prison and the hospital. You will get a better look at what is going to come in. By October Herbert will give you a clearer look at your books."

Mr. Brown: "Morissa are you going to be working here to?"

Morissa: "No dad I told you. Monday thru Friday I will be living where I lived last year with the girls. Still a full-time student. My weekends I will be doing some volunteering. My life for the next two years."

Mr. Brown: "You should do a great business on Sunday when the football games come on Everett."

Everett: "This is a college town. The student are all about Saturday football. College football. Saturday, we hope will be the day that will give us are biggest profit."

Mr. Brown: "It sounds good. I wish you all the luck you need."

Morissa: "Dad mom wants to come here and see this place. You beat her here. Are you going to call her when you get back home?"

Mr. Brown: "No I don't think so. I will wait for her to call me."

Everett: "Mr. Brown do you like bread. I have bread Cyd made. I will be right back."

Mr. Brown: "Sure I would like to try it. I don't mind if I do."

Morissa: "Dad having spent the last two years in this school. I know the kids are going to be buying a lot of these wing. Most kids have a microwave now. Just put those wings in the microwave for a couple of minutes and they are good to go. Breakfast, lunch, dinner or anytime they could eat those wings."

Everett Comes back with the bread."

Everett: "Try some of this bread. Cyd likes this type. This is one of the breads we will make the bread crumbs out of for the wings. We use six different types of bread crumbs."

Mr. Brown: "The bread is also very good. I would be so fat if I worked here. You could not stop me from eating anything I would be working on."

Morissa: "Dad you are not going to have that problem. You will not be here."

Everett: "You could come up on the weekends and see Morissa, Then you could have some of what we are making."

Morissa: "May be not. My father has his own life. If you two can excuse me for a couple of minutes I have to use the girls room."

Mr. Brown drinks the beer Morissa bought out to him before.

Everett: "I could get you another beer if you want one Mr. Brown. I am not much of a drinker. We keep some in the back room."

Mr. Brown: "I think one more would be ok. Yes, Everett thank you."

Everett goes in to the back room and brings out a couple of cold beer.

Everett: "Where are you from Mr. Brown, Where did you grow up?"

Mr. Brown: "New York. Same town Morissa and I live in now. That is where I met her mother. Morissa mother told me you lived in California your whole life. By that LA Dodger shirt, I guess you are a dodger fan."

Everett: "I did live in LA my whole life. I like LA the weather is so nice. My father is a Dodger fan. I had a friend years ago who was a crazy Dodger fan. Me not so much. I may watch a game if my father was around. I like watching him enjoying the game. I would even make him the snacks. It was a lot of fun. I would guess you are a Yankee fan."

Mr. Brown: "Met fan here. Most of the kids I knew were Yankee fans. My father became a Met fan when your Dodgers left New York. He was a Met fan so I became a Met fan. I would watch those games with my dad."

Everett: "There is a Met game on now. I will put it on for you."

Everett walks over to the TV and turns on a baseball game. The game is The Mets versus the Dodgers.

Everett and Mr. Brown are watching the baseball game when Morissa comes back down stairs. Everett and Mr. Brown are sitting at a table eating pastries and drinking beer.

Morissa: "I see we have a baseball game on how nice. I see my father sitting at a table with my boyfriend how nice. My father drinking beer when he has so far to drive. Not so nice. My boyfriend drinking beer who has to get up so early. Not so nice. What am I going to do with you two?"

Mr. Brown: "Everett suggested that I stay at the local hotel for the night. That was nice of him."

Morissa: "Yes Everett that was really nice of you to do that. I think I need to go and get some sleep. Everett I will be in the spear room to night. I guess you can bring me to Sue house tomorrow. I will not be back with you for another week. I thought you mist me this summer. I hope you have a nice sleep. Dad I love you. I will see you soon take care.

Morissa leaves Everett and her father and goes up to Everett's room for the night.

Mr. "Brown: "Everett I have known my daughter longer then you have. From what I know of her you are in trouble. Sometimes it is the way she smiles. That smile on her face is telling me, you are going to be dealing with her tomorrow."

Everett: "Yes I do agree with you on that. There is going to be somebody talking to somebody tomorrow. Would you like another beer?"

Mr. "Brown: "Sure. Why not. While you are at it can you hand me one of those chocolate covered pastries."

Everett: "I see you like those pastries a lot."

Mr. Brown: "Yes I do. I can't remember the last time I had one. I do eat too much fast food. Pastries isn't anything I ever gave a second thought about. Are you going to sell those to? I could see a lot of people liking these."

Everett: "Cyd and I have talk about it. The work we will have for the wings and bread is more than enough for just the two of us. If we can stay open for the first year then we will look in to what else we can do."

Mr. Brown: "I think it is the Mets year. They should have had more than one win back in eighty-six. I think Gooden will go down as the best pitcher they ever had."

Everett: "My father was a Tom Seaver fan. My father said he was the best pitcher he ever saw."

Mr. Brown: "Seaver was one of the best. I don't think he was the all-time best. He was a real good one. A Met legend for sure."

Everett: "My favorite player is Lou Gehrig."

Mr. Brown: "The iron man."

Everett: "I used to pitch in high school and little league. I was considered good at that level. To be that good at the pro level is to be unique. I think even if I had that kind of talent. I didn't have the drive to put the work in."

Mr. Brown: "How fast could you throw the baseball?"

Everett: "Eighty-six with no movement. The ball I through had no movement. Batting practice and a donation from my father was the reason I made the college team. How about you Mr. Brown. Did you play any sports?"

Mr. Brown: "I could hit a ball. I could hit it just far enough to make the warning track. I had the drive but lack any real talent. When I was a kid, every kid played baseball. The kids now adays don't play as much baseball like we did."

Everett: "John, Cyd kid, loves wrestling. He will watch any wrestling match. I brought him a glove and a baseball. He and I will have a catch out back. I enjoyed teaching him how to throw a baseball. The simple fun of a catch."

Mr. Brown: "I always wanted a son to have a catch with. Don't get me wrong I love my daughter Morissa. Something about having a catch with your son. When I lived at home my brother, father and I would go out and have a catch. I miss those days. Morissa told me you don't have any brothers or sisters. Everett did you and your father have a catch?"

Everett: "Sure we did. I think he enjoyed it more than me. I could have had a catch with my friends any time. He wasn't at home a lot. When he was, we had our father and son fun. After a while I could throw a baseball faster than him. I think I was around fifteen when that happen. I could do anything like that better then he could ever have done. He had his dream of seeing me in a major league uniform."

Mr. Brown: "That dream was something every kid I grew up with wanted. Now I think kids want to grow up and be wrestler. That is the sad state of baseball today. The best athlete now adays do not want to play baseball. Not enough action for them."

Everett: "I agree with that. If I wasn't pitching, I just didn't want to be there. I was the best kid at swimming in high school. If I wasn't in a race, I would want to be doing something else."

Mr. Brown: "I hope Morissa has a son someday. I could see myself having a grandson and having a catch with him."

Everett: "How do I answer that."

Mr. Brown: "I understand. You can't answer that. I see that the Mets are up a run."

Everett: "Would you like another beer. I made some ice-cream. Maybe you would like some ice cream to?"

Mr. Brown: "You make ice-cream to. Sure, I will have another beer and I will try some ice-cream.

Everett: "Give me a couple of minutes."

Everett goes in to the back. He returns back to Mr. Brown with another beer and some homemade ice cream.

Mr. Brown: "The Mets are down a run now."

Everett: "Morissa told me you were a bookie Mr. Brown."

Mr. Brown: "Yes that was a long time ago. I wasn't very big. I only had a couple of people who I made bets for. There was another guy who was a big-time bookie. I worked for him. Morissa mother and I got a divorce. She and her father paid me alimony to rase Morissa. I was a state trooper for a while. With the money from my side jobs, I resigned."

Everett: "I was one of those young guys who was a bookies best friend. I would be betting hunches on who I wanted to win. I never won enough. I have a friend named Herbert. He is the bakery bookkeeper. He made more money selling information then any money he would make betting. I stop making any bets right after I met Morissa. I don't mis it at all."

Mr. Brown: "The short time that I collect bets nobody won more than they lost. Sooner or later a better is going to lose. I am glad to hear you gave it up."

Everett: "So am I.

Mr. Brown: "Everett when I leave do you think I can take some of those pastries with me."

Everett: "No problem. We have a lot of test products, Most of the time we donate items like that to the senior center. I will get you something."

Mr. "Brown: "How do you stay in the shape you are with all the stuff you can make, If I could make what you make, I be a fat guy."

Everett: "Genetics or genes. I don't know. I do get ask that question a lot. May be when I get older, I will have a weight problem. Up to now I just burn it off."

Mr. Brown: "I saw your delivery van out front. If you want to get something a little bigger or newer let me know. If you want to get a car I could help. I see all kinds of vehicles in the car lots I go to."

Everett: "I will keep that in mind. Right now, that van is what we can afford. May be in a year or two we will see how things go."

Mr. Brown: "Morissa told me you don't have a car. When I was your age, I had a Camaro with a three nighty eight. That car was so fast. All the guys I was friends with had fast cars. We would race on this secluded road by an airport. That's the way we were. There was another group of guys across town who was all about lift kits and paint jobs. If you want, I could find you a collectable car. Or maybe something that you would like to have as a personal car."

Everett: "I like cars. In California there a lot of people who like to trick out there cars. I grew up walking everywhere I needed to go. I didn't need one. Then gambling was taking any money I could have used for any car. If I have a need for a car, I will let you know. May be you can get one for Morissa."

Mr. Brown: "Her mother would get her a new one. We would pay for it. We would give her a pre-paid gas card. It would not cost her anything. She just doesn't want one."

Everett: "That's her. Mr. Brown, I have taken her on some of the cheapest dates you could think of. She didn't complain or say she didn't want to go on any more dates with me. I had some girls who thought I had my father's money. When they found out I was just another broke guy they dumped me. Other girls just wanted to have more fun then what I was going to show them."

Everett: "The game is over. It looks like the home team won.

Mr. Brown: "I should probably be leaving soon. I can't have another beer."

Everett: "I have an extra cot. I will go and get it for you. I think you had too much to drink now. You could just crash here for the night, I think Morissa would rather have you here tonight then on the road. I know the hotel is close by. You never know what may happen."

Mr. Brown: "That sounds great Everett. I will take you up on your offer. I think your right about Morissa. That girl is the most level headed person I have known. You would not believe what a good kid she was. I had other parent tell me all the problems that there kids were giving them. I never did tell them anything like what they would tell me. She would make plans and do things to make sure everything went right. She was able to not have anything go wrong with her plans. I do wonder how she would react when she did do something wrong. Or if something happen that wasn't in her plans. Everybody has to fail at something. She hasn't had that happen to her yet.

 I thought I would be the one who would be there to pick up the pieces and help her. I never had to do it. She never came home with a broken hart. I waited for the day when she needed me. That day never came. When her mother told me Morissa found a serious boyfriend. I didn't sleep that night. She never had one. I do wish she had had that happen. I wish she failed at something. I thought that she was bound for her first broken heart. I was thinking she was now too old for her to cry on my shoulder. My little girl had grown up. Then I started to wonder who she had found. Her mother said that I would like you. I do like you. I don't think you are going to break her heart are you. I could just tell you couldn't do it.

Everett, I bet you never kicked a dog. You just couldn't do it could you. I would think everybody who meets you likes you."

Everett: "Yes I get that a lot. I like your daughter. I will do my best to keep her happy."

Mr. Brown: "I am sure you will."

Everett: "I am glad you are going to stay here tonight."

Mr. Brown: "Me two. It has been a long-time sense I had so much to drink. You are still on your second can. I guess you don't drink much do you."

Everett: "No I never did."

Mr. Brown: "Everett you seem like the perfect person. I know you are not the perfect person because there is no perfect person. I guess the best I could hope for is that you are the perfect man for my only daughter. A father can only hope for his daughter to find the right man for his daughter. When Morissa told me, she was going to have a girl my life view changed. My life became all about my daughter. The girl I didn't even know yet changed me. Then to see her grow to who she became. The questions she had for me as she grew.

Her wanting to understand why things that didn't make sense to her did happen. She just couldn't understand why people didn't try to be good people. She can't except people having problem that they can't handle without help."

Everett and Mr. Brown stay up till midnight watching old monster movies. Before they turn in for the night the two have a catch out back. The next morning Mr. Brown drives home.

Chapter Nine

Work

It is the day before school opens for Morissa third year. Morissa meets Cyd and John that day. Later that day Everett and Morissa are in back of the restaurant talking. They are on two beach chairs.

Morissa: "Everett I did have a nice relaxing time this summer. There wasn't anything I was worried about. I am going to graduate in two years. Then I will find myself a job teaching. I was thinking about what you would be doing after you graduate and where you would be living. I hoped you would be right here. I knew we would be together somehow. Everything has fallen in to place for us. I was sitting on my mother's deck thinking how happy I was. You have what you always wanted. You have your own business. I am going to have what I always wanted."

Everett: "Morissa if I didn't have this place, I would get by somehow. That is just the way I have lived my life. Having this place is just a job now. I hope I can make it work. I am grateful for having you in my life."

Morissa: "Thank you Everett. I did mis you this past summer. I hope we are never apart for that long again. I was even thinking of flying back to see you. Knowing that we would be able to spend more time together this year was enough for me to wait till summer ended."

Everett: "Starting this place took all summer. I am not sure we have everything ready for our first real day of operation. Cyd is teaching me a lot about the daily routine of a bakery. I hope it all comes together tomorrow. There are so many things that have to happen at the right time tomorrow.

There are so many times and temperature that have to be put together in the proper sequence just to get the right consistency of a texture. So many little details that get a little part for something that takes so many of them to come together as just one product. For the first day of many days. In the coming never ending of days to be."

Morissa: "You are such a good cook. I love everything you make. Everybody is going to love whatever you make. You will be great."

Everett: "Thank you Morissa. I am going to be more than a good cook here. I am going to be a worker of preparation. I am going to be a small business with a pay roll and invoices to pay. I owe my father business partners a lot of money. If I can't pay them back, I will lose everything I have here. That is something I go to sleep with every night. When I get up in the morning it is what I think of. During the day my mind is about prep for the next twenty-four hours. I hope I didn't bite off more than I can handle. There is so much that goes in to just one day."

Morissa: "I will be here for you Everett. If you need me to do a delivery or wash a dish, just ask. Anything else may not be something you would want my help with."

Everett: "Thank you Morissa. I will let you know. I want to see you get what you want. Just get thru the next two years. When you finish and become a teacher, we will work out our lives to gather."

Morissa: "Everett I was talking with my father about what I am going to be doing when I graduate. I told him that I would like to stay here and find a teaching job and be with you. He ask me if I thought if you were going to ask me to marry you. I told him that you ask me. Then I told him I told you I wanted to wait. Then do you know what he told me."

Everett: "Did he tell you to run away from me as fast as you can."

Morissa: "No that is not my father. He told me he trusted me to find the right person the first time I fell in love with a guy. Then he told me I should trust my decisions about living with you. My life with you would not be any factor with me becoming a teacher"

Everett: "I believe that about you. If one of us is going to succeed it will probably, be you. I think you were made to be a teacher. I wish you were my teacher when I was a kid."

Morissa: "Thank you Everett that is a nice thing to say. Do you think you would have been a good student and learn something every day?"

Everett: "Maybe not. I am sure that I would have had a school boy crush on you. You are going to have a lot of young boys having a crush on you."

Morissa: That isn't what I wanted you to say Everett. That isn't anything I can control. I will make sure that I dress like an old lady. I was never what the boys called the hottest girl in school. I am sure that they will find a girl there own age more interesting than some old school teacher."

Everett: "You could threaten them. Just tell them that you have a boyfriend who is a boxer."

Morissa: "I hope I can reach them without threatening them."

Everett: "I am just kidding you. I am sure you can handle any school boy crush."

Morissa: "How have you and Cyd been getting along?

Everett: "We have been getting along great. She knows a lot more about what we will be doing than me. How we are going to be operating is from her suggestions. The way we are going to make things, is going to be different than other places around here. Her French cooking experience is going to have a big influence on the finish product we offer."

Morissa: "You must think it is going to work or you would be doing something different."

Everett: "Herbert has taken some of our products to the people who work at the prison. We have used them as a test to see what people will like. From the feedback we have gotten. We do have food people like. Herbert has set up some contracts to sell what we make at the prison and the hospital. I was talking to my father yesterday about how far we have gotten and what I think the first month is going to bring us. He thinks we do have it right. If he didn't think it, he wouldn't have said it."

Morissa: "You and your father look alike but there is a difference. He has no nonsense confidence. I bet whenever he walks in to a room where a decision needs to be made. All the people in the room look to him to be the person who they can trust to make the right decision. Other people could talk for an hour hoping that they are right. Your father will say just a couple of words of what will happen and what people need to do to make it happen. Every person there will know that they have the right answers to what they didn't know. Those people may of not even know what they needed to be given the answer to."

Everett: "Morissa very good. You just describe my father to a tee. If he became president this country would be a profitable company.

He would have to take a pay cut so I don't think he would do it. The politicians can all sleep safely knowing that."

Morissa: "Everett do you know what I think your father did wrong?"

Everett: "You should be careful with that. I have known him a long time. I could only think of a couple of things. Ok Morissa tell me."

Morissa: "He made only one of you."

Everett: "Morissa there is something I have to tell you. I been waiting a long time to tell you this. I wanted the right time to tell you this. There are some things I have to tell you and I am going to do it now. I been thinking too long on when I should do this. I been thinking too much on how I should do this. I am going to tell you now."

Morissa: "Everett you know I love you."

Everett: "Yes Morissa. I love you to. This goes back to my father when he grew up in this town. You know that rock quarry I showed you."

Morissa: "Yes I remember it. I remember you didn't like being there."

Everett: "Yes you are right. Do you remember this story about my father who was playing with his older brother and some friends one summer day? I will tell it to you again. A group of kids would gather there during the hot days and go swimming in the water hole at the bottom of the quarry. My father and his brother were on the top of the hole playing around. My father's brother stepped on a lose granite slab. The slab gave way. He and the slab fell to the bottom of the quarry. The slab crushed him under the water in the bottom of that quarry. My father lost his brother that day. He said that day change him.

That day made him motivated to become good at whatever he did. He wanted to become what he thought his brother would have been. He lives with it every day he says. It is what drives him."

Morissa: "Everett, I do remember you telling me. I can't imagine how hard that is living with a sibling dyeing. Then to see it happen. That has to be so hard to get over."

Everett: "Your right having a sibling die. Then to see it happen is something that you don't get over."

Morissa starts to cry.

Morissa: "Oh no Everett. Don't tell me. That story you told me about the boy on the beach. The boy who saw the boy on the dock. You were the boy on the beach. The boy on the dock was your brother. The story you told the kids at the hospital. The second part you told me at the casino. Please tell me it wasn't you. Please."

Everett: "I was ten at the time. My brother was fifteen. My brother and his friends would drink out on the docks at night where no one could catch them. He wouldn't let me go out with them at night when they were drinking. I was half a sleep on the beech that night watching them. I was mad at him for not letting me be with him on that dock. Some time that night I saw someone roll off the dock. It wasn't anything I didn't see happen before. I was half asleep and I was thinking that person would just get themself back on the dock like they always do. I fell asleep that night. Then the next morning those guys were back on the beach. They woke me up and ask if I saw my brother. I told them I didn't. One of the guys said he probably went home because he drank too much. I went home hoping to find him there at that house my mother lives in. He wasn't there. I told my mother that I didn't know where he was. My mother called my father who was away on business.

My father told her he would come right home and she should call the police. My mother called the police. She told them I told her about him drinking on the dock and him not being there the next morning. A half hour later there were two police officers at our door. There was a teenage boy body found under the dock that morning. They wanted my mother to identify the body. It was him. My brother. His head had a gash from the dock chain. When he rolled off the dock his head hit the chain and crack his skull. Then his body got tangled up in the chain under the dock. There wasn't anything that would have saved him. We buried him a couple of days later. I had to tell my parent of what I saw that night. I thought that I should have helped him. I thought I could have saved him. They had to convince me that there was nothing I could have done. Once he hit his head, he was dead. I lived what my father lived. My father and I live with the same feelings of a failure to his brother."

Morissa: "I feel so sorry for you two. Everett I can only think of you growing up and having to live with that in your thinking every day. It is so sad."

Everett: "My brother was an athlete and fifteen years young. I was ten and wanted to be like him. He was the best at what sport he played. He had my father drive and brains. My father changed when his brother died and became who he became. It drove him. When my brother died it didn't change me. It had no effect on me. I stayed the same. At ten I was a skinny kid. At fifteen I started to grow in to this body. Everything started to come too easy for me. I started to see people around me change toward me. I could play any sport better than most guys at my age with little effort. School work was easy because I took the easiest class in high school. The girls who used to have no interest in me started to show a lot of interest in me.

I knew something was wrong with me because I had no problems at the time. Then I found my first problem Morissa. It was gambling. It was the only thing I wasn't good at. I found the challenge of my life. I could not be good at it. It wasn't easy and I wanted to be good at it. This was something my brother or father didn't do. I wanted to do this so I could be different from them. I thought it would make me different. My brother would have been a better athlete then me. My father was and will always be smarter than me. I like the rush of winning. I thought I found who I was. I dreamed of making my living at gambling. I may have had this gambling habit if my brother didn't die. For the way it worked out I became a person with a serious gambling disease. Then I found something I wanted more than the want to gamble. Morissa, do you know what that is."

Morissa: "Cooking?"

Everett: "It is you Morissa. You. I want to have you like me. I didn't want anything more then you. The joy of being with you was better than any win at gambling. I didn't need to be my brother or my father. I didn't need that vise. When we would go out on our dates. Those low-cost dates of mine was something I enjoyed because I got to be me for the first time. I was just me. Just me being with you. I didn't have to be my brother, my father or anybody.

When we went to the casino. Part of me was afraid that I would go back and lose everything we had. When I won it didn't mean anything? There wasn't any kind of rush for me. I knew I beat the gambling problem I had. The night when I gave it all back showed me, I found what I wanted in my life. I found I wanted you. When I made that first pizza for you. I found that I wanted to cook and make people happy by seeing you smiling at me. Morissa without realizing it you help me find myself and I love you for it."

Morissa: "Everett you just gave a lot of you to me. Have you ever told anybody what you just told me?"

Everett: "No. not all of it. Just parts. This is something I kept hidden from people. Everybody has parts of themselves that they keep from the world. This is just what I had in side of me. There were decision I made because I didn't know who I was. I found myself when I found you. Thank you."

Morissa: "I understand Everett. Thank you for telling me, about yourself. The girls I live with found you interesting because they didn't understand you. You have a personality like a little boy. I promise I will not tell them."

Everett: "The only person I care who knows about me is you. You are the only person that matters to me. If you tell them, it is ok. Sometimes a person says things to other people they know about someone, not thinking about it. It would not be any problem. I feel like I just had a weight taken off me now that I told you."

Morissa: "Everett. What else would you like to tell me. It can't be anything like you told me about your brother and your father's' brother."

Everett: "Morissa what I am going to tell you now no one must know. You cannot tell anybody. It will affect a couple of adults and a child."

Morissa: "Ok Everett whatever you want. You don't have to tell me anything if you don't want to."

Everett: "I have to tell you this. Cyd's young boy is my half-brother. My father had an affair with Cyd. I was told that it lasted a year. Cyd told my father that she didn't want her son to know his father was a married man. Cyd wants to tell him when he gets older. For the time those two are here no one can know.

I talk to Cyd about this before she agreed to come here and work. She asked about you and I. When I told her that you and I were serious about a long-term relationship, she said I should tell you. Herbert doesn't know and I can't tell him. You cannot tell anybody about them."

Morissa: "I understand Everett I will not say anything. I was glad to meet him."

Everett: "He is a cute little kid. He was playing outside one day this summer. He was trying to hit some small rocks with a stick. Like he was playing baseball. I couldn't help myself seeing him playing with no toys. I drove down to a toy store and bought him a bunch of toys."

Morissa: "What did Cyd say."

Everett: "She just said thank you to me. A couple of days later she ask me if I could teach him some sports. After she saw me playing with him, she told me that I was like a big kid. I am going to enjoy being his unknown big brother. I started to remember all the good times my brother and I had before he died. He taught me how to throw a ball. He taught me how to swim. I don't think I was ever as fast as he was at fifteen. Maybe I will be able to teach John how to swim. If we do good I will by a pool for him."

Morissa: What was your brother's name."

Everett: "My brother's name was Joseph. My father's brother name was Everett."

Morissa: "Everett I will always remember this night. You and I being out here talking like we are doing now. You know we do a lot of talking together. I think we will always be able to do that. Don't you."

Everett: "You are right. We do a lot of talking together. We are probably no different than any other couple."

When two people come together, they have to be able to talk with each other. The other girls I dated would ask me a lot of questions. I just felt like they wanted to tell their girlfriends what there boyfriend was like. I am sure they did the same to all the boys they dated. Morissa did you do that. When you dated other guys did you ask them questions. Then did you tell your girl friends about your boyfriend. Or were you different."

Morissa: "Everett I didn't have a lot of boyfriends like I told you before. Like other young girls we have the perfect boyfriend in our head. We do want to have a boyfriend that are girl friends are envious of. I wanted a guy my father would like. I wanted to date a guy I would like to marry."

Everett: "I did ask you. The last time I check we are not married Morissa."

Morissa: "Everett I know. Ask me when I graduate. I just may say what you want to hear."

Everett: "I will be hoping that you will say yes."

Morissa: "A woman will never let a man know till he ask her. You will just have to ask me again. This time I want you to do the old fashion thing and ask my father's permission first."

Everett: "I will keep that in mind. Thank you for letting me know that. If there is anything else you would like me to do, just let me know"

Morissa: "I will. Everett on a serious note where do you think we will be two years from now. I am trying to figure out what will be the start of the rest of our lives together."

Everett: "I think we will be talking like we are now. Just the two of us. I hope that this place is making enough to stay open. You will be looking forward to teaching full time. It may seem like a long way off now.

This coming year will go fast and before we know it, we will be right back here talking about what are next year will be like.":

Morissa: "Everett can we make a promise to each other. Can we promise to go out back where ever we are and have a talk like this. It would be nice to be able to do this."

Everett: "It sounds like a plan to me."

Morissa: "Everett I was thinking about you telling me, about your father having an affair with Cyd. Can I ask you does your mother know about Cyd and John?"

Everett: "She does. My father and mother relationship change after my brother died. He moved out. My mother wanted to be by herself more. They get along for me. They are happier apart than most people who have been together that long. I can't explain it. It is just the way they are.

Morissa: "I don't want to end up like that Everett. If you ever do that to me it will hurt me. If you get to the point that you would cheat on me, just tell me and I will let you go. I can understand you looking at other women. I will never understand or accept you cheating on me."

Everett: "I would feel the same way if you did that to me. I do understand. Couples are age don't think about those things. My father's life is so different than anything I want. I just want a simple life with you Morissa. Just you and me."

Morissa: "I like to hear that from you Everett thank you."

Everett: "Do you think it is time for us to turn in for the night."

Morissa: "What time do you plan on getting up tomorrow?"

Everett: "Cyd Herbert and I have done some dry runs. Cyd is up first and will start the day at four AM. Then I will come down at Six.

Cyd will leave to drop John off at school then comeback. Her work day will end when she picks John up later that day. I will be down in the kitchen till the next day food prep is ready. If I can't get everything done by a given time. Cyd will go back to the kitchen after she has put John to sleep. Tomorrow is for real."

Morissa: "You say Cyd is teaching you things about your business. How does she know so much?"

Everett: "Her family owns a successful pastries shop in France. She left when she became pregnant. My father wanted to give her enough money to make her comfortable. Cyd wanted to raise her child the way she wanted to. Cyd wants to have her own place one day here in America. My father has worked out payments to take care of her. When she wants to, she will leave with her son John. She says she will know when the time is right to leave and go out on her own."

Morissa: "Do you know if her parents know about her little boy."

Everett: "They know. They know that my father is the father."

Morissa: "I understand, I hope I would have done the same. I give her a lot of credit."

Everett: "Let's turn in Morissa. We start another year tomorrow."

Morissa: "Everett I am too tired to walk up those stairs. Carry me up those stair please."

Everett: "Sure."

The next day. Cyd wakes up at four and takes a shower, She dress in her white pastry chef uniform. A look at herself in the mirror. Her touted chef hat is in her hand. The temperature gauge, pen and note pad is in her chest pocket. The uniform she sees that she has earn the right to wear. A smile from her face that she still fits in to the same uniform she last wore six years ago. Cyd leaves her room and walks into her son's room. The young boy is still asleep. A kiss on his cheek.

Cyd walks out of her door and down the stairs in to a work area of stoves, bread machine, pastry machines, pots and pans. She turns the lights on and walks over to the oven and mixers. Each oven she sets the temperature to heat the dough to create the right consistency and texture. Mixers are turned on. Timers are set and the business of the day starts.

Last night prep work, is today's product that will be offered to be sold as a consumable product. The consumable product that will pay the bills for a new start up business. A new start up business for a young man with no experience in any type of retail business.

Cyd moves are timed steps from station to station. The familiar steps that take her to each station to perform the actions that are needed. The kitchen starts to smell of freshly baked bread and pastry. Flour is spread out on some cooking sheets and cutting boards. Mixer and mixing bowls start to come alive with the repetitive sounds of movement. The kitchen has come alive for its first day of life.

Everett wakes up. He rolls over and kiss Morissa on the cheek. He gets up and does his pushups and sit ups. Everett takes a shower and gets dress into blue jean pants and a white tee shirt. His wallet goes in to his back right pants pocket. A comb goes in to his back left pants pocket.

A walk over to Morissa. Another kiss on her forehead as he wakes her up.

She wishes him luck and gives him a long kiss. Everett leaves the apartment and walks down to the kitchen to join Cyd.

Everett walks in to the kitchen to find Cyd working at a mixer. He notices all the notes written with different color marker on the ovens and mixers. The notes are running time and temperature. With all the sounds being generated Everett walks up to Cyd and gives her a good morning. Cyd starts to give Everett a list of instruction from her memory. Everett just nods his head and gives her the same answer of yes. At seven o'clock Cyd tells Everett she has to leave and get John ready for school. Eight o'clock. Cyd and Herbert are in the kitchen. Herbert takes the boxes of pastries to the prison. Cyd takes some boxes of pastries to the school with her son. Everett and Cyd are trying to get a contract with the school like Herbert did with the prison and hospital.

Morissa comes down in to the kitchen to say good bye to Everett for the week. Everett and Morissa have agreed that Morissa will live with Sue and the girls. A couple of words and a kiss Morissa leaves for the week.

Everett is all alone in his new bakery. He is trying to remember the instructions given to him by Cyd. Then he starts to read the never-ending notes and instructions on the notes written around the kitchen. Cyd comes back to the bakery and goes right to work. Cyd starts to give guidance, instructions and correction to Everett.

Everett starts to lift the one hundred-pound bags that are stack by a back door. He lifts them one by one on his shoulder. Then he carries them to the staging rack. Everett throws one of the bags on to the rack. As he steps back Everett thinks of the one-hundred-pound bag as a basketball.

Twelve o'clock Everett and Cyd stop and have lunch. The two talk about supplies and John. At one o'clock the work starts for the chicken wings. Two o'clock Everett hears the phone start to ring. The calls for boxed chicken wings from the kids at college. The calls start coming if for their pick up only business. The calls keep coming in. Cyd runs out at three thirty to pick up John. Cyd comes back at four o'clock. She takes John upstairs then goes back to help Everett. Everett and Cyd take calls up to nine o'clock when Everett disconnect the phone and locks the door. The two get the last boxes of chicken wings out the front door.

Everett and Cyd just look at each other when Everett locks the door. Cyd breaks the looks and tell Everett to hire two more people from three o'clock on. Her reasoning was needing the time With her son John. There agreement was for her to have time with John. The amount of work was too much for just two people. Her last reason was for a Monday there was not enough time just to do the prep. Everett tells her he didn't know it would be so busy. He also tells her that they sold more wings the first day then he was hoping to sell in the first week. Cyd goes up stairs and checks on John.

Everett and Cyd work till after mid night till Cyd said they have enough ready for tomorrow. Cyd remines Everett to hire two people just to answer the phone and take the orders. The two talk some logistics then they go back to their room. Everett takes all the credit card receipts then goes up to Herbert's room.

Herbert not being in his room Everett drops the Daly receipts on his bed. After Everett takes a shower, he calls Morissa.

The call

Everett: "Hello Morissa. How was your day."

Morissa: "It took about an hour to get back to a school routine. How was your first day as a new business owner."

Everett: "Morissa you can't imagine how busy we were. I think we did in one day what I thought it would have taken a week to do. We have not started to advertise. Cyd wants me to hire two people. I can't believe this is the first day."

Morissa: "That sounds great. You will not believe this. Sue, Becky and Clare started to tell all the people they know to call you for food. I didn't ask them to do it. They just got that idea and they did it."

Everett: "Please tell them I said thank you. Then tell them to stop doing it for a couple of days. If you can ask them to find some people who can answer the phone and take orders. Cyd ask me to hire two people. I think I should do it."

Morissa: "Everett it is your place. She can't tell you what to do. You may want to let her know that."

Everett: "Morissa she has the experience. I am here learning from her. She knows things that I never knew that there are questions to. It may be my place. Cyd is running my place for now. If she wasn't here, I would have closed the place at two o'clock to day. Because of her we are going to start tomorrow with are feet under us."

Morissa: "I am sorry Everett. I did promise to stay out of your work. I am glad to hear you had a good day. I am sure you will make the right decision. If you want me and the girls to find some help, we will."

Everett: "Yes Morissa please do that for me. I think we made enough today to hire more people. When Herbert gets back here and starts doing the books, I will have a better picture of how we did."

Morissa: "I am surprise He didn't want to see how you did today. When do you think he will be back?"

Everett: "I hope he is back tomorrow morning. He has to pick up tomorrow's orders. He can give us some problems if he doesn't show."

Morissa: "Everett what can he be doing. Why don't you call his parents and see if he is there?"

Everett: "I can't do that. That may make a big problem for him. If he doesn't show up tomorrow, I will try and get him at work."

Morissa: "May be he has a girlfriend. You are his friend Everett has he told you he had one."

Everett: "No he hasn't told me, that he did. If he had one, he doesn't have to tell me if he does. His family always wanted to know everything about him. He enjoyed his first freedom at college. He did tell me he just wanted to come and go without those question that his parents would give him."

Morissa: "You had a lot on your plate today Everett, I should let you go. I will bet you are tired.

Everett: "No I can't say that I am. I never did so much work in one day. I should be out on my feet. Cyd told me she didn't think we would ever have a day like we had.

The place she worked in would have two hour that were busy in the morning. The rest of the time was very laid back. Tomorrow, she has to get up and do it all over again. She has to do it with a child. My father hired the right person. I like her. I could see what my father saw in her."

Morissa: "I hope you don't see everything your father has seen of her."

Everett: "You know what I mean. You are the only female I want to see. I do miss you Morissa. It is nice to have you here for the last couple of days.

When I had the chance to look at the clock. I would try to figure out where you were today and what you would be doing."

Morissa: "I was thinking the same thing about you Everett. I can't wait for this coming weekend when I can see you again. I hope you save some energy for me. We will have Friday afternoon Saturday and Sunday."

Everett: "Anything for you Morissa. I will be thinking of all the time we can now spend together. You and me and our own place. We don't have to go out and worry about how much money I can spend on a date. We could have all our dates right here."

Morissa: "That is not going to happen. You and I will not want to spend all are time there. I will treat you to some dates this year. My poor boyfriend who works so hard and so long. Maybe I will surprise you."

Everett: "You may have to wait a couple of weeks. This Saturday the school has a home football game. This place may be so busy Saturday. We will be working Sunday because there are professional Football games on."

Morissa: "We will find some time to be together. You may think about changing your hours sooner then you thought you would of."

Everett: I am going to wait till October. Cyd and I have talked about waiting till then to do it."

Morissa: "Ok Everett, I will let you go now. I am getting tired and I do have an early class. You should get some sleep to."

Everett: "Ok Morissa. Good night. Love you."

Morissa: "Love you. Dreaming of you, good night."

Tuesday Morning Herbert shows up to pick the receipts up and do his morning delivery. Everett tells Herbert that he needs to hire some people. Herbert talks to him of bills, payroll and taxes. The conversation between the two is the same for the next week every morning.

It is Monday morning after the first week of business. The first week was busier then Everett could of plan for. Most of the bakery supplies are gone. The receipts for the first week are far better than expected. Cyd voiced her displeasure with the work load, hours and the anarchy of multitasking. Everett is trying to get Cyd to have more time with her son.

Nine O'clock Monday morning The second week of business. Everett and Cyd are in the kitchen working on their prep. Everett is faxing over orders for supply's.

Herbert shows up and takes the receipts off his bed. He tells Everett he will not be back till Thursday. Everett reminded Herbert again of the very busy week and the suggestion that Cyd made to hire two people to take phone orders and work the take-out counter. Herbert talks to him of bills, payroll and taxes. Cyd enters the conversation.

She tells Herbert not to mis a morning delivery and to hire somebody or she will have him fired by calling Everett's father.

Everett and Herbert agree to hire one person for now. Everett ask Herbert if everything was ok with him. Not seeing Herbert coming back at night was a concern for him. Herbert tells Everett he has a girlfriend and that he was spending the nights with her. Herbert also tells Everett he wants to keep his room here. The two talk about everything that has gone right and wrong with the first week. Herbert tells Everett he will find the person to work for him. Herbert goes off to work with the delivery.

Everett goes back to work with Cyd. A couple of hours later Everett hears knocking on the front door. At the front door is a uniform police officer and three men in suits. Everett opens the door and steps outside.

The police officer introduce himself as sergeant O'Malley. He then introduces the building inspector, the food inspector and the parking commissioner. Everett is told that his business is in violations of numerous town regulation. The building and health inspector were sent by the town to check out some code issues. Everett lets the inspectors in to his business to inspect the place. Everett goes with them and is shown seven major and minor violations. Two hours later Everett's business is close till the violation are corrected and fixed and the fines are paid. Sergeant O'Malley hands Everett numerous fines for customer parking, and hours of retail operation. The last fine Everett gets is for the lack of trash receptacles. Sergeant O'Malley and the inspectors leave. Everett bakery is close with thousands of dollars in finds. He also tells Everett that this side of the college should stay small and local. That he should consider moving to the other side of the college.

A stunned Everett staggers back to Cyd. He ask her to stop working and to come out back with her. He has to talk to her about what just happen.

Out back Everett shows her all the violations and the fines. Cyd looks at all the violations and ask Everett what is he going to do. Everett and Cyd talk about how long the place may have to stay close. Cyd tells Everett she could move to the city and get a job if he has to close. That he doesn't need to worry about her and her son. Everett tells her not to worry about that yet. If he can't open again, he would let her know as soon as he can. Everett and Cyd talk about the supplies and keeping them fresh for as long as possible. Cyd makes a suggestion that he should call his father for some advice.

Everett not wanting to tell his father that he may have failed in his second week tells Cyd he will have to think about it. Everett and Cyd go back in to the kitchen and start to save what they can. By the end of the day Everett and Cyd have the place clean and they have saved what they can.

Five o'clock that day Everett calls his father and tells him about the violations that the city has given him. Everett's father Explains to Everett that small towns or big cities will look to raise capital for the town from parking tickets and ordinance violations. Everett's father has Everett fax over copies of the violations to him. Everett and his father talk for about an hour. Everett's father tells Everett he will look at all the Violations and call him tomorrow.

After talking to his father Everett calls Morissa. Everett tells her about the new problems he now has. Morissa also suggest that he calls his father. Everett tells her he has already done that and he would be talking to his father again tomorrow. The call last about five short minutes when Everett tells Morissa he needs to go out back and get a drink.

The call ends Everett goes out back and looks at the chairs and thinks about just getting drunk for the night and forgetting his problem.

Everett goes to his apartment and puts on gym shorts and sneakers. He then goes for a run down to the stone quarry. He sits on a ledge of the quarry and thinks about how close he was to reaching what he has wanted for so long. He then runs to the cemetery and looks at this father's brother's grave. By the time Everett gets back to the bakery the sun has set. Everett goes up to Herbert's room. Herbert was not there. He would have to talk to Herbert tomorrow.

Everett goes up to his apartment and falls asleep worrying about everything he can't control.

Tuesday.

Everett gets up Tuesday and does his pushups and sit ups. He goes down stairs to see Cyd and John sitting at a table eating breakfast. Everett gets himself a glass of orange Juice and takes a seat at the table.

Everett: "Hello Cyd and John. I see you are already for school today John."

John: "Yes. I don't want to go to school today. I want to stay here and play catch with you Everett. My mom says we can do it another day. I want to do it today. Can't I stay and play with you."

Everett: "I do not know if you know this, John. Your mother is the boss here. Your mother has to tell me what to do most of the time. She is smart enough to know what is right for me and you. I am trusting your mother and you should to."

John: "Ok Everett. Can we play when I get home."

Everett: "Sure I would like that. You can bet on it."

Cyd: "Thank you Everett. Come on John it is time to get you to school."

Cyd takes John off to school. Everett starts to look at all the violations in hope of starting to find a place to start. Herbert walks in to the kitchen and talks to Everett about the bakery. Herbert tells Everett that they will have to be back in business by October or the place will have to close. Herbert leaves for work with some yesterday left-over pastry.

Around ten AM that day Everett and Cyd are sitting at a table looking at all the things that need to be done. The conversation is about the lack of knowledge on how to fix the problems.

They do agree to try and find a plumber and contractor to start the process of getting back to opening the doors. Everett and Cyd spend the next couple of hours on the phone trying to hire someone to help them. After many hours of calls and no firm agreements Cyd leaves to pick up her son John.

Everett is out front putting new trash cans out front. A black four door car pulls up in front of his place. A man with a brief case gets out of the car and walks up to Everett. He introduces himself as Mr. Walter Becker. Then he tells Everett he works for Everett's father. His father is taking care of his fee. Mr. Becker and Everett go inside the bakery. Mr. Becker looks at all the violations and ask Everett not to hire any contractor. He would take care of everything. Everett and Mr. Becker walk around the bakery and apartment. Mr. Becker ask Everett if he had any permits and if he had to show him them. Everett shows him what he had. Mr. Becker takes them and puts them in his brief case. Everett walks Mr. Becker to his car. Mr. Becker reminds Everett not to hire anybody.

He shakes Everett hand and tells him that he is going down to city hall. He then tells Everett that he would be back tomorrow morning. Mr. Becker gives Everett his hotel phone number and room number. Mr. Becker leaves and

Everett goes back to doing some small house keeping things. Cyd calls Everett and tells him she would be back later after she picks up John at school. She wanted to go in the city on the other side of the college and see if there were other place to buy the supplies and the kind of tea she had in France. Supplies that she would like to use when they reopen. Everett appreciated the optimism.

Everett spends the rest of the day accomplishing a lot of nothing. Later that day Cyd comes back with John. Everett and John spend some time in the back of the bakery having a catch. Everett shows him how to hold a baseball. Then Everett shows him how to break in a new baseball met. Everett Cyd and John have dinner together. After dinner Cyd takes John upstairs for the night. Morissa show up about seven O'clock to find Everett out back with a beer in his hand. She gives him a kiss and tell him she will be spending the night. Everett fills her in on everything that has happen in the last two days.

Everett: "That is about all of it. Somehow after one week I may be done."

Morissa: "Everett maybe that person your father has sent can help."

Everett: "I think he may help with some of the finds. There are so many things that need to be done. Herbert thinks I have enough money till October. Then I will be done. Then I will have to go in to bankruptcy. Then I will have to go back home to California and go back to being a life guard for life."

Morissa: "Every small business has some bumpy roads. It is possible by October you are back to having your place up and running. You are just living in the bumpy part now. Now give me that smile that I love."

Everett: "I went for a run last night when I had everything on my mind. At first, I just wanted to get drunk and forget it all. I don't know if it did any good. All I could think of was the past. I couldn't think of anything I could do to help myself. It was just the past I was thinking of. I was thinking of my brother and how helpless I felt after he died. I feel the same way now. Those things that I am capable of doing have never helped me. I am a gifted athletic young man. I have found what all this god given ability is good for. It is good for nothing. There was a time when I thought I could overcome anything. It all came so easy. I don't see myself surviving this. We all have those things in life we want or think we can do. Morissa, I wanted this.

I wanted this so you could be proud of your man who can take care of you. I wanted to show my father that I could be more than his son who was always in his debt. My father never says it. I am sure he thinks my dead brother could have done a lot better than me. Talking to him last night about my problems wasn't hard at all. It was like every other talk we had when I had a problem. He would listen. There would be no lecture. It would be just him giving me the right answer. My mother would just look at me knowing that he knew best for everything and anything. I think this one is going to be different."

Morissa: "Everett, I never saw you so down on yourself. I have fallen in love with you. I love the life we are living together. Even if you lose this place, you will still have me in love with you.

You are doing something people will spend their whole life trying to do. Look at how young you are. You are just trying to succeed at something you were meant to do. When your father helps you. It is like any good father helping his son. Everett someday you may have a son or a daughter and you will be able to help them. You will be able to help him or her because you can. You will be able to help them because you saw yourself go on from this. Everett you will find a way to walk away from this and go on. You and I will be having more of these life occasion together. You may have had the ability to be a professional athlete. I think you never pushed yourself. This is a time for you to push yourself. You may still fail. You can't live thinking that your dead brother may have been a better son then you. You may lose everything. You may lose this place and all the money you have. You will still have to get up the next day. When you get up that next day, you will still be yourself. You will have me by your side. Everett you could not help your brother back then. You can help yourself. You can help us. I have to work at what I want. I am taking help when I need it. I still have to try and succeed on my own.

One day we will both have what we worked for with any luck. If we both don't get what we want for ourselves we will still have each other. You do have the ability to go on."

Everett: "Thank you Morissa. Your right everything came easy for me. I need to do this. I don't want to give up so soon. This is the first time that if I fall other people will fall with me."

Morissa: "Come on Everett I am tired. I have an early class tomorrow let's get to bed."

Everett: "You go on up. I have to call my father tonight."

Morissa goes on up to Everett's apartment. Everett tries calling his father. His father had left the country on emergency business.

When Everett gets upstairs Morissa is asleep in her clothes on his bed. He gives Morissa a kiss. Then Everett goes on down to Herbert room takes a shower and sleeps in Herbert's bed.

The next morning Everett comes down stairs and start to make Morissa, Cyd and John breakfast. The three adults talk to John about his school.

After breakfast Morissa goes off to her classes. Cyd takes John off to school. Herbert drops by in the morning and talks to Everett. Herbert tells Everett he is not going to take any salary till Everett can open up again. Everett takes the offer and tells Herbert he will pay him back like he has always done. Herbert ask Everett as a favor to him if he would hire his younger sister when they open up again. "Anything you want forever Herbert." Everett tells him. Herbert goes off to his job at the prison with some left-over bread.

Everett is by himself again looking at all the task that must be done. The words that came from Morissa the night before comes in to his thinking. The work and what has to be done cannot be found in any combination of reality and time, to a conclusion to come to a completion.

The thoughts of needing an excuse for not having anything done to get the place reopen starts to run in his mind. Then the sounds of a truck out front. Everett walks to the front door and looks out the window. At the curb is a ten-wheel truck. Across the street is the black car of Mr. Becker.

Mr. Becker walks across the street and up to Everett."

Mr. Becker: "Hello Everett. I have arranged to have a plumbing company to come in for the next couple of days. A construction company will be here in an hour to take care of all the building code violations.

With any luck by Friday the town will be here to inspect the place. All your fine were taken care of this morning when the town office open up. I will be here till you are able to open up. You know your father is taking care of everything. He is paying for everything including my fee and expenses.

I have worked for him before on several different jobs and cases for the past twenty years.

I will be up front with you; I am asking you to let these people who I have hired come in and do their job. If you see them do something that you don't like please just call me. Please do not get in there way. I am asking you do we have an agreement."

Everett: "Yes. Whatever I can do I will help."

Mr. Becker: "Everett I need to make this clear. You cannot help. Please just call me."

Everett: "Ok I got it."

Mr. Becker: "Good. One more thing I need to speak to Cyd. Is she here?"

Everett: "I see her pulling up now."

Mr. Becker see Cyd pulling up in the company van. He shakes Everett hand tells him to call him first. Then Mr. Becker walks over to Cyd. Everett sees Cyd recognize Mr. Becker. Cyd runs up to Mr. Becker and throws a running hug around him. He watches as the two talk like old friends. Cyd pulls a picture out of her purse and shows it to him. It must be a picture of John Everett thinks as the two look at it. A couple of more pickups show up. Then groups of men walk past Everett with tools and air compressors. Boxes of plumbing supplies get taken from the ten-wheel truck and in to the bakery. Cyd and Mr. Becker keep talking. Cyd is just smiling from ear to ear.

Another large truck with a giant roll off dumpster pulls up and drops the dumpster. The next truck that pulls up is a lumber truck. The truck has metal studs sheet rock and insulation on it. Everett hasn't moved a foot as men and building supplies go past him. Cyd and Mr. Becker walk past him and in to the bakery hand in hand.

An hour later a town truck pulls up to an empty spot at the curb. Four town workers get out of the truck. They go to the back of the truck and take out a gas power auger, shovels and bags of concrete.

One of the workers start to make marks on the side walk. Another takes six parking signs out of the truck. Everett can read the signs having the words thirty-minute parking. It is an hour later Everett is watching the parade of people workers and supplies come and go past him. Then he hears Cyd voice break his mindless thoughts. She is kissing Mr. Becker on the cheek and saying good bye to him. Cyd watches Mr. Becker drive away. Cyd waves to Mr. Becker. She then turns to a still stunned Everett. Everett just looks at Cyd. He starts to come out of a lost fog. Cyd has a whole of his arm. She is pulling him to the company van and telling him that she wants to show him some places in the city that she saw yesterday. Cyd drives Everett away to the city.

Everett: "Cyd, I guess you know Mr. Becker."

Cyd looks at Everett then waits a couple of minutes.

Cyd: "Mr. Becker to you is Walter to me. He is my friend Everett. We are friends. He was there for me when I became pregnant with John. I am going to tell you about your father and I. At twenty-one I had just broken up with my boyfriend. I fell for your father's charm. I met your father one night in my parent pastry shop. He was asking questions about how a shop like ours worked. He told me he had a son that may open up his own place one day.

I gave him a tour of our place. I offered to show him around some other places. A couple of days later we were having a great time being together. I soon found that I was very happy being with him. We were lovers with the want of being with each other because we liked each other. He told me before we became lovers that he was married. When I did become pregnant, I told him I was keeping the child. He said he understood and offered me anything I needed. Everett my parents had money. I wasn't going to be destitute or homeless with a child. When I told my parents, they gave me support like I knew they would. Your father Had Walter look after me. He was very kind and arrange for the best of anything I needed. I soon became friends with Walter. He was there when John was born. Walter lived next to me for a year before I told him he should get back to his own life.

Everett what your father is doing for you is for both of his sons. I don't know if you fully understand. Your father would give me my own place if I asked him. He would do it for his son John if I asked him. Sometimes a father can do something for both his sons. Everett you can help your younger brother by being a good man to him. You have to let your father do what needs to be done because he can. Then you have to do what you can to help your brother because you can."

Everett: "Ok I understand Cyd."

Cyd: "There is one more thing I should tell you Everett. I asked Walter too redo the second floor. John and I are going to have better bed rooms."

Everett and Cyd talk some more as they stop by some other restaurants and shops. They pick up John in the afternoon. They take him out to dinner. At nine o'clock the two get back to the bakery. They see all the lights on in the building.

The dumpster is full of the inside of the old building. Everett and Cyd go in to the building. They find that their living area are unlivable. Everett tells Cyd that they are going to have to find two hotel room. Everett calls Morissa and tells her where he is going to be that night. Later on, Everett is in his hotel room. Cyd and John are in there own hotel room.

The next day Everett and Cyd take John to school. Everett and Cyd return to the bakery. They are greeted by a new dumpster full of old plumbing parts. The street has new thirty-minute parking sign up and down the street on both sides.

There are new bright green trash and recycling cans also. The next couple of days are the same. Friday comes and Everett and Cyd come back to the bakery after they drop off john.

Friday they are greeted by MR Becker and a new front door and windows.

Mr. Becker greets Everett with a hands shake. Mr. Becker and Cyd have a long hug. Mr. Becker tells the two he has a tour for them. The first stop is the front glass out swing door. inside the redone bakery Everett and Cyd find fire extinguishers, smoke detectors and carbon monoxide detectors. And no smoking signs. On the floor are yellow safety tape placed near ovens and larger mixers. A table in a corner with a time clock first aide box and human resource signs. The sign are state work place law and regulation.

 Regulation from sexual harassment to hours and pay. Everything was redone to conform to all the state regulations.

The whole second floor was redone. A new updated modern bath room, living room and kitchen was added. Cyd and Johns bed rooms had all new furniture. Cyd had Mr. Becker take some storage rooms for the space. Everett floor wasn't changed. The tour ends Cyd is saying good bye to Mr. Becker in the up dated work kitchen. Everett is waiting outside by Mr. Becker's car.

Mr. Becker finish his talk with Cyd then walks out to Everett.

Everett: "Thank you Mr. Becker. I think we are going to be fine now with the local town inspectors."

Mr. Becker: "Yes you will be fine now. I had everything done to a higher stander the what would have been needed. The local inspectors will be back this afternoon. Your father had to pull a few strings to get this done. A call to a governor. Then a call from a governor, to the local mayor helped. We were able to get the right contractors and the supply's quick enough to get the job done. Everett there is going to be a bill for this. Your father and his partners has put the money up. You will be getting the invoice or all of the work and supplies by the end of next month. The invoice will have to be paid by this time next year. If it isn't paid in full by then. You will lose this place and every dollar you had put in to it. The money that was spent on Cyd apartment is not part of what you will be invoiced for. Your father and I will split that cost. My fee is being paid by your father. I wish you luck Everett. Your father and I want you to succeed. I want you to take care of Cyd. I like her. I want you to take care of John and see that he likes his home."

Everett: "I understand Mr. Becker. Thank you for the help."

Mr. Becker: "Good bye Everett. I will check in to see Cyd and you again."

Mr. Becker leaves. Everett goes back in side. Cyd is putting one of her CD in to the new radio CD player. Everett and Cyd talk about the new equipment as they wait for the local inspectors to show up and re inspect the place. Two o'clock the local inspector show up at the bakery. Within five minutes, they give Everett the sign off to reopen. That afternoon Everett and Cyd start the work for the reopening tomorrow. Cyd picks John up from school and takes him back to his new own room. Everett calls Morissa and tells her the good news that they can reopen for business.

Four thirty AM Cyd gets up for the second first day of business. At twelve o'clock Everett turns the sign over on his new front door. Everett starts to take orders for wings. The calls are light as the day turns in tonight. Everett finish up for the day by locking the door then cleaning up for the day. He calls Morissa and talks to her before turning in.

The next work week is the same routine for Everett and Cyd. Everett and Herbert talk again about bringing in Herbert's younger sister. Everett agrees to hiring his sister whose name is Jody. Jody will work the counter and take calls. Wednesday to Sunday One PM till closing.

Jody shows up for work on Friday at One PM. She is a seventeen-year-old girl with short blonde hair with purple dyed streaks in it. She is a tom boy looking girl. She walks through the front door and introduces herself to Everett who is working the counter.

Jody: "Hi. You must be Everett. My name is Jody I am Herbert sister here for the job."

Everett: "Nice to meet you, Jody. I am glad Herbert has a sister that can help us around here. We are getting very busy. I will show you around in a couple minutes. Let me ask you some questions. The first one is do you have any experience."

Jody: "If you mean working. No but I am a fast learner. Herbert told me you would want me to work the register, answer the phone and take phone orders."

Everett: "Yes that is the plan for now. If we get any busier then we can handle. I will hire someone else. Then I may change or add other responsibilities depending on what you can handle."

Jody: "I think I can handle anything you have for me to do."

Everett: "Great let me take you inside. Cyd is the person who will run the kitchen. She makes all the dough and the pastries we sell. I help her with the preparation, cooking and cleaning. I am the owner. Cyd is the one who has the experience in what this business is trying to sell.

Jody: "I got it. I will be happy to help if I can."

Everett: "Good let me show you around. Cyd is in back now she will be happy to see someone join us."

Everett takes Jody to meet Cyd. Then he shows Jody the place. Everett spends the rest of the day showing Jody how to answer the phone and take orders. Jody picks up the work she will be doing. In an hour Jody is taking the orders correctly and processing the credit cards that are given for the phone order and counter orders. By the end of her first day Jody is processing all the order and boxing the orders. The work day ends Everett walks Jody out to her car that is in the parking lot, that is alongside the building.

Everett: "Thank you for helping to day. You did pick it up really quick. Your brother was right to have me hire you."

Jody: "I was glad you like what I did today. It was easy. Tomorrow may be you can show me some other things I can do for you."

Everett: "For the next week we will see what happens. I will ask Cyd what she thinks."

Jody: "Yes Cyd to. I didn't get a chance to talk to her much today. I am sure we will get along. Herbert told me she sleep with her son upstairs to."

Everett: "Her and her son sleep on the second floor. I sleep on the third floor."

Jody: "I guess your girlfriend stays with you a lot up there. Am I right? Herbert says she is very pretty."

Everett: "She is working on being a teacher. There is a certain amount of her time where she has to do some volunteering. She will be here this week end."

Jody: "I could see why she likes you. You are so nice."

Everett: "We will be busier tomorrow. I will see you tomorrow."

Jody gets in her car and drives home. Everett goes back in side and does some work. Before he turns in, Everett calls Morissa.

Friday Everett and Cyd start their work day. Later that day Jody walks in and starts her day. Jody spends the afternoon working by herself. Later when evening comes Everett is in the front working with Jody.  It is a warm night Everett and Jody are in tee shirts and shorts. Morissa walks in to the restaurant new front door.

She see Everett and a blond girl in a tee shirt working with Everett. Jody stops and looks at Morissa.

Jody: "What can I get you to go babe"

Morissa: "Babe? You can't get me anything. I am Everett's girlfriend. It is nice to meet you, Jody.

Jody: "Hi nice to meet you Morissa."

Morissa: "Everett hello I am going up to your room. When your done down here I will be there."

Morissa blows Everett a kiss and give Jody a wink of her eye and walks around the counter on her way up to Everett's place.

Everett: "Ok Morissa I will be done about ten tonight. I will see you later."

Jody: "Nice girl friend?"

Everett: "Yes she is."

Jody: "Your girlfriend is very pretty Everett. Herbert said you have a pretty girl friend."

Everett: "I will have to say thank you to Herbert. What else did he tell you."

Jody: "He said that I would like you. He said you were a person everybody likes. He was right. I could see why the girls like you."

Everett: "That is not true. There are always people who will not like you no matter what you are like. Herbert and I got along really good. I liked your brother. He was fun to live with"

Jody: "I like you, Everett."

Everett: "Thanks Jody. Let's get back to work."

Everett and Jody go back to working. Nine o'clock Everett locks the door. Nine thirty Everett walks Jody to her car. Jody gives Everett a hug and thanks him for the job. Then tells him how much she like working with him. Everett goes back in side and finish his day. In his apartment Morissa is reading a book.

Morissa: "How was your day, Everett."

Everett: "It went by really quick. We are getting more orders every day. Cyd and I are getting a process down to making the products quicker. Without the work we were doing at first."

Morissa: "How is the money end of it."

Everett: "I think it is going to be good. I will not know till are second month for sure. Herbert who has an eye for those thing thinks that we will be ok. I hope he is right. This is costing me more than I ever thought. All those new cost are costing more than I have in the bank."

Morissa: "You will have time to get back in to the black."

Everett: "That is the good part. I have twenty-four hours a day to work at this. I never worked some much for so long at something like I do with this. Morissa, do you want to know the crazy part of this. I like doing the work."

Morissa: "How about Cyd. Do you think she is ok with all the hours that she works?"

Everett: "Right now she is ok. She wants to spend time with her son John. If her son was younger and not in school that could be a problem. Right now, it is working with us."

Morissa: "How is Herbert sister."

Everett: "A quick learner. She is able to work the front by herself most of the time. That is giving me more time in the kitchen."

Morissa: "What is she like. Is she shy like Herbert.?"

Everett: "No. I don't think so. A bit of a tomboy. A girl who always wanted to compete with the boys. You know the type."

Morissa: "I know my boyfriend is working between two females. I hope I can trust you to keep your mind on the business and not on any funny business."

Everett: "I am going to take a shower. Then I will come back and give you some business talk."

Morissa: "Promises."

Over the next days and weeks, the bakery gets very busy. The morning order for pastry and bread increases. Week day orders for chicken wings level off. On Friday Saturday and Sunday those chicken orders increases every week.

Thanksgiving week come in late November. Morissa fly's out to see her mother who has found a lump on her Brest. Her mother had the lump removed and was expected to be find. Cyd suggest to Everett that they make some pies for thanksgiving and see if they sell. Jody spends most of her free time at the bakery. Jody is a perfect fit between Everett and Cyd. Jody is the person who brings out the pastry and bread to the hospital. Cyd brings out the pastry and bread to the new account at the school that John goes to.

Thanksgiving day is a rainy day. Everett and Jody runs out the deliveries of pastry, bread and pies. Cyd and John spend the next four days with Mr. Backers family in New York city. Everett and Jody finish there deliveries around noon and end up back at the bakery.

Everett and Jody have become comfortable with each other. Morissa and Jody have had few words with each other. Most of Morissa questions to Jody is how was business for the day or where is Everett. Jody gives Morissa the answers and nothing more. Jody has turn Eighteen years old.

Everett and Jody are working at the counter on the slow holiday weekend.

Everett: "Thank you for working today Jody. With you working here Cyd was able to get a brake and take a few days. I would think you would want to be home with your family."

Jody: "No I did not want to be there. We always get in to one of those family fights every holiday. It starts off with all the cooking. Then it is the rush to eat. The guys go watch football and the girls spend the next couple of hours cleaning. Then there is the time when we are looking at each other wondering why we put ourselves thru it. I really hate it all. How about You Everett. What was your thanksgiving like?"

Everett: "Most of the time it was me and my parents. Just the three of us. When the football games came on it was just My father and I. We would bet on the game. I would bet my allowance and lose most of it if not all of it. It would been better for me if I quick gambling back then I wasn't ever any good at it."

Jody: "Herbert was always good at it. He did lose sometimes. Somehow at the end of the day Herbert had more money than he had bet. By the next day he would give most of it to my mother for food or rent or something. With a father who didn't work he helped out when he could."

Everett: "That does describe your brother. He will help people he likes. When we were in college, he would win more money than anybody else. Whenever I needed a couple of dollars your brother would be there. I do mis him. I wish he would come around here more often. When he has some free time."

Jody: "It is that girl friend of his. She controls everything about him. This is his first real girlfriend. The first one he is able to have sex with. She has him so whip it is funny to see them together."

Everett: "I wish he would bring her around here so I can meet her."

Jody: "Next time I see him I will tell him that you want to see if his girlfriend is real."

Everett: "I never had a sister. Are all younger sisters like you."

Jody: "They are when your older brother is a geeky dork."

Everett: "How about you. I haven't seen you with any guys. You are here every Saturday and Friday night. How come you didn't have any dates on those nights."

Jody: "Boobs. The guys I grew up with like girls with big boobs. I have a chest with two small bumps. The boys that like me. I don't like them."

Everett: "You have us guys figured out. It is all about boobs and nothing else."

Jody: "I wasn't born yesterday. I know what you guys like for fun. I think I am pretty enough. Maybe I will grow my hair longer. Maybe I will get a boob job. I am eighteen now."

Everett: "What would your parents think about you getting a boob job. You are still living under there roof."

Jody: "When my father found out how much you were paying me. He told me I was going to start paying him rent and help out with the food bill. He is still not working in hope of getting disability."

Everett: "What are you going to do."

Jody: "I was meaning to ask you something Everett. I guess this is as good a time as any. Can I live here with you? I am sorry I mean here upstairs. Not with you."

Everett: "There isn't another room here. You can't live with me. Morissa would not like that."

Jody: "I know. I don't think she likes me. Every time she and I are here I get this uncomfortable feeling."

Everett: "You two will get to know each other and be comfortable over time. Just give it some time."

Jody: "I hope so. I don't think she trust me around you."

Everett: "Jody, she trust me to be her boyfriend. She trust me to do right by her. Getting back to you living here there isn't a place for you to do it."

Jody: "I was talking to Cyd about it. We came up with an idea. Herbert lives with his girlfriend now. Can I move in to Herbert's room?

Everett: "I guess we can do that. We can't tell the town or we could be inspected again. If you and Cyd think it could be done, Ok. You may not have to pay your father rent any more. You will have to pay me some rent. I will talk with Herbert and see what is fair. You better start being nice to him. He controls what you will be paying for rent and what you will be paid. You should be really nice to his girlfriend so that his girlfriend is nice to him. If you get the picture young lady."

Jody: "I do thank you Everett. I am so happy."

Jody reaches up and gives Everett a kiss on the lips. Everett kiss her back.

Everett: "I wouldn't do that anymore. If anybody walked in here and saw it, we would have a problem."

Jody: "If I had bigger boobs, you would like it."

Everett: "Enough with the bigger boobs. We are all born the way we are. Some guys have muscles and some guys have looks. Some of us are smarter than other guys. It is just how it works out. It works out for you females in other ways. It is called genetics."

Jody: "You don't have to tell me about genetics. If Herbert didn't tell you. I was born with bad kidneys. When I was five, I received two new kidneys. I been fine after they did the transplant. Before that I was really sick. My parent thought I was going to die. They didn't have the money to pay for it. I was lucky enough to have a charity pay for it all. Bad kidneys and small boobs, genetics."

Everett: "That is too bad about your kidneys. Herbert never told me. You do look healthy. I would of never guess."

Jody: "I think science has a cure for anything if it is caught in time."

Everett: "You may be right. Morissa mother a lump on her Brest detected early enough. She will be fine we hope."

Jody: "Getting back to male genetics you said guys are born with muscles, looks or smarts. I guess you received two out of those three of those in your genetics."

Everett: "I don't want to know which of the two you think I have. There is no good answer for you."

Jody: "Ok it will be my secret. Sometimes looks and muscles are everything to us females. We can always buy a computer. You will just have to wonder, what I like about you."

Everett: "Let's get back to you living here. You know when you lived at home there were some ground rules you had to follow. I am going to give you some. The first one is no guys past this counter. I want to keep Cyd comfortable here. If I see or find out you had a Guy up there, I will fire you."

Jody: "Cyd told me the same thing in another way. I did promise her I would not have guys up there. I am glad that is the only one. My father had so many rules in that place."

Everett: "No that isn't the only one. I will make them up as I think you need them."

Jody: "That is so unfair. I get the same thing at home. Rules that is what I get. Do you know why I get rules at home Everett? I will tell you why. Because I am a girl. A female. Herbert or my other brother didn't get the same rules. I did because I was a girl. My brothers could come and go as they pleased. Me and my sister had more rules to follow. More rules and different rules it was unfair. Now you are doing the same thing. If I was a guy, you would have different rules. I would bet you wouldn't say anything if I was a guy with a girl up there. Would you."

Everett: "If you were a guy, I wouldn't let you sleep upstairs. Cyd wouldn't let you sleep up there. You lose that logic. Don't you Jody."

Jody: "You know what I mean. I have different rules given to me because I am a girl. That is what you are going to do isn't it."

Everett: "The best way for me to answer that is just to say you are right. Because you are a girl and living under my roof your answer is yes."

Jody: "Oh my god. How did this happen. I thought I found some freedom. Now I find myself paying rent for a smaller bedroom with rules again. When will this end? When does a girl get free of these rules? Everett, please Tell me when I can make my own rules."

Everett: "I don't know. I was never a girl. Maybe you would like to have a talk with Morissa or Cyd."

Jody: "Thanks. When can I start calling you dad?"

Everett: "You may not want to do that. Morissa may not understand it or like it."

Jody: "What do you think she is going to say when you tell her about me sleeping below you."

Everett: "The rent part she will like. She thinks Herbert is paying you too much. With you being below our bed room. I will hope for the best."

Jody: "If I was a guy, I don't think she would care. Because I am not a guy but another girl just a floor away from her boyfriend, she may not like it."

Everett: "Yes. You are right again. Because you are a girl a woman a female there are different rules. You following some rules will keep us one big happy family Jody."

Monday comes after thanksgiving and the bakery goes back to work. Morissa fly's back from seeing her mother and goes back to school. When Christmas comes to the bakery Everett is enjoying a money-making business. Cyd and Jody are getting along well together. Cyd has developed a big sister relationship with Jody. Morissa and Jody never have much to say to each other.

Spring break Morissa fly's out to her mother house. After the break she fly's back and returns to school. The bakery is always busy and making a lot of money.

Jody is living in Herbert's room. Herbert is living with his girlfriend. Cyd and John and Everett are able to enjoy their time to gather. The three of them are able to have several sit-down meals together.

The rest of the school year Everett and Morissa are able to have a relationship on the weekends. Morissa third school year ends. Morissa fly's out to spend the summer with her mother. The last week of summer she fly's back to New York to see her father.

Morissa father is driving her up for her final year of college. The two have their talk on the ride back to Morissa school.

Morissa: "Thank you dad for taking me back to school. This is the last time you will have to do it. When school ends, I will not be going to live with you. Everett and I will be living together."

Mr. Brown: "I know. I think you are with a good person Morissa. I like him."

Morissa: "Thanks Dad. He likes you. He says you could stay the night again if you want to. He wanted me to tell you that there is no baseball game on. Everett, John and Herbert will be watching a wrestling match. They were telling me how big this one was going to be. The three of them will be in the kitchen watching it all night. You will have a lot of fun being with those guys."

Mr. Brown: "I am looking forward to it. It sounds like a lot of fun."

Morissa: "Dad just think if you had a son how often you could have been doing something like that. Too bad you had a girl."

Mr. Brown: "Morissa you could not have made me any happier. To see you grow up from a little girl to a woman who makes me so proud to call you, my daughter. When I talk to your mother, we shear that same feeling for you."

Morissa: "Thank you dad."

Mr. Brown: "I am glad you spent most of your summer with your mother. I do understand you not spending as much time with me as you used to."

Morissa: "Mom is doing really well. She goes in for her treatment she does everything that she needs to. She has a new life now. She has new friends and a support group for other woman like herself."

Mr. Brown: "When we talk about you, I do ask her about her health. Like you said they caught it in the early stage. I think about the day you will be walking down that aisle seeing her crying."

Morissa: "I look forward to seeing her in that seat. Just think you two are going to be sitting together again. Then I will get my revenge with you two. When the dancing start I am going to call on both of you to be on the dance floor dancing together. It will be my wedding day. Nobody is to get the bride upset."

Mr. Brown: "For you I am sure we will be happy to do it. When do you think, he is going to ask you?"

Morissa: "I don't know. Like I told you before. He has asked me before. I am hoping this spring before I graduate. That is, if he does ask me. One never knows dad."

Mr. Brown: "I would bet he will ask you."

Morissa: "We will see dad."

Mr. Brown: "I heard your friend Tony and Pat got married. I liked them. It seems like those two were dating in grammar school. Every time I saw them, they would be together."

Morissa: "Dad Tony got pregnant. They are buying a house and going without any honey moon. It is all about practicality now. I am sorry I missed it. I really like those two."

Mr. Brown: "When you get married you can invite them to your wedding."

Morissa: "Sure. I would like that dad."

Mr. Brown: "Have you and Everett talked about moving in to your own place away from the bakery? I would think a young couple would want to have some privacy. You could find some nice house up there for a lot less money than you can find down where you grew up."

Morissa: "We talked about it. There are accouple of thinks Everett would have to do before we could do that. He would want to make sure Cyd is on board with what we do. Cyd and John are important to Everett. He gives Cyd almost anything she ask him. It isn't like Cyd ask for a lot. He doesn't question what Cyd wants. The only thing Everett hasn't done that Cyd has asked was to hire one more person. I think that may change this year. Everett just hasn't found the right person yet. The girl named Jody, Everett and Cyd like. She is the perfect fit between the two. Cyd lets Jody watch her son John. Everett wants to trust the person he hires. It is some advice his father gave him."

Mr. Brown: "How much does Everett's father get involved in the bakery."

Morissa: "Not much dad. He sent somebody to help him out the first year when the town closed him down for a week. Everett's father has the bakery's books audit twice a year. Herbert has done a great job with the books Everett tells me.

Mr. Brown: "Do you think he will open another one."

Morissa: "Dad I don't know. Dad enough questions about the bakery. Let me ask you about that woman who called for you. How come you didn't tell me you were seeing somebody."

Mr. Brown: "I didn't think you would be interested."

Morissa: "I would of like to have met her. I hope I didn't keep you from seeing other women when I was around."

Mr. Brown: "Morissa I did see other women. I just kept that part of life to myself."

Morissa: "Why dad. I would have understood you seeing somebody else."

Mr. Brown: "I never found a woman that I wanted you to be around. I wanted you to grow up with just you and I. I was afraid that another woman would have altered who you were or who you became. You had that independence about you. I didn't want you to lose it. Another woman would have tried to give you something that you didn't need. I had to tell a couple of them that I didn't want you to meet them. I lost a couple of them doing it."

Morissa: "Dad I never knew you did that for me. Thank you."

Morissa and Mr. Brown pull up to Everett's bakery. Mr. Brown gets Morissa bags and brings them in side. Everett, John, Herbert and Mr. Brown stay up all night watching a wrestling match on the tv.

Everett has made all kinds of food for the night of fun with the three guys. Everett and Mr. Brown went the night without drinking any alcohol at the request of Cyd and Morissa.

The next day Everett ask Mr. Brown permission to marry Morissa. Mr. Brown drives home not thinking about what he has said to his daughter or what he has to say to her next year.

Chapter Ten

Living.

The first week of the school year the bakery starts to get busy again. The last week of August Cyd gets up at four AM as her son is asleep. She goes down to the new kitchen and starts to finish off the dough that was prep for the daily pastries and bread. Six AM Everett comes down after his sit ups and pushups. Everett will start his work day. Cyd will leave with her son and take him to school in the company van. Herbert shows up and picks up the receipts. Herbert talks to Everett of bills, payroll and taxes. Then Herbert goes off to the prison with the deliveries.

Cyd comes back with the van at eight thirty. Everett loads the van up with pastries and bread then heads out to the hospital. Cyd goes on with working on new dough. Everett comes back at eleven. Twelve o'clock Everett and Cyd sit down at a table and have a lunch that Everett makes her. The two will talk about supply's first. Then Cyd stars to break down what she knows about dough, flower, yeast and everything else she knows and Everett doesn't. At one o'clock the two go back to work. At two o'clock Jody comes back from her school class. She count the register draw and run a tally sheet. She makes out a deposit for Everett to take to the bank. Jody next task is to do orders for stock. She makes out purchase orders and send them by fax to the suppliers.

Cyd walks out front to meet John getting off the bus. Cyd goes back to work as John goes upstairs to do his homework. Everett and Jody talk awhile about supply's and hiring a new person. Everett gives Jody permission to start interviewing a new person. He tells her that he and Cyd will have the final say.

The weeks go by quickly for the bakery. September turns in to October. A new girl has started at the bakery. The girl is a local high school student named Stacy. She goes right to work answering the phone and taking orders.

Thanksgiving holiday Morissa fly's out to see her mother. Her mother is in good health and spirits. She is now a volunteer at the local hospital. Everett, Cyd and John have a thanksgiving day turkey at the bakery. A week later Morissa return to Sue house and school.

Christmas break Morissa stays with Everett at the bakery.

Christmas morning Everett gets up and does his pushups and sit ups. He then goes down to the kitchen and collects the deliveries. He loads them up in the van and runs them out, Cyd has the day off and spends it with her son. Jody and Stacy will spend the day at their parents 'house.

Everett goes upstairs to find Morissa by the Christmas tree they set up in their apartment. Everett and Morissa start to open there gifts. An hour later there is paper, boxes and gifts around them. Morissa gives Everett a kiss and thank him for the gifts. Everett tells her he has one more gift for her. That the gift will be a surprise breakfast for her. Morissa is hoping for an engagement ring and the question would she marry him. She has her yes all set in her mind. Everett leaves the apartment and tells her he will be back in fifteen minutes. Morissa sadly and slowly starts to clean up the paper and boxes. Fifteen minutes later Everett shows up with two plates cover with small kitchen towels. Morissa smile at Everett as he place the plates on a table. The breakfast smell is familiar to her. She just can't place where she smelled that smell before.

Sitting at the table is Everett and a sad looking Morissa. Between them are the two plates with a small kitchen towel on them.

Everett: "Morissa I had this breakfast planned out for a while. This is a special breakfast for us. I don't know if you will remember it. I will never forget it. Now close your eyes, and I will remove the cover."

Morissa gives him another half of a smile and close her eyes. Everett removes the towel and ask Morissa to open her eyes. When she open them, Morissa is looking at a smiling Everett? Morissa eyes glance down to the breakfast to see a small box on top of the same eggs benedict that Everett made three years ago. Everett gets down on his knee. He reaches up and takes the small box and opens it.

Everett: "Morissa I hope this is the last time I will ask you. I love you so much. My life is yours. will you please marry me?"

Morissa eyes fill up with tears. Her hand reaches for the bright shiny ring. She goes to put it on her finger then stops. She then hands the ring to Everett then puts her finger out. Everett puts the ring on her finger then stands up.

Everett: "Morissa you are forgetting to say it."

Morissa: "I am sorry Everett how careless of me thank you. Thank you I love you so much. I been waiting for this time in our life to gather."

Everett: "That is not what I need you to say. I just ask you to marry me. I need the answer of yes I hope."

Morissa: "Oh I am sorry. I had my answer all planned out. I was hoping you would do it for Christmas. I was hoping Cyd or somebody would give me a clue. I thought maybe you told somebody. If you did nobody gave me any clue. I even try to get something out of Cyd's son John. I got nothing at all.

You have no idea what I was going thru waiting and hoping you would ask me. I can't wait to call my mother. She is going to cry I just know it. It will make her so happy. She liked you from that day we met. I am now an officially a fiancé to the best man in the world. Did I tell you how happy I am?"

Everett: "Yes you did. I still need that answer from you Morissa. We need you to say that one word to me. Morissa I will ask you again. Please will you marry me again Morissa."

Morissa: "How many times do I have to tell you. Are you playing with me?"

Everett: "Your part in this is to say yes."

Morissa: "Yes? Everett Yes a million times yes."

Everett and Morissa have a long kiss. Morissa opens her eyes and looks at her engagement ring that is behind Everett's head.

Morissa: "Everett I have to show it to Cyd first. Did Cyd know I couldn't get anything out of her. No, I have to call my mother first so she will cry. It will make her so happy. She could use the good news. This is a big day for her to have her daughter married. My father did you ask my father. If you did then my mother will know. Oh boy. I wanted to tell her first. Please tell me you didn't ask my father. No, you did. I am sure you did that is what you would do. I asked you to do that. I think I did. Everett, you have me so confused on what I should do first tell me what I should do. Oh, my girlfriends at school I can't wait to tell them that I am going to be married. I have to make so many calls. I should have planned this out better. Everett you should have told me so I could have planned it out better. Did I tell you how happy I am.

I am going to be happy being your wife. I love you, Everett. Yes, I will marry you."

Everett and Morissa set a date for the wedding the day after she graduate.

The day after new year's Everett has a visitor from one of the owner of a new casino fifty mile north of the bakery. Everett recognize the man as Tony Peri from the Atlantic city casino. The manager who he met with Morissa two years ago. Toni heard that Everett bakery made highly rated pastries and pies. Four days later Everett, Herbert and Cyd are up at the casino working out a contract for daily Pastries and pies. They make a deal that will make More money than Everett ever could have hoped for.

The bakery will now sell pastry, pies, bread, and chicken wings to the casino. Morissa spring break comes. She spends the break doing volunteering teaching in the local elementary school. Everett starts to look around for a house. Morissa talks Everett out of it till he could pay for it with what he has in the bank. Herbert assures Everett that by the end of the year Everett will have enough money in the bank to buy a house. Herbert suggest to Everett that he has a great business model and consider offering bakery franchise. Everett told Herbert he will think about it after Morissa has a full-time teaching job.

At Morissa graduation Everett closes the bakery down for two weeks. He has worked out a deal with his client's witch enable him to do it. Cyd had left for two weeks to return Home with her son John. She didn't want John to meet his father at this time in his life.

It is Morissa graduation day. Everett is the first one up he does his pushups and sit ups. Morissa wakes up next and start her day. Her day that has been a dream that took her four years to achieve. Her dress and robe are hanging up for her.

The parents that give her support to grow and complete the process of a graduation. Those two parents will be in attendance to watch their daughter achieve a goal. A goal that will be a proud point in both of their lives.

Morissa spends hour getting herself ready. She will do her hair and makeup. At twelve o'clock Morissa parents show up at the bakery together. Morissa father drove up state yesterday and pick up Miss Brown at the local airport. The two are spending the couple of days at a hotel. Everett gives Morissa parents a tour of his bakery and there apartment. Everett has already won over both parents. He reinsure them that he is totally devoted to their daughter.

Everett brings Morissa and her parents to the graduation. Accouple of hours later Morissa walks across the stage. Out of the hundreds of people Morissa waves to the three people who are her life. That night there is a small party behind the bakery.

The next day It is Morissa wedding day. The wedding will be at the local church. Morissa wakes up next and start her day. Everett has spent the night at the hotel with his parents. Her day that has been a dream that took her life time to achieve. Her wedding dress is hanging up for her. Morissa has hired a local hair dresser to do her hair and makeup.

At the local church built with the stones from the local stone quarry. Everett waits with his best man Herbert for Morissa and her father to walk up the aisle. Across from them is Sue Morissa's maid of honor. Cyd was Morissa first choice. Morissa understood Cyd choice to go home with her son. In the church was Everett's and Morissa parents and some college friends. Jody and her boyfriend with some favorite customers are an attendance.

The wedding goes on with Everett and Morissa exchanging wedding vows. Hours later Everett and Morissa are a married couple at their wedding dinner. Morissa throw the bouquet and Jody catches the bouquet. The party ends Everett's father fly's his wife and Morissa mother back home to California. A day later Morissa father drive himself home.

Everett and Morissa spend a week and a half on the same cruise ship Arwen that they visited during their first time alone together. The two spend all their time together being a happily married couple. The captain of the ship has invited them to sit at his dinner table. Everett and Morissa make a one hundred dollar bet on a roulette table. They put it all on green and lose.

Everett and Morissa stay most of the nights dancing being in love with each other. In the early mornings the two are sharing a blanket watching the sun come up over the ocean horizon. During the days Morissa catches up on her sleep or is reading books on how to teach. During the day Everett is running on the deck thinking about his bakery. He gets permission from the captain to watch everything in the ship's kitchen.

Cyd spends her vacation in France showing John all the places that she grew up in. She and John stay with Cyd's parents. Her parent love to hear there grandson speak French and English with ease. It is a sad day For Cyd's parents when Cyd and John leaves and fly back to the states.

A married Everett and Morissa get back to the bakery. Cyd returns back to the bakery with her son John a day after They do. The next Tuesday Everett and Cyd get back to work. The next September Morissa stars to teach Her first class of seven graders.

Everett and Morissa have a talk with Cyd about living away from the bakery. Cyd want Everett to stay close to John.

Cyd: "Everett I like having you spending time with my son. He likes you. He thinks of you like a big brother. I want my son to have a male role model. You are a good man, Everett."

Morissa: "He likes your son. He treats John like his younger brother. He could still do that even if he doesn't live here. I want Everett and I to live in our own place away from his place where he works. I like you and John, Cyd. You know I do. Please understand we are now a married couple. Everett and I will one day want to start a family."

Cyd: "I do understand that Morissa. I am not asking you to live here forever. I am just asking for Everett to stay here a little longer."

Everett: "How much longer would you like us to stay here Cyd?"

Cyd: "I don't know. I want to tell him that you are his brother. I want him to meet his father. I want to tell him this when I think he is ready."

Morissa: "Cyd Everett is not his father. You are asking a lot of Everett to make up for his father. I don't want to live here with my husband."

Everett: "Maybe we can find a two-family house where we can live together."

Morissa: "No Everett. I don't want to be the bad person here. I want to live with my husband. I don't want to live with Everett's work. We are not a boyfriend and girlfriend trying to spend time with each other. We are married."

Cyd: "Morissa if you were in my shoes you would understand."

Morissa: "Everett wasn't in your bed when you conceived John. It was his father. Why don't you find him and have him be the father figure?"

Cyd: "Morissa you know Everett father made it possible for Everett to get his own place. His father made it possible for Everett to get me here. There was no way somebody with my expertise and schooling would work here. This was the deal Everett, his father and I agreed to. I would work here till I wanted to leave. Everett is only paying half my salary. Everett's father is putting the other half in a trust for John. Put the money a side. I have come to like Everett being here with John. Everett's father told me that I would like Everett and that he would be a good brother to John. Morissa when it comes to doing what is right for my son. I don't mind getting ugly for him."

Morissa: "Thank you Cyd. I just lost Living away from here with my husband."

Everett: "Cyd You don't know I lost my brother when I was a little older then John. I wouldn't want to put John thru something like that. Morissa and I will be here till we find a place where we want to live. We may then move out to our own place. We are still going to be treating John the same way. We want nothing but the best for John. My father would buy you a house and pay you enough to make both of you comfortable. Your knowledge for what we make has made us successful. Morissa and I cannot control what you do with John. if we find a place, you will have to make the decision on what you and John will do."

Morissa: "Thank you Everett for those maybes and ifs."

Cyd: "When you leave here Everett. I will make my decision on what I will do or where I will take John."

Everett Cyd and Johns relationship doesn't change. Morissa and Cyd relationship becomes tense at best."

The bakery goes back to business. The pastries and bread go out in the morning. At lunch time the chicken wings get made and put in to their boxes. Everett, Jody and Stacy work the after noon's and close the bakery down at night. Everett, Cyd and John become closer as they spend more time together.

Morissa is teaching seventh graders full time. She is having a hard time with some of the parent of the kids she teaches. Morissa has explained to the parent their children are not trying hard enough. The parents tell Morissa she is too hard on their children. Those parent have gone to the principle complaining about Morissa lack of understanding for their children.

On Morissa weekends and holidays, she spend time volunteering at the city hospital. She is trying to stay away from Cyd and not letting it affect her relationship with John. Morissa enjoys her time with kids that don't have to be graded or given regulation learning criteria.

It is spring break time. Everett and Herbert have a meeting with Cyd to talk about the bakery business.

Cyd: "Everett we talked about what I would do if you moved away. I have changed my mind on that. I change my mind because I am going to tell John who his father is. And that you are his brother. This June when he finishes the school year, I will tell him then. He is starting to ask me more question about having a father. I didn't want to do it when he was in a school year. This will give him two months to think about it. Then to get used to it. I am going to ask his father to come here and meet him."

Everett: "Whatever I could do to help you two I will. If you like I will look for a two-family house."

Cyd: "No you don't need to do that. I will like you and Morissa to spend time with him. He needs to learn that his father and I are his family. That you and Morissa are his relatives."

Herbert: "Are you going to want more money going forward when Everett and Morissa leaves you here. You are going to be the one keeping an eye on his building when they leave."

Cyd: "No this isn't about money to me. This to me is about what I think is best for John. I will need someone to help me watch John some of the time."

Everett: "We could hire someone to baby sit for him when you need it."

Cyd: "I like Jody. She watches John for me some times and John likes her. Jody and her boyfriend are looking for a place to live. Everett when you leave can you let Jody live in your apartment."

Herbert: "My father will not let her live with a boy."

Cyd: "She is over eighteen now. There isn't much he could do when she moves out. Let's be real as you Americans say. If she wants to have sex with him there are a lot of bad places around a college where they could go. I have met her boyfriend and he seems like a nice person. If there is a problem, I will let you know. If you tell her not to have any male friends in the apartment, she may lie to you. I think it is a good idea."

Everett: "Sounds ok with me Herbert. I like her. We do trust her."

Herbert: "No. I don't think it is a good idea. I know I am going to sound like a big brother. I don't think it is a good liability. She can live up there with another female. There are a lot of girls looking for a safe place to live off campus. May be two girls can live up there."

Cyd: "That sounds like you have been thinking about its Herbert."

Herbert: "She has asked me if you were ever going to leave because she wanted to live there. Cyd, I think she has been planning this. Has she said anything to you Everett?"

Everett: "Yes she has asked me when Morissa and I left could she live in the apartment."

Herbert: "Do we agree. She could live in the apartment with another girl. Just one."

Cyd: "I am ok with it. I will get to approve the girl."

Everett: "Alright you will be the hen mother of two single females Cyd."

Herbert: "I will start advertising for a room to rent for a female college student starting next school year."

Cyd: "It would be nice of you Herbert to find a French major for me. I haven't asked for much."

Herbert: "I will see what I can do."

Everett: "Morissa is going to like the news. She is having a hard time with some of the parents of her students. Those parents are threatening to have her fired if she fails there kid."

Cyd: "Can they do that."

Everett: "I don't think so. Those parents probably tell every teacher that."

Herbert: "Maybe. Morissa is in her first year. They could be a problem for her. If I was in her shoes, I would just pass them along to somebody else. Live to teach another student that will try."

Everett: "That's not her. She thinks that every kid can be like you Herbert with the right teacher."

Cyd: "I think Herbert made his teacher look smart."

Everett: "Herbert thought his teachers weren't trying."

Herbert: "Everett just because you want to do something does not mean you are going to be good at it. You have a successful business because of three parts. Cyd knowledge. Your father money backed you. You work seven days a week and live here."

Cyd: "How about you Herbert. You are a part of this."

Herbert: "Number geeks are a dime a dozen. This place may have worked without your father money. Or you not working seven days a week and living here. Maybe. Take Cyd and her ability away you would have failed by now. There are people who can be good at what they do. Not everybody is a Cyd. Cyd is better at her job than most people are at their job. Cyd is the only professional here. She is here because of her talent, schooling and commitment to her craft. She has the drive of a professional.

Everett your father must have known this before he called you about her. He plan this out for you and John."

Everett: "I haven't even thought of that. I have thought of nothing else then this place failing not her."

Cyd: "When you tell Morissa that you and her are going to find that home she wanted. Everything will come together for you two. Everett I will be happy to see you have what you two have worked for. Thank you for having patience with me and John."

Everett: "I understand Cyd."

Herbert: "Your mortgage interest rate will be better if Morissa is working with a government job."

Everett: "I can't worry about that. Next fall she will be back with another group of students and their parents. What else do we have to talk about Herbert."

Herbert: "The casino wants to buy more pastry, pies and bread from us. I talked to Cyd about this possibility last month. If we want to go to the next level you will have to find a bigger place. You need to bring in another kitchen person. Closer to them would cut some overhead. That would help because your payroll would go up a lot."

Everett: "What do you think about that Cyd."

Cyd: "Everett, Herbert I have been offered a job in New York city. One of the chef I know open up a new place there. I did tell him that I wasn't looking to leave here till John went off to college. I don't want to up root John and take him away from his friends yet. I don't want him to change school. I am here. If you open up another place I am going to stay here."

Herbert: "That would be a better company plan. Everett, you go to a new place and Cyd runs this place."

Everett: "How much time do we have to come up with an answer."

Herbert: "I don't know. If they find another supplier, we could lose what we have. If we wait then they may make a bigger offer. If you do find a place to live then you open up another place you could be moving again. I think you should find a place to live. And wait for them to make you an offer you can't refuse."

Cyd: "What kind of offer would that be?"

Herbert: Everett's franchise. A bakery in each casino they own. Then you sell out fast and take the money."

Everett: "Why can't I do it now."

Herbert: "You don't have a million in the bank in case that plan doesn't work. Get the million first. Or something you can fall back on. In six months, you will own the bakery."

Cyd: "Getting back to Jody. Herbert, she needs to Figure out what she wants to do long term. She can't make any money like she is making here. She has no degree in anything. The best job she would be able to get in a bakery would be a dishwasher for no real money."

Herbert: "Everett I need your help on this. If you can tie any pay increases to some kind of college credit If she does that, I will pay for it. Please don't tell her. She wouldn't do it if it came from me. Little sister syndrome."

Everett: "Great I will do it. Anything else."

Herbert: "Nothing from me. How about you Cyd."

Cyd: "No I am A ok as you Americans say."

Everett: "A ok from this American. Let's go."

It is late June. Everett and Morissa have bought a house a couple of miles from the bakery. Everett and Herbert have handled everything after Morissa approved the house.

Jody has moved in to Everett's and Morissa apartment. She has just broken up with her boyfriend.

Cyd has interviewed a couple of girls to move in with Jody in late August.

Morissa has just been evaluated for her first school year of teaching. Seven parents have filed complaints against her for failing there kids. Other teachers have written contributing letters. Those letters state Morissa is not capable of teaching junior high school student at this time. Morissa was asked not to return to teaching at that level of education. The principle recommend that Morissa start teaching student in the early years of elementary school. Morissa drives home after her meeting. When she enters her house, it is a bottle of bailey's she goes for. Then it is her back deck of the house.

A half a bottle later Everett finds her in a deck chair with the bottle. Everett takes the deck chair next to her.

Everett: "How did it go tonight Morissa. You don't look so good."

Morissa starts crying and talking.

Morissa: "That is a nice thing to say to your wife. Hi dear. Hi love of my life. Do you know how bad you look tonight dear? You must have a big problem dear because you look like shit. Well Mr. Everett, I have some good news and some bad news for me. What would you like to hear first Everett? Well. Don't answer that. I will tell you. The good news is I will not be teaching any junior high school students next year. I may never have to worry about that. The better news it was suggested that I start with younger students like first graders. First grader so I can learn how to relate to those simpler students. Not that first grader it isn't teaching I am told. I am told that I can't do what I want to do. Everett now the bad news.

The bad news is that I am not good enough to do what I have spent my life working to do. Do you have any idea what that is like? How could you. Everything you have done came easy to you. You went thru life not even trying till you got the bakery. Then you just turn that switch in your head and that magic happen. How do you do it. I worked so hard. I worked so long. I am so smart. I was made to teach. Every place I volunteer they said I was so good with the children. My First year. I couldn't succeed my first year. Why or how did I ever think I could do it. Maybe I should of just past all the kids. I would have been given a pat on the back, It would have been like going around go and collect two hundred dollars. Now I am crying here and sitting in my own humiliation of shit. I am here getting good and drunk because I now know what I am good at.

This can't be happening to me. I did everything right. I followed all the rules to the tee. I had no grey area. I went right by the book. No favoritism. My boss could not show me what I did wrong. I know my job. I learn everything that the state said I needed to learn. I took every class I needed to take. I always received a grade of A my whole life. Give in to those parent that wanted me to give there kid a pass for not trying. Please. Give a child an excuse not to push themselves. What kind of parents would do that? Those parent should of thank me for pushing their kids to try harder. You know who gets pushed at the end Everett. MR perfect. Me that's who.

I know who could have done better Mr., Athlete who didn't even try being one. You could have related to those kids. One of them had a betting slip in class one day. Instead of bring in his homework he brought that to school. Did you do that Mr. success. I could see you walking up to any of the kids that I did not reach. You would just say something in his ear. Then that kid would be the next president.

I haven't met anybody who does it like you Everett. You didn't have to take my side or Cyd side when I wanted to leave that bakery. Did I ever tell you I hated that place? That place smells of flour. Cyd has that smell on her.

You had that smell on you. I hated that smell. Do you know why I never told you that? I did it for you. I lived there because I loved you. I hate that smell and loved you. You got what you wanted Everett.

Everett: "When you get over feeling sorry for yourself. Start thinking about finding a back bone tomorrow. Living our lives, we get those occasions to be part of another life. Occasionally a person has to face they failed a life just once, and live with it for a life time. You will have a life with many occasions to help somebody living a life. You may on one of those occasions do better than me, and save a life. You just fail once in your life time."

Later that night Morissa finds Everett laying down on the bed facing up. He has on a pair of pajama bottoms on. She crawls on top of him and drops the empty bailey's bottle to the side of the bed. She puts her head on his bare chest. Everett puts his arms around her. Morissa then whisper the words "sorry". All thru the night Morissa would wake up and cry on his chest. Everett holds her all night.

Everett and Morissa are sitting at a breakfast table.

Morissa: "Everett: "I am sorry about last night. I had never thought I couldn't do it. I wanted it so bad. I didn't think I could fail at it."

Everett: "You could still teach. Children at that age are the hard ones to reach. Some day you will be able to try it again, If you want to. Morissa those children needed somebody to teach them how important they are. How important it is to reach for their future. That there future can be found with an education.

Take the job of teaching the young children. You have so much in side of you that can help somebody who needs it. I am sorry I wasn't there for you last school year. I never asked how it was going with you. Everything was about the bakery. Maybe I could of help you with the pressure of a new job and career.

Once again, I was looking at somebody who was in need of a hand. You are always there for me."

Morissa: "Thank you Everett I will think about it."

Everett: "Did you drink that whole bottle.

Morissa: "No I spilled some on the deck. It is going to smell of baileys for a while. I will go there later if I lose this hang over and clean it."

Everett: "Do you remember what you said to me last night Morissa?"

Morissa: "Not much. I hope I didn't say anything stupid."

Everett: "You told me you hated the smell of flour. You hated when I smelled of it. Is that true."

Morissa: "Yes I am afraid so. I didn't want you to know. It is so embarrassing. Please forgive me."

Everett: "It is ok. I thought you consider it an aphrodisiac."

Morissa: "No way. At first it didn't bother me. Then you and Cyd started to smell a like. If you weren't so good looking. You would have slept alone a lot more."

Everett: "I have to thank my father next time I see him."

Morissa: "When is he coming here to meet his son John. I would like to be there."

Everett: "Cyd told me he was flying in this week end without my mother. She didn't want to make it too complicated for him. I was asked by Cyd to give them some time alone. Cyd and Jody are running the bakery this weekend."

Morissa: "I wish them luck they may need it. That boy may be so happy to have a father. Or he could wonder why his mother lied to him."

Morissa goes for an interview at the local elementary school. The school is looking for a first-grade teacher. After the interview Morissa is told that they are inviting one other teacher with more experience and seniority. Morissa goes home with little hope of landing the job. In late July Morissa is ask to come in for a second interview. The teacher with the seniority had taken a job teaching at another school. At the end of the second interview Morissa is offered the job. Morissa takes the teaching job of teaching first graders.

John meets his father and is told Everett is his brother. John is happy to hear he has a father and that Everett is his real brother.

Everett spends seven days a week at the bakery. He spends a lot of time with john teaching him about baseball. football and even soccer. Everett promises John that he will teach him how to swim. When John returns to school. Everett loses his time with John.

Morissa starts a new year of teaching in September. In October there is a parent teacher meeting. Almost all the parent are praising Morissa for her understanding of their child. Two of the parents didn't show up.

The next day Morissa and Cyd are looking out a window as Everett and John get some time playing catch with a football. Morissa starts to talk with Cyd.

Morissa: "Everett sure likes it when he gets play time with John. He thinks of John as a younger brother.

Cyd: "John talks about Everett the same way. He wants to play with Everett more then he wants to play with me. Everett is always teaching John some new sport to play. After he spends time with Everett. John comes back to me and shows me what he has learned. It could be how to hold a ball, kick a soccer ball to swing a baseball bat."

Morissa: "Everett is one of those guys who can play any sport. If we had a pool, he would show John how to swim. I raced Everett one time at a beech. I never saw anybody swim as fast as him. I think he wasn't swimming as fast as he could. He is just athletically gifted. Something about him and his gifted genes."

Cyd: "He does have a body like an athlete. I have notice."

Morissa: "I have had other girls tell me the same. Did you love his father, Cyd? If I could ask you."

Cyd: "I wasn't in love with him like you are with Everett. I was attracted to his looks and the way he carried himself. A man with some power and money.

A man who showed me a couple of months of being wine and dined. I knew he was married. I knew I wasn't is only affair. I knew I wanted him like he wanted me. When I became pregnant with John my life changed. I told Everett's father that I was going to keep my child. He told me that I could have anything. Anything but him as a father that would be there for his son. Mr. Barret became my best friend and champion. I wish I met him first. That time in my life was so complicated. Mr. Barret gave me my freedom and the means to keep John secure. He gave me the power to be me and have John in my life. Having a child has given me a bond with somebody that will always be part of me. Some day you will understand that."

Morissa: "I am thinking of when will it be the best time to have a baby. I think when Everett and I our able to spend time with a baby would be best. Sometimes I think I should have one now why we are young enough so we have more than one."

Cyd: "What does Everett want."

Morissa: "Everett and I took precautions before we got married. We are still taking the same precautions. I haven't talked to him about having any babies. Are talk being always was trying to avoid one."

Cyd: "Don't be afraid to have one because you want to teach. We as women can now do what we want to do. I have my child and the career that I want. We are both educated and have structure and people in our lives that can help us. I have talked to Jody about being a woman with an education. I think she will make the right decisions for herself. She wants to be like you Morissa."

Morissa: "I think she would like to have Everett for herself."

Cyd: "You are correct. Morissa you can trust Everett. He is a good man."

Morissa: "I do, Thank you. He hasn't given me any cause to worry about what he may do."

Cyd: "He may look like his father. After getting to know both of them I can tell you they are two different people."

Morissa: "I think it is time I take that big kid name Everett home. John is starting to tire him out"

Cyd: "I have to get John in a bath before bed. I will go and tell them that play time is over."

Morissa: "If Everett starts to cry don't worry about it. I will put a smile on his face tonight."

That night Everett and Morissa are in bed. Morissa is telling Everett how happy she is.

Morissa: "Everett Cyd and I were watching you and John playing around in the back of the bakery. Cyd was telling me John likes knowing you are his brother. I was thinking the same thing. You are his favorite person next to his mother."

Everett: "He is a lot of fun that kid. If he had his way, we would be out there playing all day and night. Give him a ball and he will want to play a game. Any game."

Morissa: "I am glad you like him, Everett. I could see how much you like him. Did you and your brother play around like that."

Everett: "It was a long time ago. My brother and I were just like any other brothers. There were times when we had lots of fun together. There were times when he took me in to the city just him and me. Nobody knew what we did. He would have been in trouble if we got caught. We did it accouple of times him and I. It was being kids in that big city. All the things we saw. Somehow, he managed to get both of us home before anybody knew we were gone. There were times when I was just a younger pain in the neck younger brother. I always had it easier when he was around. He was the one who had to be the responsible one. I just had to be the younger kid brother. Our father was always away on some business trip somewhere. My mother never wanted to go further than that deck on the beach"

My brother taught me how to swim. He gave me my first drink. Don't get him wrong. He ended up doing something good for me. I got drunk that night. The next day I got sick from the alcohol. It was a long time before I had another drink. That is why I don't drink a lot. I wish I had the chance to thank him.

He was smart enough I remember. He was the let's get a bunch of people together and have some fun. He was all about having fun. The night he died was just a night about fun.

He like my mother a lot. I think he felt sorry for her. He went away with my father and saw some things about him he shouldn't of. My brother and my mother would spend time watching soap opera during the day. My mother let him drink what she was drinking. Maybe that is why he would spend that time with her. I don't know if he just wanted to drink and it was an opportunity for him to do so. It was a sight to see those two talking about Luke and Laura and drinking together. If my mother needed to go to the city, she would let my underage brother drive her. My father saw them at times when he was home. He would just shake his head and walk on by. My father had to know his wife and my brother had a drinking problem. I never heard him say anything to either one of them till after my brother died. When the autopsy was done. My father was told my brother alcohol level was two times the legal level for a person who would be over the drinking age.

He ask my mother if she had put alcohol in his baby bottle to. It wasn't till years later I understood that he was blaming her.

My mother didn't stop drinking. She just stop drinking in front of people. There were times when my father took my mother out on business dinners.

Those dinner where you want to put a family first image, to some potential business interest before you take them for all they got. My father could do that. He would take the best and make them look so bad it would humiliate them. He had the image a stay-at-home wife and the two sons. Then it was one son. It was his one son who like to cook. Then it was his athletic son who like to gamble and cook. He would like to show off how fast I could throw a baseball.

How far I could throw a football. I was always the better athlete then anybody he was showing me off to. I can't tell you if that is why I didn't want to play school sports. I could tell you I didn't like the attention.

Somewhere along the way I found I like the rush of gambling. I didn't need to show off a talent I had. I was really bad at it. I like it better than being good at sports. It was mine to enjoyed by me. Just me. I didn't have to share it with my father. Till I ran in to money problems. Then he would bail me out. Then he would find a way for me to pay him back. That was till I met you Morissa. Thank you."

Morissa: "I understand Everett. Do you look at John as a younger brother? He is your step brother."

Everett: "I know. When I first met him, I wasn't sure how I should treat him. It all came so natural to me. I didn't have to do anything but be nice to him. He is just a good kid looking for a friend. To him I am just a friend. What is better than that,"

Morissa: "I was talking To Cyd about her and your father. She said he swept her off her feet but she never loved him. Your father took the responsibility for John. Then he hired Mr. Barret."

Everett: "That is what my father can do. If he can't fix or solve something, he knows who can."

Morissa: "Everett someday we may have a son or a daughter. I think you will make a great father to them. I could almost see you playing with your own kid."

Everett: "We all think that we will be good at it. There never were the perfect parents."

Morissa: "The kids I teach at school make me think of what are kids will be like when we have kids. I see the parents with their little ones being so proud of them."

Everett: "Those seven graders you had last year were once like the first graders. We were all first graders at one time."

Morissa: "I hope the children I am teaching now will be a better seventh grader then the ones I had."

Everett: "They will probably be a lot better seventh grader then the ones you had to deal with."

Morissa: "Someday we are going to make plans to have kids. When both of us think the time is right."

Everett: "I don't ever think the time will be right. I think one of us will just look at the other one and say it is time. Even if we try and plan it out something will change a plan."

Morissa: "Everett do you know what time it is."

Everett: "Yes. It is past eleven and we both have to go to work tomorrow."

Morissa: "It is time for us and one more."

Three months later Everett and Morissa are sitting on the deck. They are talking about Morissa recent trip to her mother.

Everett: "I am glad to hear your mother is doing fine again. It is good that she keeps getting those checkups. This being the second lump must be scary for her."

Morissa: "She is able to get the best care and has the fight to go thru the treatment. I lifted her spirits when she saw me. It was a nice surprise for her. Sometimes a simple surprise can lift a person spirit. Don't you agree with that."

Everett: "Sure why not."

Morissa: "Sometimes it is how you get that surprise makes that surprise even better."

Everett: "Sure why not."

Morissa: "Have you ever had a surprise that lifted your spirits. Maybe it was how the surprise was told to you. May be it was who told you the surprise."

Everett: "Sure why not."

Morissa: "Oh by the way how is everything with the bakery."

Everett: "Everything is going good. It is getting easier. The four of us finding ourselves with some free time during the day. John will grab me and want to have a catch in the back. Cyd has told me to stop spoiling him. I bought him a soccer net the other day."

Morissa: "You do not have to be, Herbert smart to see that. If it has anything to do with you having some fun with him. Everett, I think you are going to make the next big sport star."

Everett: "He make think that now at his age. In a couple of years when he starts to be in a competition just to make a team.

When he starts to see other boys his age faster and bigger the himself. If he wants to be the next big sports star then the reality of dedication and work is going to take over just having fun."

Morissa: "When did that reality come in to your thinking."

Everett: "I had a coach that was a bad coach. He never played at any level. He was an overweight wanted to be never got to be. It was all about the show of being a coach. He would take money from some parents to let their kid play. If a kid made a mistake that coach would humiliate that player. When a kid had a good play, he took the credit. If we won after a game, he would take the credit. If we lost, he would get on a soap box and lecture us about commitment.

His father's car lot was the sponsor of the team. I don't know how many kids he ruined. I didn't want to be a part of that again. I played on some school teams because I like just being on a team. I lost the drive to do what it takes to get to that next level."

Morissa: "Don't take this the wrong way Everett. I am glad you didn't become a professional athlete. If you did, I may have never met you. What are the odds of meeting a professional athlete on a beach?"

Everett: "I met you at a bar."

Morissa: "You have your version and I have mine. Some day when we have a kid and they ask how we met. We will have different stories won't we."

Everett: "Every kid likes to hear how their parents met. Someday will have a chance to tell them."

Morissa: "Everett what are you doing about five years from this July."

Everett: "Five years from this July. I will be working at the bakery. Why does five years from now have to do with July?"

Morissa: "I think we are going to be asked on how we met. You may want to start working on your side of the story."

Everett: "Who do you think is going to be asking us that question."

Morissa: "Everett can't you figure it out. Five years from this July. Do I have to draw you a picture?"

Everett: "No I got it. You think John will be asking us how we met. I don't think he is going to be asking that question. Morissa, are we talking about the same thing?

Morissa: "Everett sometimes you just don't understand do you."

Everett: "Ok Morissa. That was a nice conversation. I have some time left before I have to get back to the bakery what would you like to talk about now."

Morissa: "You are just going to kick yourself when I tell you what you can't figure out for yourself."

Everett: "I know we are on the deck. I know we are talking. I know I am talking to you. I have no idea what you are talking about."

Morissa: "It is about this July. Can I make it any simpler for you? Five years from now when we are going to be ask that question."

Everett: "I think I got it. July is Jody birthday and you are going to give her a party. That is good of you to do that for her. I knew you would warm up to her."

Morissa: "This isn't about Jody. This has nothing to do with her. This is about you and me and somebody else. Can't you figure it out. You are starting to make me mad with you. This should be a special time for us. I hope you are not playing with me."

Everett: "Whatever you want to do or may have done is ok. You can tell me. It can't be that big a deal can it."

Morissa: "Whatever I have done you think. What I want to do. How about what we have done. What is going to happen this July. You are so simple sometimes, My mother figured it out just by looking at me. She knew. I didn't have to give her a million clues Everett. She had been waiting for that news the day we got married. Why can't you figure it out? You are the other half to this. I can promise you that."

Everett: "May be I should get back early. This isn't going well is it."

Morissa: "Let's talk about that other bedroom we have. Let's talk about what we can use it for. Have you ever thought about what we could use it for?"

Everett: "We use it for storage. Maybe someday we will have a use for it. Right now, it is storage. I guess you want to do something with that room. Whatever you would like to do is fine with me. Just let me know what you would like me to do and I will do it. I should go now while we agree."

Morissa: "No Everett you should not go now. You should not go till you tell me what I want you to tell me. Everett this July. Using that other room. My mother knew the moment she saw me. What were we talking about a couple of months ago? Look at me can't you tell me what I am. What we are soon to be."

Everett: "Morissa please just tell me. I want you to tell me what you are trying to tell me. Tell me and we will get past it to gather. Together you and me. The way we get past everything."

Morissa: "You are just killing me. I will never forgive you for not knowing that I am pregnant and we are going to have a baby. My mother knew it when she saw me. Now what do you have to say for yourself and the hard time you just gave me. I shouldn't have told you. I should have let you figure it out for yourself. A couple of months from now I could imagine the questions from you. Gee Morissa are you putting on weight, Another dress size I see. I can't believe you ate that much."

Everett: "Morissa I been waiting for this moment. I was wondering how you would tell me. I could have never had had anybody else tell me something like that. Our lives have changed again. You have given me a family and I thank you for it."

Morissa: "How come you couldn't tell. My mother knew. When she saw me. She said I had a glow to me. I gave you every chance to tell me how happy I look. You could have told me that I look good. You weren't thinking that I was putting on weight were you."

Everett: "Could I say you always have a glow. Could I say how happy I am. Could I say how great I think you are. Can I say is it a boy or a girl."

Morissa: "I don't know yet. You and I are going down to the doctor and I will have a sonogram. I was thinking that you would want a boy. I can't make my mind up of what I would like to have. Then I think about us and who is going to be joining us. Just think that there is a person in side of me who will join us. A person, The three of us. You me and a baby. A child. The flight back it was like I was dreaming."

Everett: "When did you find out that you were pregnant. And why didn't you tell me."

Morissa: "On the flight out to my mother I got air sick. I never had gotten air sick. Then it was my mother. She saw me and told me I was pregnant. The next day I got tested and it came back positive. I called my doctor from California and told her. She scheduled me for the sonogram."

Everett: "I have to tell my mother. She is going to be ecstatic."

Morissa: "I told her. I walked down the beach and told her. I am sorry. I just thought she would be so happy. I hope you don't mind. She did call your father. I asked her not to tell you. You can call her now. She would love to talk to you. Call her before you talk to your father."

Everett: "My father is going to be hoping for a girl. He thinks that he would have spoiled a girl if he had a girl. If we have a girl, he will be spending a lot of money on her. We may never have to buy her anything."

Morissa: "I think he would be the same with a boy or girl. I hope he doesn't move here. We don't need him here."

Everett: "Have you told your father."

Morissa: "I haven't. I asked my mother not to tell him. I will call him tonight and tell him. He would love to have a boy. He would love to see a grandson playing a little league game. I could just see him be the bad grandparent yelling at the umpire for a bad call. When I had a swimming race, he would be standing up in the bleachers and yelling me on. Maybe it was just me but I thought of him as an embarrassment. I never thought of this before he is going to want a boy. If we have a boy. Take my word for it. He will find a place closer to us too live at."

Everett: "Your father and I sitting in some seats at a little league game cheering our kid on. You would like to see that wouldn't you. Every father-in-law dream, Can't wait."

Morissa: "Poor Everett. Just think of the quality time you two will have to gather. Most boys have to knock on a girl's door to go out on a date with her. You got over buddy. You never had to do that with me. I would have loved to see you standing with my father as you waited to take me out on a date. I wonder how you would have handled it. Some boys crack under the pressure.

Somehow, I don't think you would of crack. If we do have a girl. You will be the father who will greet that boy who comes and wants to take her out. I could see you asking him on his intentions. The question you will ask him, how did you meet my daughter. Then he may tell you "I saw this babe on a beach with a halter top. I just can't wait for those kind of occasion that you are going to have."

Everett: "What are you going to do about teaching this year. Then what are you going to do going forward next year."

Morissa: "I should be able to finish this coming year. Next year I think it would be nice to stay home for the first year. We will have to see what happens and how it happen as we live it. I hope you don't mind if I stay home for the first year."

Everett: "I don't if that is what you would like to do. The bakery is making enough to support us. I don't know how much money it takes to raise a kid. Don't worry about it just enjoy what we both were hoping to have one day."

Morissa: "Thank you Everett."

July Morissa has a healthy baby boy. The boy is named after Everett's brother Joseph. July Morissa has a line of relatives and friends visiting her and her new baby boy. When August comes Everett is at work getting ready for a new college year. September Morissa is not going back to any school. Her life is all about a baby.

Cyd is spending a lot of time with Morissa helping her with the changes a new mother faces. The changes of changing diapers and feeding. Waking up in the middle of the night for a crying baby. Everett spends as much time as he could with Morissa and his son.

Before Everett and Morissa knew it there son was walking and talking. The terrible twos Morissa was a season mother. The challenges that she once saw as a mother were just another day with a young child.

Everett was still working hard and spending a lot of time managing the bakery. Jody and Stacy worked the counter. Cyd was doing her same work and enjoying it. John has new friends and spends less time playing with Everett.

Herbert was able to work out a deal with the casino. The casino will pick up the daily order Monday thru Friday around mid-day.

Everett's bakery is a well-run business. Herbert is a state employee with a secured salary and pension. Herbert also get a book keeper check from the bakery. Currently he is living with his fiancé.

Cyd and John still live at the bakery. Cyd plans on living and working there till John goes off to college. When John goes away to college Cyd will take all the money Everett's father has paid her and retire to France.

Jody is enjoying her life away from home. She is making more money than her parents are. She is taking some college courses.

Stacy works part time at the counter in the afternoon and weekends.

Everett show up for work one day. He is trying to remember the instructions given to him by Cyd. Then he starts to read the never-ending notes and instructions on the notes written around the kitchen. Cyd comes back to the bakery and goes right to work.

Everett starts to lift the one hundred-pound bags that are stack by a back door. He lifts them one by one on his shoulder. Then he carries them to the staging rack. Everett throws one of the bags on to the rack. As he steps back Everett thinks of the one-hundred-pound bag as two hundred pounds. He mis places his feet and falls backwards. Everett lands on his back. Cyd sees Everett fall and goes running over to him.

Everett is laying on his back with a bag of flower on his chest, looking up at Cyd.

Cyd: "Oh my god Everett. Are you ok? You hit the floor so hard."

Everett: "Yea I hit the floor. I hit it real hard. I think I am ok. I am just hurting all over."

Cyd: "Did you break anything."

Everett: "No I don't think so. Let me gets this bag off of me. Let me sit up. I should be fine in a couple of minutes."

Everett slowly sit up on the floor."

Cyd: "Do you want me to call for an ambulance?

Everett: "No. I think I will be ok. I came off a diving board a couple of times wrong. I hit the water harder then I hit this floor. Let me get myself up and see if I can walk this off."

Cyd watches Everett get on his knees. Then Everett grabs on to the rack of flower bags and pulls himself up. With his feet under himself Everett takes a deep breath then exhales it."

Everett: "Cyd in a couple of hours I should be just fine. I need to walk this off. If I don't my whole body will get stiff."

Cyd: "I should call Morissa. She would want to know about you falling like you did."

Everett: "No Cyd. We don't want to do that. She will just rush down here for nothing. Then she will have me go for a physical. I am over twenty-five now. The morning of pushups and setups have come to an end. I lost a little muscle and weight. Nothing Strange for my age. Morissa thinks anything different with me is cause for alarm."

Cyd: "Now that you bring it up. You have lost some of your muscle. I didn't want to say anything. You are just not the same."

Everett: "I know. I think I will start working out again. Cyd maybe you will want to join me. May be we can turn this bakery in to a gym."

Cyd: "No. No I am not working out. No, I am not working out with you. No, you are not turning this place in to a gym."

Everett: "Ok Cyd you had your chance. Cyd I am going to sit down for a while. Everything still hurts. Do you have some aspirins or something I could take? That may help me start to move again."

Cyd goes up to her room and gets a couple of Tylenol. When Cyd is up in her room, she thinks about calling Morissa. Cyd does not call Morissa and goes on down to Everett.

Cyd: "Here some Tylenol and water for you Everett. I think you should call Morissa. She is going to blame me for not calling her about you. Everett, please call her."

Everett: "Give me some time Cyd. May be an hour or two. I am going to call Jody and have her come in early. I am going to lay down on Herbert old bed. Please don't call Morissa. When I come back down here, I promise to call her."

Cyd: "Ok Everett. I am giving you an ok for now. I may change my mind on that ok buddy."

Everett: "Ok Cyd you have a deal. Then you can give me some more of those pills for the beating I am going to get for not calling her sooner."

Three hours later Everett walks down the stairs and enters the kitchen. Cyd see Everett and walks up to him.

Cyd: "Everett how are you feeling. You were up there a long time."

Everett: "I am still sore all over. I think I will go home when Jody comes in."

Cyd: "Jody is up front. You can go now Everett. Please go home and take care of yourself."

Everett: "Ok let me talk to Jody for a moment before I go."

Everett walks up front and talks to Jody."

Jody: "Oh my poor superman fell down and hurt himself. Poor baby where does it hurt. Please show me and I will give your boo, boo a kiss."

Everett: "I will be ok. I just have to get in to a hot shower and get some sleep. By tomorrow I will be myself."

Jody: "You can go up to my place and take a shower. I could even scrub your back. Then you can lay down in my bed and I will be happy to make you feel better today."

Everett: "Thank you for coming in early. I will be back tomorrow. I thank you for your offer of my shower. My bed. You did make me feel better by coming in early today. You will get employee of the day. I will call our book keeper and tell him you need another rase."

Jody: "Every rase you give me Herbert takes half of it from me. I never see it."

Everett: "Stop your complaining. You know he is putting all that money he is taking from you and putting it in to a 401k. You are going to have a lot of money someday."

Jody: "Someday when I am an old lady. When I am too old to have fun with the money."

Everett: "Thank you for coming in. I am going home to my wife and kid. I am sure my wife is going to make a big deal out of me having a bad day. Bye Jody."

Jody: "Tell Morissa I said hi. Good by babe.

Everett gets in his company van and goes home. When Everett gets home Morissa is waiting at the kitchen table for him. He takes a seat by her.

Morissa: "Hi Everett. Cyd called me she said you fell at work. Are you ok?"

Everett: "I knew she would call you. I am just a little sore right now. By tomorrow I should be just fine."

Morissa: "I thanked Cyd for calling me. I would of drove down there and pick you up. I don't think you should of drove home."

Everett: "I will be just fine Morissa.'

Morissa: "Everett, I have told you there is something different with you. I could understand you losing some muscle. All you do is work in that bakery. When was the last time you had a physical? You are probably eating to many of those chicken wings.

Everett: "My first year of college. I had to have one to play."

Morissa: "You don't even have a doctor do you. For as long as I knew you, I never seen you sick. I didn't think you would ever give up on doing those sit ups and pushups. How long has it been? I don't know when you did stop doing them."

Everett: "Several weeks. I change my schedule because I was having a hard time getting up."

Morissa: "I want you to get a complete physical."

Everett: "Morissa you are making a big deal about this. Tomorrow I will be back to normal."

Morissa: "Dam this, Everett. This isn't about just you anymore. You have a son in the other room. You have a wife sitting at this table with you. She is thinking of you. There is something wrong with you. You are not going to be back to normal tomorrow. You may talk yourself in to believing that. I have seen something different with you. There have been days when you have gotten home. I think a man in his mid-fifty's has just come home. Not the man in his mid-twenties. You are not a ten-year old boy who just has to brush off a scrape knee. I am going to find you a doctor.

You are going to have a complete physical. You don't have a choice in this. You are not going to talk me out of it."

My mother was lucky they found her lump early by an exam. That is what normal people do. You are going to do it."

Everett: "I guess you are right. It would put your mind at ease with me. I am sure that I am fine. The doctor is probably going to tell me I need more exercise and to change my diet."

Morissa: "If that is what you are told. Then that is what you are going to do."

Everett gets his physical results back. The doctor told Everett he is in great shape. The doctor told him that everybody should be in the same shape as Everett. The doctor suggest Everett should start taking vitamins. Morissa and Everett are sitting at the table again talking about Everett physical.

Everett: "Vitamins he told me. That is all. No need to worry about me. I may never be what I was ten years ago."

Morissa: "No. I am not taking that. I know you better than he does. There is something wrong with you. Everett, Cyd and I have been comparing notes on you. You are dropping things that you are holding. Don't lie to me Everett. You know you are doing it. There are things I have notice about you that I can't talk to Cyd about. I ask Jody about you. She said you drop the register draw. Then she saw you have a hard time picking up the coins."

Everett: "May be I need glasses that's all."

Morissa: "Why are you being so difficult with me."

Everett: "Morissa we have gone thru this before. The doctor did say I am fine. There is nothing left for me to do. I promise I will start taking those vitamins. I promise I will start eating better. I promise I will start to exercise again."

Morissa: "You are not a boy scout Everett. Everett I was talking to your father. He is going to call a doctor he knows in New York city. When he gets you an appointment you will be there and have him do some test on you."

Everett: "I don't believe you called him. You had no right to call him. He is my father. This has nothing to do with him. Morissa sometimes I just don't understand you. I finally got to a point in my life that I don't need him to bail me out any more. It is nice to talk to him as a man who can stand on his own feet.

I call him now and talk about my son and how proud I am of him. You just do not understand what it is like for me always needing him. I was free of him coming to my rescue. I was till you called him. You did it Morissa. You did it. I am mad at you. Right now, I don't want to see you right now. My father your hero. Dam I am so mad at you. Dam it Morissa you need me I will be sleeping at the bakery. Just leave me alone please. I can't believe you called him. Bye."

Everett gets up and walks out of the house. Morissa last words to him "Everett you have a wife and a son. You son of a bitch this isn't about you. Don't come back here till you lose you could have been but never was perfect complex. You couldn't save your brother. This may be the time you save yourself for Us".

Morissa calls her mother the next morning.

Morissa: "Hi mom how are you to day."

Miss Brown: "I am right today Morissa. Thank you for calling me. It means a lot for me to have you a phone call away."

Morissa: "I can't wait to fly out and see you again."

Miss Brown: "How is my grandson. I hope you are spoiling him for me. I know that greatest son-in-law is spoiling him. He is just great Morissa you found a great man."

Morissa: "Mom Everett walked out yesterday. He left Joe and I. I was crying this morning when I didn't see him."

Miss Brown: "I am so sorry to hear that. Morissa that happens in every marriage. Sometimes it is better to leave and clear your head before something is said. He loves you so much. I am sure he will be back before you know it."

Morissa: "Mom there is more going on here then you know, This was not any simple disagreement. I think Everett has something wrong with himself. Cyd the person who works with him and I have had a talk. We both can see a difference in him. I asked Everett to get checked out by a doctor. Everett went and the doctor told Everett to take some vitamins and get some exercise. I told Everett that he should ask his father for some help in getting a second opinion. Everett got mad at me for suggesting he ask his father for help."

Mom: "I don't understand why he would have a problem with that. His father has a lot of connection. I am sure that he could be a help."

Morissa: "Male ego is part of the reason. Everett doesn't want his father's help any more. There is another part to this mom. Everett has never been sick. He just can't face he is not perfect. It is hard to explain.

Everett has something inside of him that a health company would like to bottle and sell. There is something that has change with him. If Cyd didn't feel the same way as I do maybe I would not say anything to him."

Miss Brown: "I am now concerned. There are so many places and doctors that can help anybody with anything. I am able to get the help I need. There is so much support. A person just has to look for it."

Morissa: "That is part of the problem mom. He does not want to look for it. He is in denial of something wrong. I can't reach him."

Miss Brown: "He will be back. Don't you worry about Everett coming back. He will be back. When he does you cannot back step. You will have to do what you believe is right. You get him any help that he needs that will keep him in your and Joe's life.

Years from now there will be other parts of your family's life that will need a family to be strong."

Morissa: "Thank you for understanding mom. I did trust what I was thinking, I just kept telling myself to trust in myself. This shouldn't be as hard as it has become. We have come this far without any major problems. I hope that Everett and I will be back soon and we are laughing about this."

Miss Brown: "I am going to see Miss. Stewart tomorrow. Is there anything you want me to tell her? It is just one of those days we get together and compare notes on you two and are grandson."

Morissa: "No mom. Please don't say anything about what I am thinking about Everett. You just don't want to say anything about this conversation."

Miss Brown: "Ok Morissa. I will not see her tomorrow. I will call her and tell her something came up. In a week this could be much to do about nothing."

Morissa: "Thank you mom. I was glad I could talk to you. You know you can't leave me yet. You keep yourself in great health."

Miss Brown: "I will Morissa. Like I said don't give in when you are right. You are doing it for your family."

Morissa: "Thank you mom:"

Miss Brown: "Give Joe a kiss for me. Good bye Morissa."

The next morning Everett wakes up in Herbert's bed. After twenty setups and twenty pushups Everett goes out for a run.

Everett's thoughts as he is running.

I have everything that a man could wish for. My wife is beautiful and she is in love with me. What else could I have hoped for. I have a son that is a little guy, that is the enjoyment a father could have hope for. The place I own is a successful small business. What else in my life could I have hoped for. I did it. I managed to do this by the age of twenty-five.

I don't take any part of my life for granted. I am dedicated to the people around me. I am committed to the people who work for me. The people who are a part of my work life will be rewarded for years to come.

My father who has given me every chance to succeed. I will always be in his debt for his ability to reward me with what I need at the time I need it. His ability to pay me with a check for a commitment from me to be his employee. I am just one of his employees who will perform an act for that check.

The give and take in any relationship. He gives me what I need. I gave him a grandson that is like a trophy fish on his wall.

My mother who is at home. At home with a TV and a bottle. At home with a guilt of a lost son. A son who shared her bottle. A son who was her most understanding person. The son who never needed his father's paycheck. The son who just wanted to have fun. He was just fun with whomever he was with.  My mother who can live her life as an employee to a man she once loved.

Cyd who I have come to know. Cyd who I have come to care for. Somehow Cyd was smart enough to know who my father was. No employee was she.  A young woman who has stayed free of any emotional attachment to my father. She has my father indebted to her. The payment of his ego is far more valuable than any financial payment. Cyd's one task will have him beholden to any request of hers.

John my step brother. A part of me. A part of my father. A person who innocent of any debt to anybody. Just a young boy who loves his mother. A boy who will come to the realization that Norman rock well family picture are not in everybody's family album.

Jody a young woman. A young woman who I have come to think of as a younger sister. A sister who I think of being a little careless. The older brother. No maybe like a father with the advice I give her. The support she gets from Cyd and myself. That support is more then she gets at home. I would like her to find a man to walk down an aisle with. Maybe that is what I want for her. She may want to find herself something else.

Herbert my friend my bookkeeper. My friend that I don't see enough off. My bookkeeper who I see about the numbers that I have to know about. After the numbers meet, he leaves for his own life.

Somebody liked Cyd who has found an independence from a father that I haven't.

Independence that I thought I have found. I have had it. It was better than any short lived high from an athletic achievement. I had it. My calls to my father was about what my son has learn to do. What my son was saying for the first time. When I get up in the morning my wife who loves me. A bank account that lets me never to be in need of his request. A place of work that is an enjoyment of a career.

Morissa my wife now wants to bring me in to his debt again. I can just hear her request to him. Mr. Stewart please help my husband. Mr. Stewart please help your son. Mr. Stewart once again Everett has found himself in your debt. Everett is not feeling well. Mr. Stewart Please find someone who can help him. Everett just can't find someone to tell him what is wrong with him. My husband is having problems with his health. The once physical specimen is starting to be like a normal man. Help him because he can't help himself. You must know someone who will help my Everett. Please find that person because Everett can't.

She did it. She did the only act I can't forgive her for. I am so angry at her right now. I don't know if I can ever for give her. She knows how important it is to me to not ask my father for anything anymore. I don't need him to find out if anything is wrong with me. I had a doctor tell me to start taking vitamins. It is that simple. I have to change my diet it is that simple. I need more exercise it is that simple. It is always so simple when you find out what is wrong with yourself.

Yourself I say? I don't think that there is anything wrong with me. Do I? A couple of months from now I could be back to my regular younger self.

There can't be anything really wrong with me, can there be. I am still young and strong. How many people run as far like I am running? How many in this world could do what I am doing. I have to be at two miles now. How many more mile to I want to go? May be around that cemetery.

Where was I. What was I thinking? I could be back to myself in a couple of months. I could be better than ever if I make a commitment to do some exercise. I may even impress myself. This could just be a new me.

This could be just what I need. I want to do this. I want to do the work to be a new me.

 I will show her what a commitment is. I will succeed at what I want when I put my mind to it. I don't need to have a degree to find what I want to be. I don't need any state approval. Then she has the idea that I need help. I don't need her help. I don't need anybody's help. I could do it on just my physical ability. I will show her. I will show my father. My god given physical ability. I could turn it on any time I want to. My wife doesn't have that ability. My father may have had it at one time. A long time ago maybe. That is all I need to do. Just flip that switch. It never failed me. I will show them.

I can't be wrong. Can I be. Should I try to see it from her side. Her side that is seeing something wrong with me. I have never had anything wrong with me. Maybe a simple cold once in a while. I didn't even need any medicine. There can't be anything wrong with me that can't be fixed.

I think I am five miles now. Still going strong. I should be ok so long as that sun stays hidden. Still cool enough. I wonder if I should have had some water before I left. I didn't think this college was so small. When I first came here this place seem so big. Now it is so small. I wonder who is in my old college room. I did enjoy my time with Herbert. He was a good room mate

What was I thinking? There really can't be anything really wrong with me. I know myself better than anybody. If I was sick or had something wrong with me. I would know it. I am just fine most of the time. What is a little weakness in my trunk? My core just has a bit of fatigue. I dropped a bag of flower. I need to slow up. I am feeling the run. Does anybody have an idea of how many of those bags I have lifted? There may not be a human on this planet who could have done what I have done.

My wife and Cyd thinks there is something wrong with me. I will know when there is something wrong with me.

Do I know that something is wrong? I don't think so. I keep telling myself I am ok. Why does Morissa and Cyd think there is something wrong with me. I wouldn't be lying to myself would I. If I never been sick or had something wrong with me. Would I be able to know I did have something wrong with myself?

How will I know that there is something wrong with me? That will be the day when I can't do anything. I am out for a run today. I must be in great shape. I work all the time. I haven't missed a day because I felt sick. I left early one day. If I thought I need help, would I ask for it. I would know how to ask for help.

I don't want to be in need of help. I don't need any help. If I don't want any help. Is that stopping me from seeing that I do need help. Could I be wrong.

Could I see myself like I really am. I need to think about the long picture with my family and me. Am I afraid to see myself like the people who know me do?

Three days later Everett has not returned home. He has been sleeping in Herbert's old room. Cyd has tried talking to Everett about going back home. She is getting tired of him being at the bakery twenty-four hours a day. The third night Cyd had taken John out to a parent teacher conference. Everett and Jody are alone in the bakery. Both of them are working the counter.

Jody: "Everett are you going to be staying here again tonight?"

Everett: "Yes I think so. I may just live here forever. Jody you would like that. I can keep making you pancakes in the morning. We can have dinner together at night and catch a ball game on TV. We may become close friends."

Jody: "Everett you know I like you. I wish I was your girlfriend. You need to go home to Morissa and your son Joe. They mis you. Morissa and Cyd are always talking about you. Even Cyd wants you out of here."

Everett: "How about John. I think he still likes me.

Jody: "John likes you. You are just fun for him. He is too young to know something is wrong. Everett there is something wrong with you. You have to know something is wrong with you. Can you tell me there is nothing wrong with you?"

Everett: "I can do things most people can never do. I may be a little out of shape. Jody look where I work. This place with the food we make and eat. The type of labor we do here isn't any good for me.

I spent my life on a beach with fresh air. Every day I worked there I must of swam a mile. Up and down that tower. I told Morissa that I just needed to start working out."

Jody: "Cyd and I are not a doctor. We have known you long enough to know that you are not the same. Do you know Cyd and I have both heard you slur your speech?

Everett: "I can go home and hear the same thing."

Jody: "I told you I had to have both of my kidneys replaced. The people around me knew something was wrong with me. I was too young to know anything was seriously wrong with me. If they just past off what they saw what I was going thru. I would have died. The first doctor told my parent to change my diet. They did that and it did not help me. They took me to another doctor. He did a test on me. He found what was wrong with me. Everett Morissa, Cyd and I see you more than anybody else. We all agree that there is something with you that is not right. You are not the same. A couple of days from now you may say you were right.

Then the three of us can never second guess you again. You will always have that on us. We will never second guess you again."

Everett: "Jody, Morissa call my father to help me out again. I don't need my father's help any more. I have a wife and a son. I am here to help them. That is what men do for their family. I can't be sick. I can't have anything wrong with me. My father never mis a day of work. He went to school and washed dishes. He joined the navy and became a lawyer. Whatever he does he does it better than I could have ever done.

Have you thought of who you would like to marry? I bet you have the perfect person in your mind. Don't ever marry that perfect person. You want to marry your equal. If you marry a perfect person. You will live in fear of being look down at. You can never communicate with that person. That person will always talk down to you. You will never be able to trust your own thoughts. You will grow with a fair of being judge as an incompetent person. His friends will never be your friends. You learn to have a fear of talking to his friends. You learn that your pride is safe with your silence. Then comes the alcohol that lets you enjoy a conversation with yourself. Yourself and a bottle. Then you find a family member who like the escape of a drink. Both of you are drinking for a different reason. There no fear of being asked to stop drinking. Your drinking lets your husband be free to have what he wants. What he wants is what you are not. You turn to a family first sales pitch. A show piece that isn't allowed to talk about anything then your two sons.

Then one day you lose that family member who you used to share that drink with. You will drink alone again. Then the blame will come for that son who died because you drink. Then you remember you drink because you are not his equal. You are to blame for your son dying."

Jody: "That is a lot more then I can understand Everett. Everett My father hasn't worked in years. He has five kids that he can't support. His wife my mother is a mail carrier. She has kept us feed and clothes. She has let him live with us. He makes rules for us that he thinks are good for us. What would be good for us would be him leaving."

I had it worst then you. My life isn't with my parents any more. My life is mind. Just mind right now. Your life is Morissa and your son. You are not taking care of them. You are using your father as an excuse to not be there. Morissa wants to help you.

Morissa is your wife go home and be her equal. You don't need to be perfect for her. You and her is about Joe. Go home Everett and find out what is wrong with you. Be a better man then your or my father.

Everett returns home that night, He and Morissa have a talk out side on there deck.

Everett: Morissa I am sorry I walked out the other night. I should not have handled are disagreement like that. We have never had a disagreement like that."

Morissa: "We don't even have arguments Everett. We somehow manage to work out any of our issues before they need to be worked out. We trust each other views and opinions for our life together.  Everett, I listen to what you say. I look to you as the man in this relationship. You are the person John and I need. Your love for us is your greatest strength. You are wrong about his. I am asking you to take care of yourself so you can take care of us. Please do this for us. You are free from your father Everett."

Everett: "I will do it Morissa. I will take my father's help. I hope this is the last time. I thought I was done needing his help. I was away from him. I wasn't in his debt. I wasn't be holden to him.  You don't understand what that is like. I was talking to Jody. She took your side on this.

Cyd took your side. They both told me to go home and see a doctor. Jody kind of understood me not wanting my father's help. You know her family problems are different than mine. My father is different than hers. Her father gives her family nothing. My father gives you what you earn. When I was young, I did not see it like that. He did it with my mother for years. He did it with me. My mother job was to be his home wife. A female to show a family front. The woman who bore his children. The woman who raised his children.

The care taker of his beloved beachfront property. A wife to accompany him to any event he needed her at. A wife who would never ask who he was having sex with. That was her job.

My father had a job for me. My job was to be his son. A son that he could show off. An athlete's son who played little league. A son who played high school sports. A son who could cook on those fishing trips. That summer when I met you on the beach. I told you a had to go with my father on a fishing trip. I had to go. I owned him money. He paid me to go. I wanted to stay with my mother. I wanted to spend time with the girl I just met. That girl was you Morissa. I knew I would see you back at school. If I did meet you and if you went to a different school, I may have not gone with him. Morissa, I thought of you the whole time I was up there.

I used that money to get that clown outfit out of pawn. You never ask what happen to that outfit. That outfit was my brothers. He was the one who would tell the kids in the hospital the stories. I tried to be like him. That was the last time I did it. It was a lie and I didn't want to lie to you again. That outfit is at my father's place up north. Me going back to my father for help. My father will want something from me. I am his employee when he pays me.

I talked to him before I came back here. I am going to talk with him tomorrow after he makes some phones calls. I will do what he wants me to do once again. Once again he will ask me to do something for him."

Morissa: "I understand Everett. Now that you explain it to me, I can see it. Please do what he ask you. Do it for yourself. Do it for Joe and I. You can always tell your father no. Maybe that is what your mother should have told him. You are my man, Everett. You are my husband."

The next morning Everett talks with his father on the phone. Three days later Everett takes a train ride to New York city. The next day Everett takes a train ride back home to Morissa.

Everett and Morissa are sitting at a table talking.

Morissa: "When do you think you will know if they found anything Everett."

Everett: "They told me in a day. Sometime  tomorrow afternoon they should have results from all the test they gave me. I think I gave enough blood for three people to have every test that could be done."

Morissa: "Did they give you any hint of what they thought may be wrong with you."

Everett: "No. They were all professional. They did not give me any I think it is this, that, or anything. I was just glad to get it over with. We can go forward now with are lives. Tomorrow I will get up and go to work. After I call them, you will be the first person I call. After that we will just go on. Somehow weeks from now you will find me working at the bakery. Then we will be putting Joe in to school. You will go back to teaching. Maybe I will retire when you go back to work."

Morissa: "That is not going to happen any time soon. If I work you work. Joe first year will only be a half day. After that I will go back to teaching. Maybe."

Everett: "You looked forward to teaching at one time. What happen. What changed."

Morissa: "I like being a mother more. I have my own child to teach. Thank you for giving me him. Thank you for giving me everything I always wanted.

The next day Everett gets up at his regular time. He rolls over and gives Morissa a kiss to wake her up. The two talk about who is going to call who. He takes a shower and dress for work. Before he leaves, he stop by Joes room and gives him a kiss before heading to the bakery.

Cyd is walking out the door to bring john to school when Everett walks in. John gives Everett a high five as the two greet each other. Cyd tell Everett about the day food prep as she pulls John away from Everett. Cyd gets John in the van and drives away.

Everett is all alone in his bakery. He is trying to remember the instructions given to him by Cyd. Then he starts to read the never-ending notes and instructions on the notes written around the kitchen. Cyd comes back to the bakery and goes right to work.

Everett and Cyd work there regular day with their usual task. Both of them know that the phone can ring at any time. The phone call will probably be about Everett test results. The first hour goes slowly. Herbert shows up and picks up his prison delivery. Herbert updates Everett on the bakery' numbers before he leaves. Herbert ask Everett to call him when he hears about the results. Everett pats Herbert on the back as Herbert's leaves for the day.

The morning hours past slowly as Everett and Cyd watch the clock. At twelve o'clock Everett and Cyd start their lunch. The two talk about stock, hours, to how fast they can now get the wings made. Cyd brings up the subject of hiring a new kitchen cook. Everett ask her to let her friends in the city know they are looking for a part time cook.

After lunch Everett and Cyd go back to work. The hours start to drag again. One slowly turns to two. Two slowly turns to Three. The clock turns to three when Jody walks in. Her first question is to Everett." Please tell me you heard something?"

Everett replies with laughter and a smile at Cyd. "No not yet." Jody gives Everett a hug and goes up front to start selling boxed breaded chicken wing. At three thirty Morissa calls Everett. Everett tells her that he has not heard anything yet. "I promise you will be the first person I call."

Cyd leaves to go pick up John. Everett goes up front to help Jody get the boxes of chicken wings out the door. Everett and Jody talk about hiring another person to help out Her and Stacy. Everett gives her permission to look for two-part timers. He suggest to Jody that she needs to make her mind up on what she wants to do with her life.

Everett: "Jody you know Cyd and I like you. You have to make up your mind on what you like to do with the rest of your life. You are not like Cyd and I. We like what we do. We like to make food. You may like this job right now because the pay is good and you have a fun time here. In a couple of years this place could be different. One day Cyd just may take John back to France. Then there will be someone else in the kitchen that is your boss."

Jody: "I am taking some college courses now. I did want to work here. I change my mind on that."

Herbert says I could get a bachelor degree as a paralegal from the college in a couple of years. I would like to do that. I could live here for four years and still work part time.

Everett: "I am glad to hear that. If you get a 3.0 grade or higher, I will have Herbert cut your rent in half.

Jody: "That is a deal. You cannot go back on that."

Everett: "Have I ever lied to you Jody. I will keep my word. Unless you do not live up to your end. That is not going to be easy maintaining a 3.0 grade average. You are going to be spending a lot of time up there in that apartment studying."

Jody; "I can do it. I may be smarter then Herbert. He is just good at math. I know a lot more then him. In a couple of years, you may need my help. I promise you a discount because I like you."

Everett: "Great. I can't wait. My father is a lawyer. I hope you will cost me less than he does."

Jody: "Does your father make you pay him money when he helps you. That is what my father wants when he helps me. I ask him to change a tire for me on my car. He told me to pay him twenty-five dollars. I had to remind him that I was a girl and that father do things like that for their daughter."

Everett: "No I don't have to pay him any cash. He doesn't need the cash. I just have to show up and be a part of what he wants me to do. That is what I do to repay him. Sometimes I don't mind it. Sometimes I feel like his employee."

Jody: "Everett your father has a lot of money. How come he doesn't give you enough money so you don't have to work. You work a lot of hours here. You could be having a lot of fun spending his money. I would love to do that."

Everett: "It is not that easy or simple. Cyd and I like what we do. This job lets her have the life she wants with John. I have this job, my wife Morissa and Joe my son. What I have is forever. That fun you are talking about is just fun for a short time. You get nothing from it. My father would not just hand that kind of money over to me. He helped me with this place. I had to pay him back."

Jody: "I would love to marry a guy with a lot of money. I would never work; I would just spend his money."

Everett: "Be careful what you wish for. That guy you marry may think of you as an employee. It isn't a pretty life being your husband employee. He will just have you in his house like a bird in a cage."

Jody: "I would divorce him and take him for what I can get from him."

Everett: "You would be smart to do that. You may have to lose something you love, like a beach house if you did. You may lose a part of a love one that has passed away. Sometimes people have to choose what they want in life. Sometimes you get what you want and you keep it. Sometimes you may lose something that you thought was your, till death does us apart."

Jody: "Sometimes I think I am talking to my father when you and I talk Everett. Maybe sometime you can talk to me about the birds and the bees. I think I would like to sit on your lap when we have that talk."

Everett: "I will ask your brother Herbert to do it or me. Like you said he is good with numbers. Somehow he could break down multiplying for you."

Jody: "You are so funny. I will never talk to you again if you ask him to do that. I may just become a nun. What a way to kill a visual. Does your wife know you can be so old sometimes?"

Everett: "She does. I think she likes older guys."

Jody: "I hope Morissa has a girl for her next child. I will love to see you as a father of a girl. Then you can tell her all those funny things. I hope she has a girl who grows up with big boobs. Then I will be telling you I told you so."

Everett: "What is it with thinking you girls have to have big boobs. Us guys like all kinds of girls."

Jody: "Do you like Morissa."

Everett: "I love my wife."

Jody: "I rest my case. I am going to make a great paralegal."

Everett; "Jody you are always so much fun to talk too. For such a pretty girl. For such a smart girl how come you have so many date less Saturday nights.

Jody: "I can't find someone like you Everett. I would love to meet someone like you. If you had a younger brother, I would like to have a date with him."

Everett: "Sorry Jody I have no younger brother available for you. I am not much fun on dates. I used to take Morissa out on some real low-cost dates. Some of our dates didn't cost me a five-dollar bill. You will be able to find guys who are willing to spend more than that on you. The guy you want is out there. One day you will meet him."

Jody: "I want to meet him now. I want a guy to look at me like you look at Morissa. I want a guy to treat me like you treat Morissa. I want what Morissa has Everett."

Everett: "Morissa and I are lucky to have each other. There have been people who want some of what Morissa and I share. We are just committed to each other. When you find that person meant for you. You will understand having the right person is worth the wait."

Jody: "Cyd tells me the same thing.".

Everett: "What else does Cyd tell you."

Jody: "Cyd ask me a couple of months ago if I notice something wrong with you. I told her I did notice something wrong with you. Everett, you knew there was something wrong with yourself before we did.

The people I have talk to who have the problem I have had; say they knew before they told anybody. I think you are the same way. Cyd and I never herd you complain about anything. I think you know what is wrong with you. My guess is you have had this on your mind for a year now. At night when Cyd goes up stairs, I have seen you lying down on your back on that cold floor. At first, I was thinking you were just tired. After some time, you looked like you were in pain. I didn't say anything because I wasn't sure. You were in pain. There was something in side of you that was hurting you. As I look back on the way you acted. It is clear to me now that you knew you had something wrong with you."

Everett: "You are right. It was because of the pain I was on my back. The best way for me to explain it. I just had to take the weight off my body for a while. I was hoping that it would go away. Whatever it is. It has not gone away. You are the only one who could point to a visible sign. Morissa and Cyd can't tell me anything for sure. You caught me. What do you plan on doing with what you know about me now?"

Jody start to cry a little.

Jody: "Everett, I like you. I hope there is nothing that can hurt you. You cannot have anything wrong with you."

Everett gives Jody a hug and wipes a tear from her eye."

Everett: "Please don't worry about me. I will be right here keeping an eye on you. Till the day you get a Job and leave here. I will be keeping my eye on you."

Everett's father walks into the front of the bakery with another man. They see Everett and Jody in a hug. The other man with Everett's father is the doctor who evaluated Everett in the city. Everett lets go of Jody.

Everett: "Hello dad. Hello Doctor Sims. What brings you two in our bakery on this occasion."

Mr. Stewart: "Hello Everett. It is good to see you. I have doctor Sims with me. Can we have a talk with you.

Everett: "Sure dad. Dad, doctor this is Jody. Dad you met her at the wedding. She and I have the late shift tonight.

Mr. Stewart: "Hi again Jody."

Mr. Sims: "Nice to meet you, young lady."

Jody: "Hi guys. How are you good looking rich guys doing?"

Everett: "Jody I think I am going to close early. Could you please take the register draw up stair? I will turn the sign around and clean the place up."

Jody: "Sure stud muffin. Anything for you."

Jody winks her eye at the three guys. She gets the register draw and takes it up to her room.

Everett: "Don't mind her guys. She is just trying to put on a show."

Chapter Eleven

Occasion.

Mr. Stewart: "Everett can we go somewhere and talk. Doctor Sims has something important to tell you."

Everett: "You can do it here."

Mr. Sims looks at Mr. Stewart. Mr. Stewart nods his head "ok. This is as good of a place as any." Mr. Stewart tells him.

Mr. Sims: "Everett I only had the misfortune to tell this too one other person. I hope I never have to tell anybody else this again. Everett, you have ALS. Amyotrophic lateral sclerosis. Do you know what that is?

Everett looks at his father.

Everett: "Yes I do. I am a dead man. Dad you and mom are going to lose another son."

Mr. Stewart: "I am so sorry son. Doctor Sims has told me you may have ten more years. Some people even had some remission. Right Doctor Sims."

Dr. Sims: "Very few. Sorry Everett."

Mr. Stewart: "Thank you Doctor. Can you wait out in the car for a couple of minutes. I would like to talk to my son."

Dr. Sims: "No problem. Everett, I will help you get the best help."

Everett: "Thank you."

Doctor Sims shakes Everett hand and walks out to a waiting car."

Mr. Stewart: "Everett, I will get you the best help money can find. I have already started to make phone calls. You know I have worldwide connections. Everett, money will not be any problem."

Everett: "I know dad. Does mom know. This is going to be hard on her."

Mr. Stewart: "No. I thought it would be best for you to tell her."

Everett: "I will. I will fly out as soon as I can. Then I will tell her. Are you going back there to be with her?"

Mr. Stewart: "No I have some business in the city. I will be there at weeks end again."

Everett: "I understand dad. That may be best. You should leave now. I have to let Cyd, Herbert and Jody know. Then I will go home and tell my wife she married a dead man."

Mr. Stewart: "I would like to see Cyd and John before I leave."

Everett: "Not to night please. This is going to be hard enough. Thank you for coming up and seeing me. Love you dad."

Everett and his father exchange a hug before Mr. Stewart goes out to the waiting car. Mr. Stewart and the doctor go back to the city together.

Everett goes up stairs and gets Cyd and Jody together. He tell them that he has been diagnosed with ALS. Cyd and Jody start to cry. Everett ask the two not to tell anybody till he tells them they can."

Everett lock the bakery front door and drives back home. He cries on his drive back home.

Everett enters his house and finds Morissa on the back deck reading a book. He takes the chair next to her."

Everett: "Hi Morissa how was my son today?"

Morissa; "Our son Joe was a good boy all day. His mother was thinking about you all day. I am thinking If it was good, you would have called me. If it wasn't good, you would just show up here and tell me. Tell me Everett what you don't want to tell your wife. How bad is it."

Everett: "My father came up from the city with the doctor to tell me the diagnosis. I am sorry to tell you I told Cyd and Jody before I told you. I told my father I would fly out to tell my mother. Morissa can you please help me.

I can't tell you. I have tried to think of how I would tell you. Morissa I cannot bring myself to tell you."

Morissa: "Everett what is it. What has you at a lost to tell me what is going to happen to you?"

Everett: "It is going to happen to me. It is going to happen to you. You are going to lose your husband. Your husband is going to die from ALS. Are son is going to lose his father."

Morissa: "How long have you known something was wrong?"

Everett: "About two years. At first, I thought it was just me being out of shape. I started to have a hard time with those sit ups. I should of went to a doctor then. It would have not made a difference"

Morissa: "What are we going to do now Everett. What are we going to do for our son? What are you going to do with the bakery? How am I going to help you?"

Everett: "I have a life insurance policy to protect both of you. Money isn't going to be a concern for you. The bakery

I will work out an agreement with Cyd to sell her the bakery."

Morissa: "Sounds like you have been thinking of this possibility. Have you been planning this talk?"

Everett: "I have. I have been planning this day sense we were married. My father brother died young. My brother died young. I did not think I could die young till I married you. From time to time, I would think what would happen to you. When we had our son, Joe come in to our lives I started to think what would happen to you two. Last year I took out a big life insurance policy. I been thinking that we should move out To California. It may be easier if we went and lived with my mother. Joe can start school there."

Morissa: "Thank you for having this all planned out so nicely. You have always done this. Don't tell me anything till I have to know. What a nice surprise you always have for me. You did this on are dates. You just took me to those places without telling me what you were planning. Then the thanksgiving weekend we went away for the first time. I thought we were just going to a casino to have are first love making. You just happen to surprise me with the best time I could have dreamed of. That time I spent with you as the best time in my life. That was till I had our son. Then you buy that bakery without telling me. You had me afraid that you were going to leave me at school alone without you. You even thought I may have been pregnant. Now you come and tell me you are going to die. Why would I be shocked you would have this planned out. It is just the way you think of me.  Morissa, don't you worry about anything. I am the great Everett. I have it all taken care of Morissa. I don't need your help. I can figure out how to die. I don't need your help. Please do not worry your simple mind. Is that what you are thinking.

You have always done that. You have always had to have it planned out. You are not like I first thought you were. When I first had my thoughts of you. I thought you just lived life as it came. You are not like that Everett. If there is something in your life that needs a plan you will have the plan planned out. I never saw it till now. You are like your father. You just go about it in a different way. You both get whatever you want. The way you two can make your life event work out the way you want them to.

My husband who said I was spineless. Do you remember telling me that? I remember you telling me that. I bet you were thinking of that label for some time. Now I look at you. My husband who could not tell me something that was wrong with himself for two years he tells me. I bet you were thinking I would be hysterical with sadness.

I would bet you thought I could not handle it. You were a better at one time. You would have lost if you took that bet.

I have been hysterical with worry that there was something wrong with you. Thank god for Cyd who put my mind at ease. When she asked me if I notice any different in you. I came to some kind of relief that I wasn't going crazy. I have been thinking of everything under the sun. The mental cruelty you have put me thru. Someday I will have to explain you to Joe our son."

Everett: "I have a son to think of. There are people who work with me who I have to think of. Thinking of my self is thinking of you. There is you in my life. There is you who makes me think of everybody in my life. If there, wasn't you, I would not have anybody else in my life? Morissa, I didn't want to have this happen for selfish reasons. I am going to lose you. We are going to lose us."

Morissa breaks down and falls off her chair and on to the deck crying. Everett lies next to her on the deck. He puts his arms around her.

Morissa: "I am going to lose you. I don't want to lose you. Please don't leave me. I cannot make it without you. It is us don't you remember. Just us. I love you, Everett. You are mine. You were to be mine forever. You promised me that. Please don't take us away from me. You have done everything you could have done for me. You had given me everything that I have wanted.

We are so young. This is not supposed to happen to young people like us. We were to grow old together. That is what young people do. Why you. You are as close to perfect as a person can get. You don't smoke. You are not an alcoholic. No drugs. How come it has to happen to you.


We are going to fight this. I don't care how much it will cost us. If we have to bankrupt your father, we will do it. Your father knows all kinds of people. He will get you the best care. He will get you the best doctors. There has to be hospitals that specialize in treatment for people who have ALS. There has to be a drug that will help you fight it. Everett we are going to fight it. I know you. You can fight this. You are a young strong man. You will have the fight to do it. Please tell me that you will fight it for me and our son. You are so much stronger than me.

We have to make a plan on how to fight this. I will call your father tomorrow and tell him what you have. He will start calling the best people in the world."

Everett: "Morissa stop for a minute. He knows. The doctor who saw me in the city was hired by my father. My father and the doctor showed up at the bakery to night and gave me the news. My father said he would get me the best help money can find. He has already started to make phone calls. You know he has worldwide connections. Money will not be any problem. I am sure whatever I need he will get me.

546

I asked him not to tell my mother. I will fly out to see her as soon as I can. I have to tell her. Morissa you cannot tell your mother yet. Not till I can tell my mother. I ask Cyd and Jody not to tell anybody. After I see my mother, I will tell your mother."

Morissa: "No you can't. I will call her and tell her. She still fighting her cancer. I will be the one who will tell her. Once you tell your mother I will call my mother. Then I will call my father. Then I will try to explain it to our son. I hope one day somebody can explain it to me."

Everett: "I need someone to explain to me why ALS is A Lethal Sentence. Morissa there is no cure for it. There is no drugs for its affects. You are going to be a widow before you get old."

Two days later Everett flies out to see his mother. Morissa is at home waiting for the call from Everett so she can call her mother and father.

Everett is dropped off in front of his mother's house. He walks around to the beach side. The smell of the salt air and the sand under his feet. Feels like home to him. Everett walks down to the beach. He takes a deep breath and exhales it. The first smile he has had in days comes to his face. A turn around and a slow walk with his head down to his lifelong home. Everett see the patio deck door is open. He can see his mother watching her afternoon soap opera.

Everett: "Hi mom. Surprise for you. Your son has come to say hello."

Everett hugs his mother and sit in a chair next to her.

Miss. Stewart: "Did Morissa and my grandson come to see Miss. Brown. She is doing well now. Is Morissa there now."

Everett: "No Morissa and your grandson are home for now. Joe wanted me to give you a hug. He is running around everywhere now. No walking just running."

Miss. Stewart: "He sounds just like you when you were at that age. You just were the little bundle of energy. The times I had running after you and your brother."

Everett: "Yes mom we had some fun times. I look at my son and think of my older brother. I will be doing good if I can be a good parent like you."

Miss. Stewart: "You are going to be better than me. You are stronger than me. I am just a drunk who let her family down."

Everett: "Mom we had this talk. You were not there. I saw what happen. You cannot help somebody who can't help themselves. You and dad tried to get him help. It wasn't anybody fault he die. It was his fault he died the way he died. A lot of people tried to help him. Everybody liked him. He hurt a lot of people not being able to stop drinking. He hurt you mom. I cannot forgive him for that."

Miss. Stewart: "I gave him his first drink. You can trace it back to me."

Everett: "Mom he gave me my first drink. I didn't have that problem he had. Everybody gets there first drink from someone somewhere. People get in to fast cars and don't die from it. They live to drive another day. People drink. Nobody is born to die drinking."

Miss Stewart: "Yes I know. Someday I will die. That will be the day I stop drinking."

Everett: "I know mom. You have told me that before. I wish I could help you. I can't."

Miss. Stewart: "Thank you Everett".

Everett: "Sure mom. I have to talk to you about something. You have to be strong when I tell you this. Mom I came out here to tell you."

Miss. Stewart: "Oh god is Miss brown going to die?

Everett: "No mom she is doing as good as we could of hope for. Morissa and Joe are fine. There is somebody else who is sick and going to die."

Miss. Stewart: "To bad if it is your father. I am sure you will mis him."

Everett: "No mom as far as I know dad is just fine. Mom I am going to die. Mom I have ALS. I am so sorry to tell you."

Miss. Stewart: "Not you Everett. You were never sick. You were such a healthy child. I had two healthy children. You are the picture of health. You look so healthy. It can't be you. Everett what are you trying to tell me. People in there twenty's do not die like that."

Everett: "It is rare. Mom I am going to die before you."

Miss. Stewart: "No parent should lose one of their children before they die. You can't be telling me that I am going to lose you too. Did you tell your father? He can give you anything. He will find a cure for you."

Everett: "Mom he knows. He can't save me. Nobody can. I am going to die

Miss Stewart: "Everett please tell me you are not here. Please Everett tell me I am dreaming. Please Everett wake me up. I don't want to see another child of my die. How much more can I take. Who gave me this life? Why am I living this life? Somebody help me please"

Everett: "Mom I love you. I am here to help you now. Morissa Joe and I are going to come back here and take care of you. Would you like that Mom? Just think you can watch your grandson grow up. You will get to see him more than dad will."

Miss. Stewart: "I would like that, Everett. You can come back here and be a life guard again. You can make me my meals again. I miss you making me my meals. You are a really good cook. I will go upstairs later and change the sheets. Are you going to be spending the night here?"

Everett: "Yes mom. I have a flight back tomorrow morning. I have to call Morissa now. Then I will take a walk over to Morissa mother and say hello to her. Sometime later on I will go for a swim. Tonight, it will be just you and I alone. I will make you something special for dinner. We can spend some time alone on the deck talking about the fun times. I think you will have a nice night tonight mom."

Miss. Stewart: "Stay away from that dock. I don't like that dock."

Everett: "Whatever you want mom. Mom I love having you as my mother.

Everett calls Morissa. After the call he walks down to Miss. Brown house.

The next day Everett flies back to New York. A week later Mr. Stewart flies in to New York to talk with Everett and Morissa. The three of them are sitting at a table.

Everett: "Thank you for flying out here to see me dad. I know you have a lot of places of business you could be at."

Morissa: "I am sure you rather be at a lot of other places then here Mr. Stewart. Your business trips have got to be more entertaining than coming here to see your dyeing son. You could be at home with your wife."

Mr. Stewart. "Morissa, You know I have a great deal of clout. I have a lot of contacts. I know a lot of people who know a lot of people. I have been calling everybody I know trying to find some help for my son Everett. I have even reached out to other country's looking for anything that could help him. As we are all learning there is little hope for someone who gets ALS. I would use every cent I could get my hands on to help you, Everett. You know I would."

Everett: "I know you would dad. Thank you."

Morissa: "Thank you Dad. Thank you, my ass. I see what you could do when you have an interest in something. I saw how fast you got that bakery back open. A call to the governor and you moved heaven and hell. Then you beat city hall. You arranged To get Cyd here. I saw that wing in the hospital back in California your company donated. Mr. you are going back to that rock you crawled from out from under and you find someone to help him."

Everett: "Morissa he did what he could do. There is no help for me."

Morissa: "It is his side of the family we have come to find out that has that gene. It is him who gave you it. It is him who is the cause of your mothers drinking. You know it. I know it. He knows it. We are now living that family secret. How does it feel to give till somebody else hurts Mr. Stewart?"

Mr. Stewart: "Morissa I am his father. I feel just as bad about this as you. I didn't know anything about ALS till I was told Everett had it. I am the carrier for that gene. I rather have it then give it to him. My wife and I have problems. She and I have been to counseling. She did go to AA meeting. She stopped going. You cannot help someone who can't help themselves. I do understand your anger and frustration.

I am not the blame for what Everett is going to go thru. When you are married as long as me and my wife are you will have some marriage problems."

Morissa: "The way you just put that, is like saying. Everett and I are not going to get the chance to have marriage problem like you. Lucky for are marriage Everett is going to die. We will not have a long marriage. Everett did you know a long marriage is now an excuse to impregned another woman who is not your wife.

Just think of all the women you could have screwed. I was planning on being married to you till death did us apart."

Everett: "Morissa that is not what he is saying."

Morissa: "Everett don't you take that bastard side. Every time, I look at him I see the three people life he has touch. John the poor boy he fathered. His wife who is a basket case. My husband who my son and I are going to lose. Some day when our boy Joe gets old enough, I will tell him what a pillar in the community he really is."

Mr. Stewart: "Maybe I should go."

Morissa: "Why do you have some piece tonight you are dying to get pregnant. I didn't hear you say you have to get home to your wife. Did I mis that."

Everett: "Morissa"

Morissa: "Mr. Stewart, I do not care where you go. You can go anywhere you want after you help Everett. I am telling you to find something to help him. Help him god dam it. If I find out there was help for Everett and you did not get it for him. You will never see me or my son again. I hope one day for my son's sake I don't shoot you."

Mr. Stewart: "I would help him if I could. I explain to both of you there is nothing out there that will help him."

Everett: "Yes dad you should go."

Mr. Stewart: "If is ok can I see my grandson again before I go."

Morissa: "No. No you cannot. Mr. Stewart you ever want to see your grandson again. Help someone. If you cannot help your son. Then help your wife. Show me that there is a man in side of you. You are only getting to see your grandson when and if you are with your wife."

Everett: "You can see him dad. Morissa is understandably upset right now. As long as I am here you can see him anytime."

Morissa: "Everett, I hope you are the one who can survive this disease. When you go, he is going to live with what I just said."

Mr. Stewart: "Morissa I do understand. Whatever you want. Our house back in California is available if you two want it. Everett's mother wants Everett there. I will get the best care for him."

Morissa: "Everett and I have decided to sell the bakery to Cyd. We are going to go and live with my mother. We wanted to do the move before Joe starts school. Everett and I disagree on what part of Joes life you will have."

Mr. Stewart. "You know I will give Cyd any money you want or need for that bakery."

Everett: "We know. Cyd and I have already talked about it. She doesn't want to be in your debt. She wants a clear title to the place when I sell it to her."

Mr. Stewart: "She will get it."

Morissa: "I like Cyd. Everett and I have grown close to her and John. We would like to see her succeed. She doesn't want a blank check from you.

She wants to let John know you have a wife. When she thinks he is old enough to understand your little Payton place Cyd will tell him."

Mr. Stewart: "Miss Stewart would like that."

Morissa: "Everett is going to call her tonight and tell her when we are moving out there."

Mr. Stewart: "I hope we can work together Morissa."

Morissa: "You find a way to cure what Everett has. You will have me grateful. He dies I am thinking you killed your two sons. I look at both of them, needing your help."

Two years later Everett and Morissa are living in California. Everett lives with his mother in her house. He has gone from walking with a cane to a walker. Then to a wheel chair. Then he lost the ability to sit. Everett's back was no longer able to support him when he became bed ridden. There is always a nurse in the house to take care of his needs. Everett's mother still drinks and is limited in what she can do for her son. On most days Everett and his bed are wheeled out to the deck. That has a view of the dock. Everett likes to watch the beach goers enjoying the day in the sun. Morissa lets Everett's father visit him every Wednesday and Saturday afternoon.

Morissa live with her mother at her house down the beech from Everett. She now has a five-year-old boy name Joe and a two-year-old blond hair blue eyed girl named Arwen.

Arwen was the name of the ship Everett and Morissa was on. Arwen was also the name of the bakery. She will be the last child Everett was able to have with Morissa.

The name Arwen means "Noble Maiden",

Morissa and her children spend most of their day with Everett at his bed side.

Cyd is now the owner of the bakery. She has four people working with her. Cyd has hired a new bookkeeper. John is going to school and gets to spend two weeks in the summer visiting Everett.

Herbert is still seeing the same girl. He has his steady job at the prison as a bookkeeper.

Jody is in her last year of college to become a paralegal. Mr. Stewart had called a local law firm to help Jody get a job. Jody is a part time employee till she graduate.

Sue, Clare and Becky are now living there lives as adult woman. Sue and Clare have stayed in contact with Morissa. Becky has had no contact with Morissa.

Mr. Brown Morissa father flies out to California to visit Morissa, Everett and his grand kids from time to time. He will sit beside Everett and watch whatever sport game is on tv. When Mr. Brown is visiting. Morissa is able to have dinner with both of her parents.

Just another summer California day. Everett is laying on his bed that has been wheeled out on to his mother's deck. Morissa's sitting beside him.

The bed Everett hasn't left in the last four months is a metal bed on four wheels. There is an oxygen bottle with a face mask on the side of his bed. On this wrist is a do not resuscitate bracelet. He hasn't seen the inside of a shower in a year. His body can't be held up long enough without causing too much pain.

Morissa and Everett are talking.

Morissa: "How are you doing today Everett."

Everett: "About the same as yesterday. There is a nice breeze coming off the ocean to bring in some clean air. That clean air helps me breathe easier.

I spent so much time up on those life guard towers breathing whatever air there was. I never gave it a second thought."

Morissa: "Have you had to use any oxygen today."

Everett: "Yes last night for about fifteen minutes. Then again, this morning. It helps me a lot now."

Morissa: "How about the pain. How are you handling it?"

Everett: "I had some of those large pills. They last for a while. My body is like a torcher chamber most of the time now. This body is a living hell. Almost everything hurts. What doesn't hurt I can't feel anymore. I can't move any part of my body by myself."

Morissa: "How did you sleep last night Everett. It was a nice cool night."

Everett: "I had a good night sleep. It was nice not listening to an air conditioner going all night. I didn't need Michael to help me with anything. I hate having to ask him to change my diaper. The simplest acts are now a planned-out event."

Morissa: "Michael is so good to you. You are lucky to have him."

Everett: "Yes I do like him the best. How are the kids doing today? I look forward to seeing them every day."

Morissa: "They will be here later. My mother is watching them for me this morning. Everett, you need to have a talk with Joe. He is hitting rocks in to the water with that new tennis racket. I have asked him not to do it. He is going to brake that racket or hit a rock in to somebody's eye. He just can't be good for a day."

Everett: "I will have a talk with him later on. He is now the man of the house. At five he is the man of the house. I hope he learns to handle it."

Morissa: "Don't be surprise if he starts walking over here by himself. He is now asking if he could walk down here by himself to see you. I don't want him coming down here by himself. He is too young to be by himself on the beach."

Everett: "When I was at that age, I would be all over this beach by myself. I would even sleep on the beech overnight. I didn't even ask permission to do it. I just did it."

Morissa: "Times were different back then. You shouldn't have been doing it. Please Everett stop telling him the things you did back in the day."

Everett: "I love telling him about me. I have to tell him those stories before I forget all of them. I know I am losing my memories. Now how is my two-year-old princess."

Morissa: "She has a new dress to show you later. Your father has given her a credit card with no limit. The scary part of that she understands what that means. She wants to buy a new dress every day. You can also ask your father to stop spoiling her."

Everett: "Not a chance I will do that. Maybe by the time she becomes a teenager she will bankrupt him. I hope I see that day."

Morissa: "Everett is just me to keep are kids straight. Everybody around me just wants to spoil them. When I tell our kids not to do something, there come back to me is daddy would let me. You have to understand the struggle I am having."

Everett: "I do understand Morissa. I will have a talk with Joe about doing what you ask him to do. My princess can do no wrong."

Morissa: "Everett my mother is going to be gone for a couple of days. They are going to do a mastectomy. It is just another fight in her treatment."

Everett: "I wish her luck. Your mother and I have to keep fighting don't we. I think your mother has more fight in her then I do. There are times that I want to end this fight. I know I can't win this one."

Morissa: "My mother is fighting for me and her grand kids. You are fighting for me and your kids. I still need you. Our kids still need their father. Everett, you have to give our kids memories of yourself. I want them to remember who you are. The man that is there father? It is so important. They will look back on these days they are having with you for the rest of their life. I know the questions about you will be coming from them for as long as I can answer them. Every day with you will be something that they can look back on. Please Everett let them see who you are."

Everett: "I hope that they can understand how much I mis being a real father to them. The life occasion a father has with his son. The life occasion a father has with his daughter. I remember my mother telling me about life occasion. As I think about our kids. As I think about you. I think about what that means. I think those occasion have become our memories."

Morissa: "I have some great memories of us Everett. Thank you for giving them to me."

Everett: "I am trying to remember all of them. Some of them have probably have left me forever. As my mind goes, they go."

Morissa: "Do you still remember how we met?"

Everett: "I do. My version is that I met you in a bar. Your version is that I met you on the beach. We are not going to have that talk with our kids on how we met are we. That could have been a lot of fun with them."

Morissa: "I remember the beech. I wish I turned around at that bar to see you. I wish I could go back and remember you bumping in to me. If I could do that, we would have had more time together. It would be nice if we could have had more time together.

Some people are just meant to be together Everett. We were meant to be together. I think if we met in the first grade, I would have had you as my first crush. Your mother has shown me your child photos, You were one cute little boy. I could see us sitting by each other at our desk writing little love notes to each other. If we only had more time."

Everett: "Morissa you are forgetting that I could not cook at that age. You may have not like me."

Morissa: "Not a chance Everett. I know you. I know who you are."

Everett: "Thank you Morissa."

Morissa: "How about your brother do you still have the memories of him."

Everett: "I know I have lost most of them. I just don't know which one I have lost. My mother is telling me stories about him and myself. Most of those stories I can't remember. From what I do remember and what she tells me. My brother and I had a lot of fun. It would have been nice having him here now to tell me about the fun times we had together."

Morissa: "I think he would have been telling you what a good brother you were. Does your father tell you any stories about you and your brother?"

Everett: "He does. He regrets that the three of us never got to go up north and go fishing with him. That august after my brother died was to be the first time the three of us were to go together. It never happen. That year my father didn't go. He stayed home and helped my mother and I cope as much as he could. The next year I went for the first time. I know you have problems with who my father is. I like my father. I don't like everything he did or does. I was never as good as what I could do.

Like he was at what he could do. There were times I wanted to have that part of him. I wonder what I would have been like with just some of him."

Morissa: "I love you the way you are Everett. You are the way you are for me. I don't want any part of him in you. A son and a father will have a relationship. A wife can look at it from a distance and understand it is their relationship."

Everett: "How are Cyd and John getting along. I do mis them."

Morissa: "I talked to Cyd the other night. She does mis you. The bakery is doing just fine without you. I am sorry to tell you that. She has the new people working well with each other. The freshman every year are the biggest consumer of those wing she tells me. She is trying to increase the sale of the pastry's she makes. The kids at the school are all about those wings of a chicken as she calls them."

Everett: "Those wing of a chicken as she calls them, do pay all the bills. She loves her pastry's but it is those wing that love the bakery. How about john how is he."

Morissa: "Cyd tells me he is the smart one in the school. Not the athlete like you wanted him to be. He speaks French to the teacher just to be a pane in the neck to them she says. He has his friends at school and is just like one of the other kids.

Cyd and Jody are trying to work out a time that they can both fly out here and see you. You know how those things work out. I have kept Cyd and Herbert up to date on your health. I hope they just get on a plane and come out here again soon."

Everett: "Yes it would be nice to see them again. I hope I am having a good day when they come out here to see me. This is not the way I want them to remember me."

Morissa; "They understand. If we were still living back in New York they would get to see you more often. You would be telling them to get on with their own life and spend less time with you."

Everett: "You are probably right about that. If Cyd was here, I would be worried about the bakery. We would have two things to talk about. The bakery and John. After that she would just want to get back home. I did like working with her. Every day she would leave me notes on the way she wanted things to be done. I never told her it was my bakery and we were going to do things the way I wanted them done. From the first day we worked together it was obvious that she knew a lot more about everything then me. There are a couple of things I do wonder about. The first one is if I could have made the bakery a successful business without her. The other one is if I would of ever open up a food place of my own."

Morissa: "The idea for wings was a real good idea. Any wing place could have worked. Cyd just made it something special. You had to be smart enough to see what the people around you could do. You let Cyd and Herbert work together and let them each do what was best for the business. Some people could not do that. You were smart enough to put an ego aside to make it work. Looking back on it now. You never had to do it before Everett. I think you handle that better than your father could of.

Your father would have just paid those two more, to work together. They worked together because you were you.


I did think from time to time you would rather be at a restaurant then a bakery. You did want one when we first met. You may have had the chance to do it. May be it would have been out here. Maybe it would have been out there. I guess we will never know."

Everett: "We will never know."

Morissa: "Everett do you think we both got what we wanted? I wanted to be a teacher. You wanted to own your own restaurant. I think Cyd got what she wanted. She spent her whole life doing what she wanted to do. She had the schooling the commitment and the drive."

Everett: "I don't know if you and I did. It may depend on how we look at it. At one time we were doing what we wanted to do. You were teaching. I had my own place. From the outside somebody would say we did. I think both of us know we got what we needed. We needed each other Morissa. I can't see myself without you. The bakery at the time was to let me stay and be near you. If I don't get that bakery. I am back as a life guard till I can find a way to be with you again.

What you don't know Morissa. I was talking to my father about my plans after I graduated college. He asked me what I had planned. I told him I had nothing plan after I graduated. Then I told him I didn't want to leave you. He said I should just go home and he would fine me a job. My father and I went back and forth on him finding me a job near you. That is when the restaurant my father worked at came in to the picture. My father call Pete and told him I need a job. Pete told my father that he was planning to sell the business in the future and that I would be better off working somewhere else. My father and Pete had some talks about how much Pete was looking for. My father new Cyd in France who was very good at pastries.

Somehow my father was able to put the parts and pieces together for the three of us. You Cyd and I came together because he made it happen."

Morissa: "I would like to think it would have worked without him. Everett what you don't know. I almost went to a community college. I had a scholarship for one near where I used to live. There were two factors that took me to our college. The first one was I wanted to be a teacher. Our college was a better school for any student who wanted to be a teacher. The second reason I chose that school because of where it was located. It was far enough from my father to let me live on my own. I would be close enough to him within a day's drive. Just think of all those things that had to come together for us to come together. It is amazing we had even met."

Everett: "If you live with your mother, we would have met a lot sooner. I could have been the paper boy bringing you the paper. Can't you see me bringing the paper to your door. Me knocking on your door. I could see me looking at you. You looking at me. Love at first sight. You would be going to your girlfriends telling them about the boy who likes you. They may ask you how did you know I liked you. Then you would tell them that I am always at your door looking at you."

Morissa: "Sounds like a stalker. Sounds like a school boy crush. Everett, I like the way I met you on the beach. I will always have that. I tell it to every female I can. Nobody has a better boy meets girl storied then me. I could see me telling it to our daughter one day. I do hope somebody can give her something like that to her. I have to confess I go down to the spot where you put that x in the sand. I look at that spot and think of you. I wish I took a picture of it. It means a lot to me. I was thinking about you doing at that night. I knew how special it was.

I was planning on going back to school and telling all the other girls about you doing that for me. I ask you why you did that. You said I just mark the spot where we met. Then I said a little much isn't it. Then You said Could be. You never can tell about somethings." Do you remember that.

Everett: "No Morissa I do not remember that. I still remember seeing you at the bar. I remember having pizza with you on a first kind of date. I just don't remember saying or doing that. I am sorry. It sounds nice. I just can't remember right now. I do remember taking you on some dates where we didn't spend much money. You were really good about it. I remember us winning a lot of money on green. Then I had to give it all back. I remember asking you to marry me a couple of times. There was that time when I did ask you. You still told me you could not marry me. I just would not give up on you. Something about you Morissa that I love. I may not be able to remember everything we did."

Morissa: "It is ok Everett I understand. I do thank you for those times. I will have them forever. Thank you for giving me our children. Thank you for giving me part of your life. I love you for it."

Everett: We had a good time Morissa. Lots of fun."

Morissa: "That dock is still out there Everett. Do you think of your brother looking at that dock? Every day you are out here your bed is facing that dock."

Everett: "I do. A couple of times I started to cry. This disease makes me to emotional."

Morissa: "I understand. Everett, I think of you and I as us. Do you think, you and I will ever end?"

Everett: "If you are thinking of me. I will always have us."

Morissa: "I will always be thinking of you as us."

Everett: "Morissa what are you going to do with the rest of your day?"

Morissa: "I have to get back soon and make the kids lunch. I may not be able to live up to your cooking. Joe from time to time does remind me of it. I think are daughter is going to mis out on you making her something special like you did for me."

Everett: "Tell them I am thinking about them. Good by Morissa I will always love you."

Morissa: "Till our next life occasion."

Morissa gives Everett a kiss on the cheek and walks home.

That night at the age of twenty-seven on February seventeenth Everett Stewart suffocate. The nurse who taking care of Everett calls Morissa. Morissa wakes her mother up to watch her kids. Without waking her kids Morissa runs down the beach to find Everett has passed away. On his bed side Everett mother is crying.

One week later in a cemetery there is a grave stone that has the name of Everett's brother on it. Next to that grave a new hole has been dug for Everett. At the new grave there is a small group of people. Jody, Herbert, Cyd, Sue, John, Mr. and Miss. Brown, Mr. and Miss Stewart. Morissa has her daughter in her arms. Her son Joe is standing in front of her.

The preacher has given his sermon. Each of the teary eye people there has said a few words with voices that are cracking with emotions.

Morissa drops Everett's brother Joseph old black doctor bag in to Everett's grave. She tells the people of Everett older brother dressing up as a clown at the hospital. He would read the sick kids' story's he wrote. He would be at the hospital for counseling for his drinking. Everett would leave his house and walk to the hospital to find his brother. Then a nurse name Sally would bring Everett back home.

Morissa reads the story Everett Stewart wrote about his older brother. The story Everett told her at the casino. Then she reads the story Joseph Stewart wrote about Everett his younger brother.

Younger brother.

My brother has always been there for me. Every time I need him, he was there. When I was really young, he let me share his room. It was nice knowing that I had him close by me. I would look across the room and see him. He was a lot older than me and much smarter. Anything I need to know he knows. Any thing I want to do he can do. Sometimes he even lets me play with his toys. He has the best toys. Most of my toys are for kids younger them me. Sometimes I will do something that can get me in to trouble with my parents. My brother will always protect me. Sometimes he will take the blame for it or tell them I had an accident. He even ties my shoes for me. I am learning to do it for myself.

One day I got my own room. My parents took a guest room and made it all mine. I got to pick out the color I wanted in it. I picked out this really nice blue. I got a new bed and a new bureau to put my clothes in. There was a big closet in my room. The hangers were too high to reach. I had to use something called a foot stool. I don't think I will be using it for long. I am growing a lot. It is my room now with all my stuff in it. Sometimes I will get something from my brother and put it in my room. I get some of his clothes. At first, they may be a little too big but I am growing. It is so nice to be able to get them.

My brother has a lot of friends. They come over a lot and play with him. When they do, I don't get to play with him as much. Sometimes we can find a game I can play with him and his friends. The best is hide and seek. He will always take me with him. He knows the best place to hide. That is what big brothers do for their younger brothers.

I have to go off to school soon. My big brother has been talking to me about school. He has been telling me what clothes I am going to be wearing. What I am going to be doing in school. How to get around the school. On my first day of school my mother took me. From then on, my big brother was the one who took me to school. At the end of the day, he would take me home.

My brother is old enough to go to another school now. He can't take me to school any more. He can't take me home any more. That is ok because I am big enough to do it by myself. I have my own friends now and he has his friends. Some of his new friends that he hangs out with I don't like. They keep him out past the time he should be home. He is getting in more trouble with his new friends.

My brother likes to stay out late at night with his friends to much. There are times when my brother has gotten drunk with his friends. He doesn't spend as much time with me anymore. I can often find him in his room asleep during the day. When I ask him if he wants to go and play, he sometime gets mad at me and tells me to go away. There was one weekend when he disappeared for two days. My father had to go down to the hospital and get him and bring him home. My brother was in big trouble. My parent grounded him for a week. It was nice to have my brother back for that week. We started talking again and playing outside our house again. Six month later my brother was in trouble again. He skipped a week of school.

My parents were having a lot of argument about my older brother. I didn't know what to do. I was hoping one day he would get back to being my older brother. I missed all the fun I would have with him. The things he taught me I was getting to be very good at. I wanted to be the best athlete at my age. Like he was. I wanted to challenge my brother to a swimming race. He told me he didn't have time for it. I walked away thinking he just wasn't feeling good.

Our parents had me and my brother go to a meeting with them. The four of us talk with someone who could help my brother. My brother didn't say much. When they ask me what I thought about my brother needing help. I told them I would help him any way I can. My brother hasn't finish high school and he was going to meetings

Late night I would look out my window and see my brother and his friends drinking. They would sit on a dock and drink all night. No one could catch them because they would throw the bottles in to the water. I didn't know what to do. Should I say something about what he was doing. The problem my brother had put me in a bad place. Accouple of days later I told him that I knew what he was doing on the dock.

My older brother got mad at me for the first time. He told me nobody likes a tattle tale and if I knew what was good for me, I wouldn't say anything."

Everett Stewart


Older Brother.

My parents sit me down and tell me they want to have a talk with me. What did I do this time I wonder? What could a five-year-old keep doing that my parents keep wanting to have a talk with me. side by side they sit and start to tell me our family is going to get bigger. Then they show me my mother's belly. She has around bump on her belly. Somehow in a couple of months I will have a baby brother. Oh boy, fun. Somebody to play with. A brother how happy I was that day. I went out and told every one of my friends. Then the day it happen. They bought my brother home to me. He was so small. All I could see was a little prune face wrapped up in a blanket. They even let me hold him for the first time. So, so small. Be careful they told me. I did learn the right way to hold him.


This little kid that was laying down in the living room. I sat there watching my parent making a fuss over my brother. I couldn't understand it. He wasn't doing anything but sleeping. Then other people started to show up and make such a fuss over this little brother of mind. So many people came and went. Some of them asked me how I felt to have a baby brother. I told them I liked him. He was too little to play with.

Over the next days and weeks, I learn what diapers were. I learned how much my baby brother did poops, Sometimes I could smell him. When I did smell him, I had to tell my mother his diaper had to be changed. Then there was feeding time. The food he would try to get in to his mouth was funny some times. Most of the time there was more on his face then he had eaten. My brother was doing three things at this time. He was sleeping, eating, and pooping. I didn't get to have much fun with him. All the food had helped him grow.

He could now pull himself up on the rails of his crib. When I go up to him, he would start to laugh and giggle. The funny faces I would make would make him laugh harder.

My mother and father started to put him on the floor and let him crawl around. He was able to stand up when he was holding on to a table or a chair now. Then came the day when he let go of the table and started to walk across the floor. My parents were on the floor calling to him. He looked at me and then walked to me. I caught him as he got to me. Then he looked at me and started to make some funny faces that I would make.

My room got a new bed one day. I was told that it was just a temporary thing. As soon as he was bigger my brother would be put in to his own room. I like having my brother in my room. It was nice to look over at him knowing my parent were giving me the responsibility of taking care of him.

The pooping in those never-ending stinking diapers was still going on. Sometimes at night I would go sleep in the living room.

I was teaching him how to play like a boy. We play all kinds of games. Sometimes he would break my toys trying to play with them the wrong way. I would find him playing with my toys more than his.

There were some toys of mind I wanted to keep because I like them a lot. He broke some of my special toys. I had to understand he was much younger than me. As much as I didn't like it, I knew that I was the older brother and had to be the one to understand that he was just a baby.

My brother soon found his own room. Across from me he would sleep from now on. I would get up and go to school. My brother would be there to see me leave for the day. In the afternoon my brother would be waiting by the door looking for me to play with him.

Most of the time now I would go outside and play with my friends. I like my brother but I would have more fun playing with my friends. On a rainy day when I couldn't find a friend I would play with my little brother. Sometimes I would be too rough with him. My mother would give me a lecture on he is not as strong as me so I have to be careful with him. I taught him how to tie his shoes and dress himself. I taught him the way boys go to the bathroom.

My brother is now ready to go to school. The smelly diapers are long gone. He has everything that he will need for school. I had to tell him about school and what goes on there. He was telling me that he wanted to go to school. I guess I did at that age to. I told him about the teacher he was going to have in his first year. The teacher should remember me because I was so smart. I warned him about some rules that the school has that he would have to follow. I think he will be ok. I will be in the same school for a couple more years.

My brother found his own friends now. Some of them come over and play with him. They play the same games as I use to play with my friends. Sometimes on a rainy day he and I would find something to play together, maybe watch something on tv or get in to a fight. I think all brothers must do that sometimes.

I am still watching him. Our parent go out some time and we will be by ourselves at home. Me being the oldest puts me in charge. I don't have to tell him anything. He is the best little brother to watch over.

John Stewart

Eight years later Cyd still has the bakery. Her son John is making plans on going to college. Herbert is now married. Herbert's wife has given birth to twins. Jody has a full-time job in a law office.

Morissa is living in her mother's house with her mother and her kids. Morissa is sitting on her deck talking to her father Mr. Brown. Mr. Brown will visit Morissa twice a year. Once at the last week of August before his grand kids go to school. Then again at Christmas.

Morissa: "Dad I am glad you had a nice flight in from New York. It is too far for you to drive anymore."

Mr. Brown. "It wasn't the distance that bothered me so much. It was the amount of times that I had to stop and find a restroom. I like seeing the country as I drove through it coming here. When I went back home, I would go a different way to see something different."

Morissa: "I notice that restroom need on that last ride you gave me to college. I am starting to understand why you wanted to give me that ride to school back then. I see my two kids and someday I may be doing what you did for me. Dad I did not want to be in a car with you for that long. For six months after you dropped me off. I would be thinking of what I may have told you that I didn't want to tell you.

Then for the next six months I would be thinking what I don't want to tell you the next time you drove me back to college."

Mr. Brown: "I understand. I am grateful for you letting me have that time with you. I do think of those talks we had. You gave me something I will always remember."

Morissa: "You are welcome dad. When Joe goes off to college, I will let you bring him to school."

Mr. Brown: "Not me. I had my time. It is all on you now."

Morissa: "Thanks dad. Maybe I can get mom to do it."

Mr. Brown: "Sure I would like to see that. Could you tape that for me."

Morissa: "No problem. I would like to see it too. We would have a ball watching it."

Mr. Brown: "Morissa where are your kids now."

Morissa: "Mom has taken them out for ice-cream. There is a new ice cream shop close by. The shop was once a bar. Then it became a sushi bar. Now it sells ice-cream."

Mr. Brown: "Your mother and I have been getting along great. I was not sure we would. Our phone calls about you was always a pleasant conversation. Our talks now at the dinner table are still a pleasant and enjoyable conversation."

Morissa: "Thank you for doing that for me. I can't tell you how much I do enjoy being at a table with you two. I tell my kids how important it is to have a family sit down dinner. Most of the time Joe will have some other place he rather be. Arwen wants to be on a phone talking to her friends"

Mr. Brown. They get along nicely from what I see of them. I think you are raising two good kids Morissa."

Morissa: "Thank you dad. I have my hands full sometimes. Sometimes I just enjoy being there mother. I look at them and see parts of there father. Arwen has a competitive side to her I don't understand.

 I don't know where she got it from. Joe can draw a picture of anything. I don't know where he got that from. He loves to draw."

Mr. Brown: "Morissa you are nothing like your mother or I. Somehow you became your own person.  Kids will grow up with their own personality.

A parent can give their kids a good foundation. Your two kids will give you some heartaches along the way. You will worry about them. You will be proud of them. You will have them as your kids. No one can ever take that away from you. From the first day you were born you were my child. Morissa your mother and I am so proud of you.

The next day Morissa is with her ten-year old daughter Arwen. Arwen is writing a story in her journal. Joe her son is playing on the beach with his friends.

Morissa sees Joe and his friends run up to a man walking his dog. The man starts to sign his autograph for the kids. Joe leaves his friends and the man then he runs up to his mother. He tells her that the Super bowl winning quarterback Earl Miller is the man walking the dog and he wants his autograph. Morissa takes Joe and Arwen down to the man on the beach.

Morissa walks up to Earl Miller with her kids.

Morissa: "Hello Earl it has been a long time. Can I have your autograph."

Earl: "Hello to you. Do I know you. I cannot place where I saw you before."

Morissa: "We met about ten years ago. You were playing the piano for me and some other people."

Earl: "Were you the girl who was at the casino."

Morissa: "Your last song was Every passing heart beat."

Earl: "I remember you. I was playing a piano and you were sitting by me. It seems like yesterday when we were doing that."

Morissa: "We were so much younger back then."

Earl: "I was just starting my career. I have two rings now."

Morissa: "I saw you win those championship games. I told my son I met you. I don't think he believed me."

Earl: "She is right young man. We met at a piano"

Morissa: "What brings you to this beech?"

Earl: "I am divorce from my wife. I just bought that house down the beach. The one with the jacuzzi. May be you know the house."

Morissa: "What a small world. I live in the house behind us. I live there with my mother and my kids."


The End.

Edward Licciardello

Book two sometime later.

I had a brother who died of ALS. Joseph

I had a brother who died because he could not stop drinking. John

I had two young brothers who were born as twins.

I had two brothers who died four months apart.

There is no message in this story.

I would like to thank two men.

Donald and John D.

# © 2021

www.ingramcontent.com/pod-product-compliance
Lightning Source LLC
Chambersburg PA
CBHW060239030726
47493CB00024B/1382